Marz

Gary

Ilan

Marilyn

WELCOME
to
FEAR CITY

Sarah Dvojack

U

**UNION
SQUARE
&CO.**

NEW YORK

For the Haran Irish Dancers
and for the City of New York.
Past, present, and future.

UNION
SQUARE
&CO.
NEW YORK

UNION SQUARE & CO. and the distinctive Union Square & Co. logo are
trademarks of Sterling Publishing Co., Inc.

Union Square & Co., LLC, is a subsidiary of Sterling Publishing Co., Inc.

© 2024 Sarah Dvojack

ISBN 978-1-4549-5390-6 (hardcover)
ISBN 978-1-4549-5392-0 (paperback)
ISBN 978-1-4549-5391-3 (e-book)

Library of Congress Control Number: 2023052239

For information about custom editions, special sales, and premium purchases,
please contact specialsales@unionsquareandco.com.

Printed in the United States of America

2 4 6 8 10 9 7 5 3 1

unionsquareandco.com

Cover and interior design by Marcie Lawrence

What's past is prologue.
The Tempest, Act 2, Scene I

Or

*Hello from the cracks in the sidewalks of N.Y.C.
and from the ants that dwell in these cracks and
feed in the dried blood of the dead that
has settled into the cracks.*
Son of Sam, May 30, 1977

PROLOGUE

THE VALLEY
THE CAST-IRON DISTRICT
HELL'S HUNDRED ACRES
SOUTH HOUSTON INDUSTRIAL AREA
"SOHO"

November 9th, 1965

Sylvie Stroud was watching an episode of *Where the Action Is*. At five years old, she was hopped up on the day's top hits as they piped through the old black-and-white set, dancing wildly within the confines of the woven rug beneath her bare feet. (Stray one toe outside of it, and you were sure to get a splinter from the old floor.)

As Little Richard ended his performance and the jerking teenagers on the screen stopped to clap and screech, the screen began to flicker. Sylvie didn't notice it, but even if she had, it wouldn't have bothered her. The TV was forever doing funny things like that, both because it was ten years old, and because the loft didn't have reliable electricity.

She was home alone—in a way. Her dad and brother were out, but her mom was downstairs in the other studio reupholstering a chair they'd fished from an industrial dumpster. Sylvie could hear her radio through the thin floorboards, so she started dancing to that instead. *Hey, you, get off of my cloud!*

But then the TV started spitting out incomprehensible garbage, and Sylvie turned to see the image whirring whirring whirring at a frenetic pace until, with a soft *pop*, the screen went black. And with it went all the lights, and the sound of her mom's radio. Sylvie could see her surprised face in the smudged glass of the TV set, lit up now only by the moonlight coming through the tall windows.

Sometimes that happened, too, when the old fuses couldn't take the pressure. But there was something different about it this time because Sylvie quickly realized that moonlight was *all* there was. The buildings across narrow Greene Street were as dark as her own, including the factory that made cheap plastic dolls and women's underwear.

Outside, an empty truck rattled by and people on the sidewalks called to each other. *You seein' this? What in the hell!*

All the warmth from her dancing left her very quickly. Her skin felt like it was buzzing, all the hairs on her arms shivering. The silence was so thick that it was loud inside her head. And the rest of the unfinished loft was dark and deep as a cave—Sylvie had never noticed that before. It had always seemed bright and open.

A tickling sensation on her foot made her jump, and she looked down to see a couple of ants crawling over her toes. Like everything else, that didn't surprise her, either—the building had holes and cracks at every seam, and rats still kept a functioning highway between the floors.

It had been at least two minutes and her mom hadn't come upstairs and Sylvie didn't want to be sort-of-home-alone anymore.

She sat down to brush off the ants and pull on her socks, and when she got back up again, she put her bare hand down on the floorboards for leverage.

All at once, she wasn't alone anymore. A whole entire world burst into her own. Instead of furniture and art and stacks of sheet-rock, there were machines and noises and the foulest smells. Old oil and dirty fabric and rancid smoke and things she had absolutely no names for because she was only five years old.

People wearing old, unfamiliar clothes marched into and over each other, talking and laughing and yelling in equal measure as they moved through and around piles of acrid furs or thundering machines. The floor was covered in discarded waste all knotted together. Were those boxes of buttons? No. Piles of fabric? Mounds of wool? Her street was still covered in bales of fabric and clippings, but not in here! Like staring at ten slides all stacked up and held to the light, the images didn't make sense. She was frozen in the middle of it, unable to move for shock. The moon glowed through the people, turning them to ghosts. They had to be ghosts. Her house was haunted.

She shut her eyes.

The people disappeared when she ran, screaming, for her mother, her sock-covered feet beating a path to the door—a path that these strange people had already taken. Were probably the reason the floor was so worn out in the first place.

She couldn't explain what had happened, so she pretended she had been afraid of the dark, and her mom believed her.

But then she made the mistake of touching the windows to see down into the dark street, and all the ghosts erupted from the walls again. This was how Sylvie learned that they only showed up if she touched the old parts of her building. The windows, the floor, the exposed brick walls. Then she learned that objects held ghosts, too, even the old typewriter her dad found sitting on a curb (there had been a note taped to it—NOT BROKEN). Several ladies in shirtwaists typed when Sylvie typed, so Sylvie never used it again.

She wore mittens indoors and her parents laughed it off because it was nearly winter, and the loft was cold. But she wouldn't take off the mittens at school, and she wouldn't take them off in bed, and when her parents fixed the boiler, she wouldn't take them off then, either. Every surface was a perpetual game of hot lava, but she appeared to really believe it would burn her.

By spring, she was in front of an NYU psychoanalyst, her now six-year-old mind trying to come up with a lie because she didn't understand the truth but knew it was too unbelievable to convey. He said she would probably grow out of this behavior, that kids sometimes developed anxiety around starting school, but he still looked at her funny and she still had to see him every other Wednesday.

Forced to think about it, she began to wonder—if these were ghosts, shouldn't others see them when she did? Why weren't they lurking under her bed or shouting "*BOO!*" from dark corners? They never even looked at her.

4

In the fall, she went on a field trip to the Metropolitan Museum of Art with her first-grade class and leaned against a pillar in the patio from the Castillo de Vélez-Blanco. A mere sliver of her wrist brushed the marble—and as both a Spanish castle and a Park Avenue mansion suddenly overlaid the staid museum, Sylvie realized that she wasn't seeing *ghosts* at all.

She was seeing the past.

Almost immediately filled with relief, she wanted to tell everyone she knew, but her teacher simply praised her vivid imagination and joked with the chaperones about some ladies who time-traveled at Versailles.

Not being afraid didn't make it any easier to endure the chaotic mess that is the passage of time. She was sick of wearing mittens and sick of going to the analyst. When she read X-Men comics with her older brother, she thought of the young mutants who could control the uncontrollable and decided to figure out how to sort the pile of slides into an orderly projection that could be switched on and off when she wanted.

It took years, but it worked, and she learned a lot about her powers as she spent all her time with them. When she began to need glasses, she called the power her 20/20—because her hindsight was particularly good.

She learned that she couldn't use it on living things, like people. She learned that history had to steep for something near a decade before she could consume it, so new objects gave up nothing. She learned that she couldn't interact or change anything, and that no one could interact with her. She even learned how to focus on one memory at a time (it helped to know what you were looking for). More and more she thought of the visions, the memories, the slides, as movies to be preserved.

Because once obliterated, some memories were lost for good. She couldn't find Collect Pond or even an inch of pre-European Manhattan underneath all the concrete and steel. When she watched *West Side Story*, her parents told her the neighborhood was beneath Lincoln Center. When she learned that Penn Station was finally getting demolished, she made her parents take her there nearly every weekend, and she would prowl the exterior, trying to collect stories that were about to be thrown away, writing things down in notebooks she refused to let anyone read, though her brother often tried.

Her own neighborhood was as vulnerable as Penn Station and San Juan Hill. While the adults organized, she wrote furious letters to Robert Moses like it was a hobby. Her dad found one and hung it at a gallery opening. An art dealer bought it for $50 and turned it into a mimeo that was spread around the neighborhood, then into the Village and beyond: ROBERT MOSES STOP PUTTING ROADS THROUGH OUR HOMES!!!

After four years, she stopped wearing mittens (even in winter) because she could finally move through the world like other kids again, putting her bare hands and bare feet wherever she pleased and only seeing things when she felt like it.

By the time she was ten, she had been kicked out of every museum in the city because she couldn't (wouldn't) stop touching everything. She was banned from school trips until her parents explained that the oils from her skin could damage old things. (They wondered if touching too much was compensating for all those years in the mittens, but they stopped taking her to the shrink.)

Of course, she didn't keep it to herself, but still no one believed her. She pretended to be a reverse psychic, able to tell anyone anything about their school building as long as it happened years ago. She made two dollars doing it, but a teacher stopped her, asked her how Encyclopedia Stroud knew all that.

Oh, I just touch the building and it shows me.

It gave her a sense of ownership of her city that no one else could have. She made a game of looking through old photographs at the public library her mom worked at. She would find a famous face, a famous event, and scour the past to find them. She learned how much of New York was reused, some buildings on their fifth or fiftieth iteration. Square pegs in round holes, either chopping off their corners or crudely busting out more space (like her neighborhood). Some buildings wore their history proudly. Others covered it up.

For years she would peek at every building she passed, creating parades of moments around her like episodes of TV, seeing everything without fully comprehending how real it all had been, despite the smells, despite the sounds. Too young to grapple with the ugly parts, until she wasn't anymore.

The history in and around her neighborhood had its own particularly bitter flavor, full of dregs. Rat pits and frozen bodies. A man sleeping on the steaming corpse of a horse and children keeping warm on a grate. A family thrown from their apartment, their possessions already on the sidewalk, the children thin with bellies distended. Gangs of men shooting and slashing at each other—several with their innards spilling out or blood gushing from their necks and gasping mouths. Police raiding brothels and dragging women down the steps. Black men beaten by raging white men. The kidnapping of a scarlet-haired dancer from the ghost of a Bowery theatre, her head—identifiable only by that scarlet hair—dumped where an old wood-frame house used to be. An unconscious girl Sylvie's age hauled onto a cart and carried away. A woman with sharpened teeth picking flesh from long, brass nails on the tips of her fingers. Fires. So many fires. Young women falling from the sky to escape a raging inferno that burned Sylvie's skin and hair and filled her nostrils as though it were still happening.

In the sixth grade, Sylvie kept her hands to herself for almost an entire year. For months, she had night terrors. It was back to the analyst, where she decided she couldn't be so adventurous or so callous. Her focus shifted to the present, to dance class and crushes, to the only friends who actually believed her. She visited the same places and always vetted new ones, letting go of the idea that she could learn everything buried in the surfaces around her, realizing that no one could.

The country thought her city was dying, but Sylvie knew it couldn't. She could see through Manhattan, right to its beating heart.

At least, she thought there was a heart there.

CHAPTER ONE

HELL'S KITCHEN

May 30th, 1977

The gunshot severed the scream.

A teenage girl hit the sidewalk and collapsed over the curb, into the street. Her splayed arms nearly flung beneath the wheels of a Ford Pinto.

The Pinto didn't sound its horn. A nearby dog-walker didn't flinch, nor did her little Pomeranian.

Sure, this was Hell's Kitchen, but unless the Westies and Gambinos had changed their targets, there was no reason for a teenage girl to be shot during the dinner rush on a Monday evening. There was less of a reason for no one to care about it.

The *Post* would probably say this was the moment the City of New York finally lost the battle for its soul. Earth to city: GIRL DROPS DEAD.

If, in fact, a teenage girl had been shot at all.

Her body was already gone.

Sylvie's heart thudded in her ears, pumping her head so full of blood that it felt like her brain was being smothered. She gripped her dance duffel and tripped down the last two steps of the row house stoop. Her knee hit the iron gate, chipping off bits of black paint and knocking the small, wooden sign affixed to the rungs: BYRNE SCHOOL OF IRISH DANCE.

"Wow, Sylvie," said one of the girls coming up behind her. Nessa Murray, of strawberry hair and a pale face full of freckles and erythema. "You gotta open it first."

Sylvie couldn't think of a reply.

The accordion music began again, two floors up, proudly striding out an open window, while the rest of her dance class dispersed over the sidewalk. A few of them waved to a pair of girls smoking by a scraggly but determined tree.

Sylvie didn't even feel the impact of the gate on her knee. She had to keep moving, had to spread the block between herself and whatever *that* was. Whatever *that* was, wasn't supposed to happen. Sylvie thought she knew how it worked, the palimpsest that only she could read.

After all these years, she didn't want to be wrong.

The two girls by the tree flicked their cigarettes away and dropped beside her. Marzelline Hallan, a Black girl with her hair in braids she'd done during homeroom, moved her eyebrows in different directions and folded her arms. Her leather jacket squeaked at the elbows. In that moment, she was the epitome of skepticism and looked exactly like her contralto mother, rather than the soprano who fronted a punk band. (It was the formation of that punk band that had Marzelline switching out her nickname from Lina to Marz. Marz and the Martians. Her opera diva mom hated it.)

"Hello to you, too," said Marz. "Where's the fire?"

"I thought I forgot my hardshoes for a sec," Sylvie said, rescuing her voice from her bone-dry throat. "So, did you find a new drummer?"

On Sylvie's other side, Marybeth Huang laughed, though it came out as a snort that seemed rather undignified coming from someone in a gleaming ballet bun and pink tights.

"Smooth," said Marz. "Subject expertly changed."

Talk through it, Sylvie. "I'm not changing the subject; I'm making conversation."

Marz looked at Sylvie in astonishment. "Okay, babe. Sure. *No,* I didn't find a new drummer in the last two hours."

Sylvie hugged the strap of her duffel harder. "Sorry for asking! Damn."

"Now why are you getting all shitty?"

Marybeth looked down at Sylvie's leg. "You just fell down the stairs. Did you notice?"

When Sylvie didn't answer, Marz took hold of her ponytail and tugged it once.

"Space."

Twice.

"Ca-"

Three times.

"-*det.*"

Sylvie grabbed her ponytail back. "It's—"

CRACK

Sylvie's entire body jolted, and she spun around to see the teenage girl already prone on the ground. With no car in the way this time, the scene continued to play, and Sylvie couldn't stop watching it.

The girl wasn't dead at all. She clawed at the ground, dragging herself forward with one arm, heedless of the road in front of her and the people walking by. The people walking right through her. From this distance, Sylvie couldn't see the girl's face, but she noticed how something grabbed her hair and began pulling her back. And as it pulled, her body faded and was gone again.

She had never seen anything so clear before, so isolated. It was sickening to behold.

"Sylvie?" said Marybeth, who actually sounded concerned now.

Sylvie's gaze flickered from Marybeth and back to the empty sidewalk, where the ground floor of a row house had recently been gutted to make way for some sort of something. A café, one of the dance moms said. A sure sign of either money laundering or the next wave of neighborhood reform, or both.

In the minutes that had passed since the gunshot, since the girl, since the Pinto, since the Pomeranian, no one had even looked out their apartment windows on the top three floors of the maybe-café, where the girl had fled, and screamed, and been shot all at once.

Sylvie felt sick and cold. She readjusted her bags. "I gotta get home for dinner."

Marz leaned over to close the space between the three friends.

"Hey, I'm serious, what's going on?"

"Nothing!"

"Did you, like, *see* something?" Marybeth whispered as they restarted their walk to the train.

"Because you got that look," finished Marz.

Sylvie shook her head and untied her ponytail. A sheet of long, tangled brown hair hung around her face. "Forget it."

"Why are you hiding?"

"I'm *not!*"

But Marz nudged her to the side, until Sylvie was pressed against the iron fence of the nearest apartment building. Flies buzzed around the garbage bins. Ants had control of a banana peel.

"Stop—*damn!*" Sylvie protested.

"Tell us or else."

"Or else *what?*"

"I don't know—you'll feel guilty? C'mon, you saw something! Did you finally look at Deirdre's cellar? Was that book right about the crazy doctor who butchered his patients? Is there a for real ghost? Sorry if so. I didn't actually believe it."

Part of their friendship was spent looking up haunted houses to confirm or deny their apocryphal origins, Marz's second favorite pastime after music. They looked for places easy to vet, easy to research, but were rarely ever successful, and nothing was ever scary. They started that hobby in junior high, with the old Merchant's House Museum near Marz's place.

Sylvie pushed her hair over her shoulder and squared off with her. "You gave up your chance to find out when you gave up your chance to be the first Black Irish dancer in New York."

"I made my choice, girl. I see what you wear and it's *not* decent."

"Oh, it's not *so* bad," said Marybeth, who had joined Irish dance lessons with Sylvie before committing to ballet.

"Okay, Miss Tutus," countered Marz.

Dance was a topic Sylvie could run along like a track, so run along it she did. Anything to put distance between herself and the probable murder tumbling around her brain. "I'm getting a new dress this summer. What would you approve of, Marzy? Should it be leather and safety pins?"

Marz made a scoffing noise.

Marybeth laughed. "No, no, Sylvie. Disco, Marz's favorite-and-a-*half*! Make it gold lamé!"

Marz sighed. "*I'm* not the one who'll be wearing it in front of people."

Sylvie ignored her. "Ooh, totally! Sequins all over."

"Just covered in rhinestones," said Marybeth.

"Ah, rhinestones. The most Irish of stones," said Marz. "Blarney, Swarovski . . ."

Sylvie interrupted her. "I've told you a hundred times. Being Irish doesn't even matter. My parents aren't Irish, and Marilyn is . . . I guess I've never asked her."

"Real talk, babe, I probably *am* Irish—"

"We are so far off the point, guys," Marybeth interrupted. "What did you see? You know we'll believe you."

It wasn't a question of belief. It was a question of acknowledgment. Acknowledgment that maybe her powers were going wrong. But there was no reason to lie, either. She would tell her friends eventually. They were the only people she *could* tell.

"Okay. Look. I saw something, and it was weird, but the weird stuff isn't the weird part—I shouldn't have seen it at all. I didn't touch anything!"

"You ran into the gate," said Marz.

"That doesn't count," said Sylvie. "Anyway, see these jeans covering my legs?"

"Oh, she's a bitch today!"

"It's hard to—to always know what *you* know," said Marybeth.

"What was it?" asked Marz.

Sylvie sighed and lowered her voice. "Some girl got shot. But it was across the street from Deirdre's."

Marz turned her head as though she would see the body, but she knew enough by now to realize she wouldn't see anything. She knew enough because there wasn't all that much to know.

Unlike in the comics Sylvie and her brother used to read, there wasn't a mad scientist or celestial being she could turn to for help. No mystical tome, vat of radioactive insects, or faraway galaxy to explain her origins. Even her adoption was wide open. Her birth mom, Marilyn, having been a student at the Brooklyn high school where Sylvie's mom once worked, was now a journalist or something on the other side of the city. They usually saw her at Christmas. Not exactly a mystery.

"You don't think . . ." Marz bit her lip.

Sylvie waited half a second before pushing Marz's shoulder. "What? You don't think what?"

"What if it's, like, something to do with the .44 caliber killer."

"What?" said Marybeth.

15

"*How?*" said Sylvie.

Marz threw out her arms. "He shoots people, right? College girls!"

"Yeah, in *Queens* outside *discos*, not in Manhattan outside Irish dance schools."

"If he heard all that accordion music . . ."

Sylvie sighed. "Okay, Don Rickles."

"He can't take the train?"

"Don Rickles?"

"The *shooter!*" Marz looked over her shoulder to be sure no one was paying her attention. "I mean, people been shot here, too. Shot and bombed. And bombed again. Dunno why your teacher doesn't move."

"She grew up here."

"*I'm just saying*, it's not out of the *realm of possibility* some multiple murderer would come over here. Maybe it's too hot for him out there. Or, shit, maybe it's a copycat."

"Ugh, Marz, stop," said Marybeth. "You're creeping me out. My studio's over here, too."

"I should quit meeting you dance nerds and stay home. Anyway, Sylvie, what d'you think? Maybe it's some astral-projecting ghost of his victim!"

Sylvie shook her head as though to push the words away from her. "No way, bub. I'm not *psychic*. Whatever happened already happened, and it must've happened years ago. That's how it's . . ." Sylvie trailed off. Did any of her rules, her observations of her own abilities, even matter now? Maybe it *was* from yesterday. Maybe it was a girl who liked to dress a little retro, like Elvis fans her age.

Marz sighed this time, tapping her bitten nails against a scratched-up New York Dolls badge on her lapel. "The bigger mystery is how you saw her at all, right? She was at one place, you were at another."

"Maybe I didn't drink enough water."

"I feel ya, I feel ya. That's gotta be it."

"Maybe it's something different. Maybe it has nothing to do with the normal stuff you see. You know how people say some kinds of ghosts repeat their lives and don't know they're dead? Maybe it's that," said Marybeth.

"Yo, that's not a bad theory!"

"See, I listen to you, *ghost nerd*," said Marybeth.

Sylvie was grateful for the hypothesizing, really, and almost didn't want to poke holes in the idea. But. "But you didn't see anything—or hear anything? I heard a gunshot. And she screamed."

Despite herself, despite everything she knew, Sylvie hoped.

But Marybeth shook her head.

And Marz did, too. "Man, I wish you could record it and we could see what it's like. Not—not the murder!" (Sylvie had looked at her.) "Just your visions."

The weight of her bags was pulling at knots in Sylvie's shoulders, so she sped up.

Her friends were quick on her heels. Marz began walking backward in front of her, her worn-out Chucks expertly navigating the broken sidewalks and oncoming foot traffic. "Okay, so you've never asked Marilyn about being Irish, but have you ever asked her about . . . *your powers?*"

Sylvie snorted at the word *powers*. She couldn't help it. It sounded so grand and so important and also plain-old-fashioned ridiculous. If she were in X-Men, she would be Random Background Student. "I've thought about it, but I've also thought she might tell me something else. Like, her whole family's nuts or something."

"Obviously you're nuts, but you could still have powers."

"Thanks, bub."

"You should ask her. It's not like she'd ask you. Probably for the same reason, y'know?" said Marybeth.

Sylvie sighed. "Maybe she fell in the Gowanus Canal when she was pregnant. That's sorta like a vat of radioactive goo."

Marz looked Sylvie up and down. "It woulda been so ironic if you were the first Irish dancer with, like, ten arms."

Despite herself, Sylvie laughed.

CHAPTER TWO

Sylvie and Marz once lived in facing cast-iron warehouses on either side of Greene Street. Along with Marybeth, who lived around the corner on Broome, they were three of the few children in all of SoHo because, at the time, no one was supposed to be living in SoHo at all. When the threat of the expressway became too real, Marz's family moved into an East Village townhouse.

But all three girls still attended the same schools, and Marz's dad still owned their Greene Street loft. He even played freeform jazz there on the weekends, or at Ali's Alley, like the old days. Sometimes Marz's mom would practice her arias there, too. Loft opera, Marz's dad called it. Then they would all go to FOOD on Prince Street and have the soup, even though the prices went up once the tourists arrived in the neighborhood. People constantly worried that SoHo's future was already lost, the artists' days numbered in favor of uptown or out-of-town yuppie bohemians in Earth Shoes. But Sylvie thought the adults were freaking out for no reason. There were still too many rats and trucks in the streets.

Marybeth's family had called this part of the city home for almost a hundred years. Her great-grandfather opened the first electric light shop on Canal Street. Her father was an installation artist who used neon bulbs. Their loft was twice the size of Sylvie's in order to have enough room.

They were all rooted to the mercantile wasteland, addicted to the space, to the DIY spirit of organizing and self-expression. Defeating Robert Moses was a point of pride and deepest honor.

With the threat of demolition and illegal living no longer looming over them, it was hard to imagine going anywhere else. Even when Sylvie's mom lost her job when the city closed her library and her dad, fearing layoffs, jumped from CUNY to teach at the School of Visual Arts. Her parents were raised in Brooklyn (her mom) and the Bronx (her dad), but they liked charting this strange new/old cobbled ground. Her mom got into ceramics.

With Marz on a crosstown bus for home, Marybeth and Sylvie walked together from the train and parted ways at Sylvie's door.

"Chin up, kiddo," said Marybeth. "We'll figure it out. Don't worry about tonight."

"I won't." Sylvie hoped it wasn't a lie. "See ya tomorrow."

"Later days." Marybeth waved, then had to wave a second time when a neighbor spotted her across the street. An older lady whose paintings of melting pet portraits were always in the Prince Street art fair. Sylvie waved, too, then she turned around and took out the keys to get inside. One for the street door, another for the elevator, and two more for the apartment. She would only need the deadbolt since her parents were home.

Geneva Stroud was surrounded by steam heat from a pot of something on the stove. Her thick, dark hair slowly falling out of the twist pinned with sticks at the top of her head.

"Woo!" She waved her hand through the cloud and moved away from the burners.

Stepping out of the elevator, Sylvie dumped her bags on the unvarnished floor and wrenched off her sneakers as her six-year-old golden retriever ran, tongue out, from the other side of the loft.

Sylvie scoured her fingers through fistfuls of her dog's warm fur. "Hi, Jessie Baby!"

"How was class?" asked Sylvie's mom.

As Jessie Baby ran circles around the brand-new kitchen island, Sylvie slid onto one of the mismatched stools. She shrugged, admiring the way her big toe stuck out of a hole in her left sock. This toe had lost and regrown its nail three times and now had more ridges than the Appalachian Trail. It wasn't a toenail—it was a formality.

"Fine. Marz needs a new drummer, so her sister's filling in."

"Which one?"

"Mom, which do you think? Gigi is *eight*."

Marz had two younger sisters, Alcina (Cee, mostly), and Gioconda (Gigi, always).

"I dunno, I hear she plays a mean flute."

"Didn't she hit someone with it?" The floorboards creaked as Bernard Stroud, Sylvie's dad, walked past, throwing a kitchen towel over his shoulder. He had a bald spot, a ponytail, and a well-groomed mustache. Sylvie hadn't seen his upper lip in years.

"With the case," said Sylvie. "And she was right to do it."

"Your toe looks cold, Silverado."

"Yeah, well, I'm gonna go downstairs and practice."

"You just had practice. You don't have homework?" asked Geneva.

Sylvie groaned. "Homework doesn't count this close to June."

"Then why do they hand it out?"

"A quota. Like cops and parking tickets."

Geneva gave her a look of motherly cynicism and went to the sink while Bernard laid out vegetables to chop.

"Speaking of school," she said, "Gary's coming home next Thursday, so take all your trophies and dirty socks out of his room, please. And do me a solid by tossing the socks in the hamper."

Sylvie spun on the stool once, twice, three times, listening to it squeal. It once belonged to her dad's drafting table and was covered in ink and paint. "Lucky him. I've got junioritis."

"There's no such thing as junioritis."

"Mom, come on! I need to practice my new set! Deirdre says adjudicators at the Worlds sometimes ask for *three*."

"All right. It's *your* future."

"Future *World Champion*."

Geneva ignored her. Sylvie tried not to take it personally. "You've got until supper. Then it's homework. And it's *lights-out* at ten, and I mean it. If I wake up to the sound of your hardshoes at midnight, so help me God, I'll throw them out and you right after."

Bernard pointed the paring knife at her. "There's probably a box down there you could move into."

Sylvie slid off the stool. "10-4, good buddies!"

Dropping her dance bag across her shoulder, she went to grab the key for the elevator before her dad shouted, "Stairs!"

Sylvie sighed and unlocked the front door.

The Strouds occupied floors four and five of their building. With loft living gone legal, floor five was home. Floor four was her parents' studio and storage, though neither went down there as often these days. As a result, what was finished upstairs was never going to be finished downstairs.

Sylvie was three when her parents moved from Brooklyn to SoHo (it wasn't even called SoHo back then), buying their space from a man who snagged the whole building for next to nothing when the button factory packed up and moved out. The ninety-year-old proprietor had finally retired to the country (New Jersey). For a while, that left only the Strouds and one other tenant—a wholesale fabric distributor had the third floor and only used the place to store rag clippings. And they were still around, sort of, but a burgeoning co-op had taken over the first two floors and revamped the gallery. They were currently negotiating with Sylvie's parents to install an automatic elevator.

As a result of the general condition of the place, and the fact that the fabric company may have forgotten it was even there, Sylvie could continue to beat up the already beaten-up fourth floor with impunity. No one had respected these floors in a hundred years, anyway—hardshoes were the least of its problems. Sometimes she still found stray buttons from the factory wedged in cracks and seams, and when her parents put in the studio bathroom, they uncovered hundreds of pins between the floorboards from the time a millinery had occupied the floor, before the buttons.

SARAH DVOJACK

The stairwell was dark because the skylight hadn't been scraped clean since World War Two. The stairs hadn't been repaired since World War One. The tread was uneven and sloped to one side or the other, depending on which floor you passed. Usually that was the only thing that made Sylvie nervous. Now it was the darkness, too, that slowed her descent.

Her steps bounced off the old walls and slipped into nothingness below. Without even street noise to ground her, her thoughts strayed back to Hell's Kitchen, and the girl, and the shotgun blast that rocked Sylvie's brain.

Clenching her teeth, Sylvie skipped down to the landing below and jammed her dad's studio keys into the locks. She shoved the door open as fast as she could, sliding the chain lock on even though she never did that.

Then she shivered.

Then she laughed.

"Calm down. Damn."

The air was cold and dusty, and the horizontal sun carved deep shadows across drafting tables and easels and bookcases and stack upon stack of archival boxes filled with her dad's old cartoons. Even her (previously her brother's) old crib was down here, taken apart and wedged between a desk and several boxes marked X-MAS.

Just like upstairs, just like every floor, cast-iron pillars ran down the center of the space. The only real room was the bathroom squared off by drywall that didn't even reach the warped, tin-tiled ceiling. It was back there that her mom had started working after she was laid off, stacks of bowls and plates and mugs occupying a new wooden shelving unit. Her potter's wheel sat on a plastic sheet covered in dried white clay.

Sylvie flung her bag on one of her dad's wooden flat files and pulled out her hardshoes. They smelled like sweat and warm leather, and most of the black polish had come off the toes. In ten years of dancing, she couldn't fathom how many shoes she'd gone through and how hardshoe shapes had evolved, but each pair smelled the same and reminded her of the first lessons she ever had, when the steps and politics were simple, and she wore Mary Janes with little taps.

Exposed pipes and ventilation poised like serpents above her head and down the walls as she walked to a beaten side table and plugged in the stereo, switching it on. Sylvie and Gary had bought it for their dad's birthday two years earlier (with their mom's money), and it was already covered in dried clay and paint. More than one button had, on different occasions, been stuck to the next and required a palette knife to break free. It was a friendly machine.

Then it spat AM static into the room and Sylvie's heart hit the back of her throat with such force that she saw a pop of white behind her eyes. She hurriedly smashed the 8-track button just to get the hissing to stop, but then it began to blast mid-song.

"Eject, eject!" she yelled at it. They would probably hear her upstairs—the floors weren't exactly insulated.

Rubber Soul, her brother's third-favorite Beatles album and her dad's first, popped out of the slot, and Sylvie shoved the cartridge into its bent sleeve.

Her heartbeat filled the space the noise had occupied as she dug out a record of *Dónal Ó Maonaigh Set Dances Vol. II.*

When she turned around, the nearest pillar seemed to jump at her, and she ducked down and fell as her hardshoes slipped beneath her.

"Cripes!"

A sliver of the dry floorboard went into her palm, and she could barely look while sliding it back out. Once, when she was seven, a splinter in her thumb caused her to see three women making silk flowers for four days straight. She'd barely slept or walked in a straight line until the last trace of wood was pulled free. Her dad had to use a magnifying glass to find it. Everyone thought she had a bout of vertigo from the pain.

Sylvie almost thought it would happen again as she closed her hand. The little bead of blood spread into the folds of her skin. Life line, fate line. She licked it off. The room stayed empty.

"Oh, you're really gonna qualify for the Worlds like this."

Three years in a row she had tried, and three years in a row she had been stopped at the starting line. A high fever. A broken ankle (which healed as soon as Sylvie didn't need to dance on it anymore; two weeks later and her X-ray looked like it had never been fractured at all). An errant bobby pin that made her fall hard on her ass in front of the adjudicator's table.

This year the curse was getting even more creative.

Accordion music filled the studio, but it was almost too loud, too abrasive. Never in her life had "Fiddler Around the Fairy

Tree" seemed menacing. She didn't want to listen to any music at all, suddenly—even music played on a piano accordion by an ancient Irish man.

Sylvie stood up and tucked her jeans into her socks.

She knew pretty much where to drop the needle to reach her track, but each time she went to lift the needle and repeat, it let the silence back in, and she found she didn't like that, either.

"It doesn't matter," she muttered, accidentally landing in the middle of the previous track with a mighty scratch. "It wasn't really there. It doesn't matter anymore."

It.

She could not repeat what happened after dance class again. She wouldn't invoke it.

Instead, she loudly counted off the bars until the start of her dance, then beat her steps into the floor.

CRACK

The first heel click reverberated off the walls, sharper than Sylvie could ever remember. Had they always sounded like gunfire?

Every toe hit, every slam, every treble.

BAM BAM BAM

The teenage girl's body fell in rapid succession, over and over and over.

Every time Sylvie moved within sight of a column, it was the girl standing there, light pouring through a shotgun blast through her chest.

The visions, the pantomimes, the memories—they were no threat. They never noticed her. They couldn't. They were the tape inside the 8-track, rewinding and replaying back and forth. Or the grooves of a record, Sylvie the needle.

But she hadn't touched that row house, possibly ever in her life. It was as though the girl had run out to be noticed, and now that she was noticed, she was somehow alive.

Every once in a while, it seemed like history tried to remind her that it was real, not some kind of tableau vivant for her childish amusement.

It didn't make sense, but it did fill Sylvie with dread that not a single beat of her set could drive out. She stopped the record and looked around. She had so much of this room's history memorized, so many revisited moments. A man singing "Melancholy Baby" to another man. A woman trying on every hat and doing impressions with each one. A surreptitious affair between an errand boy and (probably) a secretary. A young woman sneaking cheese to a rat, then one day taking it home in her skirt pocket.

Sylvie hesitated and sat down, pushing her hand to the floor until she had what she wanted—herself, ten years earlier, mittens on her fists and slippers on her feet as she danced her first reel steps in bold but messy circles. Those mittens—a blockade against an assault to her senses. Sylvie's stomach dropped as a new thought occurred to her: what if that seven-year-old girl didn't go back in? What if *none* of the memories went back in? What if this mental stopper Sylvie had developed no longer worked? What if she was supposed to have been looking all this time, after all, and now she was going to be punished by seeing everything, everywhere, always?

She wasn't religious, but *damn* did it sometimes feel like a curse.

She closed her eyes as she lifted her hand away, and even though she could no longer hear her younger self in the room, she had to breathe in and out before she was ready to look.

Alone. She was alone. She was freaking out for no reason.

You'll get over it tomorrow. It's just shock. You'll get over it tomorrow, or maybe the day after that, and everything will be normal again.

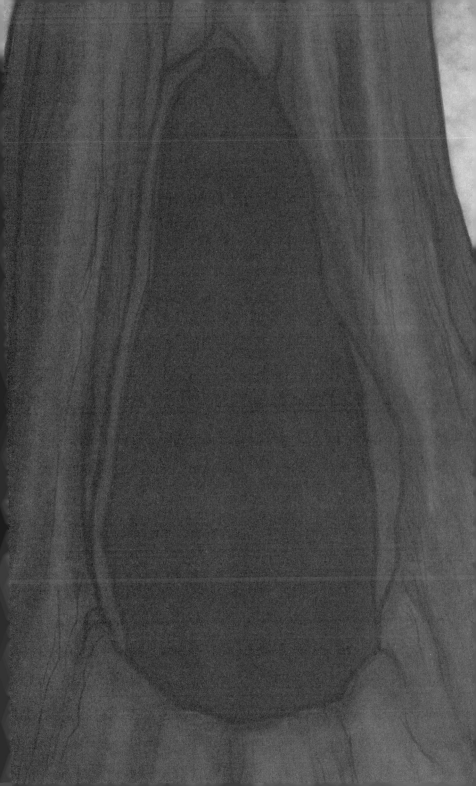

CHAPTER THREE

Normal was dance, and dance was normal. New York City was full of people who shared that understanding. New York City was for people who wanted the stage. They slummed it on cigarettes and bed bugs and Howard Johnson's to break out in Fosse, Balanchine, or Ailey. The kinds of capital R Romantic and gritty and Chorus Line-y that people loved and lauded, teased in Page Six, and made movies out of. Prestige covered in sweat and tights.

Irish dance, though. What was Irish dance? It didn't get you to Lincoln Center or Radio City. One day a year you might make it on Broadway, in the St. Pat's parade, hidden behind twelve pipe bands (Scottish) and their Highland dance troupes (also Scottish). It didn't get you on the front pages of the most local of local newsletters. Sometimes it got your recital flier stuck to the bulletin board at Wally's ice cream parlor. It definitely got you teased when your friends saw you in your costumes or came over to your apartment and saw your Fleetwood Mac and Peter Frampton posters overlaid with banners of medals and sashes.

Sylvie took Irish dance seriously because no one else did. No one knew what it looked like, and no amount of explanation could stop the patronizing chuckles. Everyone imagined quaint country folks dancing around in circles.

Unlike most people at her dance school, Sylvie didn't fall into it through cultural inheritance or a parental legacy. She only learned about it when a girl in first grade danced a slip jig for show-and-tell, and Sylvie needed something to distract herself. To give her hands nothing to do. She was a rare outside case, but no one on the inside cared. They were happy to have her there. It was everyone else she wanted to prove wrong.

Four years after she started dancing, she was handed a tangible goal to make legitimacy happen. The World Championships were created. And five years after that, the very first American won the title, some teenage boy from Chicago. She wrote it on a calendar when Deirdre told them. Of course, it was a boy who won first—clearly women's lib hadn't reached the adjudicators—but the possibility felt much closer than it had before.

What kind of dancing is it you do?

Irish dancing.

Oh, how interesting.

I'm a World Champion, actually.

She'd had three chances to make it to the Worlds. If another cosmic fluke stopped her a fourth time, maybe she really *was* cursed. In another year, most of her class would be off to college and adulthood, and they would leave their dance shoes and memories behind. This wasn't her last chance, not by any means, but it felt like the end of an era stood on the horizon, pointing down at her.

Up in Hell's Kitchen, Sylvie slowed as she approached the street corner. It was utterly against code, putting the brakes on in the middle of the sidewalk, but she did it without thinking because all of her thoughts were on what she would see when she turned that corner.

Part of her was convinced she had nothing to worry about. Part of her rehearsed this moment all day at school. The relief she would feel. The lightness. The new appreciation for the order of things, the expectations she had for her hindsight.

But there the girl was, already flat on the sidewalk, the invisible hook already in her hair, dragging her back. Sylvie was so consumed by disappointment that she let her eyes linger on the vicious wound to the girl's chest and shoulder, how her arm was limp. Then the vision broke up and was gone again.

Sylvie's legs and arms felt like they weighed a thousand pounds, like she couldn't move. Then the terror of seeing it again sent her running across the street.

As she waited at Deirdre's door, she reached out her hand to trace the brick facade like she often did. Deirdre's entire life was laid out here, from the days she wore Shirley Temple curls and pinafores and barely reached Sylvie's knees to her very first students (who also barely reached Sylvie's knees). As a kid, Sylvie used to slip bits of what Deirdre's parents said or what Deirdre did into conversation, just to see what her teacher would do. ("That reminds me of something my dad would say," was what Deirdre would say.) Sylvie loved knowing these things about her. But today Sylvie looked at her exposed hand and quickly shoved it into her jeans pocket.

Then she heard the gunshot again. She looked back like someone had her head in their hands and forced her to do it.

She thought she saw the girl glance at her, as though to mock her before throwing herself on the ground, but it was just a trick of the late afternoon light.

"Cripes," Sylvie whispered.

"You—"

"Cripes!" Sylvie shouted.

Bushy-haired Caitlin Haley stepped backward, the open door in her hand. "Sorry! Didn't mean to freak you out. I was already downstairs, so Deirdre told me to let you in."

"I thought I forgot my hardshoes," was all Sylvie could think of saying. She hated being this rattled. She hated that there was no authority she could talk to.

"It's figures tonight, anyway, remember?" Caitlin looked expectantly at Sylvie. "You coming in?"

"10-4." Sylvie couldn't even look at Caitlin because she would have to smile, and she was still working through a lot of different feelings.

Of course it was figure class tonight. Group dances. Other people depended on her. Deirdre had fundraised the previous spring so they could afford to send a whole team to Ireland if they qualified. They'd chosen *Three Tunes* for the oireachtas—a perennial favorite that gave her only slight incentive not to run the fuck home again.

Sylvie usually preferred a spot near the middle window that faced the street below, but tonight she forced Devon Slocum out of his favorite corner. She pretended not to notice the change, and for a while she even found herself relaxing again.

It wasn't until she heard the shot again, sounding above the stereo, that Sylvie began to lose it. First, she tripped on her own feet. She claimed she suddenly had to sneeze and it threw her off. Then she began to anticipate each shot, so that her whole body would stop moving altogether, causing people to collide with her. She ran for a drink of water despite having a water bottle just to get out of the room and away from the window.

"Sylvie," Deirdre kept having to say, which was not something she usually had to say. "Earth to Sylvie. Are you here with us, Sylvie?"

Everyone, seven pairs of teenage eyes, stared at Sylvie. "Sorry—earache." *Earache?*

"Do you need to go home early?"

Sylvie thought about it. Hesitated. She could run out the door and look like a fool without any of her classmates noticing, but figures were probably her best chance at the Worlds if she fell on her butt during her solos again, and leaving early, especially without an earache, gave her the irrational feeling that she would forget how to dance at all.

"I'll be fine," she said instead.

"You're jumpier than when I saw *The Omen* last year," said Devon as they packed their things and changed out of their shoes at the end of class. "Did you see that one? Does your friend Marz like horror movies or just the real-life stuff?"

"Yeah, we saw it," said Sylvie.

"It reminded me of this creepy story my sister told me—"

Sylvie snorted and shoved her softshoes into her bag. Marz and Devon had embarked on a never-ending bet three years earlier—that he would find a New York horror story she hadn't heard. So far she had only paid out fifty cents (the price was a quarter per story).

"Spill it." She both wanted to leave and didn't want to go outside at all.

"Okay, so there was this mansion in Brooklyn."

"Mansion in Brooklyn. Check."

"This rich German family lived there, I dunno, a hundred years ago. Anyway, they had two kids, and one day the son jumps off the balcony. He lived but he couldn't walk anymore. He said a headless lady wanted his sister to die, so he tried to sacrifice himself. Turns out there were bodies buried in the basement. They moved out after that."

"I dunno why the idea of a bunch of headless women wandering around is almost funny. Like, you'd think their neighbors would notice."

Devon shrugged and helped Sylvie stand up. "Hey, I'm just the middleman. Tell me if Marz knows that one."

But Sylvie forgot to relay it.

She loitered in Deirdre's front hall until most of her class was gone, then bolted out the front door.

Marz and Marybeth ran after her.

"Hey, what the fuck are we? Chopped liver?" called Marz.

Sylvie kept walking. "The girl's still there."

"The girl—wait, the murdered girl?" whispered Marz.

Sylvie nodded.

"Okay, well, we'll figure it out, babe."

"Let's meet at the end of the block from now on," said Marybeth. "Would that help?"

"Thanks for not thinking I'm crazy," Sylvie said.

Marz slung her arm around Sylvie's shoulders. "You gotta appease crazy people."

"Ha ha."

"It really must have something to do with the renovation," said Marybeth, almost to herself.

Sylvie doubted it, but what did she know? Maybe Marybeth was right. "But I don't want to see it four days a week until they're done—and what if it just doesn't go away?"

Then she began to think back to when the renovation began. Earlier in the spring. April, maybe. It was now freshly June. What took the girl so long?

She was there the next afternoon, too.

She was probably there at all hours every single day, falling and falling and falling again, a record skipping and skipping and skipping and no one but Sylvie could make it right.

But she also knew she *couldn't* make it right.

This helplessness left Sylvie feeling like an invasive species had taken root inside her. It was so much like the way it felt when she was just an overwhelmed kid with no way to reach the brakes. She hadn't felt afraid of her hindsight in a long time. She had hoped she would never feel that way again. And she felt bad that the thing upsetting her the most wasn't the murder, but the lack of under-standing, the lack of control.

At her next class, Sylvie wore her sunglasses so the world was dim and slightly blurry, and let her hair hang around her face. Cait-lin asked her if she was high or something.

And at the next one, she skipped the sunglasses and left her regular glasses in her bookbag. Every few minutes, the window at her back and open to the sunny afternoon, Sylvie heard the gunshot down below. And each time she did, she forgot where she was in her step and ended up wandering aimlessly without muscle memory like she had never even seen someone dance, let alone done it herself.

"Sylvie! You just cut Nessa and Brigid off again!" Deirdre snapped at her, marching to the stereo and stopping the music. "Start again. Sylvie, sit this out until you've got your mind in the present. Everyone else here is going to be competing this summer, and until today I assumed that included you."

Deirdre could be strict, and Deirdre could be demanding, but Deirdre never really got angry. It left the rest of the class silent and Sylvie feeling more embarrassed than she could ever remember. Her face burned, and she didn't think she'd worked up enough of a sweat to hide it.

"Sorry, Deirdre, I'm sorry," she mumbled, her voice lost some-where in her nerves.

Deirdre gave her a pitying sort of look, but Sylvie didn't wait to see if she was going to impart sympathy or concern. The last thing she wanted was a talk. Deirdre rarely called up the parents, but if she thought Sylvie was Troubled, she would make an exception.

Sylvie went into the bathroom and turned on the taps to disguise the stupidly fast breathing she needed to get under control. On the other side of the wall, the floor thundered, life went on.

Wednesday was free from lessons, and she was so relieved that she immediately felt guilty instead. Dance class was supposed to make her happy, was supposed to motivate her through difficult school days and the looming question of her future. Without it, she wasn't even sure that she was good at anything. Even her hindsight was ultimately useless and impossible to prove.

As a kid, she fancied herself a real Nancy Drew for about a second. There was a two-hundred-year-old well in the basement of a place on Spring Street that was supposed to be the site of a famous murder. She knew she could prove whether or not that murder happened, but she couldn't get people to even believe the well was there, let alone to excavate it. And why would they? She was just a kid with a vivid imagination.

Sylvie tried to push her frustration aside as she hung out in Marz's neighborhood until it was time to meet Marybeth and distribute themselves among their homes. While Marz considered new boots, Sylvie tried flirting with guys in pomade and creepers but couldn't quite empty her brain enough to enjoy it. She finally did remember to tell Marz Devon's ghost story and Marz said there were too many stories that involved headless women, but it was probably about the Penzig brewing family. No quarter lost today.

Soon it was a full week since the teenage girl first appeared, and she showed no sign of letting up.

Stressing about it gave her wilder fears. What if all these years of reading buildings were nothing more than a break with reality? Or maybe her whole entire history was a fabrication. There'd been all those Senate hearings and news reports about MKUltra over the last few years. Maybe she was an experiment, some kid the CIA had injected with LSD to try and build a super spy, able to suss out where the Soviets kept secret labs or some shit. Maybe her parents or Marilyn were agents, monitoring her progress.

All right, maybe not. But something was wrong with her, and something else was broken on top of that. There was always a first time for every mental disease. Patient zero.

Maybe she wasn't Random Background Student. Maybe she was something else entirely.

CHAPTER FOUR

The E train squealed along a turn. An empty whipped cream canister rolled over the floor. A kid in an NYU sweatshirt with the sleeves cut off smoked a cigarette while he carved something into the doors. Someone had tagged SAVE BOSWIJCK in bloodred paint across the seats in front of them. A bright yellow happy face sticker was framed in the *O*.

Marybeth hummed ABBA as she knitted a pair of warm-up shorts for dance. Marz kicked the canister away, her army-navy backpack balanced on her knees. Sylvie kept staring at the happy face sticker without really seeing it.

"I know I ask you this every Thursday, and like every Thursday I am extending the invitation to hit up *Rocky Horror* with us tomorrow," said Marz.

Another shrill whine along the tracks. One of the hapless tourists covered one ear.

"Maybe," said Sylvie.

Marybeth stopped humming. "Whoa!"

"No way," teased Marz. "That's the first maybe in *years*."

"Shut up. If I'm tired in the morning, big whoop," Sylvie said. She only ever went out late on a Friday night if Marz's band was playing. Not even a boyfriend could get her to change her mind, which was probably why she'd never had a steady one. Not a huge loss, really.

But tonight, Sylvie was humbled and humiliated. She'd had to use the small practice room like she was a little kid first learning her steps. At least it faced the back garden.

"It's so fucking annoying. Everything's good. I'm dancing. I'm concentrating. It's all normal. And then I hear the——" She mimed a gun blast to her chest. "I pretend it's a car or something, but I know it's not."

"Yeah, that'd be distracting," said Marz.

"It's not even that she gets shot! That sounds bad. But I've seen people—it's that it happened for no reason. I didn't touch anything! I didn't do anything different than I usually do. And I keep worrying I'll see something somewhere else. Maybe eventually I won't be able to control it again, and it'll be worse this time. I'll see things all day long no matter what. You know how overwhelming it is to have a thousand people walking and talking all over? I'd go crazy inside of a day."

Marz helpfully patted Sylvie's knee. "Babe, I get it, but it's stupid to think like that until you have more proof."

"God, don't be so *reasonable*."

"Look, girl, you can *see the past*. Me and Marybeth *have* to be the reasonable ones."

"But if it does go haywire," said Marybeth, "you can just stop wearing glasses and then you won't see it as well."

Sylvie snorted. "I've tried that."

"*And* I'll knit you mittens."

"I guess I just wish I could find someone who knew what the hell was going on, y'know? I've got nothing to go on, here."

The train slowed, the breaks squealed even louder. The canister wound back toward them and knocked against Sylvie's toe just as the kid in the NYU sweatshirt dropped his cigarette and the doors opened. Marz stood up. Paper fluttered in the breeze.

"I'll walk home with you guys, if you want," said Marz.

Sylvie shook her head. "It's fine."

"You sure?"

Sylvie nodded without thinking about it. Nodded because Marz needed to get out, and she didn't want her to worry. What could any of them do?

Marz and Marybeth had no reason to believe Sylvie saw the past in the present, but they did, and they always had. Marybeth had even learned to knit to help support Sylvie's odd sartorial habit (though it took a few tries to get mittens that a person could feasibly wear).

"I'll call you," Marz said as she shouldered her bag.

Sylvie saluted her. Marybeth flashed a peace sign.

As the train moved on, Sylvie compulsively tapped her foot on the dusty floor, kicking away the canister whenever it drifted near and staring at an ad for Virginia Slims. The model's head was blackened out with a thick dot of paint that dripped down one side of her body. Someone had put a happy face sticker right in the middle of that, too.

She had two stops to go, but ten seconds after leaving Fourteenth Street, she made a decision.

"I'm gonna see Marilyn."

Marybeth looked up from where she was gathering her knitting back into her bag. "Right now?"

Sylvie was already shouldering her bag. "Yeah. Before I realize it's a bad idea."

"Should I tell your parents where you are if they phone?"

"Sure. Yeah. Or plead the Fifth if you need to. But maybe call Marz so she doesn't call my place first, looking for me."

Marybeth nodded as the doors opened and they got off at West Fourth together, as usual. "Sure thing! Good luck, I guess."

Waving to Marybeth at the station entrance, Sylvie hurried up and around the block, barreled onto a crosstown bus, then shoved her way onto the 6 train.

She did all of this without thinking beyond her immediate surroundings and the burden of speed walking with a rucksack and a dance bag. If she ventured any deeper into her thoughts, she would ask herself what in the world she was going to say after the doorman let her up.

"Sylvie!" was what Marilyn said, once she'd unhitched the chain lock. They were a match for height now, which left Sylvie to assume that she was either done growing or would officially become tall.

They looked alike in almost every obvious way, except that Marilyn had golden blonde hair (dyed) she kept above her shoulders and blown out into perfect currents that bounced around her heart-shaped, Sylvie-like face. A face with kind of small, wide-set brown eyes, straight brows (Marilyn's plucked into a rail-thin arch), and no freckles or moles, though Marilyn had a small scar on her cheekbone. She also needed glasses, like Sylvie, but her frames were from Bergdorf Goodman on Fifth Avenue, not Sol Moscot's on Delancey.

Marilyn wasn't rich, but her mother had some money once, when she was a child star on the dying vaudeville stage. Then she was a bit player on Broadway. Then there were other things that involved Forty-Second Street theatres that Sylvie wasn't supposed to know about. Then she married an airman from the Pacific Theater who came into an inheritance when his parents died instead of him.

Then they had Marilyn. Then Marilyn had Sylvie, but Marilyn was only in the ninth grade, and fortunately for Marilyn, Geneva Stroud was a young librarian at her high school who had adopted a son already, and the rest was history. Or, well, the rest was present.

"Hello." Sylvie almost cringed at the plastic sound of her voice, like she'd never even talked to this woman before.

Marilyn gave her a sympathetic look and said, "Come in, Applesauce."

The apartment was a real apartment, always meant to be lived in, but to Sylvie it was suffocating in its railroad narrowness. An abundance of patterned, metallic wallpaper made the living space even smaller and more chaotic, centering the focus on a plastic-covered velour sofa Marilyn's mom had given her.

Sylvie's parents liked minimalism and macramé, but mostly they liked the furniture they bought after marrying twenty-five years ago, and they had a lot of square footage to spread it out in. And plants. They had plants covering their oversized windows and hanging beneath the skylight. Half the people in SoHo did. Marilyn just had a vase of fresh, white flowers sitting on a side table. She'd had some on display every time Sylvie visited, which was infrequent.

She had read Marilyn's apartment only once and was surprised by how calm its layers were compared to her own loft. Not having machinery in its past would do that.

"It's already dinnertime, so I'd guess you've eaten," said Marilyn, who was so far the only person to speak at all, other than Walter Cronkite. She walked away to switch off the tube.

"No, I just finished dance," Sylvie finally said, dropping her bags near the chrome and Formica dining table and sitting down. The dining chairs had plastic-covered cushions, too. Marilyn moved to the adjacent kitchen and piled dirty dishes into the sink.

"Hungry? I had Chinese, but I could nuke the leftovers."

"No, I'll—" Sylvie's parents were going to be angry she was late. Probably two or three hours late, at the rate things were going. It would be dark out, and no matter where she was, she wasn't supposed to be out after dark. *It's ten o'clock: Do you know where your children are?* If she was lucky, her mom wouldn't phone the local precinct. If she was *really* lucky, her mom wouldn't call Marz and Marybeth. She didn't want to tell her parents she was here, in case of awkward questions, but that was going to be inevitable.

She decided to put it off.

Marilyn stared at her, waiting for the rest of the sentence.

"Actually, yeah. If that's all right."

"I shouldn't eat it so often, anyway. It's just lo mein left. That okay?"

"Totally. I eat all Chinese food."

"Me, too. And I think I do." Marilyn laughed her clear, happy laugh. "I don't know how you knew to drop in today. This is the first time in weeks I'm home before seven."

Sylvie realized she should have rehearsed something. Even written something down on the back of her hand. Or her palm, so she could hide it, though she would have sweated it off.

"I guess I'm psychic," she said, wincing inwardly.

How does anyone ask if they have special powers? Fiction said superheroes (or villains) could demonstrate something when needed. What could Sylvie do? Marilyn hadn't lived here long enough for her own memories to appear and be cited as proof.

"Wish I was," said Marilyn. "My job would be a piece of cake."

Well, that didn't work. Or maybe that was the answer. "So, uh, work must be busy, I guess," Sylvie said. She couldn't remember what paper or magazine Marilyn worked for.

Marilyn scraped the food into a bowl and dropped it in the microwave. "A real pain in the ass. Thank God tomorrow's Friday. How was school?"

Sylvie shrugged. "School's okay. We're almost out."

"How was dance?"

"School was better."

Marilyn bit back a laugh. "Really? Why? I thought you liked dancing."

A girl from the past keeps getting shot and dying right across the street every time I'm there, and it's because I have special but useless powers, probably, and do you have special but useless powers?

"Are you Irish?" Sylvie said instead. Then she couldn't believe she'd said it. Marilyn was going to think she was having Issues.

"Am I—uh, I don't think so. Mom always *said* she was Spanish and French, but I'm pretty sure that was just for her act. I think my grandma was Polish or something. Or whatever Poland was back then. Not sure about Dad's family. Atler could be German or something."

"I guess I should be doing Flamenco," said Sylvie, and she meant it as a joke, but it came out a little too moody, so Marilyn walked out of the kitchen and sat down in a chair next to her while the lo mein spun and spun and spun in the microwave.

Danger, Will Robinson, danger!

"Did someone pick on you at dance? So what if you're not Irish? I bet you're better than most of those kids."

Quickly, Sylvie shook her head. "No, it's not that. They don't care. I just realized I never asked, that's all. I might need to know someday, like if I donate blood."

"They don't need to know your ethnic background to donate blood. I don't think . . ."

"Bad example. I guess I was just curious."

Marilyn laughed and leaned back in her chair, looking somewhat more serene than she had a minute ago. "So you schlepped over here to ask if I'm Irish?"

Marilyn was definitely going to tell Sylvie's parents all about this if she didn't stop acting like a sulking teenager, so Sylvie quickly lied and said, "I was with Marz and Marybeth and she's looking for a new drummer so I was late coming home, anyway, and sort of nearby so I thought I'd say hi."

"Well, hi, then. It's nice to see you." Marilyn looked even more serene and even went back into the kitchen. "Who're Marz and Marybeth, again?"

"My best friends."

"Right, right. How's the fam?"

Sylvie began tracing the chrome ribbing around the table. "Fine. Mom's still looking for a job. There's a listing at a private school."

"She'll get it. She's the best. You still got that boyfriend?"

Sylvie didn't want to explain she'd had a few since the last time she saw Marilyn (at Christmas). "Nope."

Marilyn laughed.

"So, your mom's fake French and Spanish and your dad was maybe German. Anything else weird in there? Like, uh, anyone have superpowers or been accused of witchcraft?" Sylvie asked hopefully.

Marilyn laughed. "I mean, my mom could go through men like toilet paper, which is sort of a superpower. They might still invoke her name in Times Square, but I don't know what that would do. Say her name five times in the bathroom mirror of—well, Mom's still alive so I don't think anything would happen. I guess it'd still summon her."

Sylvie snorted as Marilyn dug a fork out of the utensil drawer and pulled the steaming bowl out of the microwave.

"Cheers, toots," she said as she dropped it on the table. "The bowl's hot."

"Thanks." Looking at the food, Sylvie's stomach turned over, and she couldn't quite tell if it was hunger or anxiety about this weird predicament she'd put herself in.

"So, no one did witchcraft?"

Back in the kitchen, Marilyn was scrubbing the harvest gold Formica counters. "Are you reading *The Crucible* in school or something?"

"We did in the fall, actually. I asked Mom and Dad the same question back then," she lied. "They're squeaky clean."

"Honestly, I don't really know, but I think if we had some relative who was burned or hanged or drowned for witchcraft, Mom would've told me. But I only know anything back to my grandparents, anyhow. I suppose if Mom's really French, there could be a chance. Maybe we're related to Joan of Arc."

"Why'd they burn her again?" Sylvie asked.

"Politics? It's always politics. I think she saw holy visions or something."

Visions. Sylvie didn't see true visions, unless Joan of Arc mistook her abilities for visions when they were actually inconvenient history lessons.

Marilyn continued. "I doubt she did. She probably had what Sybil had. Did you watch that? How wild. I almost don't believe that could be true, either, having so many personalities. But what do I know? The brain's complicated. I've gotta read the book."

Sometimes when Marilyn spoke, the old Brooklyn came out. She had a much stronger accent when Sylvie was little, but when she came back from college it had mostly gone away.

"What—what about prophecies? Do we have any prophecies?"

The brain's complicated. Maybe that was good enough.

"I could ask my mom's favorite psychic."

"She's got a favorite?"

Marilyn dumped the takeout carton in the garbage and retrieved an unfinished glass of white wine from the living room. "Delilah Marie," she said. "God knows she'll probably stick her name on Mom's will someday. If anyone doesn't have visions or prophecies or premonitions or even a real personality, it's Delilah Marie. But you can't convince my mother otherwise. You know what she tells her?"

Sylvie shook her head.

"Satanic murder cults. Delilah Marie goes on and on about Satanic murder cults. That's why kids are getting shot here. That's why kids are going missing on Staten Island. She thinks that Cropsey urban legend is real. Y'know, that escaped mental patient with an ax or a hook for a hand or whatever."

"Yeah, I've heard of it." Marz had told her when they were barely out of kindergarten. "He lives in an abandoned hospital or something."

"So they say. And she told my mom that all the rich and power-ful folks in this city have demons that make them successful."

"Honestly . . ."

Marilyn laughed. "Okay, maybe she got some of that right. But I also wish I was psychic just so I could get my mom away from her."

"Have you ever tried?"

"Every time I talk to her I try—or do you mean tried to be psychic? I don't think it's something you try if you actually are. I think it just, y'know, happens. And if it happens, the *Post* will write about it first."

So Marilyn probably didn't write for the *Post*. That was a relief. "Not you?"

Marilyn swirled her wine. "I don't play dirty enough."

"I guess if I find someone with crazy powers, I'll tell you first."

"That's very thoughtful of you, Sylvie."

Sylvie had only occasionally wondered if her ability was inher-ited. She had never attached too strongly to the idea or envisioned some grand revelation where her birth mother explained that, yes, this was a burden passed down a hundred years and here is how to fully control it.

Or that maybe the boy who knocked Marilyn up was sent away to a facility somewhere after manifesting extraordinary behavior and hadn't been seen since. Sylvie knew nothing about him, so it seemed possible.

But now that it was very, very clear that Marilyn was unbur-dened (or a good liar), Sylvie couldn't finish her dinner. She was disappointed, and more than disappointed, she was embarrassed for coming, embarrassed for asking absurd questions that would probably be flagged as some sort of teenage crisis. And if Deirdre had finally given up hope and called, Sylvie was doubly screwed. Back to the shrink.

Marilyn had never ratted her out for anything—that wasn't her place in Sylvie's life—but Sylvie's hindsight used to abide by rules, so there was always the chance for change.

Ten minutes later, after Sylvie had washed her bowl and Marilyn had finished her wine, she knew she had to leave before she dug too deep a grave. Her curfew was dark, and the sky was a deep purple.

"I should walk you to the train," Marilyn said, surprising her.

"Why? Worried about Satanic cults?"

"It's late and I don't want you getting snatched up by an ax-wielding maniac. Or shot."

At the word "shot," Sylvie could almost hear the shotgun firing in her head. "I—Marz talks about that killer sometimes. He's in Queens, anyway."

"You're remarkably close up here compared to downtown, Applesauce. Queens is just across the river."

Sylvie's throat had gone dry as she shrugged on her bags again. "But what if *you* get shot walking back from the train? Or he shoots both of us?"

Marilyn sighed and set her wine glass in the sink. "Just let me walk with you, all right? You're a kid, and I'm the grown-up. I don't wanna put you in a cab, but it might be safer . . ."

"No, I can take the train. I've never been mugged, but I've got hardshoes and they'll put a dent in anything if you hit hard enough."

"Well, thank God you've got a weapon. Now deal with having me tag along to the station."

Marilyn left her reluctantly. She even offered to wait on the platform, until she realized she only had her keys and no tokens.

Alone again, Sylvie relished the station lights and counted the rats on the track. A group of drunk college kids pushed through the turnstiles and filled up the grimy space with noise. Raised voices, mostly, and some warbling laughter. They entered the same car as Sylvie and sat at the other end, leaving only scattered papers and other trash between them. There was the smell of fresh paint on the stale air.

The fluorescents jittered as the train thundered beneath the city. Sylvie stared at her reflection in the opposite window until her face lost all meaning. She waved a hand in front of her face and half-expected her reflection not to move.

When she reached her station, the drunk kids followed her out. Sylvie hurried ahead of them and up to the street to wait for the bus. They walked in the other direction, toward the east and probably a dive bar. For lack of anything else to look at, Sylvie watched them. Then one of the stragglers turned his head and looked back—she turned her head in the other direction and jammed her hands into her pockets as her heart thumped unhappily.

But he left her alone.

He probably hadn't even been looking at her. More likely he was checking to make sure they were going in the right direction. Like you always do when you get out of a station you don't know.

It was probably even more necessary when drunk.

Sylvie exhaled and rubbed her nose and realized she wasn't alone at the stop at all. The sudden appearance of a woman in a calfskin coat scared her so badly that she had to pretend to sneeze to cover the awkward movement her body made.

The woman didn't flinch. She didn't look at Sylvie, either, and somehow that was worse than if she had.

When the bus finally came, the woman didn't move until Sylvie did, and she sat in the row behind her despite all the empty seats at the back. The only other people were half-asleep. One held a copy of the *Village Voice*, and it was starting to slip from his fingers. Sylvie looked out her window and caught the reflection of the woman behind her. She sat straight in the seat, seeming to stare right at Sylvie's head.

Sylvie slowly moved to the outside seat. The woman looked down and pulled a book out of her bag. Sylvie breathed out.

It's not weird to sit behind the only other girl on the bus, Sylvie thought. Gotta look out for the sisterhood and all that.

Houston Street was quiet, for the most part. The bridge and tunnel crowd didn't come during the week—no street parking. The NYU students were holed up in the Village—East and West. The trucks wouldn't begin loading up until close to dawn.

Tonight she wished change would come faster to her neighborhood and install more twenty-four-hour delis and bars and late-night crowds. The places open late catered to the manufacturing crowd and weren't necessarily welcoming to teenage girls. There was only one real bodega, and it was out of Sylvie's way. Though lights were on in many of the lofts, the street level was comparatively dark. And with no gallery openings or shows crossing her path, there were few people out. In the shadows she could hear more than see the ubiquitous rats—ubiquitous because of the garbage and the lack of cats to herd them. Newspapers rustled, pages scattered over the paving stones and loading docks.

Walking alone with her bags on her shoulders, Sylvie couldn't help imagining a sudden tug as someone, some nameless, faceless someone grabbed her rucksack and pulled her into the dark, never to be seen again.

Sure, that had never happened in SoHo before (not since the term SoHo was coined, anyway), but whatever it lacked in typical comforts, it more than made up for in places to hide. Dumpsters filled with the guts of buildings. Bales bursting at the seams with scraps and rags. Empty floors abandoned by struggling merchants. And if she could run, she'd probably trip on the cobblestones and uneven pavement, uncared for and unmaintained for a generation.

She imagined what it would look like to be shot outside her building. How her blood would probably slip through those geometric cracks. She could see the girl from the vision's blood, a spatter here and a trail there as some unknown someone dragged her away. And now that she was back in Sylvie's thoughts, the girl began to fall again. And again and again until the pavement had scrubbed her face away.

Sylvie's heart beat a hard rhythm in her temples as she passed a darkened lot that, in daylight, was a small Federal-style house that had absolutely no business among the cast-iron behemoths of industry. It still had dormers with wooden shutters, but at some point, the brick had been punched through for the convenience of a trucking business. The later attempts to fix the damage had never been completed in any meaningful way, and both holes—one a very large rectangle, the other in the shape of a T—were now boarded up like a grotesque face. The city deemed it unsafe decades earlier, but what wasn't unsafe in this city? It was Sylvie's favorite building on Greene Street (apart from her own building), and it looked unoccupied even though it wasn't.

Stepping off the sidewalk, Sylvie sat down on the chipped marble steps and—just sat there. Her instinctive push to flip the pages of history open wouldn't come. She didn't want it to, despite her familiarity with this building and its inhabitants. It wasn't fair that the places she once looked to for comfort or an anchor point were now almost a threat. She was still unconvinced that the visions wouldn't stay exposed forever. That the proverbial cookie jar would no longer have a lid.

"God, Sylvie, you big dumb chicken," she muttered. Then she closed her eyes and put her hands to the step and heard the world come to life a hundred times over.

This place had sold hats, furs, and human companionship—not in that order, and not all at once. Though it was dimly lit, the phantom of proper windows and doors restored themselves and a quorum of people—women in crinolines and men in coveralls who could have been their great-grandsons—erupted from the dark. Signage and rooms to rent appeared and disappeared, and the missing carriage light glowed yellow and sometimes red. It was nice not to be so alone, even if these people didn't know she was there. She had their movements and faces and clothing nearly memorized. She even knew some of their names.

The home was built for a family called Arnoux, when the area was still respectably middle class. By the Civil War, it was a series of brothels, like most of Greene Street back then. One raid yielded the names of the women who worked there at the time—*inmates*, the newspapers called them. Isabella, Annie, Ida, Celia, Emma, Nettie, and another Nettie. She had no idea who was who. There was even a fire in one of the upper rooms.

Through the haze of long-dead people, Sylvie saw a shadow sift through the layers. Just a dark, formless mass slipping in and out of the mirage. She didn't recognize it, but it could have been something newly revealed from the last ten years. Still, she tried following it, until she realized that one of the women, one of the inmates or maybe one of the bakers or milliners, was staring at her.

Sylvie immediately jumped up and just like that, the sidewalk was empty, the house dark and scarred by time.

Sylvie shuddered and began walking again. She still had two blocks to go. The buildings were only going to get taller, the narrow street even darker. She heard her footsteps, but she heard other footsteps, and she quickened her pace, which only freaked her out even more.

Bolting now, because if she was going to panic to death, she might as well give it all she had, Sylvie launched across Spring Street, almost losing her footing on the metal plates that made up half the width of the sidewalk. She was almost home now, and it was only when she saw the lights on upstairs that the panic of being chased gave way to the stale panic of being late.

Breathing hard, cheeks hot, armpits damp, Sylvie bit her lip as the front door squeaked on old hinges. She eased it shut just as carefully but expected a hand to shoot through the gap at any second. Fear made her slam it and turn the locks.

Inside the tight entryway, there were two doors—one for the elevator, the other for the stairs. The door to the stairs was usually kept wide open, but tonight it had closed to reveal only a strip of pitch. Sylvie thought she heard a clanging echo from somewhere up above, and quickly unlatched the elevator door and the metal grille.

She couldn't wait to be punished. She couldn't wait to hear her parents' voices and feel Jessie Baby's fur.

As she pulled the grille open and stepped into the apartment, a figure jumped right into her face. She backed up, screaming, into the corner of the elevator.

CHAPTER FIVE

"Jesus Christ, Cool Breeze. Is the 'stache that bad?"

"Gary! I swear to *God*! What is *wrong* with you!"

Sylvie's older brother held up his hands and backed away as she lobbed her duffel at him.

"Thanks for the warm welcome, Sylvie!"

Sylvie's dad was on the sofa in front of the television, finishing an episode of *Barney Miller*. "Who died?" he called, getting up to turn off the set.

"Gary's about to!"

"I think I scared her," he said as Sylvie shoved past him, dragging her bag along the floor. Her heart raged in her ears, pounded against her throat. She had forgotten her brother would be coming home today.

Her dad folded his arms and leaned against the back of the sofa. "Dare I ask where you've been?"

"I went to Marilyn's."

Bernard's face softened at once. For a brief moment, Sylvie was taken with how easily her parents believed her—not that she was lying, but how easily she *could*. She'd never given them a reason to doubt her.

"Oh yeah? How is she?"

"Fine. She says she never gets home before seven, no one has superpowers in her family, but also no one's nuts or a witch, and her mom goes to a psychic named Delilah Marie who's probably trying to steal from her."

"Interesting."

Sylvie dropped her bags and stretched out on the floor, allowing Jessie Baby to lick her face. Arms and legs outstretched, she attempted to sink into the floorboards.

Geneva Stroud came down the hall from the back of the loft. "Where were you?"

"She was at Marilyn's," said Bernard.

Geneva wasn't as moved. "You're not supposed to be out after dark. Please tell me you didn't take the train alone."

When Sylvie didn't answer, her mother threw out her arms.

"Sylvie!"

"It's no biggie!"

"It is a *big* biggie. You're not supposed to be on the train after dark, either! And you missed your brother's welcome-home dinner."

"Sorry. I forgot." She tried harder to sink into the floor. Her mom had probably reminded her of the dinner before school, but Sylvie's mind was a bag of loose marbles.

"You forgot about me," said Gary. "Thanks a lot."

"Sorry again. What'd you guys do?"

"We went to Oh Ho So. Dad was gonna cook steaks, but you were late," said her mom.

"See—I had a psychic intuition! I ate Chinese food with you, long distance."

Geneva leaned against the kitchen island and sighed. "How was dance?"

"Fine."

"You ate at Marilyn's?"

"I ate her leftovers."

Geneva grabbed a hand towel to wipe at some crumbs. "How is she?"

"Fine. She's not Irish, either."

"Isn't that nice. Get off the floor, hug your brother, send the elevator back, and do your homework."

Sylvie had been naive to think her parents would actually ground her. They never grounded her. She never did anything worth grounding her for, so they were probably out of practice. Neither did Gary, although he walked the line more than she ever did.

Gary, staring down at her beneath a head of thick, shaggy, dark brown hair, with his dark eyebrows, denim shirt, and Lee Riders with the hems all torn up. And a new handlebar mustache almost like their dad's.

"You look like Bert," Sylvie told him.

Gary immediately smoothed his mustache. "Burt Reynolds? Really? That's cool, I guess. I was going for Glenn Frey."

"No, like, you look like you have Bert's unibrow on your mou—hey!"

Gary grabbed Sylvie's ankles and began dragging her back toward the elevator while Jessie Baby's frantic tail wound her body into wild circles around them. "Okay, bye, Sylvie. I've missed being an only child."

Sylvie twisted her legs and tried sitting up. The roughened floorboards caught in her hair and snagged her shirt. "I'm gonna get stabbed by a splinter! All right, all right! You do look a little like Glenn Frey."

"Thank you."

"If Glenn Frey was ugly—ow!"

Back on her feet, she couldn't avoid Gary as he hooked her around the neck and smothered her with her own hair. "Smart-ass."

"Thank you."

Once Gary freed her, she dragged her bags to her room, passing her brother's on the way. His door was ajar, and she caught a glimpse of last year's trophies she still hadn't put away. Before anyone could say anything about it, she ducked inside and began gathering them up.

Neither his room, nor hers, had windows. Their parents built their master at the back, taking two windows and building the bathroom around the third so that neither of their kids would argue over it. Where windows might be, there was whitewashed brick—or would be, but both of their rooms were covered in posters and photographs.

Darkness in the apartment had felt threatening only once in Sylvie's life, and it happened so long ago that it was more of a fragmented dream than a reality. The walls were so poorly fitted that shimmers of light peeked through the seams at the high ceiling. The loft was a space where people had once worked elbow-to-elbow, and try as the Strouds did to turn it into a habitable space, to put up boundaries where there were none, total privacy really only existed when you were home alone.

But standing in Gary's darkened room, Sylvie suddenly felt aware of the unlit corners and the faces in the posters leering down at her. She thought of the shadow, of the dead woman's stare (impossible), the lady on the bus, and hurried through her task, determined to make this a one-time trip.

The light flipped on, and Sylvie dropped everything she was holding.

"*Damn it!*"

"You are jumpy as hell," said Gary, who was leaning against his doorway without a care in the world.

Sylvie hurriedly knelt down to pick everything back up. Her hands trembled and her spine felt hollow, like the shock had cored it out.

"I lost my grip," she lied.

He knelt down to help her. "Stick some of these in the kitchen so they're useful instead of taking up space."

"Yeah, I'm totally gonna eat cereal out of a trophy."

Gary ignored her. "Did you *really* go to Marilyn's?"

The way he said it prompted Sylvie to rush to her own defense. "Yeah. Where else would I be?"

Gary shrugged. "Beats me. I don't know what you get up to since I left home."

"Left home? I wish."

"Brutal, Sylvie."

"I get up to the same things as always."

"Okay, so nothing."

With her arms full again, Sylvie struggled to flip him off.

"So, uh, what brought you to Marilyn's?"

"I went to ask her if there are superpowers in her family."

Gary had never believed her, but he never seemed to disbelieve her, either. She wondered when the day would come that her teasing him with the truth would actually sink in. And what he'd do when it did. He was three years older than Sylvie, and when she first saw their loft come (back) to life, he was old enough to carry those memories with him. Memories of Sylvie hollering about men and machines, her eyes wide, almost devouring the room. The TV had gone into their dad's studio for two months—no eight-year-old would forget that, either.

"Of course."

Sylvie carefully stood and backed out the door, avoiding eye contact with him. Gary, holding three small trophies, followed her, then cut across her path to nudge open the door to her room.

"And does she?"

"Nope," she said as she dumped her trophies on her bed. "She's not even psychic."

Gary gingerly placed the small trophies on her desk. "So it's just you who's weird."

"Some people have precognition, and I've got postcognition."

"Really fucking useful that's been. Remember when you were like eight and you walked into my room and told me a man lost three fingers right where my bed is? Ran off cackling like the dwarf killer in *Don't Look Now*."

"He gets them—*got* them caught in some kind of machine. They just popped like a couple of—"

"Okay! Cool! Channel your postcog into bilking rubes for their hard-earned money again. I'll manage your career."

Sylvie turned to face Gary before leaving to fetch her bags from his room. "Seriously, you have to shave that mustache. You look forty years old."

He followed her. "Quit taking pot shots at my lip mane!"

"Please never call it that again, or I'll talk about the girl who gets her hair ripped out—"

Stop, Sylvie, damn.

Gary changed the subject. "*Anyway*, is Ilan home yet?"

Sylvie shrugged. "I haven't heard from him. Wouldn't he tell you, too?"

"So I guess you weren't actually out with him, then."

"Why would I be?"

Gary raised his eyebrows at her. "No reason."

Sylvie shoved his arm and walked back into her room. "God, you are *beyond* annoying."

"You forgot about me, and I didn't get any steak," he said.

Guilt bloomed in her chest, but she couldn't bring herself to jump up and grin and hug him and join him in front of the TV until it went off the air.

"I really am sorry, okay? It wasn't on purpose. But I need to do homework. Some of us still have school tomorrow." She dropped into her desk chair and shoved some nearly due library books into her bookbag.

Gary leaned on the doorjamb. "Sounds awful."

"Well, it is!"

But it wasn't school that was awful. Her days were a breeze of loosening focus as the end of the year approached. She even went with Marz and Marybeth to see *Rocky Horror* at the Waverly. She told them about her visit to Marilyn and how she hadn't learned anything useful. Marz wanted to meet Delilah Marie.

Then came Saturday and her morning lesson and Sylvie's body was rigid with tension. It was a feeling she hadn't experienced since she was a little kid—that heightened sense of reality, the dryness in her throat and thickening tongue. Her cereal felt like rocks in her belly.

She never felt deep anxiety anymore. Not during competitions. Not during performances. Not even last semester, when she had to perform a one-person play about a worker in a Chicago sausage factory. The Deep Throat jokes persisted.

The day was cool, the sky cloudy. It had been cloudy all week, but no rain fell. Sylvie hopped off the train two stops early so she could walk. And think. And overthink. Her only recourse for getting help with her hindsight turned out not to be a recourse at all. Where could she even go from here? How could she fix it?

Each step she took was slower than the one before it. She counted the streets as though she hoped they would suddenly run out. At the last corner, she stopped. She stopped every time, but this time she couldn't figure out how to start again. Her legs simply wouldn't move. Nothing was firing at her feet to tell her to go, that she had to go, that dance was going to start.

The idea of skipping dance frightened her almost as much as the reason why she was considering skipping in the first place, but she just couldn't do it. Inside her head was an image of the girl standing on the sidewalk, a hole through her chest, blood curdling over her lips as she choked out Sylvie's name and begged her for help. It was the stupidest, most ludicrous image in the world, but it was there all the same.

Fuck.

She needed a break—just one day, just one second. She needed to think about how to stopper that girl back up, return her to the brick and stone that was supposed to cradle her memory.

Suddenly Sylvie was doubling back, retracing her steps but skipping the station and turning down the next block instead. She had more than an hour to kill before she would meet Marybeth after her ballet class, and she couldn't go back home yet anyway. So she beat an old path through the city, the way she used to do when she was young and way too unafraid of the things she might see.

It pissed her off. It really pissed her off. She wanted to be that little kid again—hell, she wanted to be the version of herself from two weeks ago.

Her heart pumped hot, guilty blood through her head, and she defiantly began to shove her hand against every surface, pulling out and shoving back memory after memory.

Hello. Goodbye. Hello. Goodbye. Come out, go away. I'll never see any of you again.

I'll never see any of you again. Sylvie felt like she was being a bit of a dick, but if that girl really wanted her attention so badly, maybe she would give it to her, undivided. Maybe Sylvie would step into her domain and find all her secrets, prove she wasn't frightened. Maybe touching that place, looking at its innards, would flip a fuse back into place.

As she made a wide turn back toward Marybeth's ballet studio, Sylvie suddenly laughed. Breaking into a construction site? Was that really where things were at?

She thought of her dance class going on without her, of Deirdre being relieved she wouldn't have to fight with Sylvie's chaos tonight, and she sighed and knew that yes, that was exactly where things were at. But she wasn't ready to take that step.

CHAPTER SIX

June 11th, 1977

Sylvie met up with Marybeth outside her ballet studio as they usually did, and the pair hopped on the train for home. She decided not to admit she had skipped class.

It was approaching lunch hour, and the afternoon turned sunny enough to head to Wally's for a cone. With Marz in her family's old loft trying out drummers, Marybeth and Sylvie went alone.

Wally's was packed and out of room, so they ate outside, around the corner on Wooster Street. They sat on the metal loading dock of a print shop, closed today, which gave them a good view of the tiny flea market in the narrow parking lot next door. Tourists did their Saturday stroll, popping into and out of new galleries and new restaurants and planning to end their day at one of the new clubs, or even the new disco (called, of course, Loft, and which the Ad Hoc Committee to Ban Disco had spent last year trying to prevent). Those people had their world, and the kids who grew up here occupied another.

Between the parked cars, a group of kids played some kind of quasi-basketball game using trash fished out of the dumpsters, not caring if debris or a dusty rubber ball bounced off the windshield of a LeBaron. They used a paint-covered barrel for a hoop while a kid stood over them holding a strip of crown molding like a bat and played goalie. Up in the lofts, with the jazz festival coming up, slips of music fell over the crowds like so much smoke.

Sylvie let the sunlight dry out her thoughts and her guilt about skipping dance. If Deirdre called, Sylvie would tell her a kind of truth: she wasn't up for it today but only figured it out at the last minute.

After they finished their cones, they wandered to the SoHo Music Gallery and browsed the albums before heading back to Sylvie's place. The elevator was up, breaking the daytime rule of sending it down again, so they were forced up the stairs.

Once inside and breathing hard from the climb, Sylvie sent the elevator back to the lobby and kicked off her shoes. Her feet reeked, so she stripped off her socks. No one was home except for Jessie Baby, who roused herself from a nap to come wag her tail at the girls.

"The window's open across the street," said Marybeth as Sylvie went to pour two glasses of water—and to grab a Pepsi can from the fridge.

"Are they playing?" Sylvie asked.

"I think so. Let's go watch!"

Drinks forgotten, the girls went to one of the windows and cracked it open on squeaking hinges. Then they climbed over the narrow bookcase that enclosed the old radiator and eased out onto the fire escape.

Marz's family's loft was directly across from Sylvie's and had one extra window owing to the building's extra width. All of the windows were open, and through them rose and fell the staccato sounds of drums and fragmented guitar as Marz danced erratically (well-practiced in her bedroom mirror) between her bandmates, occasionally sliding into a run of lyrics that were impossible to pick apart. Marybeth and Sylvie started their own careful dance, mindful of all the cracking paint on the ironwork beneath their feet, and also that the whole structure likely needed another inspection. A few people passing below them looked up.

"MARZY!" Marybeth yelled, while Sylvie stuck two fingers in her mouth and cut the air with her whistle.

Marybeth winced. "Ow! Jeez Louise! Why'd you *ever* learn that?"

"To get revenge on Gary for learning it first."

Marz came to the window and flipped them off and as Sylvie and Marybeth laughed, the ladder above their heads shuddered.

"Oh shit," said Sylvie.

The girls froze, looked at each other, and hurriedly climbed back inside, where they went to Sylvie's room and talked about nothing until they heard the elevator doors open.

"Password!" shouted Sylvie.

"Hey, Cool Breeze!" It was Gary. "Come look at what I found in the dumpster!"

Sylvie rolled off her bed and Marybeth followed her out the door, where they quickly realized that it wasn't a *what*, but a *who*. Sylvie's stomach lurched like she had missed a step.

"Ilan!" *Yes!*

Ilan Holt, looking a little wider in the shoulders, his blond hair longer and blonder after a year at Stanford. He was the first kid Sylvie and Gary met when their parents moved into the neighborhood, a year older than Sylvie and two years younger than Gary. Until he skipped the ninth grade. Which was about the same time that Sylvie felt the distinct pull of a crush—which she liked, and therefore kept stoking. It was fun to have crushes. Fun and easy and frivolous.

She hadn't seen him at all since last summer (his parents had left for Mamaroneck), so there was always the chance she no longer cared a fig. But no, he had gone and made himself even prettier. She was delighted.

As Gary swiped the sweating Pepsi can off the kitchen counter, Sylvie bounced her way across the living room to give Ilan a thorough hug. He nearly lifted her off the ground.

"Sorry. I probably smell like sweat," she said, not actually caring at all.

"You're not the worst thing I've smelled today," he said as he let her go.

"Gee, I'm flattered."

"She's being way nicer to you than she was when I got home," muttered Gary, who flopped over the back of the sofa and landed in a sprawl, popping the tab on the soda.

Ilan waved at Marybeth as they all found different places in the living room to lounge. "Is that Marz out there?"

"Yeah," said Marybeth.

"What've you two been up to?" asked Gary.

"We went to Wally's. It was crazy," said Sylvie.

"Oh, shit, let's go to Wally's!" Ilan said to Gary, nudging the torn knee of his jeans with one bare foot.

"I'd rather go for Dave's," said Gary. "I want fries with my egg cream."

Sylvie dropped next to her brother. "So, what dumpster did you find him in?"

"Almost literally ran into him in the Village," said Gary, scratching at his side. He wore a denim button-down shirt that was barely buttoned up at all.

"I'm subletting a place on West Tenth for a couple months. No way was I gonna spend all summer up in Westchester."

"And no way were we gonna head up there," said Gary.

Sylvie nodded. "Yeah. No car anymore."

"No interest in Westchester either," said Gary.

"Your friendship means the world to me, too," said Ilan in all mock sincerity as he leaned back in the old rocker and tossed his wavy fringe out of his eyes. "Winter break was the most boring week of my life. Dad complains every other phone call that he has to mow the lawn, and I'm all, whose fault is that? They have the same square footage inside. It's stupid."

"How's it out in the Wild West?" asked Sylvie. The furthest west Sylvie ever got was when her parents took them camping at the Grand Canyon. They had to rent everything, even the car—they flew back.

"Nice," said Ilan. "Real nice, actually. Soon as summer hits New York, I'm gonna wish I was back there. You guys on break yet?"

"Almost," said Marybeth.

"The junior-senior just happened, right? What was this year's theme?"

"Yeah. It was supposed to be a Night in Paris, but it kinda looked more like a Night in Jersey City," said Sylvie, who immediately weighed how much detail she should get into about her date just to see what Ilan would do. But with her brother there, she didn't elaborate.

"You're both still dancing, right?"

"Mmhmm," Sylvie and Marybeth replied.

A pinch of guilt returned. Sylvie's stomach dropped again, much less pleasant of a sensation this time. What if Deirdre had taught them some amazing new step?

Then you'll learn it next week!

"Right on. I'll come see you this summer, like the old days." When Gary was forced to tag along to Sylvie's feiseanna, he sometimes took Ilan, and the two of them would spend the afternoon running around and being generally irritating with the other bored siblings.

"Eh, it gets kind of crazy. I don't even take my friends," she said.

Ilan leaned back, put his hands behind his head, and began to slowly rock the chair. It bumped into the overgrown ficus. "What? I'm not your friend anymore?"

"Okay, then even more reason for me to say no, since I *don't take my friends*."

"I haven't gone to a feis in years," said Marybeth, who had competed for a brief period. "It would be kinda fun to go again."

"No, it really wouldn't," said Sylvie.

"I haven't seen her dance since I got back," said Gary.

"It's been three days!" said Sylvie.

"Jesus, that long? I've usually been woken up by your shoes at least once in a three-day period."

She shrugged. "I'm learning how to be a more respectful member of the household so that they don't kick me out as soon as I turn eighteen."

"If they kick you out, you can crash at my place, free of charge," said Ilan. (Sylvie tried imagining crashing at Ilan's place but stopped. She'd save that for when she was alone.)

Gary rolled his eyes anyway, but Ilan didn't notice. Marybeth did, though, and she giggled. Sylvie nudged her, but not discreetly.

"Actually, speaking of crashing," Ilan continued, "we're gonna hang with a couple people later. Not at my pad, but nearby. Come with. Bring Marz if she's done by then."

"Who's gonna be there?" asked Sylvie.

"Don't worry," said Gary through a yawn. "You've probably only dated a couple of them."

Sylvie flipped him off. "Marybeth? You up for it?"

Marybeth shrugged. "I'm down. Let me call my parents."

She got up and walked into the kitchen, where the goldenrod phone hung crookedly on the wall, cord overlong and knotted from years of Sylvie twisting it around her fingers while she talked.

Sylvie didn't mind parties, or hang-outs, or whatever. She didn't go to many, but they also didn't rate very high on her list of priorities (dance). Besides, Gary mostly hung out with wannabe beatniks who wished they had been born in time to haunt the Gaslight Café and were planning to write in Dave Van Ronk for mayor. But going to parties with Ilan made them much more appealing.

Once Marz and Marybeth were cleared to go (and to spend the night at Sylvie's after), they dispersed to have lunch and get ready. Sylvie finally showered off the day, slid combs in her hair, and pulled on her peasant dress with the laced-up bodice because it made her boobs look good. She followed that with a couple of necklaces, and as many rings and bangles as she could find. She held up her beringed hands to her poster of Fleetwood Mac. Praise Stevie. Maybe this year she'd try a shag cut.

Probably not.

CHAPTER SEVEN

On the walk up to the Village, they stopped for a slice and Mary-beth went to get an Orange Julius, and it really felt like summer had come and relaxed all the fibers of the world. Sylvie's mind slipped pleasantly into the space of heightened reality and pantomime that naturally occurs in front of a crush who actually knows you exist. The marbles in her head stopped cracking off each other.

They headed to a third-floor apartment in a russet row house on Christopher Street. It wasn't too far from their old elementary school; they'd probably walked by it a thousand times before. Sylvie brushed her hand against the facade without really thinking about it—because it had been normal not to think about it until recently. And her heart spiked for a second, but only a second, as she watched long-ago tenants march up the stoop with them. Still, she pulled her hand away and rubbed it on her hip as though that would wipe away the evidence.

It's fine, Sylvie.

Once they were buzzed inside, they clambered up the linoleum stairs onto a stiflingly warm landing that still had its old tile. It already smelled like smoke out here—weed, cigarette, and incense all at once.

"What it is, what it is!" said the young man who opened the battered door. Marty, Sylvie was fairly sure. He wore a too-small

Vampirella t-shirt and had a mop of black, curly hair. She couldn't tell if he was high or if it was just his disposition, but he moved as though partially submerged in water as he let them through.

They filed through a narrow hall that opened into a living room. The door to the bathroom was closed, and the bedroom and kitchenette were packed with people. Already, disembodied voices called Ilan's and Gary's names, people coming out of nowhere to hug or high-five their welcome-homes. A girl with golden waves kissed Ilan right on the neck, an ex-girlfriend hooked his arm, and Sylvie tugged at Marz and Marybeth to separate herself before she did something embarrassing.

On the floor in the living room was a kid in the middle of prepping for a drag show at Max's Kansas City. He sat on the unpolished floorboards with a portable vanity set while everyone else occupied ratty curbside sofas and a twin mattress that doubled as a coat rack.

The windows were open to let out all the smoke. Beneath the din of conversation, someone had put on Patti Smith's *Horses*. It wasn't quite Sylvie's, Marz's, or Marybeth's taste in music, but they feigned cool appreciation as they wandered through the crowd, catching a few greetings of their own.

As Marz went to score some grass, Sylvie noticed a boy with slick dark hair and a white t-shirt with the sleeves rolled up. "Oh, no," she sighed, feeling a rush of warmth up her torso.

"What?" asked Marybeth, who had lit up a cigarette.

"It's Jason. Do not leave me alone with him or I'm screwed."

"Yes, we know," said Marz, who had returned, successful, and passed a blunt to Sylvie.

They played dodge the ex for several minutes, until Sylvie felt quite at peace and mostly forgot he was there. Ilan had a beer and was wrapped in conversation with a girl named Carole, who had a curtain of perfectly straight jet-black, Cher-like hair that threw off light like a crystal. Or maybe Sylvie was just getting too high.

Eventually, though, as more people left sobriety behind, Sylvie had to do her party trick. It was inevitable. People she didn't even know would begin to seek her out, finding the whole concept infinitely amusing. "Hey, I heard you're a reverse psychic. What happened in this place?"

An hour earlier and she would have hesitated or lied, but her head was in the clouds and her mind was switching between wherever Ilan was, and wherever Jason might be.

Sitting on the sofa, lounging between Marybeth and Marz with her shoes off, she skimmed her toes against the bare floor and watched what unfolded. At least this time there was an interesting scene in the early 1920s, of two women having sex on a wet canvas right where the kid had transformed himself into an (as yet) bald drag queen. He had to pause the application of a lash to look down at the floor. "Good for them, I guess."

No one ever believed her, which made her feel freer to do it. And the higher people were, the less likely they would remember any of it, anyway.

"What goes on in that imagination?" said a voice from above her—Jason's voice, rumbling right on through her. She smirked up at him as Marybeth put her hand on Sylvie's leg and gripped. His eyes were on her cleavage.

"Nothing you haven't seen."

Ilan always made her reckless. She wanted him to notice her, though he always noticed her, and she wanted him to think about her and wonder what it'd be like to be in Jason's position. And she wanted to spend her reckless energy on people who didn't matter the way Ilan did. People she could mess up with. People who wouldn't mean anything if she never saw them again.

Jason raised a dark brow beneath his pomaded hair and walked off, and she watched his ass in his rolled jeans and groaned.

"Sylvie," Marz hissed in her ear. "You've had that one before."

Marybeth pushed harder on Sylvie's leg. "Stay. Put."

"Your *brother* is here," whispered Marz.

"I don't see him."

"Does that *matter*?"

Sylvie wasn't even listening anymore. "Ugh. But Jason's so *hot*."

She had never been so conscious of the rise and fall of her chest as she breathed. She pushed Marybeth away and jumped up and around the couch and slipped into the hall, where Jason was waiting, leaning against the wall like the greaser he thought he was and, at least right now, Sylvie wanted him to be.

She returned from the bathroom fifteen minutes later, chugging a beer. Jason returned to the crowded kitchenette, where someone was passing around a bong.

"I should be ashamed," said Marz. She took the beer away, looked at it, looked at Sylvie, then handed it back. "Never mind. I'll get my own."

Marz left and returned. Sylvie could finally uncurl her toes, even when Ilan walked by and dropped onto the floor next to her, leaning against her legs. Thank God he hadn't done that earlier or she would have been on the floor, between the boards, melting onto the poor tenants below.

As Gary came into the room and dropped on to an ancient futon, Sylvie received a couple more requests about what had gone on in the apartment—mostly demands for more information about the women. To those who didn't know Sylvie, hadn't gone to school with her or with Gary, the routine must have seemed bizarre.

"For some reason, whenever she tells me stories, they're always full of carnage. Everyone else gets fun shit," Gary said, arms spread over the back of the futon. On his left was a Black kid in a wide-collared paisley shirt and pristine polyester pants. He and Gary dated off and on and must have been on again. His name was Nelson, but he went by Sonny.

Ilan lit up a cigarette. Sylvie could easily have tangled her fingers in his wonderful blond hair, but she didn't. (He was the only blond boy she'd ever even liked.)

Carole returned to the room, her hair still hypnotizing even to Sylvie's slightly more sober mind. "So, speaking of buildings, did y'all know Ilan moved across the street from a haunted house?"

"Which house?" asked a white girl named Jenny who was seated in the window with her brand-new fiancé at her feet. She was petting his shaggy hair the way Sylvie imagined touching Ilan.

"The Mark Twain house. On West Tenth. They also call it the House of Death, which is a little—"

"No shit!" Marz almost shouted, almost leapt off the sofa and out of her beloved winklepickers she'd bought at Trash & Vaudeville. "I read this book by some actress who lived in that one and the one next to it—the one next to it seems way more haunted, but apparently people started dropping dead when she moved into the Mark Twain house."

Marz had already gotten Sylvie to touch the building sans Mark Twain, but it didn't reveal anything unusual—on the outside, anyway.

Sylvie could tell what someone's next question would be. *Well, Sylvie, can't you tell us if it's all true?*

"I've never been in them," she said.

"You couldn't get into the Mark Twain house, anyway," said Carole. "It's boarded up."

"When did that actress live there?" asked Ilan, who had turned a little and put one arm across Sylvie's knees. She stretched her legs to set one foot on his knee in return.

"The '50s and '60s. The book was mostly a lotta talk about reincarnation and psychic abilities, though. Boring as shit by the end, but good for her and her journey, I guess," said Marz.

Sonny shook his head. "Sounds like she wanted to sell some books."

"Nothing sounds less scary than the ghost of Mark Twain. Even if he does murder people or something," said Jenny.

"The deaths in the Twain house were real, though," insisted Carole. "You can look all that up. A dozen people just dropped dead or killed themselves in, like, a year. Folks who had lived in it for years and years, too. One after another."

"Yeah. That's what the book says," agreed Marz.

"Well, they've got obituaries, is what I'm saying."

"Maybe that lady killed 'em," said the queen at the makeup kit. Half the people laughed.

"The Mark Twain place is fully abandoned," said Carole. "That's part of what proves it's haunted. An abandoned townhouse in the Village? Get real."

"Did it have fire damage or something?" asked Gary. "Maybe the landlord can't be bothered to make it habitable, and it's not allowed to be torn down because Twain lived in it."

"I think you've hit on it, man," said Sonny, giving Gary's knee a supportive squeeze.

"It does have a plaque," said Ilan. "It's all tagged over, but it's there."

"Half the houses in New York are haunted," said a guy who was prone on the floor behind the futon, visible only by the worn soles of his shoes.

Jenny's fiancé, whose name Sylvie didn't know, had to move when she got up to go to the bathroom, and he yawned and took her seat in the window. "If you want an actual murder house, my cousin told me about one."

"I think this is my fault," muttered Gary. "I said *carnage*. I attract carnage."

"Honey, I'm not carnage," said Sonny. Gary laughed.

"Go on," said Marz to the fiancé. "I wanna know if I've heard of it."

"Dunno if it's haunted but it should be. I guess it happened to my cousin's neighbor. Well, not *to* him. But he lived there when it happened. Anyway, I looked it up and he wasn't lying."

For a second, no one said anything.

"Wait—what?" asked party host Marty, leaning in the doorway from the cloudy kitchenette where he had been listening in.

"You forgot the story, baby," said Jenny, reemerging from behind Marty.

"Oh, shit. Right. It's the Bushwick Murder Mansion. You ever heard of that one?"

"Bushwick Murder Mansion?" repeated Marz, who was clearly annoyed she hadn't and therefore skeptical it was real. A name like that seemed like it belonged in every basic book of New York hauntings.

"Maybe my cousin made the name up."

"Explain it and maybe someone'll know," said Jenny.

"Okay. Well, it's like this. This guy killed his whole family and himself. People thought the house was cursed and no one even lived on the block anymore, after it happened. All the houses were abandoned. Every single one of 'em. Far out, yeah?"

"This is Bushwick?" asked Sonny.

"Yep. Pretty sure."

"There's your answer. They let the South Bronx burn, they let Bushwick burn."

"Yeah, true. But they abandoned it back in the '50s, and it's still abandoned now. Seems weird to me."

Sonny shrugged. "I think it's just an excuse."

The no-name fiancé shrugged. "Sure. But the murders are real. That part's real."

"Wouldn't be the only time some guy killed his family," said Ilan.

"Nope. I gotta friend in Westfield—that happened in his town," said a random voice from the kitchenette. "The dad killed his family, then went on the lam. He said he was saving their souls from hell or something, but he was really just in debt. He's still missing. The house burned down after they discovered the bodies."

"Oh, shit! That reminds me—I forgot part of it!" said Jenny's fiancé.

Everyone in the room and several people outside of it chorused *what* at the same time.

"One person lived. Some neighbor girl who was over there ran off before she could get it. But then *she* went missing, and her family was also killed."

"Yikes," said Carole. "She totally did both."

"Nah, nah, I bet she's that actress lady who wrote the book," said Sonny.

"She's dead, actually," said Marz. "She died before the book was published."

"Mark Twain strikes again!" someone called.

"That'd be stone cold. If she did all that—the girl, not the actress," said Ilan. "Probably the dad was in the mob."

"Oh." This seemed to have taken the wind out of Jenny's fiancé's sails. "Good point. Maybe he was in trouble and then the girl figured something out and had to die, too. Hm. Yeah. Probably that's it. Case closed, except that she went missing."

"Check the rivers," said Gary.

"Wait a sec," said the kid in drag. He had just closed his makeup kit and could rejoin the conversation. "I know what you're talking about. They tore that place down."

"When did they tear it down?" Sylvie asked.

"Probably right after the murders, before someone could burn it down like that place in Westfield," said the voice in the kitchenette.

"Man, sucks that it's gone. I'd love to check it out," said Marz.

"Yeah, it was really old," said the queen. "Hundred-something years old. Probably didn't want to preserve it anymore, though."

"Ugh, it's gonna be dark soon. We can't keep talking about this shit. Let's go back to the stuff Sylvie was talking about before," said Jenny. "Lesbians. The bohemian lesbians."

Sylvie and her friends probably had another fifteen minutes before they would need to start walking back to make curfew. Gary's presence would give them a little extra time, but he didn't seem in any mood to leave. Neither did Ilan, which was mildly disappointing. But Sylvie needed a break from boys tonight. She was feeling drowsy.

Besides, she knew exactly what was going to happen as soon as they left, and it was better not to have Gary and Ilan with them.

Down in the vestibule, Marz turned to Sylvie and said, "Mark Twain house, *please*."

CHAPTER EIGHT

The girls swung north, passing the Jefferson Market Library, once the country's first night court, then a women's prison (Sylvie had learned too much there, too young). They then crossed Sixth Avenue. For the first few minutes, Sylvie walked without hesitation or dragging her steps, as though, yes, she *would* walk right up to the old house and push her hand to its tagged-up front and tell Marz the truth (at least the truth that happened outside). One more haunted house to tick off the list. Her mind was still just addled enough to trick her into doing it.

But as they crossed onto Tenth, Sylvie felt a barometric shift in her mindset, a heavy reluctance rolling over her and slowing her steps. The leafy trees caused a quickening of the dark, though it wasn't true velvet (when was it ever true velvet in the city?). But besides that, the street was still relatively busy with foot traffic. Warm windows glowed around them, and people sat on their stoops and smoked or let their dogs take one last whiz. Music poured out of open windows. A car passed, tried to find somewhere to park. There was nothing out of place.

They had to walk nearly the whole length of the block to get where they were going. On their right, along the south side of the street, was just another row house in a line of row houses. It didn't even have its original stoop, and the entry was now below street level, the door covered by heavily tagged and rotting plywood. Where the original entrance once was, the bricks were partly discolored. A giant patch between enormous windows, like someone had cut off its nose.

"Well," appraised Sylvie. "Here we are."

Marz looked up at the dark windows as though she would notice anything, like there would be anything to notice but reflections of the sky.

"For a place with a name like House of Death, you'd think it'd have more stories than just what some lady wrote in a book," she said. "That's a heavy name."

"Yep. Pretty sure we all agreed on that when you read the book, bub," said Sylvie, who was trying to casually stand near the tree at the curb. Now that she was here, and looking at the noseless face, she felt nearly all right again. Nothing had lunged out of the walls and gotten itself murdered in front of her. The Hell's Kitchen vision was a fluke, and she would fix it. (Was that confidence the grass, the beer, or the crush on Ilan?)

"It's just the Mark Twain thing, probably. And he didn't, like, *live* here. This wasn't his childhood home or even where he died," Marz continued.

"See, that's what I don't understand. When people think a place is haunted by someone who didn't die there," said Marybeth. "But people are gonna think we're being creeps. Let's get back to Sylvie's."

"That doesn't explain why the landlord gave up on it," Marz continued. "*That's* the weird part. Kinda corroborates that lady's story."

"Or she wrote that after it was already abandoned and fit her details to match," said Marybeth.

"Okay, got me," said Marz, walking backward toward Sylvie and Marybeth at the curb. "But, like, why abandon it? And why hasn't the city taken it and auctioned it off or whatever?"

Sylvie sighed. "Maybe the landlord died, and the city hasn't noticed. I don't know. Can we go now? The sun, it is setting." She gestured above her head, where they couldn't quite see the sky through the leaves.

Marybeth began to slowly walk away. Marz didn't notice. "You'd think someone around here would complain."

Marz turned to Sylvie, beseeching. "*Please*, Sylvie. Just one little, tiny look."

"You are so predictable," said Sylvie.

"Hey, Marz," interrupted Marybeth. "Can we please convince Sylvie to hook up with Ilan this year?"

"Oh, my God!" Sylvie and Marz said together, taking steps in opposite directions.

"You wasted tonight on fucking *Jason*," said Marz.

"We didn't—"

"The *fucking* was emphasis! This could have been it, Sylvie. Ilan would have done anything you asked him tonight."

"He would *not*!"

Marz looked at Sylvie, who had stepped across the sidewalk in one swift move. "I mean, when she wears that dress, *I* stare at her tits, too, and I don't go for white girls."

Sylvie looked back down the street. Even wearing her glasses, she was too near-sighted in the failing light to tell who was approaching. It would be so typical if Ilan showed up right this second, just as Marybeth and Marz were going on and on about how she was always doing stupid shit to torture him and one day he would just give up.

Finally, the House of Death would claim a real victim or two.

"You guys! Can we *go*?"

Marz spun around. "Quit stringing him along and jump him. You barely dated this year because Ilan wasn't around to catch you making out."

"Marz!"

"This has gone on long enough. It's all fun for you but we have to see you drooling over *Jason*. Again! You already dated that one! And you went with *Steve* to the prom? You dated that one before, too!"

Sylvie shook her head. "It's not that easy! I've known Ilan forever, and I like being friends with him. I don't wanna fuck it up!"

"You're not gonna fuck it up!"

Marybeth shrugged. "Honestly, Sylvie. She's right. Summer thing with Ilan. Make him pine for you until next summer, then you throw him over so he has to work for your affection every time he comes home. That way it'll always be new and exciting."

"Okay, *you* watch too many soaps," said Marz.

"I do and I love them," said Marybeth.

"Can we please deep-six this convo," said Sylvie.

Marz kept going. "In any case, aren't you worried about him dating some college girl? What'll you do then, eh?"

"Fine! All right. This is what I'm gonna do," said Sylvie, and with her embarrassment pumping all the blood in her body right into her ears, she walked down the steps to the shadowed front entrance to the House of Death and pushed her hand to the stone facade. She barely remembered to close her eyes—she always closed her eyes first at unfamiliar places. Twelve years did not make the scale of history any less staggering to behold.

She could no longer hear Marz and Marybeth behind the whirlwind of sound and chaos around her. When she opened her eyes again, it was to see people coming and going and talking and shouting and carrying bags and furniture and boxes—people who could have been by yesterday and people who would be too old to see yesterday at all. Some people walked up a ghostly stoop, while others came and went through the door now hidden behind the plywood.

She tried to calm her breathing and think to herself, *Mark Twain. Mark Twain. What does he look like? Does he have white hair? Or is that because the pictures are black and white? Wait, how old was he when he lived here? Did he have a mustache or is that Colonel Sanders? Was Colonel Sanders real? I have no idea what Mark Twain looks like, do I? Is that bad? Wait! That could be—no, that's a hat. Wait—no, yes, that's a hat.*

Thus far, she could spot no death happening on the outside, and for that she was grateful. Whatever cursed this place must have occurred indoors, assuming anything had cursed it at all. Marz was forever reading True Stories that were only true in that they were stories.

In the crowd of filmy people, Sylvie suddenly noticed a dog. It was an inky black stain on the ephemeral slideshow, and it walked up the steps and onto the sidewalk. The size of it was what caused Sylvie to stop and pull her hand away. It looked like a tall, slightly shaggy retriever with large, pointed ears, but it was so dark in color and the air was so dusky that she couldn't even see its eyes. More significantly, it didn't disappear with the rest of the past.

Marybeth and Marz had moved away, just a little, and Sylvie headed back up the steps to join them.

She had to be sure the dog belonged here in the present. "You see that?"

"Uh. Hard not to, babe," said Marz.

"Did you see where it came from?" Sylvie asked, relieved.

"Somewhere in front of the house. It's too shadowy down there to see."

"It must have been sleeping in the gardens and you woke it up," said Marybeth.

The dog did nothing but sit on its rigid haunches in the shadow of the tree. It didn't pant or whine or try to greet them. It didn't wag its tail.

Sylvie felt a breeze stir the air around her, playing at the hem of her dress. It was warm, like the building had breathed on her. She looked up at the windows, still dark where they weren't a mirror of the sky. She dreaded seeing a light turn on somewhere, but nothing did.

"Still here, eh?"

The girls looked up as Gary and Ilan approached.

"I knew you'd check this place out," said Ilan. "I could see the maniacal glint in Marz's eye."

"Yeah," said Marz. "Just wanted to solve the mystery once and for all."

"Mark Twain show up?" Gary took notice of the dog, then, and frowned. "Whose dog?"

"Dunno. Probably lost," said Sylvie. "It was in the front garden."

"Everybody's got a dog around here," said Ilan.

"Doesn't look very friendly," said Gary.

Sylvie felt someone run a hand through her hair and she looked at her friends, but neither was near enough to have done it. No one had even come down this side of the street except Gary and Ilan, though distant music pumped out a window in the house next door. Distant music and quiet talking. She couldn't really tell where it came from.

Marybeth had looked up, too. Even Ilan turned.

"Um, well, I'm gonna call it. See you guys later," Ilan said, giving Gary and Sylvie hugs (Sylvie couldn't even fully appreciate it with that dog sitting there) and waving at Marz and Marybeth as he crossed to the north side of the street.

The rest of the group started walking toward Fifth Avenue, only a short distance away. At the end of the block, Sylvie looked back once more, but the dog was either gone or swallowed up by the dark.

They turned south and cut through Washington Square Park, its marble arch streaked with tags and tiny masterpieces. Declarations and nicknames.

The fountain was quiet and the night was cool, but people still hung about the edges playing guitar and laughing, singing, smoking, indulging in and creating the atmosphere that drew people to the park, to the neighborhood, in the first place.

Sylvie's thoughts pulled her to the east side of the park, to a potter's grave most people didn't know they were walking over. Suddenly she imagined the ground stirring, bodies rising, cloudy eyes rolling over the people until they saw Sylvie and her friends and began to follow.

Her barometer twitched again. She scanned the crowd, tried to ground herself back to the mundane. The nearby families had walked their kids for the last time and were home, and the burnouts came back out to take the evening across the finish line. She focused on a bearded man in a wizard's cap pushing along a cart of Bella Abzug for Mayor buttons. Then on the guy with a boombox, and a group of young women laughing and passing a roach clip with a feather on one end, and a skateboarder tripping and nearly wiping out. A roller-skater in a crocheted duster wove her way between stationary groups of friends and couples. The duster spread dramatically behind her.

Sylvie caught the eye of a guy with curly brown hair—or rather, he caught her eye, as he was already watching, head tuned to Sylvie's movement like an antenna. Then she remembered her dress and its tight bodice and almost laughed—but she didn't want to smile and make him think she was flirting.

She quickly moved her gaze to a man and a woman just behind him. They sat by the fountain but instead of facing toward it, they turned to watch Sylvie, as though that was what you were supposed to do.

"Please look at those people by the fountain and tell me I'm not crazy," Sylvie whispered.

"I cannot tell you that," said Marz.

"What is it?" asked Marybeth.

Sylvie almost didn't want to say anything, but when she looked back, the man with shaggy hair was still watching her. "I swear people are staring at me."

"At your tits," said Marz.

"It's not just guys!"

"Lesbians have hormones, too."

"No—there's something weird about it!"

"Sylvie, I don't see nobody being any weirder than usual," Marz assured her.

"I felt weird back at the house, too. Like somebody touched my hair or something," Sylvie insisted. She wanted to say she regretted touching the building, touching any building at all, but with Gary here she decided not to. And her friends would have called her paranoid. Nothing had happened. All of the memories had behaved as normal.

"It was probably one of us on accident."

"No, it—"

"I think that's the kibosh on ghost stories for tonight," said Marybeth.

"See, I knew these interests of yours weren't healthy," said Gary, but he moved noticeably closer to his sister, anyway. "You two staying over?"

"Yep," said Marz.

Once they were through the park, Sylvie decided Marybeth was right. Too many ghost stories. Too much weed while listening to them. Too much internal anxiety about reading buildings again. Too many adults yelling that they'll get shot by a random maniac with a gun if they're out too late and having too much fun while doing it. Too much, well, too much of a lot of stuff over the last few weeks. Sylvie's mind was primed to overthink in ways it wasn't used to, and now she didn't know how to handle it. That was all it was. Once she fixed the problem up in Hell's Kitchen—and she was determined to fix it—she would feel better.

All the same, though, they all walked home a little faster than usual.

CHAPTER NINE

The memory of Saturday night felt distant and toothless by Sunday morning. Most of it had to do with daylight and sleep, but the rest was swept out of Sylvie's mind when Ilan came by. Sylvie wore her favorite crop top, and they went for dim sum in Chinatown with Gary and her parents, then caught a late-afternoon showing of *Smokey and the Bandit.* Ilan had bumped her foot with his through half the movie and gave her something to fall asleep thinking about instead of what excuse she would use to cover her ass in dance class on Monday.

Sylvie walked up the east side of the block, head down, hair down, hand gripping the strap of her bag in what she felt was defiance. That girl wouldn't drive her away again.

Before ringing Deirdre's buzzer, she turned and stared across the street, at the leafy trees that served to shade the front of the future café, her current nightmare.

I'm gonna figure you out. I'm gonna figure you out and you won't be able to win anymore.

(Is being murdered winning?)

Out the girl would come, any second now, bursting through a door that was concealed by the barricade of construction.

Don't look away. It's not really happening. Not anymore.

As soon as the air began to shimmer, Sylvie turned around and hit the buzzer to the beat of the shot.

Watching that scene was still a lot to ask for.

As though she was riddled with contagion, Deirdre immediately bundled Sylvie into the small practice room away from the other dancers. Sylvie wasn't even embarrassed. At least, not until Deirdre sighed and shut the door with both of them inside.

"Sylvie, can we talk?"

Now a jolt went through her, and she braced her whole body for whatever Deirdre said next. Goodbye, summer feiseanna. Goodbye, oireachtas. Goodbye, Worlds.

"Is everything all right at home?"

Oh, boy, the universal question for the Troubled Teen, straight out of a movie of the week. *Go Ask Alice.* If Sylvie didn't answer this expertly, her parents were absolutely, no question, going to get a phone call. Telling everyone she was on uppers, downers, and diagonals would be easier than the truth. She told the truth all the time—but no one believed her.

"Sure! Everything's fine," she said, jumping between too chipper and too somber in an attempt to be casual. "I swear. I just got— um." *Think, for cripes' sake.* "It's like a weird block. It's like, I just—"

This was more difficult to explain away than Sylvie had anticipated. The struggle showed on her face.

Deirdre tilted her head in that way all adults do when they think they see what's really going on, and it's not as bad as they thought. "I know you must feel like the universe has it out for you every year—God knows that's how I feel as your teacher. But I promise, Sylvie, if you're thinking ahead and worrying over how successful you will be or won't be in the fall, stop it now. Don't sabotage yourself. You're more than capable of doing very well and of qualifying for the Worlds, but don't look so far ahead. Remember what it meant when you were young, and remember the joy of learning and coming to class."

Sylvie didn't know if she should protest. In many ways, Deirdre wasn't actually that far off.

"I know. I try."

Deirdre sighed again. "Sometimes I wish they hadn't formed the World Championships, and I know the pressure goes up every year. But I wouldn't let you go to the oireachtas if I didn't believe in you. It wouldn't be fair to you. Remember, you and your class are ambassadors for this school and my name, and I trust in and believe in all of you. Don't let one mistake or one bad day snowball like this, Sylvie. I don't want to see you looking so terrified anymore, all right?"

Sylvie nodded.

On any other day, this would have been the sort of speech that won a medal for the underdog. And most of it did settle happily into Sylvie's marrow, warming her up in all the places that had cooled. But it didn't solve the real problem, which had nothing to do with dancing at all. For that, she had only herself to rely on. Over the weekend it had stopped feeling so daunting. But now the break was over, and it was back to reality. Unreality. Surreality.

"Please just tell me if you're not planning to be here. We have to think about the figure team, and your classmates are going to rely on you being ready. I know you can do it, they know you can do it, but *you* need to do it. Forget all that other noise and remember this is just a dance. We're not saving lives here."

All she could do was thank Deirdre and promise that she would get over this wall in time for the first feis. And Deirdre smiled at her and let her practice in the large room again, in close proximity to other people—in close proximity to the windows, which Sylvie mostly ignored. She had to. She wasn't saving a life, but she was screwing up part of her own. Like hell the frozen memory of a girl was going to get her kicked off the figure team.

And with Ilan around, she didn't dwell on the Hell's Kitchen Enigma when she was away from it. He usually came over after dinner and would join Sylvie and Gary on the sofa in front of the TV. He'd sling his arm over the back so that her hair fell against him, and anything involving the past seemed about as interesting as counting grains of sand.

Ilan had never come over this much, even when they were all just kids, even when he lived a block away. Sylvie no longer had anything much in the way of homework, so when she got home from dance or class, she and Ilan and Gary would go out, smoke in parking lots, hit up junk shops (where she *used* to enjoy looking at the history of any object Gary thought looked especially cursed), wander into galleries, or bond over fries and a Coke for dinner. Sometimes Ilan would give her a piggyback ride between destinations, which was something he and Gary used to do when Sylvie still wore mittens and hated touching surfaces. They never went to Ilan's place because both he and Gary—who *had* been there—said it was empty and boring as shit. The guy Ilan had sublet from had taken the stereo out.

Sylvie decided not to push it. She wanted to savor her crush instead of devouring it, and this gave her time to consider how to investigate the Hell's Kitchen building while she still could. Deirdre would take her summer break until August, so Sylvie's excuses for going into the West Fifties would be few and far between. And Sylvie wanted it done and over with, because that violent aberration was the one thing ruining the bliss of having Ilan home.

✦

Sylvie stood on the curb outside the dance studio with her hands grasping her rucksack and her duffel. Sweat licked at her forehead and the back of her neck, beneath her braid.

"I'm doing it now," she said, and Marz and Marybeth looked at each other, then at her, then across the street.

"You two should wait at the end of the block, in case I get caught or something." Sylvie had no idea what would happen if she did, but her mind was wrapped around other things—that scene from up close, and what the building was concealing—and she didn't even care.

Maybe this plan was stupid. Maybe it wouldn't work. But Sylvie felt like it had to. What else could she do?

"We'll go to Hansen's. Meet us there when you're done. And good luck. You'll be fine. I doubt anyone'll give two shits about finding you in there," said Marz.

Marybeth gave her an encouraging smile and the pair walked off.

Cabs and cars passed and parked and double parked and then the air shivered, and Sylvie shivered, and as she did, the girl erupted from her building, careening for safety as fast as she could. Sylvie was about to bow her head when she noticed a man emerging from the building, through an opening in the wooden barricade. He fit so perfectly into the scene that for the first time, Sylvie wanted to shout for the girl to turn left or right or anywhere but into traffic and the path of a bullet.

The construction worker scratched his forehead beneath the hard hat and lit a cigarette. Then he just leaned there, jeans covered in dust, boots covered in dust, unaware as someone took hold of the girl's hair and dragged her back over the sidewalk, right through him.

A second man left the construction and nodded at the first, but he didn't stay. He snapped closed a chain lock over the doorway and left. The first man walked after him, a dusty jacket under one arm. He looked back only once, then he was gone, too.

Inexperienced in the art of breaking-and-entering, Sylvie didn't know if a crowded block during rush hour was a burden or a boon.

This is crazy, she thought.

This is crazy.

115

Sylvie crossed the street, her thoughts jumping between getting caught and what she would see if she didn't get caught. If it was this bad on the outside, what was waiting for her on the inside?

The shotgun blast stopped Sylvie in her tracks. She looked away, and down, and noticed a sizable gap beneath the flimsy barricade. Reaching into her duffel, Sylvie pulled out her water bottle and dropped it, then took a dramatic step forward that included a solid kick, and the bottle rolled right under the gap.

"Cripes!" She thought she sounded convincingly annoyed. Annoyed enough for two people walking by to look at what happened. One of them laughed, and Sylvie took her chances and knelt down on the sidewalk.

"Dang it," she said, peering through the gap. "I need that." *Enough with the exposition.*

The water bottle sat in a pile of plaster mere inches from her fingers. Beyond that, the front of the building was dark, the windows boarded up.

This is crazy.

When there was a gap in the pedestrians, Sylvie pushed her bags through. Now she had no choice but to follow.

"Here goes nothing," she muttered to herself, and then she wriggled her way beneath. Broken concrete and dust scratched at her chest and stomach. Her hair caught in the jagged edges of wood above her. But she made it through, and no one seemed to have reacted. She'd find out soon if someone called the precinct.

She rescued her water bottle, wiped it off on her dusty jeans, and looked at the front door of the building—well, where a front door had been. There was no door on it at all now, just a gap with a makeshift plywood door with a simple barrel bolt lock, and piles of stone reliefs probably meant for decorating the facade.

Sylvie took a deep breath. The sidewalk and the street were just a foot away from her, separated only by a makeshift wall. The sky was still bright above her. But she felt like someone had clamped hands over her ears. She gripped her water bottle and didn't make another move until she knew she had waited too long, and suddenly the teenage girl was on top of her, running through her, beyond the barricade and out onto the sidewalk. Gasping, Sylvie ran inside, unlocking the makeshift door as the shotgun felled the girl.

Inside the building, breathing hard through a knot of panic, Sylvie saw quite a lot of nothing. The only light she had was the sun coming through the door. The walls were stripped down to the bricks, the tiled floor was covered in dust, and the beams in the ceiling were exposed. Wires and pipes, and places where wires and pipes were destined to be, punctured the walls and floor all around her. A small generator sat in the middle of the room. From above, she could hear the distant, muffled footsteps of the tenant in the apartment overhead, and what sounded like a TV. In this unfinished state, it kind of looked like your average SoHo loft, but small and square.

She waited, still clutching her water bottle like a buoy on rough seas. Any second now, the rest of the scene would unfold before her. Maybe the girl would run from the back, where an actual door led who-knew-where. A minute passed, feeling like an hour, but the teenage girl never came. Never set a single, terrified foot into the building. This fact was almost as disconcerting as the teenage girl's presence at all.

And Sylvie knew she was still there, still replaying out of sight, because she could still hear the earth-shattering sound of the shotgun and her scream.

Now, though—now Sylvie was confused.

Hesitating, she worried at a chapped spot on her lip before carefully pressing the pads of her fingers to the brick wall just inside the door. Waiting another beat, closing her eyes, then getting scared about closing her eyes in here, Sylvie woke the building up. (Of course, buildings never slept, unless their memories were dreams.)

And right now, the building looked like a dive bar, or a pub, with a mix of hard-looking men and decades of scraping chairs and stools and tumblers. The old brass rail and mirrored wall behind it had clearly not been altered until they were ripped out completely, as their continual presence was a sturdy anchor in the tide of history. She smelled cigar smoke. She smelled spilled alcohol and sawdust. She even smelled urine and sweat and god-awful, terrible things that don't come through in old pictures.

There was what sounded like a fight somewhere at the back, maybe beyond that other door, but it was of some official capacity, maybe boxing—legal or not. Probably not. She'd seen things like that in places all over SoHo and Chinatown. There was laughter and betting slips. And there were teenage girls, but they clearly worked here, or worked the patrons here, and were dressed decades out of date, even compared to the murdered girl. There wasn't a man with a shotgun, either, though she wouldn't have been shocked to find out that people had been shot in this bar or pub or tavern or inn that seemed to have evolved over the course of a century.

And then she moved her hand away and there was nothing.

Nothing at all.

Frowning, Sylvie tried again, this time gripping the doorway. Even if there was a fluke outside, if that girl was ever in this building, she should have been here. She should have run through that door or been dragged back inside. Sylvie heard no female screams above the din of the chatter, and each person who came near her, smelling of tobacco or stale sweat, looked like they belonged to a time long before that girl was ever born.

She tried a third time, desperate now. Sometimes it was hard to parse, and she had to focus, really focus, to get the layers to separate themselves. New sweat formed on her brow. Her hand gripped the brick as though she wanted to push down the wall.

She scoured the people, the floor, the overlapping stools and chairs and bar overly stocked with decades of drink.

Sylvie felt a breeze push through the building, and she stopped. It was useless. The girl hadn't been inside this place.

So she went to the facade and put her hand there. Her heart was beating rapidly, dizzily, a combination of adrenaline and desperation. As the girl ran from the building, patrons came and went over the course of generations. Sylvie could not see who pursued the girl, and the scene still started and stopped abruptly.

"God *damn* it," she said, forgetting to whisper. Nothing, there was nothing. The scene was still broken. She had learned nothing and instead managed to depress herself.

She shuffled back onto her stomach to slide out under the barricade, then turned around to pull her bags through. She freed her dance duffel first, then reached back in for her bookbag. As her hands closed around the strap, she noticed something in the doorway. A pair of large, long-fingered hands, black as pitch and barely visible against the shadowy threshold—which she had forgotten to lock back up.

It was as though someone was standing on their hands in the doorway, and it was one of the most unnatural things Sylvie had ever seen. She forgot even the girl, the gunshot, everything, and wrenched her bookbag free, knocking off her Give Earth a Chance button in the process. She left it there in the rubble, jumped to her feet, and ran.

CHAPTER TEN

Home. Sylvie wanted to go home, but she couldn't go home. She had to find her friends, but she also wanted to pace and chew her thumbnail and wash her hands and take a shower and scrub her eyeballs and her brain.

Marz and Marybeth took in the whites of her eyes and high flush and immediately assumed she had seen the whole murder, and that it was gruesome, and that she needed a Pepsi from Hans Hansen, but all Sylvie could do was splutter, "Black hands! Just these black hands—they just appeared there in the doorway like a pair of feet!"

"Black hands? What kind of black?" asked Marz, with slightly less sympathy.

"Black like a shadow black!" Sylvie almost screeched. "Like not human! Like it sucked up all the sunlight black! Outer space black!"

Marybeth held her shoulders. "Breathe, please."

"Hold up—go back. Hang on. We gotta sit." Marz took Sylvie's elbow and they dropped onto a bench outside of Hansen's Deli. There was every possibility Hans Hansen would come outside and ask if Sylvie wanted her usual turkey on rye, but Sylvie could barely remember where she was. She hadn't been this scared before, even as a little kid during the blackout of '65. Those people, those ghosts, looked like people and behaved like people did. Even the murdered girl wasn't existentially awful, just the regular, nihilistic awful.

"Let's do this in order. You went in there, right?" asked Marz.

Sylvie nodded. "Yes. And there's nothing—she's not in there. She's not even outside."

"But—I'm fully confused, babe. You always see her outside, yes?"

"Yes!"

"Okay, banshee. Please stop shrieking."

"My heart is gonna explode," Sylvie whined, leaning her forehead on her knees, which had lost all feeling and strength. Marybeth tentatively rubbed her back.

"So you didn't see her inside the building."

Sylvie shook her head. "No. Nowhere. She's not in there. And then." She sucked in a breath and sat back against the bench. "I went outside to check out there and the only thing is the vision I already see. I don't see before or after or even the person who shoots her."

"How's that possible?" asked Marz.

"I don't know. It's not like—it's not like I see everything that's ever happened. Sometimes I can miss things in all that chaos."

"We know," said her friends, who didn't really know at all, but still believed.

Marz once said that watching Sylvie's face was proof enough. She had offered to film it with her dad's old Super 8 so Sylvie could see, but Sylvie didn't want to know how unhinged she looked.

"That place was just a bar. Or, a lot of bars over a lot of decades. I was really stupid enough to think that would do something. Touching it would do something. But that girl's still there."

"But like you said, it's hard to see it all. You really could have missed her," Marybeth offered.

"I tried four different times. The last time—I never got anything so fixed in my mind before. It was like looking through index cards. I thought I would pass out. She wasn't there."

"But something else was," said Marz. "You saw a shadow."

Sylvie groaned. "I don't know what it was. I just know I regret ever going in there because of it."

"Explain. You saw hands. Shadow hands."

Sylvie's heart began to beat even more rapidly as her thoughts returned to what she had seen in the doorway. She thought her breathing would stop. She almost wanted to jump to her feet and start jogging.

"Okay. I was crawling back out and I just got one bag out and I was reaching in for the second, and . . ." She shuddered. "In the doorway were these hands. There were arms, too, but obviously I wasn't gonna stick my head in and look any further than that."

"Like, severed hands? Severed arms?" asked Marz.

Sylvie shook her head. "I wish! That would have been easier to deal with, I swear to God. No, it was like someone was doing a handstand in the doorway. Who fucking does that? Even if they weren't a shadow, I'd be strung the hell out."

"That is possibly the strangest thing I've ever heard," said Marz.

"It was worse than strange!"

"Are you sure it wasn't just some shadows and weird construction stuff?" asked Marybeth.

"No way. It was clear as anything."

"But it was a shadow, though."

"Yes, but—"

"Have you ever seen anything like that before?" Marybeth continued.

"No. Never in my life."

"See?"

"I'm telling you guys—I saw it. That's what it was. It couldn't have been anything else because there wasn't anything there. Just some stacks of building material on one side, and lots of broken pieces of concrete. Nothing that would look like *hands*, Marybeth."

"I just think it's better to think rationally first. If you've never seen something like that, even in all those haunted houses Marz drags us to—" ("I don't drag you nowhere!") "—then it's most likely just nothing."

"So you don't believe me," said Sylvie, and she wasn't used to her two best friends not believing her, and was not prepared for how to deal with it. She would have no one else to turn to.

"I believe that you saw something," said Marybeth carefully, "but I don't think it's what you thought."

"I need something to do," said Sylvie. "I need something—I just want to stop this one part. This part with the girl. I want to stop that part before I have to deal with something else."

Marz slung her arm around Sylvie's shoulders. "Look, babe, I'll check my books and see if that place is supposed to be haunted. But you know what you should do now? You should look it up, too, and see if you can find anything about that murder."

"Honestly, I'd rather see that girl get shot than ever see that shadow again. And if that starts showing up, too, I'll never be able to go to Deirdre's again." Sylvie sounded like a small, melodramatic child, but she felt like one, too.

"Maybe the murder is unsolved and the body is buried in the building and if you figure that out, it'll go away. Maybe the shadow is some kind of weird ghost—I dunno—situation. Like a harbinger. Maybe you were on to something."

"Nothing like that has ever happened before," Sylvie countered. "And I've seen unsolved murders a million times."

"Maybe it takes special circumstances. I don't know. This is beyond the scope of human understanding here, girl."

Sylvie could only nod. The library. She had to go to the library, anyway, to return some books. They'd been sitting like bricks in her bookbag since Gary got home.

After another minute or two, the girls got up and went to the train. As they walked, Sylvie thought, and she realized she'd never quite sat and analyzed when she supposed the murder took place. The girl didn't look alien to the modern landscape, as she was wearing tight-fitting cigarette pants and a purple sweater. But she was still out-of-place from today, with blunt bangs and a different kind of pageboy than the one girls like Marybeth had now.

"It's not hopeless," Marybeth said as they waited for the train. "I know it must be scary, but there has to be a reason it started, and if there's a reason it started, there has to be a way to stop it."

Marz nodded. "We'll solve this, Nancy Drew."

Sylvie craned her neck to look down the platform. She imagined the shadow figure slinking upside down out of the dark tunnel and quickly stepped back.

"Feels more like a case for Mystery, Inc."

Marz hooked Sylvie's arm and pushed Sylvie's glasses up her nose. "We'll solve this, Velma Dinkley."

It was the last day of school on Friday, and Sylvie was going to the library no matter what. She'd had to sleep with her lamp on every night, and she leapt into bed to avoid the dark gap beneath it (though that gap was actually full of shoe and sweater boxes). She was the only kid at school still hauling around a bookbag.

Marz had band practice and Marybeth ballet, but they met by their lockers before parting ways. Summer didn't make much difference to them—they'd see each other just as often, if not more.

"You're going now, right?" asked Marz.

"Yep."

"If you need help—I can be late. They'll struggle without me, but that's on them."

Sylvie shook her head. "I'll call you both tonight. Don't expect good news."

"Negative Nancy over here."

"Oh—hey, look who it is!" Marybeth suddenly stood on her elegant toes and waved at someone behind Sylvie. Sylvie turned around to find Ilan coming toward them, smiling, the fluorescents somehow looking lovely and warm on his blond waves. Oh, the Frampton of it all.

"Enrolling for next year?" Sylvie asked him as he stopped beside her.

"Yeah. They took back that year I skipped. Turns out it was a mistake," he said, slinging an arm casually over her shoulders. He smelled like cigarettes and Brut aftershave.

"Didn't we tell you that already?" said Marz.

Ilan pulled at Sylvie's bag. "Isn't it the last day?"

"Why are you up here, though? You gonna teach a class now, too?" said Sylvie.

"Oh, Sylvie, better avoid his class or you'll get him in trouble," said Marz.

Sylvie swatted at her.

"You couldn't pay me a million bucks to teach high schoolers. They're brutal. *You're* brutal. I was just saying howdy to the locals. Poking around the place. Visiting my old locker. Y'know. When you graduate next year, you'll do the same thing."

"They'll never see me again," said Marz.

"They'll see me at the reunion," said Sylvie.

"You say that now."

"Yeah, I'm not going to the reunion."

"Aw, I was hoping we'd all go together," said Marybeth. "Not you, Ilan. The three of us."

"I wouldn't get in the way of your little ménage à trois," said Ilan.

"Well, I'm breaking it up because I got practice and I need to hoof it," said Marz. She pushed away from her locker and grabbed Marybeth. Then she gave Sylvie a meaningful, but obvious, look, and Sylvie kicked the back of her combat boot. Marz probably didn't even feel it.

Ilan kept his arm across Sylvie's shoulders as the four of them left the building together. Marybeth waved her goodbye, unlit cigarette in hand as she crossed the street to walk to her ballet class.

"Don't do anything I wouldn't do," said Marz as she turned east. "Ilan's an exception, though. Anyway, later!"

"Marz, I swear to God!" Sylvie shouted after her.

"Going to dance?" Ilan asked, unhooking his arm from Sylvie. The loss of his weight almost tipped her forward. She hadn't realized she was enjoying it quite that much.

Sylvie shook her head, trying to be calm, trying to be less of a high schooler than she presently felt. "Not tonight. I'm going to the library, actually. That's what's in my bag. Books. Gotta return them."

"Sounds like a blast."

"I'll see you at home?"

"You wanna ditch me that badly?"

"I didn't think you'd want to come."

"I've got nothing on my schedule."

"I—okay. I'm sure you say that to all the Strouds."

Ilan grinned at her. (Oh, she really did love having a crush.) "Probably."

CHAPTER ELEVEN

Ilan tagging along made research a little more complicated, and Sylvie briefly considered coming back to the library on Saturday after dance. But going to dance meant going by *that building*, and going by *that building* now gave her a second wave of horror that was even worse than the first. And she just didn't want to go to the library tomorrow.

Sylvie skipped ahead of Ilan as they walked, treading backward ahead of him whenever they crossed a street. "Is it weird to visit? You'd be graduating this year if you hadn't decided to be a know-it-all."

Ilan snorted a laugh. "It's not weird, it just puts things in perspective. You wonder why you were freaked out by any of it."

"I could remind you, if you want."

He reached out and gently tugged on the hair swinging around her face. "Nah. Thanks, I'm good."

She laughed and spun back to his side, tossing her hair over her shoulders, maybe so he could see them.

"How's Stanford, anyway? You never talk about it."

Ilan shrugged. "I like California. I hiked the Pacific Trail with some guys from my dorm. I mean, not the whole Pacific Trail, obviously, but we wanna try going up into Washington and Vancouver. Go to Seattle, maybe. Next summer. You should come."

"I'm not a big nature gal."

"I didn't think I was a nature guy, but it's pretty cool. Anyway, I think I shoulda gone to a smaller school, maybe. Not like it's bad, but half my class have dads in the military and it's fucking boring."

"Shoulda gone to Juilliard after all," said Sylvie. "Or at least Berkeley."

"My parents thought Stanford would open more doors. Music is hard, y'know. But I'm not gonna be an engineer."

"Here I thought California was still full of hippies."

"Hey, my sister's there. She's hippie enough." He laughed. "What about you? You must be thinking about college by now."

"So they say."

"Really? You're not?" Ilan sounded incredulous, making Sylvie instantly self-conscious. Ilan had always been smart, but he wasn't buried-in-books smart. It was easy to forget his perfect grades and scholarships when his bag was music and yours dance.

"Not even for a second."

"For real?"

Sylvie hoped Ilan would get distracted by her hair again, or something. Crushes were fun; college was not.

"I'm gonna be a dance teacher. That's what I'm good at," she said. "I'll turn Mom and Dad's studio into a school. It's bigger than my dance teacher's place."

She felt his hand brush the back of hers—felt it all the way up her arm, up her neck, into her chest. She waited, holding her arm right there so he could find it again, but the moment passed, if it had been a moment at all.

"Come on. That's not all you're good at. You're one of the most interesting people I know."

Sylvie laughed to defuse the tension. *Crushes are supposed to be fun.* "Interesting is what you say when you can't think of anything else."

"Bull. Not everyone is interesting. They might be fun or entertaining but not *interesting.* Interesting lasts longer."

Sylvie felt herself flush, but she powered through it. "Okay, then. Thanks."

"Anyway, you've always been into buildings and history. You and Marybeth and Marz. You were the only kids in the neighborhood who went through the dumpsters and sourced where things came from. Remember when they did the landmark preservation stuff and those art historians went around documenting the buildings? You followed them around and they let you because you knew what businesses used to occupy all the buildings. And you were like eleven."

Sylvie looked at him. "You remember that?"

"It was weird, so yeah!"

"Weird or *interesting*?"

He paused. "Weird."

Sylvie flicked his shoulder.

They were nearly at the library doors now, and she needed to tell him the real reason she was here—well, half of the real reason. She wasn't sure if they had a mood going, but she was about to squelch anything that was there.

Oh, well. Priorities.

Sylvie tucked her hair behind her ear and pushed up her glasses. "Actually, I have something else to do at the library, too, if that's all right. You don't have to stay if you wanna go meet up with Gary."

"Unless you're burning the place down, I can handle bumming around a library in the summer. What's up?"

"I need to look up the history of this building by my dance studio."

Ilan laughed, and loud. "What did I *just* say?"

Sylvie flicked him again. "Shut *up*!"

Still laughing, Ilan said, "You set your own trap—so what's the skinny on this building?"

"Keep laughing, I guess, because there's kind of—there's a murder that may have happened there once, and we're just curious. Marz and Marybeth and me."

And he did keep laughing. "I see that you're trying to spread the blame out, but we all know Marz is more interested in that shit than Marybeth and you."

"Actually, this one's on me."

At the library doors, Ilan held them open for Sylvie and a girl rushing in behind her. Sylvie slipped off her bookbag and pulled out the library books.

"I'll nab one of the microfiche machines. What era is your murder from?"

"You don't have to do all that," said Sylvie.

"What era?" he repeated. "And where's the building at?"

She sighed and gave him the address first. "I don't really know the era. Maybe the '50s?"

"Right on. Come meet me when you're done." He gave her one brief, too-long look before grinning and turning toward the stairs. Sylvie watched him until she worried he would turn around and see her standing there mooning like a middle schooler.

The library was full of kids fresh out of their respective schools, some of them in disheveled uniforms, others in ringer tees and cut off shorts. They chattered and chewed gum, homework no longer an issue for most of them. They were here out of habit, somewhere to go before they could go home. Safer than *out there*, where killers prowled for young blood.

An elderly woman in a tropical muumuu and rain bonnet came up the stairs from the reference section, one hand holding a collection of print-outs from the microfiche, the other on the arm of a librarian, who held the woman's cane.

Sylvie thought about how she would look in fifty years, browsing the events of her youth in whatever buildings still remained, watching herself standing here and remembering the conflict of a murder, a ghost, and lusting after a boy. It wasn't that she time traveled, but she could almost sense her elderly self laughing right behind her. She even turned to look. *See you in the twenty-first century, if this city makes it out alive.*

Alone with her own thoughts, as soon as Sylvie returned her books and took two steps down to the reference section, she realized how daunting this task was going to be. How it would probably take many visits to get a single answer. And this fact weighed on her as she dropped her bookbag by the machine Ilan was setting up, then went off to browse an aisle of New York history. Maybe a book of old headlines or local crime stories would call out to her.

New York was way too big for this, and she was only one person. She gently dragged her fingers along the spines of rebound volumes and old, cracked leather. As a girl, she liked to see who had read the books before her. Many of the oldest volumes came from the gilded mansions of Millionaire's Row, their libraries donated when the family ran out of funds or the building was demolished. Uncut pages, unread and untouched by anything but a printing press. All for show on mahogany shelves, until they arrived here.

Behind her, Sylvie felt someone brush past her and she turned to look, but no one was there. No one was in the aisle at all, or the one behind her. When she turned back to the books in front of her, she noticed a shadow standing just on the other side of the shelf. Her heart dropped and her hand dropped, and she took a wary step to her right, toward the desks and machines and librarians and people—all of which seemed very far away now. The shadow didn't move, but something was clearly there.

The aisle felt like a tunnel. She thought of the hands in the doorway and her skin crawled. Turning, balling her fists to keep herself from even accidentally using her hindsight, she felt more than saw the shadow move with her. And as she approached the end, she prepared for a pair of wicked hands to grab her. But nothing did.

The aisle was empty. All the aisles were empty.

Jesus Christ, Sylvie. Marybeth is right. You're getting strung out over nothing.

All the same, she gave up on the books and went to Ilan, who was sitting at the machine and idly scrolling through headlines. Sylvie leaned on the back of his chair and tried to slow her heart.

"Solve it yet?" she asked him, sucking in a quick breath, and nudging him over so she could squeeze onto the chair. She could have grabbed a free chair, sure, but there was no fun in that.

"Possibly. Here, let me go back. These are crime reports from different papers for different years. This is '55," he said. "I figured, start in the middle and work up and back."

Sylvie nudged him with her entire body. His left leg slipped off the chair, as did her right. To keep her from falling off, he hooked an arm around her waist as she leaned forward to see the scans with her fuzzy vision. She pushed her hair over her shoulder and took over the job of scrolling.

It was difficult to concentrate, especially with so many clipped headlines and brief articles of varying quality and preservation. A few headlines were gruesome enough to shock her away from thinking about how Ilan had a prime view of her shoulder and neck and wondering if he was looking at her. And once in a while she saw a headline about an event she had witnessed.

"Oh, wait, I've seen—" And she would stop herself mid-sentence and continue as though she hadn't spoken.

But mostly Sylvie found herself overwhelmed to the point of frustration. She simply didn't believe she would find something. And if she found something, she simply didn't believe it would help.

They moved from 1955 to 1954, and Sylvie felt like she was starting to see double. Ilan hauled her fully onto his lap, and she thought she was seeing triple.

Among the incidents in Hell's Kitchen were gang murders, bombings, stabbings, arson, brothel raids, a man gone missing on the Appalachian Trail, ransom, kidnappings, more ransom, dismemberment, shootings, more shootings—men, lots of men. Almost exclusively men, both victims and perpetrators. None at the building across from Deirdre's. None on her block at all.

Distilled to its worst, the city didn't seem all that different twenty years later. Today's papers made it sound like the end times every day. Though, for those who came up against people like the .44 caliber killer, it was.

If a teenage girl had been shot anywhere in Hell's Kitchen, then or now, she would have rated at *least* an inch of column space, especially if a gang member caused it, and most especially if she was collateral damage. Maybe she had her own Capeman, this one never caught. But if she did, no one cared.

Maybe it wasn't a man who shot her.

That *definitely* would have been in the news.

There was no folder for 1953, so they jumped up to 1956 and quickly ran into the story Jenny's fiancé had told at the party. The story of the Bushwick Murder Mansion—which the papers called the Herkimer-Cropsey House.

"Cropsey," said Sylvie with a huff of laughter. "What're the odds?"

"What d'you think came first? The urban legend or the real people?" asked Ilan.

Sylvie shrugged.

Sure enough, the story of the Bushwick Murder Mansion was true. At least, the part about the father who killed his family and himself, and there being one survivor. A friend of the children. There were poorly scanned photos of what looked like yearbook and studio portraits of the family. On follow-up stories, some of the photos (if there were any) were slightly better quality.

FATHER FELLS FAMILY

An infamous Brooklyn mansion is the scene of another grisly tragedy.

In the early evening hours, neighbors reported hearing a scream and gunshots from the historic Colonial Herkimer-Cropsey house in the Bushwick neighborhood of Brooklyn. When authorities arrived, it was to a scene of indescribable carnage.

Vittorio Albero, 48, allegedly shot and killed his wife, Teresa (44), and all four of their children,

before turning a second gun on himself. Vittorio, Jr. (18), Dolores (16), Louis (13), and Patricia (9) were pronounced dead at the scene. A seventh victim was a friend of the children, who was rushed to _____ Municipal Hospital with life-threatening injuries. Her name has not yet been released to the public. She is not expected to survive.

Vito Albero, Sr., fled Italy for Queens sometime in 1938, according to a family friend who did not provide their name. He worked as an electrician and bought the derelict mansion from the city in 1955. Neighbors said — (cont'd page 8)

"That is some far out shit," said Ilan.

"No kidding."

"But, see? He's Italian. Gotta be the mob."

"Or he was just a shitty person."

Sylvie scrolled fast through the rest of the paper, then several others, her eyes glazing over until they fell upon a new photograph, and she gasped so hard she almost swallowed her tongue.

BROOKLYN GIRL SURVIVES SHOOTING

"It's her!" Sylvie yelled, her heart thumping wildly in her chest. She almost launched to her feet, almost grabbed the machine and shook it. She didn't even remember that Ilan wouldn't get it, until he said, "Whoa, Sylvie. We're in a library."

She didn't hear him, though. There was so much kinetic energy moving through her that she started biting her thumbnail and furiously tapping her feet.

There was a yearbook photo. A girl with dark, shoulder-length hair, short bangs, and a boatneck shirt framing a small strand of pearls. She smiled brightly out through the ink, a dimple in one cheek but not the other. Sylvie didn't know that. She had never seen her smile.

Rynn Marquardt. Her name was Rynn Marquardt. And with her name unfolded her life—her very improbable life.

Shot five times . . .

Shoulder and ribs badly broken . . .

Expected to make a full recovery . . .

Miracle . . .

Sent home to her parents . . .

Unbelievable. What Sylvie saw, just one gunshot of the five seemed *impossible* to have survived. It gave Sylvie doubts that this could be her.

But the photo was so similar to the girl she'd seen dozens of times now. And what kind of coincidence would it be to have two girls who looked so much alike be attacked and injured in the same way?

"How did she *live*?" Sylvie said to the universe.

Mr. and Mrs. Walter Marquardt [oh, those poor people] **claim their daughter never had problems with anyone at the Albero home, nor had she spoken of tension between the family members. She had been**

invited to the house many times prior and recently attended the senior prom with the eldest son, Vito, Jr.

"We hope she won't remember what happened," Mrs. Marquardt told us. "We wouldn't want her burdened with something like that."

Sylvie was torn between the lingering feeling of having violated Rynn's life by seeing her at her lowest, and a new sense of relief knowing that she hadn't been murdered that day, after all. It was, in actuality, much worse than she knew, much worse than she had ever seen, but Rynn had survived.

"But it happened in *Brooklyn*," she said, again forgetting that Ilan didn't know what she did.

"Yeah? And?"

Sylvie pushed up her glasses and looked at him, an instant flush creeping over her face. "I don't know why I said it like that."

Ilan laughed. "This has you psyched. If I didn't know you, I'd be scared of you right now."

She gently elbowed him, but she was already hunting for a follow-up. She had to know more. She *had* to.

She jumped to 1957 and even the fact that Ilan was her chair was forgotten. They had only minutes before the library would close.

GIRL MISSING AFTER BUSHWICK MASSACRE—FAMILY DEAD
Another family butchered in their own home, cause not released, and their oldest daughter missing.

Walter (44), Phyllis (40), and Avis (13) Marquardt of ___ Bushwick Ave., in Brooklyn, were found dead yesterday evening after several calls and visits from friends, family, and employers went unanswered.

Rynn Marquardt, 19, the sole survivor of a vicious attack that left another family dead in July of 1956, was not at the scene, and authorities admit they have little hope of finding her alive.

No ransom note was left.

The residence is only blocks from the historic Herkimer-Cropsey house, where all six members of the Albero family were killed by the father, Vito Albero, 48, who then turned the gun on himself.

Rynn, a classmate of the eldest Albero children, was reported by friends, who wished to remain anonymous, to have had a difficult year since the slayings.

"She started going around with a strange crowd," said one. "Lots of older men."

Neighbors admitted that the young woman came and went at all hours and that her parents expressed concern for her well-being.

"They said they thought she was into something dangerous," said one neighbor. "Like maybe she wasn't God-fearing no more. They were talking about moving away. Well, it's not surprising. She spent too much time at that mansion. They need to tear it down."

Tragedy has long dogged the Herkimer-Cropsey house, alternatively known as the Dutch House, which was originally a wood frame cottage built by

Frederick Herkimer in 1710. In the 1750s, the English Cropsey family expanded the home into a mansion, but the American Revolution ruined them.

In 1801, William Cropsey's surviving son, Isaac, was accused of murdering a young woman and two male associates in the home. He was found dead at the scene.

During a renovation in 1886, five additional bodies were unearthed in the cellar presumed to be more victims of Isaac Cropsey.

The last family to live in the house before Mr. Albero was a German brewing family by the name of Penzig. They bought the house in 1893 and left only a year later, citing at the time that no one had told them about the skeletons before the purchase.

Unoccupied until 1955, locals feared the home had become a sanctuary for strange rituals and cultist group meetings. Local rumor claims that no animals will cross the property — (cont'd page 14)

Strange rituals and cultist group meetings reminded Sylvie of Marilyn's mother's psychic. If anywhere was going to be the site of a Satanic murder cult, a house with repeated mass killings across three centuries seemed like a good candidate.

"Penzig. That sounds familiar," said Sylvie.

"We need to return all this," said Ilan. "We can come back, though. Print stuff out next time."

Sylvie nodded and stood up. She realized now that her whole body was trembling as though she had just let go of something heavy.

People began to filter back upstairs. With the machine off and reference materials returned, Sylvie grabbed her bag and fell into step beside Ilan. The only other person in the reference section now, aside from the librarian scuttling around in the back, was a woman packing up her fringed suede bag. As Sylvie and Ilan passed her, she stopped what she was doing and turned her head to look at them. Her gaze followed them long enough that Sylvie raced ahead of Ilan up the stairs.

He laughed, but Sylvie didn't feel relaxed again until they were out in the daylight.

"You still coming over?" she asked. "I didn't freak you out completely?"

"Of course you didn't." Then, surprising her and turning her thoughts into a buzzing sound, Ilan took her hand. Really took it, too, lacing his fingers right between hers as though they'd done this a thousand times. Both had probably imagined it, anyway.

Sylvie almost wanted to walk the whole way back, just to see what would happen. She'd been carefully watering this crush for four years and the idea of pruning it just to have something lovely and fleeting—potentially—scared her as much as it did anything else. They were friends first, and for so long. Maybe it was good to just hold hands. Maybe it wouldn't be so fleeting.

"So, I guess you found something, after all," he said.

"Hm?" Her thoughts were still incoherent.

"I thought you were looking up something in Hell's Kitchen."

"Oh. Oh! Right. Yeah, I totally was, I swear. But it was kinda fun to find what that guy was talking about. Well, not fun."

"You gonna go out to that place and take a look at it with your psychic powers?"

These were always just jokes, but they always caught her by surprise.

"Hell no. I don't need to see that." She had already seen a fraction of that, and it was terrible.

"I'm glad you've moved on from the time when you kept telling us there were murdered women in a well buried in the cellar of that place on Prince——"

"Spring," she corrected.

"Terrific. You remember."

"Look, I didn't tell you to scare you. I'm burdened with exceptional knowledge. I have to share it sometimes," she said with more sincerity than she meant to. But Ilan just laughed.

"What about this place?" Ilan nodded toward the brick apartment building that faced the sidewalk. It was an ordinary tenement, with ordinary garbage cans and ordinary ants crawling in ordinary patterns through the cracks in the front steps. Lace curtains were caught in one of the windows.

Sylvie considered it and, because Ilan was holding her hand and she'd just discovered who the teenage girl was, she skated her fingers along the brick and watched decades of people bloom like a polaroid around them.

"There's a stagedoor johnny at that first-floor window," she said, and she stopped. "A girl's in the window with her hair in pin-curls, and he's giving her some kind of box and flowers. Like, a *huge* bouquet. It's not gonna fit in that window."

Ilan wasn't looking at the window, though. Ilan was looking at Sylvie. She pulled her hand away from the building and met his gaze and thought about grabbing his shirt and pulling him against the wall. They kept walking.

"Wait, what's a stagedoor johnny again?" he said.

"Guys who would go after actresses and dancers and people like that. Some of them would give these women crazy shit, like cars and houses."

"Right, yeah."

She couldn't tell if he was actually listening. He rubbed her hand with his thumb, and she felt it right in her chest as they walked to the station.

It was a Friday night, and the sidewalks of SoHo were festooned with larger items for disposal—bookshelves and couches and desks and chairs. Already, people would have picked over most of the best pieces, but almost everything was guaranteed to go somewhere other than the dump. The clutter, and the usual detritus of rag bales, boxes, and barrels, not to mention the scattered mercantile trash, cast long shadows over the street.

Passing down Prince and within sight of Greene Street, Sylvie was staring up at the two real lit windows in a trompe l'oeil mural, when Ilan suddenly stopped. He didn't let go of Sylvie's hand, forcing her to stop with him.

"What?" she asked, looking up at him.

He took one step backward and said nothing.

Sylvie didn't like the way his face looked. His color seemed to be slipping away, and his eyes were wide.

"Ilan?"

"I need to go," he said, his voice low and caught in his throat.

"What?"

He was really scaring her now, and his grip on her hand began to tighten, like he had forgotten she was there. Sylvie followed his gaze, trying to look where he was looking, but she couldn't find anything out of place. And that scared her even more.

"Seriously, Ilan, quit. You're freaking me out."

"You can't see it?"

She didn't want to know what she wasn't seeing, but she had to ask. "See *what*?"

They weren't alone out here—the post office was directly across from them, near closing, and a man ran in carrying packing tubes, almost colliding with one of the wholesale workers who had just left Hy Gus Luncheonette.

She squinted hard, willing her glasses to sharpen her vision in ways they couldn't, but the only thing she could see was a black dog on the corner of Greene Street. It was barely visible, as it was sitting in front of the dark grating on the doors of the SoHo Center's library. Someone had probably tied it there and gone into a gallery.

"I don't see anything," she said. "Let's go."

She attempted to pull on him, but Ilan wouldn't move.

"You don't see that dog?" he murmured.

"That black dog?" She looked back at Ilan, when he suddenly jumped, almost pulling her over.

The dog was now on their side of the street, sitting just as it had been before, its eyeless face trained upon them.

CHAPTER TWELVE

The dog was so dark that it seemed like a hole in the fabric of the universe. It cast no shadow. It did not breathe. How had it ever looked normal to her? How had she just dismissed it?

Ilan backed up without turning his back. Without even blinking. He kept telling Sylvie to go but not to go home, but she didn't want to be left out here. Maybe she could run into a shop—but what then?

"I'm coming with you."

Ilan immediately looked a little more human again, a little more normal. Not because he was relaxed, but because he was freaked out in a new way that Sylvie wasn't ready for. "No way."

She frowned, surprised and a little offended. "Ilan! Come *on.*"

"No, Sylvie! It's not safe up there. I see it *all the time!*"

"You can't leave me here with that thing!"

"Maybe it'll follow me." He didn't sound certain enough for Sylvie's liking.

"It's in *my* neighborhood!"

She still had a couple hours before it got dark, but what was more dangerous—walking in the dark, or something that looked like walking darkness?

Ilan sighed. It was short and sharp and full of reluctance. "Fine. Okay. Let's go."

He hadn't stopped holding her hand, and he pulled her with him, back the way they had come. Back down Prince Street, back up Broadway, and they didn't slow until they were on Houston, where Ilan instantly started flagging taxis.

Sylvie had almost forgotten where Ilan lived, and as they passed the Mark Twain house, she remembered the dog that had come out of the garden. (Had it come out of the garden?) At the time, it seemed like nothing. So much nothing that she had forgotten about it. She must have been more buzzed than she realized.

The front door of Ilan's ivy-covered building wasn't locked, so he shoved his way in and headed upstairs. Two flights, three flights—he was on the top floor, one of two apartments, one on the east and one on the west, at least according to the doors off the hall (Ilan's was on the west side). There was one additional door that said ROOF, but it was padlocked. The air up here was stuffy despite the day being cool.

Inside the dim apartment, Sylvie found herself in a long hall that smelled of cigarettes and skunky weed. At the end of the hall to her right was a door that was only just cracked, so most of the ambient light spilled in from the other end, toward the front. She peeled off her shoes and followed Ilan that way, toward the light. They passed a doorway to the galley kitchen, a door to the bathroom, and a narrow door that had to be a linen closet. The original telephone niche was still in the wall, though it had been painted over several times and was now home to a cascading philodendron sitting on an out-of-date Manhattan telephone directory. The phone was on the wall, instead.

Ilan pushed through the curtain of beads separating the living room from the rest of the space. They clacked together pleasantly. On any other day, in any other mood, Sylvie would have made a joke about it, but she couldn't. She dropped her bag next to the futon that sat beneath two small, square windows. A woven rug covered most of the dinged-up parquet floor. There was a stack of records with no player, and a closed guitar case and trumpet case. The shades were drawn except for a sliver, and Sylvie could see (and hear) that the window was cracked open. The ivy rustled. A soft breeze slipped through the room.

To her, used to thousands of unimpeded square footage, the space was small and could be cozy. But it was also very stark. Nothing hung on the walls but nails where art used to be.

"Um—I'll just remind you now that none of the furniture is mine." He laughed a little, but he was plainly still rattled. He grabbed something off the TV stand, which didn't have a TV on it, and dropped onto the futon. He slid a half-full ashtray along the coffee table in front of him. Sylvie watched him pull a cigarette from a pack and a matchbook from his pocket, and he lit up.

He offered her the pack, but she shook her head.

Sylvie could tell he was still trying to recalibrate his thoughts, his mood. But she had to do the same.

"How often do you see it?"

Ilan shook his head, took a drag, blew the smoke away from Sylvie.

"Ilan. I'm gonna keep asking. What's been going on?"

"I—" He paused, brow furrowed, head slightly raised, chin slightly tilted, as though he was concentrating on something. "Wish I had a TV here. Undecided if I should buy one or rent one. I should at least buy a stereo. Which feels stupid because my system is at my parents', and they could just bring it here. Or I could go get it."

Sylvie's turn to furrow her brow. "What?"

"We could check the nabes, see what's good," Ilan continued.

"I don't want to see a movie right now. Answer me. What is that thing?"

Ilan seemed to flinch. She saw him look over his shoulder, toward the shaded window. "I dunno. A dog."

"A dog."

He pulled and pulled on the cigarette, and she stood there, not wanting to push but absolutely needing to.

"You gotta tell me what's up, Ilan. Come on. You see it all the time? Where?"

Ilan must have come to the conclusion that Sylvie wasn't going to stop asking, or maybe he wanted to get some of this out.

"Half the time I go outside it's out there," he said, dropping his voice so that Sylvie had to step closer to the coffee table. She sat down on the rug.

"Since when?"

"Since the night of the party. Don't you remember it?"

"I kinda forgot, actually," she admitted. She hoped it would make him feel better. That she hadn't been frightened.

155

Ilan flipped the matchbook lid over and over. "Good. Because I don't even like talking about it. Feels like it knows."

"It doesn't . . . it doesn't come in here, does it?" Sylvie imagined the beads clacking behind her and turning to see the mass of shadow looming over them, stopping their only way out. She turned to look, just in case. Nothing was there.

Ilan looked gray. He shook his head tightly, pursed his lips around the cigarette. He pulled hard, exhaling a storm cloud. He coughed. "Sometimes it's sitting on the stoop. I've almost fallen down the damn stairs. Maybe that's what it wants me to do."

"Where does it come from?"

He inclined his head over his shoulder. "That house. The Mark Twain house. I've seen it standing on the roof."

"Fuck off." Sylvie felt cold.

"Feels like a sheepdog and I'm the sheep. Only I don't know where it wants me to go or what it wants me to do. Or maybe it doesn't. Maybe it's nothing but a freaky shadow. Other people see it. They point at it."

"See? So it's nothing to do with you. Maybe it just kind of haunts this street and . . ." Sylvie trailed off because she didn't know why it would be in SoHo. SoHo was *her* neighborhood, *her* home.

She sucked in a deep breath, let it settle against her diaphragm, let it ground her long enough to say, "I saw something freaky recently, too."

Ilan looked at her through the smoke. She couldn't tell if he thought she was humoring him.

"It wasn't that dog, but—" God, how was she going to explain this? "It was why I wanted to look up that building. In Hell's Kitchen. I saw something weird, where it's being renovated."

She had to take another breath and focus on the breeze and the ivy and the evening sunlight. The strangeness of the apparition unsettled her as badly now as it had then. "There was a weird shadow person. I could only see part of it through the partition, but it was just these hands on the ground. It was so fucking strange."

"Hands? Human hands?"

Sylvie nodded. "Like a man's hands."

Ilan pushed his cigarette into the ashtray.

"It sounds wacky saying it out loud, but it was like they were doing a handstand. I could only see up to the elbows, sort of. It was standing in the doorway and the doorway was dark, and it was dark." She shook her head. "Awful."

"Doubt it was a man."

Sylvie frowned. "What do you mean?"

"I mean, I doubt it was—it wasn't a person. It wasn't a human." He was already lighting a new cigarette.

"What, like, the dog has human hands?"

Before Sylvie could tell Ilan off for creeping her out even more, he said, "You think Marz would know what any of this stuff is?"

"I told her what I saw. Want me to ask her about the dog?"

At first, Ilan shrugged. Then he shook his head.

"What if I don't say you saw it. What if I just, like, remind her of the one we all saw that night."

When he didn't shake his head again, Sylvie leaned over the table and skimmed her fingers over Ilan's hand. She took his cigarette so he could hold her, instead. His palm was sweaty. "We'll figure it out."

He watched her hand for a moment before laughing softly. "I was hoping this afternoon would be a little different."

So did Sylvie, but she didn't want to make him feel worse.

"Maybe we should go for a walk," he said, his voice suddenly brisk. "Get some food, maybe."

Sylvie stood up and sat down next to him. She could feel the breeze better here, hear the gentle ivy and the traffic down below— foot and car in equal measure. A little dog barked. She wanted to open the shades. She also didn't want to see the house. But it wasn't directly across from them; it was diagonal and could easily be lost behind lush tree canopies from this high up.

"Hey," she said, the universal start to any conversation when you're concerned. "We're okay, right? If you wanna come crash at my place, you know we've got room."

Ilan didn't look at her. He was leaning forward so that she couldn't see him, anyway, with his hair falling around his face. She wanted to touch his back—so she did.

"Yeah," he said. "We're okay. It doesn't do anything. It's just creepy." *Just creepy* was underselling it, and they both knew it. Then he leaned back, and Sylvie barely had time to move her arm to avoid it getting trapped against him and the futon.

He shook his head, stuck his cigarette back in his mouth, patted Sylvie's knee, and stood up. He stretched. His back cracked.

"You wanna get pizza?" he said.

"Okay." Sylvie didn't want to go outside yet, but she didn't want to make Ilan stay where he was clearly uncomfortable.

While he went to the bathroom, Sylvie got up and went to look at his records. As she filed through the pile (Sun Ra, Herbie Hancock, Chick Corea, Miles Davis, Chet Baker), she could hear someone talking—someone other than Ilan and too muffled to be down on the sidewalk.

When Ilan came back into the room, she said, "I forget what it's like to live in a normal apartment. You hear everybody."

"Someone in the apartment next to me is in an Off-Off-Way-Off-in-the-Boonies-Broadway show right now. I heard *all* about it 'cause she talks on the phone on the landing. The cord's gonna be chopped in half soon, the way she shuts it in the door. Hope it happens in the next few days."

He went to the open window and shut it with a crack and pop of old paint, then dropped the shade the rest of the way.

"Blow your trumpet at her while she talks. Do you practice much?" she asked him.

"I get people banging on the walls and floor sometimes, so no. One more reason to miss the old loft."

"You're way too good for people to get pissed at your music," she said, affronted. "People around here used to like art."

"They probably do it because I play at like midnight." His voice was shot through with that smoker's rasp.

"You can come practice at our place any time you want," she said. "Well, not at midnight. Mom and Dad don't even let me dance at midnight."

Sylvie knew she ought to call her parents. Really, she should call Marz or Marybeth first, since she was supposed to meet up once all three were free. They would be ready with a cover story for missing dinner.

But she didn't want to explain where she was, and why, and she didn't want to go home yet. They'd been halfway to something this afternoon, and it still hovered between them. Especially when she realized that Ilan was watching her instead of looking at his albums. He sat down behind her instead of putting on his shoes.

"You should stay with us more, anyway, because this place has nothing in it. You're gonna get cabin fever."

He looked relaxed, almost back to normal. He'd smoked through a couple cigarettes to get there, and she smiled a little awkwardly at him. She leaned against his arm. Saw his gaze flicker to her mouth, briefly. Then he stood up again.

She looked down at the albums to cover a frown. Why didn't he just kiss her? Man, maybe he thought she was too fast or too flighty. Maybe it was revenge for every time he'd turned a corner in school and found her in front of some boy's locker. She'd overplayed her hand.

You're overthinking. Ilan dated, too.

Ilan went back out in the hall to grab his shoes. As the beads clattered, Sylvie heard the voices again, but this time they formed something distinctive.

Syyyylvieeee

Sylvie dropped the record and stood up. Sunlight glowed through the closed shades, and she walked over to them and pulled one up. She didn't even think about it—she just did it. Across the street and to her left was the Mark Twain house, and she looked at the empty, square windows in the top floor as though someone was leaning out them and shouting for her.

"Sylvie?"

Sylvie jumped when she felt Ilan's hand on her back.

"Let's go," he said. "Pizza."

She nodded. She grabbed her bag, which now held only her battered old pencil case that rattled childishly with every step. Ilan shoved his cigarettes in his back pocket and led her out the door. She almost expected to see something on the landing, but no one was there.

Outside, she avoided looking at the Mark Twain house, and was surprised when Ilan crossed the street in its direction.

"Hey, do you mind if we, like, go around the other way?" she asked after him, but he didn't hear her.

There were no dogs, no phantoms, no shadows, only people. Real people. It was the dawn of the weekend, after all, and a nice evening. The trees were full with leaves, planters bursting with color. It wasn't scary here. It couldn't be scary here.

Ilan paused to wait for her, though he didn't look back. He must have been nervous, still. Seeing the dog seemed to have inspired some kind of primordial fear that touched the surface of his mind, and it was hard to shake those deep-seated instincts. She got it. She felt it when she saw that girl—no, *Rynn*. She had a name now, and somehow that made her less formidable. Or maybe it was that other things had happened which were far more alarming.

She wanted to tell him it was okay, but she didn't really know if it was. So Sylvie reached for his hand and he took it, then held it, really held it. Laced each finger into hers. She breathed out. He turned away from the house, heading west so they wouldn't have to cross its path, after all. Though she couldn't help looking back, just in case.

Nothing was there.

CHAPTER THIRTEEN

"*Before* dark, Sylvie. *Before* dark!"

Sylvie's parents weren't the easiest people to anger, but they were angry now. She thought about lying and saying she had been with Marz or Marybeth, but the odds were way too high that either or both of them had called or come by, not knowing where she was. She should have called, but what difference did that make now?

"It wasn't totally dark when we left!" Sylvie insisted, dropping her deflated bookbag but not having time or ability to do anything else. Her parents had sprung up from the sofa like a pair of jackrabbits and cornered her at the door.

"Don't look for loopholes. The rule is *home* before dark. Not *on your way* before dark," said her mom.

"We don't have a lot of rules for you, Sylvie, so don't make us start adding more this late in the game," said her dad.

"You've known Ilan a long time, and we do trust him, but it doesn't matter. If you want to hang out with him, keep it to daylight or bring him back here."

"We just went out for pizza! It's no big deal."

"It's not a big deal that you were with Ilan—it's a big deal that you keep coming home after your curfew," said her mom. "That's two strikes this month, kiddo!"

"Sylvie—there are reasons we want you home before dark, and you know what they are," said her dad. "You think you're protected and safe down here because we've always let you kids do what you want, go where you want. But it's the illusion of safety, Silverado. We're still in a big city with a lot of people. You might feel immortal, but that's because you're a teenager."

"I know I'm not immortal. I know teenagers aren't immortal."

"Then act like it. Don't walk around the city after dark," said her mom. "Unless we're with you, or Gary's with you, don't do it. Period. End of."

"Gary stays out all the time!" Even as Sylvie said it, she knew it was a stupid argument, something a little kid would think. *He's twenty*, was what her parents were going to say.

"He's twenty." (Bingo.) "We've told him we don't like it. We've told him if he's out late, stay with a friend. But he's also a man, Sylvie," said her mom. "He gets some privileges that you don't."

Sylvie sighed. "So much for women's lib."

Her parents didn't laugh. "Think about those poor kids getting shot over in Queens. Just having a date, seeing a movie, and then their lives are over because the wrong person crossed their paths."

Or visiting a friend, safe in their home, when their dad goes nuts and kills everyone there.

164

"I know! I know, I know. I'll be home before dark from now on, okay? I swear."

"Until you turn eighteen. And that's not much longer, so you can sit tight," said her dad. "Our house, our rules."

"No practicing tonight. You've got dance in the morning, anyway. And no going anywhere this weekend, either. Be grateful that's your only punishment," said her mom.

Sylvie nodded and picked her bookbag up. *Let summer vacation begin.*

After getting cannoli at a bakery on Bleecker, Ilan had walked her as far as Houston. His mood had crested and fallen and even Sylvie found herself staring hard into shadowy corners, and ordinary dogs on ordinary leashes made her look twice. She didn't really know what to do when they stopped at Sixth Avenue to wait for the light. Insist that he stay? She didn't like to think of him sitting in that barren apartment, listening to the ivy scuttle against the windows, unable even to listen to music, dwelling on a ghost that didn't haunt his building.

"You *sure* you don't want to just crash here?" she asked him.

"I'm fine. I don't want . . . I don't want to make your parents worry," he said. "They probably already are, so go ahead and blame me."

"Listen. Ilan. If you're worried about seeing it by my place tonight, I'll just walk from here, okay? You don't have to come any nearer." She squeezed his hand and all he did was reluctantly nod. She tried not to take that personally. She had sort of hoped he'd be more worried.

No, Sylvie, I don't want you on your own. I don't know what's going on with that dog, but I don't want to take any chances since it seems to know where you live.

She was being unfair. Ilan had to walk back alone, too. And he didn't have parents and a brother waiting for him once he got back inside. She'd been terrified, though, as soon as she turned down Houston on her own. To avoid the corner where she'd seen the dog that afternoon, she approached Greene Street from the south, looping down West Broadway and along Broome Street. Enough people were out eating late dinners that her mood eased once she was in sight of her front door. But she paused before going inside and looked up, wishing she had dragged Ilan with her, wishing she had refused to let him go. Dread stirred in her brain as a breeze kicked up and rustled the trash along the curb.

✦

After showering and changing into her PJs, Sylvie kicked her bookbag under her bed, where it would probably stay until the next school year, then dropped down onto her bed. She didn't know where to take her mind first, so she thought of nothing and listened to the muffled sound of Gary's music next door.

Music. That would relax her. She got up and rummaged through her records. No Frampton. She wasn't ready for a Frampton moment.

Rumours it was. She'd spun that thing to death for all of February and March. She and Gary had tickets to see the Fleetwood Mac tour at Madison Square in a couple weeks, but she hadn't thought much about it this month.

Flopping on her bed again, Sylvie stared up at her tiled ceiling and folded the image of herself over the top of ephemeral witch Stevie Nicks. Two years ago, Sylvie wanted to change her name to Rhiannon. Now she'd decided that would work better if she ever had a daughter. *A daughter.* God help that kid if her condition was hereditary. But it must skip generations because Marilyn seemed fine.

As soon as she closed her eyes, a grainy photograph surfaced on the waters of Sylvie's mind and dispelled all of her other thoughts. *Rynn.* The teenage girl had a name. She had found it only hours ago and had no time to dwell on it.

Rynn smiled a bright smile, a pearl necklace at her throat, her hair curled for the occasion. She didn't know. She had no idea what waited for her. That easy, oblivious face the newspaper shared was not the face Sylvie knew, stretched white with terror, eyes riveted on her escape, then bright with pain and desperation. Blood soaking through her sweater, her hair wrenched from her scalp by invisible hands. Hands. Shadowy hands in the dark of the building, a figure standing in the corner, watching Sylvie watch the past, waiting for her back to turn. Waiting for her, still, as she moved down the library aisles. Waiting for her now, standing above her bed, or tucked into a corner of her ceiling.

"Fuck *that*."

Sylvie sat up and pulled off her headphones. A pipe thumped across the loft, somewhere near the bathroom.

She got up and lifted the needle, switched off the system, and left the room.

The loft was mostly dark, except for slivers of light coming from Gary's half-open door and her parents' room at the end of the hall. It comforted her to know that everyone else was awake, but she still went right to the tube and turned it on. Dialing mindlessly through the channels, she stopped at the last half hour of *Battle for the Planet of the Apes*, then folded herself up on the sofa and turned on a lamp.

"Which Planet of the Apes movie is this one?" Gary said, coming out of his room and ambling to the kitchen. "There's like fifty of them."

"It was either this or a repeat of *Quincy, M.E.*"

She heard Gary crack open a can of something and he sat down at the other end of the sofa and stretched his legs onto the coffee table. A copy of *Parade* from last Sunday's paper slipped to the floor.

"So." He sipped his Pepsi. "You and Ilan, eh?"

"What about him?" she asked, voice either uninterested or warning him off, depending on how determined he was to get a juicy answer out of her. (There was no juicy answer.)

"You dating?"

"No."

Gary raised his eyebrows.

Sylvie was glad for the semi-dark, so he couldn't quite see how she was turning red. "You probably already heard everything I said to Mom and Dad. What's it matter to you?"

"Because you're my sister, that's why."

"You never asked about any other dates I've had."

"Yeah, but Ilan's *Ilan*, not a try-hard loser."

Sylvie rolled her eyes—really rolled them, hoping that Gary would see it, hear it, feel how much she didn't want to talk about this. She didn't even know what she and Ilan were or would be.

"I don't want you driving him off," he said.

"Oh, please."

Gary folded his arms. "So you were gone from the end of school until dark, but all you did was eat pizza and go to the library."

"I mean, we hung out at his place for a sec before going to get pizza. You were right. There's nothing to do there. It's kind of sad."

"Mm." The skepticism dripped from him, and Sylvie wasn't used to that, not from Gary. Not from her brother, about her. Almost worse than that was how stupid she knew her story sounded. Gone for hours with nothing to show for it (or to replay while falling asleep). It burned her up worse than embarrassment.

"What is your *problem*?"

"I just wish I'd known you went up there."

Sylvie wrinkled her nose. "You go up there all the time."

"Sorry for looking out for my little sister when she's out in the dark and her friends are calling and stopping by and don't know where she is." Now his tone had changed. Now Gary was properly angry. Or afraid. Or—

"Are you *jealous*?"

"*Jesus*, Sylvie, don't be a brat."

169

"Ilan was always my friend, too, y'know. Just because you're both in college now doesn't mean I'm—"

"I don't care if you date Ilan, or hook up, or whatever! Just do it here. But not when I'm here."

"Why?"

"Because I don't want to see it."

"You know what I meant."

"You just shouldn't go over there, okay? Not by yourself."

Sylvie felt a thread begin to pull at the back of her mind, tugging at the stability of her indignation. Despite herself, despite how cornered she felt and how wrong Gary was, there was doubt, now, seeping in.

"Come on." She smiled a little, offered a weak laugh. "It's Ilan."

"It's not about *Ilan*."

"If it's not Ilan, then—" *Then.* "You know what's going on with him."

Gary gave her a look she couldn't read. Absolutely could not read what it meant at all. It made her second-guess this tactic, but it didn't stop her. "And you believe him. Because you've seen it."

No answer.

"Tell me the truth."

"Sure. I saw it same as you. Night of the party." Gary tried to look relaxed, but he kept touching his mustache.

"Saw what?" She knew what he meant, of course.

"That . . . whatever it was."

She opened her mouth to tell him she'd actually seen the dog just up the street, but the words wouldn't come. She wouldn't let them. The more she spoke, the more she envisioned it outside their building, slipping through the cracks around the door, like a dark breeze off a stagnant pool.

"I didn't see anything weird up there tonight, for whatever that's worth," she said instead.

"Let it go, Sylvie." Gary turned the Pepsi can around and around in his hands. He was faintly lit by his bedroom light and despite the mustache, he suddenly looked as young as he had when they were growing up.

"That's not fair. Ilan told me everything."

He dropped his voice even lower. "I wish he hadn't."

Sylvie folded her arms hard across her chest and stared at the glowing screen. "That's stupid. You're both—you're both overreacting."

"Maybe we are but don't go up there. Get him to come here. And that's all I'm gonna say about it ever again. Capiche?"

"No! Not capiche!"

"Too bad." Gary stood up and went back to his room, shutting the door completely.

✦

For once, Sylvie wanted Rynn to show herself.

She stood on the corner, waiting. It was a warm morning but not warm enough to account for the sweat she felt beneath the strap of her duffel. People walked by her, but she didn't pay attention to them. She could almost count her breathing, count her heartbeat, and it seemed like Rynn was taking forever this time.

Sylvie didn't want to be out there, so close to the building, so close to the partition that kept whatever was inside of it, inside. She didn't look at the gap above the sidewalk—categorically refused.

Then there she was. Rynn burst from the invisible door of time and space and careened over the sidewalk, right through an elderly couple carrying a reused Zabar's bag.

Taking a deep breath, and feeling like she ought to be committed, Sylvie walked several steps closer and said, quickly and under her breath, "Rynn Marquardt? That's your name. Rynn Marquardt."

It would look like the worst black comedy if anyone else could appreciate the whole scene. Sylvie calmly talking to a girl who had just been blasted through by a shotgun and was now crawling desperately over the ground, sobbing and choking and trying to get to a place of safety that did not exist.

As the unseen hand grabbed hold of Rynn's hair and pulled her back, Sylvie could see the fear on her face, in the shocked whites of her bright blue eyes—it outweighed the pain she had to be feeling in her obliterated shoulder. Blood soaked her chest, bubbling up from her sweater as her heart no doubt raced harder than it ever had in her life. She looked like she was trying to scream but her voice died at the back of her throat. She was wearing a pearl necklace. It was probably the same strand she had on in her yearbook photo.

You're going to live, Sylvie thought. *Through this part, anyway.* She felt ill and closed her eyes. Had she really thought saying Rynn's name would work? Like a talisman or a spell? She'd read too many Zilpha Keatley Snyder novels.

Up in Deirdre's studio, her revulsion turned to that familiar, lead weight disappointment. She hadn't realized how much she was counting on it to work, until it didn't. Then all she was left with was the knowledge that something terrible had happened, and she was going to have to live with it at the periphery of her life until Deirdre moved or Sylvie moved on. And she couldn't move on. Not yet.

By afternoon, though intermittent clouds floated in front of the sun, the city broiled. Sylvie couldn't remember the last time it had rained. Hello, summer, and the first real scorcher of the year.

As soon as Sylvie got back home, ate lunch, and showered, she and Marz and Marybeth went to Paracelso to look at vintage clothes, then out to the playground by NYU when they decided the idea of clothes in this kind of heat was unappealing. Someone had hitched up a sprinkler head to the chain link fence and a gaggle of kids was congregated beneath it, running bare-footed and bare-headed and bare-bottomed through the spray, over to the giant wooden play sculpture that could give you a splinter just by looking at it, and not putting on the brakes until they were tearing through the overgrown baseball field. No one touched the slides today. Just the reflection could bake the skin off your legs.

The girls had come to this park since their own toddlerhood, and most of the adults sweating and suffering in the treeless afternoon waved to them or came by where they were sitting together at the farthest and highest point of the big, old, wooden beams, just to ask how school was, how their parents were, what they were up to this summer, and would they see them at this talk or that show opening.

But mostly they were left alone, which was what they wanted, anyway.

Sylvie liked being surrounded by happy activity. Normal life in their normal neighborhood, doing normal things like playing freeze tag, Mother May I, and digging in the dirt. People drifted along the sidewalk outside the fencing, going north or going south, toward shadier parks or shadier buildings. A white woman with long, straight, blonde hair stared longingly at the sprinkler.

All of that made it a lot easier to finally unload everything on her friends. She kept her voice down, not wanting parents overhearing the details.

"Remember at the party the other week, that guy was talking about a mass murder and the girl who disappeared?"

"Hm?" said Marz. "Oh, yeah. That house that was torn down. Sucks."

Sylvie tightened her grip on the wood beneath her and watched as the four-year-old version of herself, barefooted and bare-handed, ran wild laps around her brother, her hair in high pigtails.

"What if I told you that the girl in the story is the same one I keep seeing."

First, Marybeth gasped, almost throwing her knitting to the ground. And as she gasped, Marz shouted, "No *fucking* way!"

Well, that got some of the parents to cast them meaningful but polite looks of reproach. A few of the kids laughed conspiratorially before darting away.

Preschool Marz, her hair in twists with baubles clacking, jumped onto Sylvie's back with a wild whoop. Marybeth laughed around the thumb in her mouth as tow-headed Ilan broke away from Gary (cropped hair and far before a mustache) and said something to Marz that made her laugh hysterically.

Sylvie waved her hands at her friends and the memories retreated. "Shh!"

Marz lowered her voice. "First of all, how'd you figure that out? And second, you and Ilan *actually went to the library?*"

"Yes, *we actually went to the library.* Her picture was in the papers. I know it's the same girl."

"But you still don't see anyone else. You don't see the dad," said Marz.

"I've never seen him. I don't know." Sylvie suddenly wondered what the circumstances of the girl's disappearance even were. Was she shot again and dragged away? Was Sylvie actually watching the kidnapping and not the massacre? Rynn had disappeared, not died. She could be anywhere or nowhere at all. And Sylvie wondered if she was supposed to go find her, avenge the unsolved deaths of her family like a girl detective in a pulpy novel.

She wasn't going to do that. She wasn't even going to try.

Marybeth frowned. "But wait, didn't that murder happen in Brooklyn?"

Marz's brown eyes, rimmed in cat-like black liner, were sparkling with sunlight and ideas. "Remember how people thought the dad coulda been in the mob? Maybe they took her to Hell's Kitchen and killed her family because she really *did* know something. Did you find anything about that place in the papers?"

But Sylvie was already shaking her head. "No. But I didn't see *any* of that when I looked in the building, remember?"

"What if they never got inside all the way—"

Sylvie just kept shaking her head. She brushed a wayward ant off her knee.

Marz sighed, heavy and annoyed.

Sylvie noticed the same couple walking by the park again. She recognized the woman with the long, blonde hair. This time, the woman was looking placidly at Sylvie.

Sylvie quickly looked away.

"What's the girl's name?" asked Marybeth.

"Rynn."

"Kinda unusual," said Marz.

"I tried saying it to her, at dance. Like, *I know your name, please go away now*," Sylvie finally admitted. "Didn't work, obviously. Stupid, right?"

"I was actually gonna tell you to try that," said Marybeth, her focus back on her knitting.

Marz leaned back a little, then winced and pulled a splinter out of her palm. "So, touching the building didn't set it right. And learning her name didn't set it right." She drummed her slender, ring-covered fingers on the wood. "Maybe finding her will do it."

"That's *impossible*."

"Look, you don't really know your 20/20 hindsight that well, babe. It's not like you've got a mentor you can ask or whatever. Maybe there are parts of it that are more, like, alive or real or whatever. Not just a copy."

"That just doesn't make sense," Sylvie insisted.

"Then I guess the only thing to do is see what happens when the construction is done," said Marybeth.

"I wonder . . . I should talk to Marilyn. She works at a paper, and I bet she can go look at archives or something."

"Hold on. Didn't you mention her mom goes to some kind of psychic?"

"*Fake* psychic," Sylvie reminded her. "Anyway, she's more concerned about Satanic cults." Not that Sylvie could be certain there wasn't one involved in Rynn's story. But she was certain there wasn't one involved in her own.

Fairly certain.

"Delilah Marie! I wouldn't forget that name," said Marz. "You could just try. Look at yourself. You're proof there's more out there than meets the eye."

"I don't even know how to find her. And I don't have enough money for her to be interested."

"Just an idea to keep in your back pocket," said Marz. "So. Sylvie. What'd you and Ilan do? I went by your place after dinner, but you weren't back, so. Y'know." Marz winked obnoxiously in Sylvie's direction and Sylvie shoved at her.

"He held my hand," she said.

"And?"

There was the blonde woman again, walking even slower now, eyes fixated on Sylvie like sonar seeking prey. This time Sylvie watched her until she was out of view. Her skin itched, a breeze caught the loose hair around her face.

"You are such a perv for wanting the details!" said Marybeth. "Leave it alone."

"After all these years, you think I'm gonna just leave it alone?" said Marz.

"Nothing happened," said Sylvie. "Ilan's . . . hey. D'you guys remember that dog we saw at the house? The Mark Twain house?"

"Barely," said Marz. "I was still kinda wrecked."

"Ilan says he's, like, being haunted by some kind of phantom dog."

Marz turned her entire body toward Sylvie and crossed her legs on the wooden beam. "Yo, *what*?"

Sylvie tried to explain the afternoon, the progression from holding his hand to encountering the dog, to how frightened he was after. Then she mentioned that Gary believed him.

Marybeth stopped knitting.

"Phantom dogs are pretty common. Like, pick a place and there's a story about a scary black dog. Black Shuck, Church Grim, Padfoot, Yeth Hound—okay, those are basically all English. But anyway, it's almost always bad luck to see one. They're basically the devil or a demon or even an *unbaptized child*," said Marz, her tone mocking as she finished. "If you believe any of this stuff, anyway. I

178

try not to, otherwise there's no way I'd hang out with you right now. No offense."

"I wouldn't blame you if you stopped."

"Don't wallow, babe. Anyway, I know one New York story. There's another old place somewhere in the hinterlands of Brooklyn that Hessians took over during the war, and legend says they ran off screaming about phantom dogs and scary voices. Probably inspired *Sleepy Hollow*, to be honest. Or the other way around, knowing how many ghost stories Victorian people just made up from nothing. Who knows."

"I can't help thinking of that weird . . . whatever it was I saw in that building," said Sylvie, reaching back compulsively for the wood and the memories contained within it. "Obviously it wasn't a dog, but it was a shadow like that."

"Seriously, what is that lady's hangup?" asked Marz.

The blonde woman was back, alone. She had retraced her steps instead of going around the block, her vacant stare boring right into Sylvie. Sylvie heard a whisper, somewhere in the still air, and turned her head to look. It was only kids, running and jumping and sweating the day away.

"Maybe that dad wasn't in the mob," said Marz. "Maybe he was in a cult. Ugh."

Sylvie's mind went to Rynn. To her anonymous neighbors and their fears of a *bad crowd*.

"Don't say that," whispered Marybeth, who was clutching her knitting needles in preparation of putting them away.

The blonde woman was standing still, now, hands on the chain link fence, eyes on Sylvie.

A gaggle of kids ran past, and the woman didn't even look at them. Then a man stopped next to her, his body slackening at the shoulders, the plastic bag of takeout in his hand falling to the sidewalk, and he slowly turned his head to look at Sylvie, too, as the blonde woman opened her mouth.

Syyylvieee . . .

CHAPTER FOURTEEN

"Nope. I'm out. I'm gone. Goodbye."

Sylvie's body was covered in goosebumps, icy with the sort of chill you can only feel from within. She leapt off the play structure with Marz already beside her, an arm on Marybeth's shoulder.

They casually, then quickly, bolted from the park, not looking back until they were up in Sylvie's loft. The curtains were already drawn against the heat of the day, but Sylvie closed the blinds in her parents' room, Jessie Baby following her excitedly down the hall.

Despite the rules of the day requiring the elevator to always be sent down, the girls called it up and chain locked the door. Sylvie wished she could cover the skylight—she kept thinking the woman was leering at them through the glass, but it was only the planters hanging beneath it.

And she couldn't stop pacing. "I knew there was something wrong in the park. And the lady in the library. I knew it. I knew I wasn't imagining it!"

A note on the kitchen island said her parents had gone to get groceries, and Gary was who-knew-where.

The girls were tense, waiting for someone to lean on the buzzer or start banging up the stairs and on the door. The fire escapes at the front and back end would be their only recourse.

"I was only joking about a fucking cult, but I take it back. I put it in the universe, and I'm taking it back!" said Marz.

"But Sylvie hasn't even done anything!" said Marybeth, still clutching her knitting. "You haven't gone looking for—for that girl."

"I went to the library!"

"You didn't know what you were doing there," said Marz. "You were just looking at the building."

"Cults don't know the difference!"

Marz breathed out. "It's not a cult. It can't be a cult. It was just some lady out of her mind on something."

"She said my name." And still the sound of it scratched at the base of Sylvie's brain.

"I didn't hear her say anything," said Marybeth.

"Me neither," said Marz.

"Well, I did! And I swear I heard my name when I was at Ilan's, too—y'know, one time I wondered if I was some kind of experiment gone wrong, and now I think I am. Now they're all looking for me to drag me back to the institution." Sylvie sat heavily on the sofa but immediately bounced back to her feet.

"You're just freaking out," said Marz. "Hey. Stop pacing and look at me."

Sylvie froze where she was, her face flushed, her body cold. The ceiling fan whirred above their heads, flickering the light.

Marz put her hands on Sylvie's face. "Breathe. In and out now. You're not an experiment. Say it."

"You're not an experiment."

"Sylvie."

Marybeth was at the window, pushing aside the curtain to stare cautiously out. "No one's out there. I mean, those people aren't out there, I don't think. Everyone's acting normal."

"See?"

"Maybe that dog really is a bad omen," said Sylvie.

"Did you see it lately?"

"Not today."

"Look, if Ilan is seeing it more, then you're not its target, anyway. So forget it. Just forget all of that."

"But why's *he* seeing it at all?"

"Because they're neighbors? I don't know, Sylvie."

When Marz let Sylvie go, Sylvie immediately paced again. (Marz sighed.) "What if you're right? What if I'm supposed to solve this?"

"I mean . . . I guess you could try," said Marz, who went into the living room to watch with Marybeth.

"I don't know *how!*" Around and around the kitchen Sylvie walked. Down the hall. Back to the living room. Then she stopped. "I'm calling Marilyn now. That's what I'm doing. She can find me articles about—about Rynn or that place in Hell's Kitchen. And then . . . I don't know."

Sylvie had to go through her parents' address book to find Marilyn's number, not having called it much in her life. She wondered what Marilyn did over the weekends. Maybe she still had to work, like her dad did when he still drew editorial cartoons.

Marz and Marybeth stayed in the living room as Sylvie went to the kitchen phone and spun the dial.

Sylvie took a short breath. *Here goes nothing. Please do not think I'm a total creep.*

It took several rings, but Marilyn eventually answered. She sounded harried, at least until Sylvie started talking.

"Oh, hey, Applesauce! What's cracking?"

"Are you busy or something? I can call back."

"No, no! Not busy, at least not for a couple hours."

"This won't take long. I just thought—you work at a newspaper so I thought maybe you could help us out."

"Who? The fam?"

"No, no, me and my friends. We're, uh, trying to look up a couple things. One's a place in Hell's Kitchen and the other is this girl who disappeared."

Marilyn laughed. It sounded lighter, maybe relieved. "So you want me to check the archives, eh? Should be a cinch, but I might not be able to get in there right away. Lemme get a notepad so I can remember what to look for."

"No prob. It's not life-or-death." Hopefully.

Sylvie listened as Marilyn scooted through her kitchen, probably opening a junk drawer and rifling around for a ballpoint with ink left. After several seconds, she said, "Okay! Shoot."

"The first thing is this place in Hell's Kitchen. We're not sure but we think a crime happened there, or it's haunted. It's across from my dance school and it's getting renovated right now." Sylvie gave Marilyn the address.

"I'll see what I can dig up. What's the other thing?"

"Okay. So, we're not sure if it's related or . . . whatever, but it's about this girl who disappeared like twenty years ago. Her name's Rynn Marquardt. R-Y—"

"When'd you hear about Rynn Marquardt?" asked Marilyn, cutting her off.

Sylvie was caught off-guard. "Um. Old articles at the library. I was actually trying to look up the building, but no luck."

"How much do you know already?" Marilyn's tone had Sylvie on edge again. She didn't sound angry, or confused, but there was no smile or laughter anymore.

Sylvie wound the phone cord between her fingers, pressing the coils together. Maybe it was all over the news back then. "Uh. A guy killed his family and shot Rynn, too, but she lived. And then someone killed her family and kidnapped her."

"No, not kidnapped. She disappeared." Marilyn paused just long enough that Sylvie felt compelled to speak, but then she added, "See, Rynn used to babysit me."

"No *shit!*" Sylvie knew that Marilyn was from Brooklyn— Bed-Stuy or Bushwick, she could never remember which neighborhood—and she knew where she'd gone to high school, but she'd never imagined the world could be this small.

Without thinking, Sylvie frantically waved at her friends, pointing to her room and to Gary's and miming picking up the receiver. They bolted over the couch, landing with ungainly thuds on the ground—even graceful Marybeth tripped over her own feet. Jessie Baby ran after one girl, then after the other, then she went to get a squeaky toy.

Marz picked up the receiver in Sylvie's room, and Marybeth picked up Gary's. Sylvie hoped Marilyn wouldn't notice the sounds, but she was talking right over them.

"Yup. She lived a couple houses down from me on Bushwick Ave. I used to walk by that house—the house where the first set of murders happened—all the time. We called it the Dutch house, or just The Mansion. It was abandoned up until that family moved in. We all thought it was haunted."

She knew Marz had to stop herself from interjecting then, as there was a funny rustling sound on the line. Sylvie laughed enough to cover for it. "Duh. An abandoned mansion? Guaranteed haunted."

"We were half-disappointed when people actually moved into it. Anyway, about Rynn. I always had a sitter as a little kid, but she was the last one. She had a little sister, too, who would sometimes watch me instead. Her name was Avis. I probably wouldn't even remember them if it weren't for, y'know, what happened. We stayed with my grandparents for a month after Rynn's family died."

"What was she like?"

"She let me get away with anything. Sometimes she took me with her to see her friends. I had stars in my eyes around all these high school kids. Before that family moved into the Dutch house, she would take me out there and pick wildflowers and tell spooky stories. Rynn had these notions from her grandma, I remember, about the wildflowers. That they were good luck against evil. But we never went inside or anything. Not until someone bought it and Rynn started dating that boy. She took me over there once more after that and I finally got to go in. I must have been nine."

"You met those people?" Sylvie knew she didn't know much about Marilyn's life, but this was like finding out she was a Russian sleeper agent or had gone to the moon.

"Only the one time. Before you ask, I don't remember them. I was more interested in going to the house. It was this grand old Colonial mansion, but it wasn't in good shape. It smelled weird, I remember. Moldy. I think they'd only just moved in, so that's probably why. After everything happened, nobody bought that place again. But when we got older, my friends and I would sneak out there and—look around." Sylvie caught the pause and every unmentioned thing in it.

"What was it like?"

"Creepy as shit!" Marilyn laughed again. "The fact that I knew Rynn made it creepier to me, I'm sure. I never told my friends that, though. I don't know why."

"Did you ever see anything out there?"

Marilyn paused, a much more pronounced one this time, and Sylvie worried she was coming off insensitive.

"It's hard to remember what was real and what we just kinda made up to scare ourselves. See, after the murders happened, people started leaving that block for good. It made the houses vulnerable, y'know, to vandalism and bored kids like us. By the time I was thirteen or fourteen, no one had been in that house in three or four years, and no one was vandalizing the other houses anymore, either. I think that made it eerier than anything else."

"Someone said no one lives on that block anymore."

"I couldn't say what it's like these days. I imagine landlords torched all the buildings by now." She sighed heavily into the receiver. "But back when we were there, you wouldn't see anybody, not anybody at all, not even a squatter or a stray cat. Darkest block in the city, and I mean that literally. There was one working streetlamp and it would buzz on and off. And no one ever came by when we—don't do what I did, but we would light a little fire in the yard and just crawl all over the place, go into the house, all kinds of stuff you just shouldn't do. It's dangerous. Probably full of black mold and broken floorboards. But not even the police ever came by, which of course was the real appeal. It was like walking into space. You could do anything out there, absolutely anything, and no one would notice."

Marilyn laughed, once. "Which means you could break your neck and no one would notice that, either. Stupid, stupid stuff, girl. Don't do what we did. But yeah, we did see things we thought were ghosts. Except we were always there at night, and we were always up to something, so I don't really trust my memory. We thought we were smart little shits. Grown adults at fourteen. Well, my mother sure thought I was. Ha!"

Sylvie didn't know what to say. She knew she was born during Marilyn's freshman year of high school, and hearing that she had been hanging out where Rynn was shot and a family murdered gave Sylvie marrow-deep creeps. That was too close. That made the Hell's Kitchen Enigma too coincidental to be a coincidence at all.

"I'll just say that I'm glad they tore it down."

"What do you think happened to Rynn?"

Marilyn blew out a gust of air. "Not a damn clue, honestly. I never thought about it much. I didn't know it had happened at the time. One morning I woke up and Mom helped me pack an overnight bag and it was off to grandma and grandpa's. They lived in this cool house in Ditmas Park. Mom's childhood paid for that, probably. Anyway, I never got a new sitter, so I didn't really care a fig. When I was a little older, maybe eleven or twelve, kids at school would whisper about it. Sometimes people said they saw her around. A lot of people were convinced she killed her family. Some people thought that man faked his own death and came back for Rynn. She lived through a lot of shots—"

"Five. And he had a shotgun. Who survives that?" asked Sylvie.

"No one. So people thought they had to be exaggerating in the papers. Maybe the dad had mob connections and bought reporters off."

Sylvie didn't hear it on the line, but she saw Marybeth stick her head out of the door and mouth, "See!"

Oblivious to it, Marilyn kept talking. "It gets pretty silly. Some of the rumors I heard were over the top. I think the two events were essentially unrelated."

"But that's a serious case of bad luck, isn't it?"

"Worst I've heard of! Probably someone saw the address in the papers, saw they lived in a big house, and things got outta hand."

"They were rich?"

"Not rich. They just lived in a big old Bushwick Ave house. I think her family inherited it or something. I remember my mom talking about that. They had some old connection to a German brewing family, but there was no brewery or money left by then."

Another German brewing family. Or maybe it was the same one. Sylvie couldn't remember the name from the article, but Bushwick had once been full of families like that.

"If people thought she was rich, maybe they meant to ransom her. Maybe they got caught in the act and killed everyone. Leave no witnesses, that sorta deal."

"I think that's the most likely explanation," agreed Marilyn. "She was pretty high profile, at least locally. So, y'know, not some big conspiracy."

"They really never found her?"

"Not that I know. But I'll go into the archives, anyway, just to check. You've got my curiosity piqued, too."

"I still can't believe you knew her," said Sylvie.

"Imagine how I felt when you brought it up! I haven't thought about Rynn in years. Now I've got the heebie-jeebies."

"Sorry. If it helps, so do I."

Marilyn laughed a little, then paused as though she was considering something. Sylvie waited.

"Look, I'll tell you one last thing. It won't help your heebie-jeebies, but . . . That year after the shooting and before Rynn disappeared—I saw her out a couple times and she wouldn't even look at me. Like she didn't know who I was. The second time it happened, I went and cried to my mom, and she said Rynn was a lost soul. And if *my* mom thinks that, God knows how bad it must be."

"Do you know anything about that year before she disappeared? Other than that?"

"Not really. Like I said, some of the rumors were really out there. But basically it was like she fell in with a bad crowd. But who could really blame her for acting out? Look at what she went through."

"I really don't understand how she recovered."

"It's possible she never really did."

When they hung up a few minutes later, winding the conversation down to *how's dance* and *how's work,* and Marilyn hoping she wouldn't be too scared on her date tonight, Marz and Marybeth ran out of the bedrooms and all three girls looked at each other and yelled.

"Oh, my *God*!"

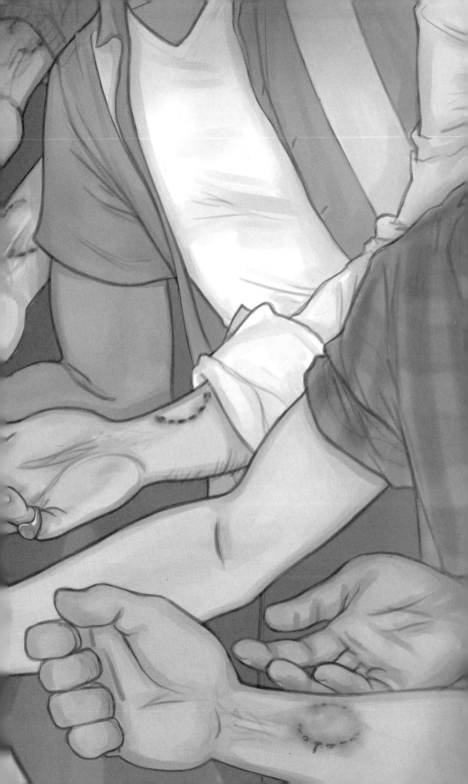

CHAPTER FIFTEEN

"That's no coincidence."

Sylvie started shaking her head before Marz had finished speaking. "Oh, don't even *say* that."

"It's a coincidence. Don't listen to her," said Marybeth.

Marz was frowning, though, apparently not relishing the creep factor at all. "I feel like you should go out there and look around, but at the same time, I don't want you snooping at someplace cursed."

Sylvie laughed purely out of shock. "Wow. Marz Hallan doesn't want to chase down a haunted house."

Marz flopped back on the sofa and held up one finger, black polish artfully chipped. "First of all, it ain't there anymore. Second of all, I didn't really believe in half those other ones. If you go into a haunted house believing, you're guaranteed to see shit, and I wanted to see something *real*, not something my brain put there. And last, after that crazy white lady out there, I think you gotta be more careful."

"But you still think I should go?"

"*I* don't," said Marybeth, who went to the windows and looked out each one of them. Satisfied with whatever she saw (or didn't see), she dropped into the rocker.

"I don't *want* you to go out there, but today proved something's up, and it feels like the only way to get answers is to go to the source. *Carefully.*"

Sylvie sighed and sat on one of the kitchen stools. "I don't want to go out there. I don't want to solve a mystery. Not this mystery. This one is too awful. And it's not going to fix what's happening, either."

Marz got up and joined her on another stool. "But what if it does? Anyway, wait for Marilyn to find stuff in the archives before you decide anything."

Sylvie nodded, then groaned and put her head in her arms on the counter. "You're right. It's too coincidental to be a coincidence, and I don't want to know why or how or any of it. I want to go back to being a fluke."

Sylvie couldn't explain why it bugged her to know that Marilyn was out there roaming around that property on a timeline where she could have been pregnant with her. It wasn't because the whole thing was probably irresponsible—she didn't care about that. It was everything Marilyn didn't want to go into. It was the fact that Marilyn knew Rynn, and Rynn had disappeared with a trail of bodies behind her.

All these weeks, Sylvie had looked at the girl with sympathy and anguish, but part of her brain was pricking at her now. Fight or flight. *A lot of people were convinced she killed her family.*

A memory can't be a lure. A memory can't be sentient.

She thought of the hands in the doorway. The figure waiting for her in the dark.

That night, it took her hours to fall asleep. She kept her desk lamp on. Sometimes her mind would drift, and she imagined people lining up along the street outside her building, staring up at their windows. Thank God she didn't have a window in her room.

✦

Without school, going to dance was more and less of a production. A longer commute, but only one bag to carry. The ride uptown in the summer was for reading or shuffling her steps as she slumped against the plastic seats, and on Monday it was no different. Marybeth went with her, but their schedules would soon be diverted. Really soon. The very next day, Marybeth started her summer ballet intensive, and Sylvie was alone, and alone with her thoughts.

The car wasn't very full. A couple people looked over open subway maps, heads bowed together as they pointed from one line to the next. A man had cracked the window and dropped his cigarette onto the track. A couple girls held the straps and laughed at something one of them had said. An elderly woman held a bag of groceries and clutched a *Reader's Digest*.

At West Fourth, several college-aged kids hopped on, not bothering to sit even though there was room.

After West Fourth, there were no stops until Thirty-Fourth Street and the train barreled north. Sylvie lost herself in thoughts of her steps, bouncing her bag on her knees, her hands compulsively gripping the edge of the orange seat. The car she was on was too new to give up its memories, so eventually she stopped trying and folded her hands, instead.

A soft thump caught her attention. The woman across from her had dropped her knit purse and her wallet tumbled over the dirty linoleum. When she failed to pick it back up, Sylvie pulled her eyes up to meet the woman's face. She was staring at Sylvie, almost unseeing, her expression slack except for how she didn't blink.

Sylvie stood up. She had nowhere to go but she couldn't just *sit*, and when she looked back, the woman still stared at her, head turned now, mouth slightly open as in sleep. Sylvie looked away quickly but in doing so, noticed a man at the pole was staring at her, too.

Over the roar of the train through one of the opened windows, Sylvie thought she heard someone speaking to her. It was a distant, buzzing noise in her head that must have been words, but she couldn't understand them. Or maybe it was her heart trying to beat its way out from behind her ribs. *Escape!*

Suddenly, the woman made a sharp movement and Sylvie jumped, hurrying awkwardly for the farthest set of doors and refusing to look at anyone at all. The thirty blocks between stations had never seemed so long or so claustrophobic. Dark tunnels, bright stations she wished she could escape into, then dark tunnels again. Until, finally, they pulled into Thirty-Fourth Street. Then it was the agonizing seconds until the car came to a stop and the doors finally opened.

She didn't look to see if she was being followed. She rushed off the platform, her bag thumping against her hip, and wound her way through the packed station, taking the first exit she found without even looking at the street numbers. She pushed against the downward current of commuters heading home from work and careened through knots of shoppers carrying bags from Korvettes and Gimbels and Macy's.

Sprinting up the stairs to daylight, it was only then that she remembered why she was on the train at all. Dance. She had twenty blocks left and ten minutes to cover them.

Ducking into the doorway of a wig shop, she squatted down to comb through her dance bag, seeking out her wallet. She didn't have enough money for a cab.

"Come *on.*"

Something washed over her—not supernatural, but very raw human anger. She didn't even know what to shake her fist at, where the problem was, and that made her even more desperate. If she had been close enough to walk back home, she would have gone right inside and told her parents and her brother everything about herself, again, but not let up until they realized she wasn't joking. If they carted her off to the psych ward, so be it. At least Deirdre wouldn't think she was flaking out on her.

For the full ten minutes, Sylvie ran. She cut through traffic and leapt around people, but it felt like no progress at all. Seventh and Eighth Avenues were clogged beyond reasonable passage, a mess of tourists exiting matinees and curiosity seekers loitering in front of peep shows and porn theatres. Sylvie wasn't really allowed up here, certainly not on her own, but nothing could have compelled her back onto a train. And it was stupid, because missing dance should be incentive enough, but she couldn't get the woman's gaze out of her mind. One day, one of these spaced-out people might have a gun, and then what?

Eventually, sweat collecting on her brow and soaking through her shirt, Sylvie stopped, and gave up, and turned south.

Where her anger ebbed, humiliation attempted to flow in. Class had started. She could see Deirdre's disappointment, her confusion. She would ask people if they had talked to Sylvie, seen Sylvie. She might even call Sylvie's home before warm-ups were complete. It's what *she* would do, Sylvie supposed.

Waiting for a light, she shut her eyes and willed it out of her brain. *Later, later, deal with it later.* For now, she had a lot of blocks to cover and time to kill.

She hadn't seen or talked to Ilan since Friday and the only reason it hadn't bothered her was because their evening together was a question mark at the end of a blank phrase. He owed her nothing and she wouldn't know what she wanted, anyway. But she didn't want to leave it like that, or to leave him alone.

At Twenty-Third Street, she started to feel a little less brave. At Tenth, she couldn't help holding her breath. The dog was still pretty creepy, regardless of where it ranked compared to all the other bullshit going on. But it wasn't there. All the dogs were warm and living, all the people occupied with their own thoughts instead of Sylvie. All the memories were quiet. Normal, everything normal. Sylvie just wished she wasn't so sweaty.

At Ilan's building, she had to pause for a minute to remember his apartment number (the peeling name outside wasn't his). As she pushed the buzzer, she briefly wondered where his friend had gone, the one whose name was on the lease. Did that guy know? Seemed a suck-off move not to warn Ilan. And what about the other people in the building or on the block? Why did it bother Ilan more than anyone else?

Seconds passed. Maybe he wasn't there. She could go home now and not look suspiciously early, but she didn't want to, so she hit the buzzer again. Finally, a crackling sound responded, and Ilan's muffled voice fell through the old speaker, "Hello?"

"Good afternoon, sir, I'm selling encyclopedias. Would you like to buy a set?"

There was another muffled noise that may have been a laugh. "Sylvie?"

"Is the front door still broken? I'll come up—"

Another pop and fizzle from the speaker. "Hold on! I'm coming down."

Another couple seconds and she heard someone thunder down the stairs. Ilan came through the vestibule, opened the door and, instead of letting her in, came outside.

"Let's get outta here," he said instead of hello.

"Uh—yeah. Okay."

Ilan nodded. He smiled at her (his stupid beautiful smile), but it lasted only a second and Sylvie noticed one eye looked a little bloodshot. The scent of cigarette smoke rose off him. He hopped down the stoop, casting glances up and down the block as though looking for car traffic on the sidewalk, then kept going east. He didn't take her hand or even look at her. When he kept going, crossing Fifth Avenue, Sylvie frowned.

"You don't wanna go back to my place?"

"I need a walk," he said, at least finally looking at her and realizing she was a good three feet behind him. She couldn't figure out his expression—it wasn't sad, but it lived within spitting distance of it. He stopped for a second to let her catch up, but he still hadn't taken her hand and she began to worry she had misjudged everything between them, somehow, or that maybe he'd come to realize it was a bad idea. Maybe he was worried about their friendship, or maybe he thought she was too weird or too *high school*. They were only a year apart, but college was the majors, and she was out here in the bush league. The last thing she wanted was to be so white bread that Ed Sullivan would have thought she was cool.

That crush had been a lot more fun the week before.

Then, just like that, he slung his arm over her shoulders, and she breathed out. She didn't even mind how wet the armpit of his shirt was as it settled on her bare skin, though she wondered how he was already this damp after only a couple blocks. His apartment was stuffy, but this was like he'd gone running.

Well, she supposed, she wasn't any less gross herself.

Tentatively, because she couldn't really gauge him, Sylvie slipped her arm around his waist. It was a natural movement, made it easier to walk with the weight of his arm on her. She hooked her thumb into a worn belt loop as though to keep him from drifting off.

CHAPTER SIXTEEN

They didn't really have a plan, they just wandered. The more blocks they covered, the easier Ilan stepped and the more he began to sound like his old self. When they reached Broadway, he took her hand and pulled her over to the Strand to look at the carts of used books. She tried to find the strangest titles, the weirdest topics, and he laughed again and held her gaze and she could see, in the sun, that it really didn't look like he'd slept in days. He tucked her hair behind her ear. His fingers were tobacco-stained.

"You wanna go in?" she asked him.

"Sure."

She grabbed his waist and pushed him toward the door, sinking her hands into his back pockets to guide him into the store.

Through the displays they walked, parting and reuniting. Sometimes he found something and actually stopped to look. "I already read the book I brought," he said.

She leaned around him, feeling the warmth of his back against her chest, putting her hand around his waist again as she moved to stand next to him instead. There were some kids in here—she couldn't be *completely* rude.

"You only brought one book?"

"I thought I'd be able to watch the tube and listen to music."

"You need to stay with us. I'm serious. We've got a TV, a few stereos, and plenty of books," she said. She felt the muscles in his back shift with his shrug, and he looked down at her as he put the book away, took her hand, and tugged her along to another aisle.

"Your parents don't need all that," he said.

"Well, two of the stereos are mine and Gary's."

Ilan laughed. He kept slipping his fingers through her long hair, gathering it loosely in his fist and letting it go, then gathering it again as he looked at titles and read the cover copy. The motion almost stopped her talking, but it was also making her more determined to get him to safety.

"Come on. They won't care. Seriously. They'll help you find somewhere else, if you really can't stand the thought of staying with us."

"You know that's not it."

"I don't know that, actually."

"Okay, well, it's not."

As Ilan took interest in another book on another shelf, she swept by him again, dragging her hand over his back, hitching her fingers into his shirt. He paused with the book in his hand, and she smiled a little.

"Prove it's not, then." She leaned against the shelves, some of the spines shifting beneath her weight, and he put his book away and leaned over her, resting his hands on the shelf behind her shoulder. He searched her face and she tried to hold his gaze, to hold it and keep holding it. She hooked two fingers into his belt loops.

But, damn, his eyes really were red. His lips looked chapped, though she stared at them, anyway.

"Please?" she said, softer and more serious than she meant to. "You look tired."

Ilan sighed and stepped away from her, heading down the rest of the aisle.

Fucking good job, Sylvie. Way to kill the moment.

But wait—why was she mad at *herself*? She was genuinely concerned and offering him an out!

"What?" she asked him. "What's the problem?"

"There's no problem," he said, but he no longer touched her hair or her back when she came up beside him. Instead, he walked away.

"It's safer with us, isn't it? Why are you torturing yourself?"

He didn't answer her. He walked around another display, now making his way to the doors. Sylvie wanted to push people over to follow him, but then she stopped. No, she wasn't going to be some kind of kicked puppy or lovesick child. If Ilan insisted on living in a place that bothered him even when she gave him an escape, that was his problem.

She just couldn't fucking stand how he kept holding her hand and taking it back.

When he locked eyes on some collection of poetry, Sylvie gave up. "Whatever. I'm going home. Come or don't."

She was surprised, then, that he actually followed. They didn't talk the entire way back, and she kept her hands on her duffel and her step ahead of him, regretting that she ever thought it was worth breaking open the crush for this. This was exactly what had once scared her off. Fantasy and reality gone at once, and for what? In the old worst-case scenario, she at least got one hook-up before their friendship was dashed on the rocks.

When she got home, Sylvie was too angry to care if Deirdre called. Her parents looked at her a little oddly when she walked in the door with Ilan behind her, but they said nothing incriminating.

"How was class?" asked her dad. He was in the kitchen, looking at a recipe clipped from *Good Housekeeping*. Her mom was on the sofa watching the news, glass of white wine in hand.

"Fine. I need to practice," she said through almost gritted teeth.

"Don't go dancing near my stuff, honey. I've got the drying rack out," said her mom. Then, "Hey, Ilan."

"Stay for dinner?" asked Bernard.

"Sounds good," said Ilan.

Gary looked far more suspicious than her parents. After giving Ilan a brief hug hello, he gave Sylvie a look, eyebrow raised and head nodding in Ilan's direction. She shook her head at him, thought of throwing her whole bag at him.

Ilan went with Gary into the living room. Gary sat down in the old rocker and dropped his leg over the arm. "Mom, do we have to watch the news?"

"It's important to watch the news."

"Just let my brain rot. I want to be happy and ignorant this summer. Ilan, go change it."

"I don't think *Zoom*'s on right now," said Ilan.

As Sylvie shut the door behind her, she heard the muffled impact of a thrown pillow.

She hurried downstairs even before the echo of the slamming door had faded and slid into the studio. Light poured in at both ends of the floor, but especially at the front. It was muggy and the heat had warmed up the old paint and her mom's clay and made everything smell like art supplies, so Sylvie cranked one of the windows as far as it could budge.

Everyone else's windows were open, too. There was music coming from some—dance studios and music studios and just general enjoyment. The warm weather brought her neighbors out and into her mind as she turned on the radio.

She kicked off her sneakers and pulled on her softshoes. She didn't let herself have any time to think a single thought, though dozens were threatening to spill out.

After changing the music, Sylvie ran through a series of half-hearted stretches and drills and launched into her reel.

She didn't feel comfortable, and she couldn't let her thoughts go, but she danced. She expertly dodged the columns and the most uneven, damaged spots, but her body felt stiff and heavy. So she stopped and went to the stereo to pick up the needle. And she stood there for as long as it took her to pick up a hardshoe and throw it at the wall. It hit with a resounding crack and left a dent in the drywall. Then she sat down, folding her legs beneath her.

Deirdre would call. Deirdre would cut her from the team.

Her parents would think she was having problems and take her to the shrink again.

Rynn would still be there. Whatever lurked in that building would be waiting.

And there was a strange black dog that kept Ilan so petrified he wouldn't even do anything to fix his situation. Or maybe it was just an excuse to get away from her. Or maybe Gary had warned him off.

And everywhere Sylvie went, someone would start staring at her as though hypnotized.

Sylvie heard footsteps on the stairs. Someone passed by her floor and continued on, down to the street level. It was probably Ilan, she supposed, and she rubbed her temples and stood up to grab her hardshoe back from where it had fallen onto a stack of manila folders.

When she turned around, Ilan was standing in the doorway. She hadn't even heard the door open, and her heart leapt right into her mouth.

"Jesus Christ. Ever hear of knocking?" she said, so frightened that it only made her more annoyed.

Ilan stepped inside and let the door gently shut behind him. "Look, Sylvie . . ."

"Please don't," she said. "I don't know what you're going to say, but don't say it. It doesn't matter. Sorry for inviting you over. Apparently you hate it here."

"I don't hate it here," he said.

"Coulda fooled me. Why aren't you upstairs with Gary?"

"Your mom made him go to the supermarket for something," he said, walking not to Sylvie but over to the window, beneath which (like upstairs) was the radiator. But unlike upstairs, which had been closed in and turned into a bookshelf for plants, this wall was raw and bare.

Ilan sat in the open sill and the breeze stirred his hair. He pulled a crushed pack of cigarettes out of his back pocket.

Sylvie didn't know what to say to him, though she knew what she'd *like* to say. *What's the real reason you won't stay with us? Why'd you flirt with me if you won't follow through?*

But all she could do was stand there, watching him smoke out the window.

She went back to the stereo and switched records just to have something to do with herself. She couldn't practice now. Her heart and her brain weren't interested.

"I'm sorry, Sylvie," he said. "I know I'm being an ass."

Sylvie turned around again, mostly unmoved. "Then stop. Because it's really annoying."

"Look. You're right. I need to move."

Damn his stupid roughened voice and his stupid blonde waves. Damn how vulnerable he seemed. She walked over to him, lowered herself onto the windowsill beside him.

"You're smoking too much," she said.

"Yeah. I know."

God, how she wanted to ask him what was happening, why he was obviously still so scared, but it was clearly the last thing he needed or wanted, and as long as she could get him out of that place, the rest could wait until a time when they could laugh at everything again.

So she dropped her legs onto his like she would have done in the old days, and she was relieved when he dropped his hand onto her bare knee. They didn't say anything for a while. She watched the people down below them, listened to the last of the trucks roll through.

Though Ilan was tired, though he was preparing to smoke himself out, he held the cigarette between two fingers and regarded her like she was a sign to read.

"Yeah. I'll move out," he said. "I'm done there. This week, I'm gone."

"I'll help you pack."

"Send your brother. I'll carry one box and he can carry the other."

Sylvie laughed a little, the knot of anger in her chest almost free.

"I'm serious. I'm gone. Hell, forget waiting a week. I'll come back tonight."

"You swear?" asked Sylvie.

"I swear, Sylvie. On my life."

"That's too dramatic." But she felt better. Nothing had changed yet, but she felt better. There was a gentle breeze and she looked out over the fire escape, over the street, when she felt Ilan's hand slide past her knee, just a little. She could see him shift at the corner of her vision, so she turned to face him, and to slide her legs off him so she could move her whole body closer, instead—because there was that wanting, not-going-back kind of look on his face, in his eyes and his slightly parted lips. She knew that look but it had never felt this good before. She didn't even care if anyone saw them—someone would, and it might even be Gary.

Ilan put the cigarette out on the dusty sill without even looking away from her, which for some reason was the hottest thing Sylvie had ever seen in her life, and just like that, he was delicate inches from her, tucking her hair behind her ear again, then sliding his hand to her jaw. But just as she felt the brief graze of his mouth—a gentle spark of static—the speakers popped and the needle fell with a walloping scratch. She would have ignored it if Ilan hadn't frozen there, all the rising color in his neck and jaw leaving with a rapidity that seemed impossible. And then the music started to play backward.

Sylvie leapt up and ran for the stereo.

"Fucking *stop*!" she yelled at it, pulling the whole plug from the wall.

"Sylvie—" Something passed in front of the windows and Ilan jumped up and stumbled back inside.

Outside, the music and ambient noise suddenly seemed muffled and distant. Despite every kind of common sense telling her not to, Sylvie walked over to the windows. Tall and old and in desperate need of better glass, Sylvie had always loved them. Hundreds of people had looked through them, hundreds of reflections had stared back. She was one of them, a part of their history, and she liked that.

"Sylvie, wait," said Ilan. "Don't go over there."

Across the street, she could see one of her neighbors lost in painting a giant canvas. Another neighbor was talking to someone, his back to her, sitting on the sill. Another was dancing, just as she had been, but in a different, whole-bodied way.

There was nothing strange out there, but she still wound the window shut.

Behind her, Ilan made a strange sound—not a groan, not a cry, but something strangled in his throat.

"I gotta get outta here." His voice was strained, clipped, stressed beyond capacity despite how quietly he spoke.

"Wait—Ilan!"

Sylvie was quick on his heels, but he had already thrown open the door. She could hear his echoing footsteps as they took the stairs at almost a run. She hurried onto the landing. "Ilan!"

The knot was back, tighter than before, as she rushed back into the studio and grabbed her dance bag.

Syyyylvieee . . .

Sylvie froze.

She could hear scratching. It filled the room with sound—terrible sound. Like the creaking of a jaw or the scraping of teeth. It emanated from the back of the studio, in the shadows of her mother's drying racks. But Sylvie didn't wait to see what it was. She ran.

She slammed the door behind her and didn't take the time to lock it. In the stairwell, the air felt cold, like a wind had curled up from below and above, and Sylvie ran upstairs for home.

When she burst into the kitchen and locked the door behind her, her parents stared at her in alarm.

"Can we go out to eat tonight?" she said, breathless.

"You weren't down there very long," said her mom, who was standing in the kitchen while her dad held open the fridge. "Where's Ilan?"

"Is Gary back yet?" Sylvie asked, knowing he wasn't because she hadn't heard anyone come in.

"He went to the Grand Union for me," said her mom. "Hey, Sylvie, I just got a call from Deirdre."

Cripes. Fucking cripes.

"Can we go out to eat, though? Anywhere? Like, can we go?"

Her parents exchanged a look as Sylvie walked deeper into the loft, almost weaving a figure eight between two of the columns. She was sweating. The fan wasn't fast enough. The air was stagnant.

"Hey, come over here," said her mom, who had now moved into the living room. "Calm down. What's the matter? Did something happen just now?"

No, she couldn't sit. She needed to keep moving. Maybe they could run up on the roof. Was the fire escape still secure? Had anyone checked it recently? "No! Nothing!"

"Deirdre said you've missed two classes these past two weeks. That's news to us," said her dad.

"Deirdre and I already talked about—"

"She's concerned about you. She says you've been going to class distracted and unfocused. What's going on?" asked Geneva.

All these weeks (or years), and Sylvie had no excuse. She hoped it would never come to this. "Nothing!"

Nothing? Her parents weren't stupid. Sylvie was sweating and pale and couldn't stop looking out the window, at the door.

"Are you on something right now? Did something happen between you and Ilan?"

Oh, no. "No!" Calmer. "No. No, I'm not. Nothing happened! Ilan just had to go home."

214

Geneva beckoned to her daughter. "Come sit with me. We need to talk."

Slowly, Sylvie came toward her. Slowly, she sank down on the end of the sofa. But her heart still raced. She bounced her knee.

"Sylvie, you've never skipped a dance class in your life. Are you losing interest or are you more interested in Ilan?"

"No!" Sylvie hadn't meant to shout. It wouldn't help her case. "No. Sorry. No. Ilan and I aren't anything—and I'm not losing interest, I swear I'm not." How could she convey how badly she wanted to dance but kept finding things thrown in her way?

"Because you're getting a new dress next month, and we don't have to spend the money if you want to quit. And we won't judge you if you want to quit. You've been going for a long time—"

Sylvie stood up. "I don't want to quit!" She'd yelled again but now it was either yell or cry. "I don't want to quit. There's nothing wrong. I swear. I'm not doing drugs. Today I just had a train problem, and I didn't have fare for a cab or anything and it was just too late. I tried walking but I couldn't get there! I swear I don't want to quit. I don't. I want to compete. I want to go to the Worlds more than anything."

"But look at you right now, Sylvie. You're all over the place," said her dad.

"It's—I got spooked downstairs. The record player started freaking out and playing backward and I flipped out. I think Marz tells us too many ghost stories." *Oh, sure, Sylvie, go on and blame Marz.*

She could tell her parents weren't really satisfied. Why should they be? Their daughter had been downstairs, alone, with a boy they clearly knew she liked, and now she was up here white-faced, sweating, and near to tears—without the boy. But she knew she couldn't give them a real answer, either, because they regarded the truth as a long-standing joke.

"Okay. We trust you, Sylvie," said her mom. "But if you skip again without telling us or Deirdre why, no dress. Got it? If you have train problems, find a phone and call her or call us. Don't let everyone worry."

"And keep some cab fare on you at all times," added her dad.

Sylvie nodded. She felt like she hadn't taken a breath in hours.

When Gary returned, their parents agreed to go out.

"But I just went to the store!"

CHAPTER SEVENTEEN

Sylvie had never walked so much in her life, and of course it was June, and rain never fell anymore, so she arrived at her dance studio already sweating. Because every day she walked half her journey uptown, hopping on a train or the bus only above Twenty-Third Street, and never sitting down or even touching the poles or straps, just in case. She didn't want anyone—anything—to know she was there.

Not that walking really felt any easier. Going outside among crowds gave her a nervous energy, even in her own neighborhood, where half the faces were ones she recognized. One look in her direction and she wanted to bolt. Every bale of rags or barrel of junk or stack of boxes gave her reason to pause, briefly. Just in case it wasn't what it looked like. And she never went into the studio.

But she didn't miss a single dance class. She made her apologies and decided those would be the last ones she had to give. Walking and dancing and walking again in the rising heat wrung her whole body out, but she would do it for as long as she had to. Plus, it made her so tired that she didn't struggle to fall asleep.

Ilan was trickier. She hadn't seen him in days. When she called him the day after he left, he hung up just as she began to speak. After that, the phone simply rang. Not even Gary could get him to answer.

Often she walked by his block and stood on the far side of Fifth Avenue, watching the shady street for a while before moving on. She did it without thinking, and he never came outside. After what happened in the studio, Sylvie knew better than to take his avoidance personally, but it was there all the same. He swore on his life he would come back. If it were her, she thought, she'd have moved already.

"Can't you get him to go somewhere?" she asked Gary, leaning in the door to his room. "Y'all got heaps of friends still around."

Gary was replacing film in his camera and didn't look up. He'd tied his hair back from his face in a ponytail that barely functioned, as layers were already slipping out. "I tried."

"When was the last time *you* saw him?"

"Same day as you."

"I'm worried."

"You need to chill." He snapped the back of the camera shut and wound it.

Thinking she heard one of her parents coming up the stairs, Sylvie came into the room and shut the door. "Chill? How? He won't answer our calls, and the last time I saw him, it looked like he wasn't sleeping. That's not like him."

"Maybe it is, Sylvie. He's been away at school. Habits change. Let it go."

"He was fine the first week back. You said yourself something is up. You warned me away from his place, and you're gonna let him stay there? What if he's in danger?"

Gary looked sharply at her and pushed his camera onto his bedside table. "How would he be in danger?"

Sylvie paused. Then she flipped on his light—it was way too dim in the room to tell him any of this. "The day he was over here, when the stereo started playing backward, I swear something was in the studio with us."

Her brother didn't react.

"I swear, Gary. I heard something whisper my name. That's not even the first time. And Ilan heard it, or he heard something. And that's why he bolted."

Gary looked at her and she prepared for him to tell her she was overreacting or scaring herself. Or that she was lying and something had gone wrong between them, just like he knew would happen.

Instead, he said, "You're right. I told you not to keep going up there. You gonna listen to me now?"

"You believe me."

Gary scrubbed his mustache, rubbed his forehead, and stood up. "It's not—just let him deal with his own problems."

"Should we get someone to help him? Are exorcisms only for Catholics?"

He snorted and extracted the rubber band from his hair with a wince. "Don't be dramatic."

"I'm serious! You're just gonna abandon him like that? Your oldest friend?"

"There you are, still being dramatic. If he wanted our help, he'd be staying with us, wouldn't he?" Then Gary dropped his voice and leaned closer to Sylvie—they could hear their parents coming in with

Jessie Baby. "Listen. I invited him down here the first time he told me he saw that dog creeping around. I invite him every chance I get. He says no dice, so what else can I do?"

"I don't understand why he won't move out," Sylvie whispered.

"It is what it is."

"But this is messed up! What if something happens to him?"

"Nothing's going to! Just trust me. He's doing the right thing."

Sylvie shook her head, unable to comprehend anything Gary was telling her. "That's insane. Do you hear how insane that is? Sounds like you know something I don't."

"Sylvie? Gary?" called their dad. "You guys home?"

Gary walked toward his door but stopped in front of Sylvie and put his hands on her shoulders. "I'm just saying, if he says don't make it our problem, *don't make it our problem.*"

✦

"I'm starting to think Rynn's not the real problem here," Sylvie admitted. She and Marz and Marybeth were over on Wooster, picking through a dumpster in the summer sun like the old, normal days. This one was half-filled with empty paper tubes and broken sheetrock, but someone had dumped broken planters in, and someone else had tossed out a pile of artistically graffitied fragments of egg-and-dart molding.

Marz pulled one of the tubes out and brandished it like a sword. Like the *old*, old, normal days, when they were still kids playing pirates and maidens and fighting over who won the sword fight and if the maiden could have a sword, too.

"How's that?" she asked, poking Marybeth with the tube.

It was now or it was never. "You remember how I told you Ilan and I saw that black dog, and he thinks it's haunting him."

Sylvie suddenly didn't want to say it out loud. Any of it. She shut her eyes as though that would help, as though that would stop anything from being summoned.

"Yeah?" said Marz.

Sylvie was perched on the edge of the dumpster, dust all down her bare legs, and she thumped her foot against the side and switched her gaze between Marz and Marybeth. With a sigh, she explained her strange afternoon with Ilan, skipping only that they were a second away from kissing. She didn't want Marz to get distracted.

"And now he won't answer our calls. Mine or Gary's. Actually, he straight hung up on me the first time I phoned him."

"Maybe you're right," said Marz.

"It's almost like misdirection," added Marybeth, who had been going through the molding. "We're obsessing over that place uptown, but the creepy stuff was happening in front of us down here."

"Except for that shadow I saw—unless that had something to do with the place on Tenth, too," said Sylvie. "Which I hate a lot more because that means these creepy things can go wherever. And I don't even know what that was."

"I still think you saw something that wasn't really there," said Marybeth.

"But people must touch that place on Tenth all the time," said Marz. "And that lady who wrote that book—she never talked about ghost dogs and shit. A ghost cat, but not a dog."

Sylvie no longer felt the sweltering heat. "No one touches it like I did," she said, staring across the street, past her friends, seeing nothing at all.

"So there's something out there that noticed you've got magic and . . ." None of them knew how to complete Marz's sentence.

"But it's haunting Ilan, not me," said Sylvie, though even as she said it, she began to doubt her words. She remembered the sound of her name from the depths of the loft. "And, God, I've touched thousands of places, and this has never happened! Not ever!"

"None of it makes sense," said Marybeth.

"Gary didn't want me going up there. To Ilan's. I did it, anyway."

"He doesn't want you going there because of the dog or because he thinks you're hooking up?" said Marz.

Sylvie sighed. "First I thought it was the second thing. Now I don't. And I think he knows something. Something other than what Ilan's told me."

"Gary seems like his normal self, though," said Marybeth.

Sylvie scratched her shoulder and shrugged. With her sneaker, she nudged at some of the discarded egg-and-dart molding and wondered what would happen if she touched it and played their usual game of finding out where it came from.

"Ilan remembered our dumpster game. He mentioned it on the way to the library. He said we were weird."

Marz picked up one of the planters. "Maybe we are, but he's—"

"Oh, my God." Sylvie bolted fully upright, almost tipping backward onto the sidewalk.

It was like lightning, the way the thoughts hit her. From the molding to Ilan to the library to Rynn to Marilyn to the house to the hole in the ground it had become, then right up to the front door of a small brick row house in the West Fifties.

"I'm such an idiot. I'm such an idiot! I know why she's up there, and it's so stupid and so *obvious*!"

"What?" her friends asked, going from startled to eager in a matter of whiplash.

"They demolished the house. They demolished the house, but it's like—when they tore down Penn Station, they put things from it in other places." (Sylvie had wanted to keep a lot of it.) "That's what they did. That's totally what they did to that house in Bushwick. They tore it down, but because it's historical, they saved things from it and now they've got something up there on that building that wasn't there before, and it brought Rynn *here*!"

"Actually," breathed Marz, "that *was* super obvious."

"It doesn't explain why I see her the way I see her," Sylvie continued. "So it's only half an answer."

"D'you think it messed with your powers—no, that can't be right. Otherwise anything demolished would set it off, wouldn't it?" said Marybeth.

Sylvie jumped down to the sidewalk. Only one corner of the puzzle was solved, but it felt good to solve any of it at all. It was progress.

"We don't even really need a solution to that, though," said Marz, climbing out on the other side. Sylvie helped Marybeth down next. "I mean, we don't need to cure you or something."

"Why?" Sylvie asked.

"Figure out what pieces on the building are from the Bushwick place and try to get rid of them."

"*That* seems easier said than done," said Marybeth. "You are so much the optimist."

"One of us has to be."

Sylvie dusted off her legs. "*How?* I don't wanna go back in that place after what happened. I know Marybeth thinks it was just a trick, but it didn't look like no trick to me!"

"Look, it's desperate times, babe. Maybe it's not even on the building yet, just sitting in a pile of materials," insisted Marz. "You can grab it and chuck it into the Hudson. Then, poof! One part of the problem is fixed, and we never have to think about it again."

"Unless they used that building on other places, too," said Sylvie.

"Don't build a bridge out of murder house rubble before you even need to cross it. Damn," said Marz.

They started walking south toward Broome, seeking out their next dumpster.

"I'm more concerned about Ilan," said Sylvie. "For two seconds I really thought Rynn was gonna be some kinda sinister puppetmaster. I really stopped feeling bad for her. I kinda hated her, even. Now I almost don't care. Everything else got a lot worse, and she just stays the same."

"Also, fixing Ilan's problem's the only way you're ever gonna get to fuck him," said Marz.

Both Sylvie and Marybeth chased her the rest of the way down the block.

They found their next target and clambered in. Sylvie half-expected to find more of Rynn already, even though she knew it wasn't very likely. At least, not yet. That *yet* sank with a thud to the bottom of her stomach like it was another industrial dumpster. But Marz was right—*don't think about it until you need to, Sylvie.*

The loot in this one was also picked over. Lots of damaged canvas and planks with the nails still in. A chair with a broken leg and moth-eaten upholstery that might be a fun project for Sylvie's mom but none of them wanted to carry it. The girls moved on again. Marz had band practice in a few hours, so they made their way vaguely over to Wally's, egg creams on the brain. Without thinking, fixed to the habit, Sylvie brushed her hand along a nearby loading dock. As soon as old trucks and men in coveralls flickered to life around her, she pulled her hand away and balled it into a fist.

The air was still and though the day wasn't atrociously hot, there was something stale about it, like walking through a yawn. Some of the streets were surprisingly quiet for a Friday workday. The ordinary jam of trucks had skipped some streets.

There was a yellowing *Daily News* page caught by the next dumpster. It sat along the cobblestones as though it had been baking there for weeks, and fluttered weakly in the breeze but could not move. The headline was, predictably, about the .44 caliber killer. It would have been that or budget cuts or arson. There was nothing else to discuss about New York.

COPS: .44 KILLER 'IS TAUNTING US'

"The one thing about all this stuff you're going through is that I forget there's a maniac with a gun roaming around," said Marz.

"My parents haven't," said Sylvie. "They flipped out on me for missing curfew when I was at Ilan's. Don't let them see this." Sylvie mostly meant it as a joke, but she grabbed the paper, anyway, to toss it in the dumpster.

Underneath it was a half-eaten rat, ants covering its patchy fur and the open wound that exposed its ribs and putrefied innards. It, too, had been broiling in the heat.

Marybeth gasped. "Oh, gross!"

Sylvie dropped the paper and scampered backward, rubbing her hand on her thigh. "Oh, ew! Ew!"

"*That* is how plagues start," said Marz, who had backed up even further.

Sylvie shuddered. "God, give me a hundred live rats over *that*."

As Sylvie danced around, she realized that people were staring at her from across the street. And maybe it was because she had yelled. Maybe it was because they had moved so abruptly. That's what Sylvie hoped it was, but she knew it wasn't. They weren't walking by or watching with interest. They didn't even seem interested. It was like they had to do this but didn't care why.

"Oh, no," Sylvie whispered. "No."

Marz and Marybeth noticed and backed up.

"Let's go," whispered Sylvie, grabbing both of their arms. They didn't know where to go, just *away*. Keep walking, keep turning, until the fabric of the universe smoothed itself out again.

"They know. They know when I do it. They know when I use my hindsight. They do."

"I wasn't really joking about that cult," admitted Marz.

"It can't be a cult," said Marybeth. "Why's it always just random people like that?"

"Random people can be in a cult."

Sylvie expected to see some new terror on every block they passed, but there was nothing. Just familiar faces and curious tourists. Blankets and bare walls covered in renegade art for sale. Bins of rubbish and rags. The tide of litter that drifted in and out along the cobblestones. Tagged walls and open galleries. Narrow streets and tall buildings. Home. This was home. Focus on home.

She was afraid to go inside, but Marz had practice and Sylvie and Marybeth were going to go this time. And ordinarily those nights were fun, full of people from scenes Sylvie and Marybeth didn't often frequent. They couldn't get away with smoking or drinking in Marz's parents' loft, but high-octane music was enough fuel for hours.

Except that today Sylvie felt hollow. She couldn't focus on anything going on around her, only a fear that she would look up and see everyone in the room, even her friends, watching her like a Saturday morning television program. Uncaring but obsessed. And then what would happen if Sylvie just stayed there or couldn't get out? What would those empty-eyed people do with her? What could they even want with her? She left early, without saying goodbye. She covered her hand in her shirt to open the door, used her hip to swing it.

She would never touch a building again, she thought. She would wear gloves, mittens, socks. Encase herself in long johns and turtlenecks. Summer could boil up around her and she would suffer through it.

Rynn really wasn't the problem anymore. Something worse had entered Sylvie's world. Something worse because it knew she was there, and Rynn never did. Never could. Never would.

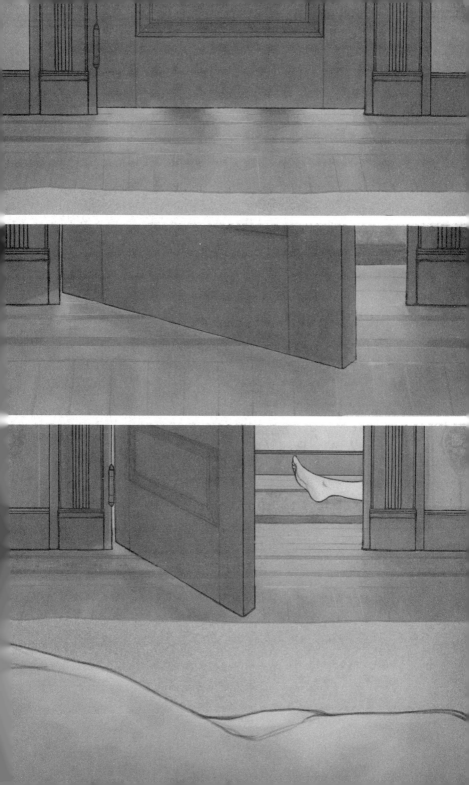

CHAPTER EIGHTEEN

June 27th, 1977

Sylvie lay in bed staring at the wall, concentrating on what she thought was the echo of a sound in her ears that had woken her up. Then she heard the fridge door shut. Someone was up—that was it—but her parents didn't usually go for midnight snacks.

It had to be Gary, so Sylvie closed her eyes and turned over, intending to go right back to sleep. He'd gone out somewhere after dinner, said he'd be back in the morning, but maybe plans had changed. Gary didn't have a curfew, after all.

Then she heard him open a bottle of something, and the cap hit the counter and delicately rolled onto the floor. He laughed, but she didn't hear anyone else with him (and neither she nor Gary usually brought dates up here, where privacy was a non-starter). She turned just enough to look at her clock—3:28 AM.

Then another door opened, and her dad said, "Sylvie? Is that you?"

"No, Pops, just your son!" Gary called to him as though it was the middle of the afternoon and everyone was wide awake. Sylvie groaned and rolled off her bed, padding over to her door in sock-covered, slightly sweaty feet.

"It's after three," said Bernard, whose voice was heavy with sleep. "I thought you were staying over at Ilan's. How did you get back?"

Staying over at Ilan's? Sylvie, her door just wide enough to stick her face through, felt like she hadn't heard correctly. Sure, *Gary* could go up there. Ilan wouldn't ignore *him*. But then she was relieved because it meant Ilan was okay. Gary hadn't abandoned him, after all. Maybe things would pick up.

"Don't worry about it," said Gary.

"Gary. How did you get back?"

"Walked!"

"Gary."

"That's my name, don't wear——"

"You shouldn't be out walking at this hour."

"——it out. What? I'm *fiiine*. Fine like wine, as the philosophers say. I even found a c-note flapping in the breeze outside."

Sylvie frowned. It wasn't that he sounded high or drunk, but he didn't sound normal, either. She opened her door wider. "Thanks for the wake-up. How's Ilan?"

"Even better than I am," he said. And to be sure, Gary looked pretty damn perky for the back half of the witching hour.

"He didn't come with you?"

"Why should he?"

"Sylvie, you can talk in the morning. Go back to bed," said her dad.

"I just wanted him to know how loud he's being."

"Thank you, Sylvie. Good night. But she's right, Gary."

Gary sighed. "Why don't *all* of you go back to bed? That sounds like a grand plan to me."

"Gary?" Now their mom had come out of their room, her hair in a very messy braid at one shoulder. Jessie Baby wriggled out from behind her and came prancing down the hall, but instead of greeting Gary, she stopped just outside Sylvie's room, and so did the wagging of her flowy tail. She growled, low in the back of her throat, but only Sylvie heard it, and it arrested her attention.

"Jessie Baby?"

"What are you doing back?" asked Geneva.

"Didn't need to stay anymore," said Gary. He flopped down on the rocking chair and took a swig of whatever he had grabbed from the fridge. It looked like a bottle of beer, which was pretty damn bold.

"Did something happen? This is a little unusual, kid," said their dad.

Gary considered his dad's question, tilting his head a little this way, then that, and making a thoughtful humming noise. "Yes and no. But Ilan doesn't need my help anymore, so I thought I'd come home! Home is where the heart is, and Ilan's pad is boring as hell."

"Wow, such poetry," said Sylvie.

"You shouldn't be out alone at this hour. You should have stayed with him until the morning," said Geneva. "I don't care how boring his *pad* is. You should have been asleep, anyway."

"Hold on—is that a *beer*?" Their dad had noticed the bottle as he got closer to the living room, their mom right behind.

Geneva gasped. "Gary! It's the middle of the night! You have to be up in four hours, don't you?"

Gary shrugged and jumped back to his feet, leaving the beer on a side table. Jessie Baby noticed the movement and barked, and it wasn't a friendly bark.

"Jessie Baby," said Sylvie, attempting to reach for her collar. "It's okay, girl."

Jessie Baby backed up, throaty barks mixed with low growls. Her ears were down, teeth bared.

"Jessie girl! Jessie Wessie Baby, come give me a gross, slobbery kiss!" Gary cooed at her, as though she was playing. She snapped at him, though she was yards away.

"Whoa, Jessie, girl, it's all right. It's just Gary," said Bernard. "Sylvie, put her in your room or something."

Gary said nothing. His face still looked freakishly at ease.

"Come on, girl! C'mere!" Sylvie whistled at Jessie Baby, nervous to touch her, nervous to come near her.

Jessie Baby slowly backed into Sylvie's room, tail firm between her legs as Sylvie closed her in. But even then, she could hear her growling at the door.

Bernard finally switched on a lamp. Coming back into the hall, Sylvie squinted until her eyes got used to the light, then raised her brows. Gary was sweaty. Flushed and sweaty, like he had run the whole way home.

"No more drinking tonight," said their mom. "Absolutely not."

Gary walked into the kitchen and dumped the rest of the beer down the sink. "No problemo, comrades. It's gone."

"What did Ilan need your help with?" asked their dad. "Should we call his parents tomorrow? I'd want to know if it were you."

"Nah. I mean, it turned out to be no big deal."

Sylvie couldn't believe that. But Gary was so cheerful that maybe they really had gone out and found a rabbi and a priest and an imam and sent the stupid dog back down whatever crack it slipped out of. But then why wasn't Ilan with him, equally cheerful?

"Like I said, his place is boring," Gary continued. "No extra pillows. No TV. No stereo. Just a copy of *Fear and Loathing in Las Vegas*. The guy he sublet from took all the good stuff with." As he talked, he couldn't stop walking or moving. He tapped his fingers along the kitchen counter, sat on one of the stools, spun several times, then hopped off again.

Geneva's hard stare was following him. "So what did you do? Because it looks to me like you did something."

Gary laughed again. "We talked and talked. We walked and walked."

"You know you've got the march tomorrow," his mom reminded him. "Are you gonna be good to go?"

He waved an arm at her. Sylvie thought she saw something on his wrist but was too far away to pick it out. If her parents noticed, they didn't say anything about it. "Yes! Sure. Of course."

"Gary, stand still," said Bernard, coming over to him. Gary took a step backward and for a second, Sylvie thought his convivial expression faltered.

"What?"

Bernard held one of his shoulders with one hand and tilted his chin with the other. He must have been looking at Gary's eyes, and he must have been satisfied with what he saw, because he let him go.

When Gary laughed it off, it didn't sound quite as confident. "What? Jesus, Dad. We didn't even smoke. Ilan's got no stash left."

"You're sweating," said their dad.

"It was more of a jog than a walk."

"You jogged from the Village. In the middle of the night," said their mom.

"Sure! You don't want me out late, so I ran back."

"Don't get smart."

"I don't think he has, if he's walking alone at this hour," said Bernard.

"Hey! Low blow, Pops."

"Since when am I 'Pops'?" Bernard stepped back toward Gary and folded his arms, but Gary backed up.

Gary flourished his arms. "I dunno. Better than Bernard, right?"

"I don't like how you're acting right now," said their mom.

Sylvie didn't know what to make of this show he was putting on, but it left her feeling less like they had fixed something and more like they had covered something up.

Suddenly, their mom gasped. "What on earth happened to your arm?" Geneva reached out to grab for him, but Gary stepped back even further. He shook his head and the smile left.

"Nothing!"

"Did you fight? Did you and Ilan have a fight? What is that?"

Bernard noticed, too. "Good lord, Gary, is that a bite——"

"It's nothing!" He held his forearm to his chest.

"Did something happen between you and Ilan?"

"No! But——but something sure happened between Ilan and Sylvie!"

Their parents looked at her standing there in her oversized shirt and sagging socks, and she shook her head, stepping away from her door where Jessie Baby kept whining. "Ex*cuse* me?"

"Sylvie, we don't——" began Bernard, but Gary kept talking.

"If you're gonna worry about anyone, you should worry about her! This one needs to stay indoors more."

"Gary, we're not talking about your sister right now," interrupted their mom. "We're focused on you. You're out running in the middle of the night with an injury to your arm. I don't care how old you are, we want to know what happened. Were you even *with* Ilan? Because he's always had his head on straight."

"You shouldn't be worrying about *me*," Gary continued. "Sylvie skips dance like the place is on fire. She goes to hook up with Ilan instead."

Sylvie couldn't believe what she was hearing. Couldn't believe he had just roped her into this.

"That's a total lie! What is *wrong* with you?" she snapped at him. Their parents moved to stop her marching over to him. "I'm not the one walking in here high!"

Gary snorted. "I'm not high, Silverado. I'm completely present!"

"Then you'll feel it when I deck you——"

"Gary—Sylvie, enough!" said their dad.

"Sylvie, are you still skipping dance?" said her mom.

Oh, no. They were *not* steering this conversation to *her.* Not with Gary acting like he had snorted a variety of white powders. "Mom! No! I've never done anything with Ilan except hold his hand! He's lying!"

"Okay, but you've done plenty of shit with other guys!" Gary continued, smiling as though he was enjoying this, waiting for this, had dreamt of it. And Sylvie was so flabbergasted, so unprepared to hear him throw her into the fire, that she barely knew how to defend herself.

"I—I don't do *shit!*"

"I'm telling you. You shoulda seen her at the last party we went to. Blazed, drunk—"

"Oh, *please*! You were smoking shit, too!"

"Sylvie—Gary, stop it," said Bernard. "I mean it. Stop it!"

"Even Marilyn called to ask us how you've been. If that isn't a sign something's up, kiddo, I don't know what is," said her mom.

"What? Marilyn called? When?"

"A week or so ago."

Sylvie was lost. What would have prompted that? Asking about Rynn? Surely not. Sylvie's parents wouldn't care if she was asking about ghost stories, anyway. Not with Marz for a best friend.

"I'm *fine!*" Sylvie pointed at her brother. "I'm not the one sweating and twitching over there!"

Gary started laughing, then. "All I'm saying is you should ground her indefinitely."

Sylvie rounded on them. "Why are you being such a *jackass*?"

"Okay—both of you—I said *enough*!" shouted Bernard. "Gary, we're not grounding her. You are on *thin ice*, kid!"

"Under the ice," said Geneva.

But Gary was still laughing.

"Everybody here needs to go to bed. *Now*," ordered their mom.

Sylvie gave Gary a disgusted look. "God, would you stop *laughing*?"

"Sylvie. Go," said her dad. "Now."

"Fine. Fine!" she said. "I'll go to my room and finish doing all the drugs I do, and then y'all can ground me!" To make a final statement, she shut her door hard enough to shake the sheetrock (it didn't take much to do that).

It wasn't easy to fall back asleep. Sylvie kept ruminating on why Marilyn would have phoned up. She wouldn't have known when or how or why Sylvie skipped dance, so that couldn't have been it. God, maybe she really had narced on Sylvie for asking about family secrets. Maybe the talk about the Bushwick house was some sort of last straw. Maybe she was worried Sylvie would go out there and do stupid teenage stunts and wind up pregnant.

Gary and her parents fought for a few minutes longer—more of a one-sided fight, really, with Bernard and Geneva raising their voices and Gary laughing or outright ignoring them until, finally, he went into his room. Sylvie could see a light crack along the ceiling and hear his door shut.

Jessie Baby would not fall asleep at all. She wouldn't even lie down. As soon as Gary entered his room, she stared at the wall they shared and kept up a continuous, low growl that Sylvie couldn't have slept through if she tried.

What the hell had Gary been up to? Had he even been with Ilan at all? Their mom was right: Ilan was pretty straight-laced, all things considered. Sylvie wished she was at Marz's, or Marybeth's, or just anywhere other than this close to her brother, who seemed to have become a different person.

But sleep came to her, eventually, because the next thing she saw was Ilan sitting at an adjudicator's table, smiling his insouciant, white-toothed smile that made her knees go rubber.

He doesn't know anything about judging Irish dance, she thought. *This doesn't make sense.*

"Sure it does," said Ilan, and it did not faze her that he heard her thoughts. Maybe she'd spoken aloud.

Yes, she must have, which wasn't appropriate at all. You weren't supposed to speak to the adjudicator.

But never mind, maybe you were allowed at the Worlds.

She wasn't in the lineup anymore. She was waiting backstage at the Mansion House in Dublin, which suddenly looked like the Metropolitan Opera House. Outside of her periphery, she could hear the audience cheering as the accordion player stopped and the dancer took her bows. She wondered where Ilan went, then promptly forgot he had been there.

She didn't feel nervous or afraid. She didn't run through her steps, either, because of course she knew them. They were threaded through her muscles. She belonged here, and she had always belonged here.

Skip 2 3 double hop and down

What had she been so worried for?

There was a dancer in front of her, suddenly, but she had always been there. In the shadows, the stagehand, who looked very much like Gary, directed them out. Sylvie and the other dancer emerged into the bright stage lights and stood a few yards apart. They didn't look at each other. They looked into the miles-deep crowd.

The music started and, counting off, Sylvie pointed her foot, rose onto her toes, and began to dance.

She couldn't really feel her legs, not because they were numb, but because they moved without her having to think much about it. Every piece of the step came through her. She didn't have to meet it. She didn't have to consider it. It just happened.

It was strange and should have been terrifying. She knew it should have been terrifying because there was a twinge of it at the start, but then the feeling left her completely. She could have been flying. The crowd roared its approval. The faceless adjudicators—Ilan, forgotten now, no longer among them—applauded, too. They weren't supposed to do that, but of course they would for Sylvie. She was the best they'd ever seen.

Her shoes changed without her changing them. Softshoe to hardshoe. Slip jig to treble jig in the blink of an eye. She forgot the other girl dancing with her, turned to her right and kicked her heels together. As she landed again, she saw the girl's face. She recognized it, and in the dream, she was torn between her step and a great feeling of unease that had not been there before.

Rynn, that was her name. Oh, Rynn needed a hospital. Her arm was hanging loose at the shoulder, blood pooling down her hands and legs, staining her white dress pink.

Then Sylvie turned again and forgot what had happened. She was alone on stage now, a sea of faces staring at her from the seats below as she finished her final round and bowed.

No one had to wait for results. The podium was already there, and she was already on top, a heavy crown atop her head, a heavy trophy in her arms.

The woman who handed it to her was not Deirdre, but someone Sylvie didn't recognize. She was taller than Sylvie, even standing on the podium, and had long, golden blonde hair and wore no clothes at all. This didn't surprise her. It seemed normal, in fact, that this woman in particular would not wear clothes. How could any even fit her, tall as she was?

The crown slipped and cut Sylvie's scalp, but she continued to smile as a thin trickle of blood filled her eye. The woman held her hand and raised her arm, not to cheer with her, but to sink her teeth into Sylvie's wrist.

How odd, Sylvie thought. How very odd that it didn't hurt. In fact, it felt quite nice in a way it shouldn't. She stared at the woman's lips on her skin, licking her own, her heart racing. The trophy was gone, now, and so was the crown. So was the podium. The auditorium was empty. The woman disappeared.

Ilan was there, instead, lifting his mouth from her arm. He pulled her to him, and he was all she could see.

"I love to watch you," he whispered to her neck. She felt his teeth against her pulse, and she gripped his shirt to keep them there. "Everyone loves to watch you. They'll never be able to tear their eyes away from you."

He felt hot, like a fire burned inside his body instead of blood and tissue. He pulled her closer and she was sure he was going to devour her, but that was what she wanted.

But no, no, that wasn't the right feeling. Something crept up the back of her mind, an unstable sensation that, in a blink, this scene would change and a nightmare would curdle her reality.

And then she was awake again, suddenly as before, but this time it was Jessie Baby who had stirred her. She was still staring at the wall, whining now. There was a puddle beneath her feet.

"Jessie?" Sylvie murmured, voice slurred with sleep.

What a weird dream—weird and embarrassing. Weird and embarrassing and, for a moment, kind of nice. The crown and trophy, she liked the crown and trophy. Sylvie focused on that, on the podium, but as sleep left her, so did the nice feeling, the delusion that drowsiness brings. She thought of Rynn, and she lifted her arm to check that no one had bitten it. Then she sat up, preparing to go get a towel to clean up after her dog. And maybe to bring Jessie Baby to her parents.

But on the other side of her wall, she heard a gentle thump. No, not a thump. Gary was walking. Pacing around his room. She could hear the boards creak, and creak again when he returned. Worse still, he was talking. It was too quiet for her to understand, but she strained to listen, anyway.

Maybe he was on the phone, but it didn't seem that way. He wasn't pausing to wait for someone to respond. It wasn't a proper conversation. And it was awfully early in the morning for any of his friends to be awake.

Carefully, Sylvie eased out of bed and grabbed her desk chair. She leaned the back beneath her doorknob, not knowing if that would really work, or why she felt she needed it to, but she wasn't going to be able to sleep without it there.

Then she raced back to her bed and quickly pulled her feet off the floor. She stared up at the seam where their walls didn't quite fit along the ceiling, and wished she could block the light that came through.

CHAPTER NINETEEN

Gary was gone before Sylvie was up. She knew it before her parents told her because Jessie Baby was sleeping on her legs.

Bafflingly, her parents didn't mention the previous night's episode at all. Not at breakfast, not as they got ready for the Pride march and joined up with the other families, not even as they walked up Seventh Ave, ANITA SUCKS signs everywhere you looked—not once the entire day. It left Sylvie feeling like she had dreamt the entire thing.

Maybe they talked about it with him before Sylvie woke up, which was fair enough, she guessed, but Gary had involved her. And, really, the whole episode was too strange not to talk about. But she didn't want to bring it up and risk her neck.

Thankfully, this year's march ended at Central Park instead of the other way around. On top of everything else, if she'd had to navigate through a party in the Village, she wouldn't know what to do. She wasn't likely to spot Ilan in the thousands of revelers (and who knew if he would even go), but she didn't want to go near his street anymore. Occasionally she would catch the eye of someone, and they would look just a second too long in her direction, and her heart would turn over like a struggling car engine.

Afterward, she had to double back to go to dance. It was a nice enough day that her parents didn't question why she decided to walk twenty blocks instead of jumping on the train. They walked with her.

No one expected Gary home until late, of course. He had his own friends, his own traditions, his own feelings that his family didn't need to be a part of. At twenty, all his parents expected of him was a phone call. *Where are you, and please be safe.* Maybe next year he'd find a place of his own. Maybe he wouldn't even come home over the summer. That would be weird, but inevitable.

After class and a quick bite, Sylvie and Marybeth met up to spend the night at Marz's. Her parents were out to watch some jazz musicians, leaving Marz and the girls with Marz's little sisters, who were watching *Bugsy Malone* on the new TV. Cee kept bursting into song and Gigi would yell at her to quit.

Up in Marz's room, sitting in the opened windows that looked down on the street below, Sylvie wasted no time at all in relaying the entire night, from Gary, to Jessie Baby, to the dream. Unable to talk about any of it for the entire day, she felt like a shaken soda can in the hot sun.

"I know it was just a stress dream because I'm gonna be competing in, like, a week, but it was just so creepy on top of everything else. Jessie Baby actually peed—she peed on my floor from fright!"

Marz had started shaking her head as soon as Sylvie mentioned Gary's bite wound, and she hadn't stopped. "Uhn-uh. Hell no."

"Do you know for sure he went to see Ilan?" asked Marybeth, whose knitting had stalled completely (she had moved on from the shorts, which she wore that day after dance, to make Sylvie a new pair of mittens).

"No. But why would he lie?" Sylvie's left leg hung off the sill, where the heel of her overheating tube-socked foot brushed the stone facade.

"To make you mad? Or jealous?" suggested Marybeth, and Sylvie sighed.

"But I wasn't. I was kinda relieved, honestly, 'cause I thought that meant Ilan was okay. But I don't know shit from Shinola, do I?"

"Yeah, this is pretty clear it's just shit," said Marz. "I was gonna just say let it go and have Gary make his own bed, but the Jessie Baby thing. . . ."

"I know," said Sylvie, who almost wished she hadn't mentioned that part. She wanted some impractical, comforting speech that would make her see reason and reality. Gary got into a bad stash. Or did something harder. The bite wasn't a bite—or maybe it was. The loft had been pretty dark.

But Jessie Baby took all that reason and reality and turned it on its head.

"Maybe he was with some kind of weird animal. Maybe he met someone who had, I dunno, a baby tiger for a pet," said Marybeth. "And Jessie was nervous."

"I'm just not even gonna laugh at that because I kinda want it to be true," said Marz.

"Yeah," said Sylvie.

They decided to join Cee and Gigi for the end of the movie, and they stayed out in front of the TV until Marz's parents came back home.

And they came home with news.

"I don't know why you gals didn't wanna come along with us," said Kenneth Hallan, taking a silk scarf from his neck. "That Holt boy was playing. Thought for sure you'd be there for that. Though he did say he only got the call this afternoon. Still, though. Too bad!"

"Ilan?" said Marz. Sylvie's mouth had gone dry.

Mr. Hallan nodded. "On that brass of his, sounding like a whole new Chet Baker. Let's hope it's just that California air's doing and nothing else," he said as he returned to the foyer, where Winnie Hallan had kicked off her heels and was taking her earrings off.

"Cee and Gigi upstairs?" was what she asked the girls first, and when Marz said yes, her mom added, "Dad tell you who was in the group tonight?"

Then she paused in the doorway. "Lina, those hose have more rips each time I suffer to see them. Can't believe you make your friends look at those things."

Marz stuck out her long legs to admire her torn-up fishnets and pink toenails. "Did you talk to Ilan, Mama?"

"Not long. Asked him how he is, his parents, sister, all that." Mrs. Hallan shook her head as if in disbelief as she went toward the stairs. "I remember he was good, but that year at college has done something extra to him. Where's he at, again?"

"Stanford," Marz called after her.

"*Stanford.*" She clucked her tongue. "What's he thinking? Musta been his dad's doing. Shoulda sent that boy to Juilliard— could be teaching at Juilliard! Don't stay up too late! I don't care it's summer! And no more TV!" Mrs. Hallan had ascended the stairs as she spoke, and her voice was now slightly muffled by the second-floor landing.

"Yes, ma'am!"

The ceiling creaked as Marz's parents entered their bedroom.

Sylvie wished her friends weren't looking at her. She didn't know what to say, so she adopted an unaffected expression, one shoulder slightly shrugged against a tufted pillow. "Your dad said he only just got the invite," she said, watching as Marz got up to turn off the TV.

"True," said Marybeth.

But Sylvie couldn't help her bitterness. "He must be feeling a lot better, then. Maybe he'll bother picking up the phone."

✦

The next day, after lunch and an excursion to Pearl Paint with Marybeth and her mom, Nancy, Sylvie finally schlepped home. Her mom was on the phone, looking agitated, her dad standing just off to the side, frowning and scrubbing his mustache.

As she walked in, Bernard beckoned to her and went over to the living area, giving Geneva space to talk. Sylvie felt a quick flush of nerves, hoping she hadn't forgotten something, hoping no one had called about her—except Ilan, maybe.

"Have you seen your brother today?" he asked her before she had a chance to even ask him what was up. Jessie Baby came over with a toy and dropped it at her feet.

"No. Why?" Instead of relief that it wasn't about her, Sylvie felt the barest tug at her chest, like someone pulling at the laces of a shoe. She picked up the slobbery toy and tossed it. "Isn't he back yet?"

Sylvie could tell that her dad was struggling to figure out how much to let her in on, but eventually he simply said, "Doesn't seem like it. Your mom's calling around to his friends."

"I'm sure he'll *love* that," said Sylvie.

Bernard smiled. "Yeah, well, he's asking for it."

"Don't make him too mad. He's gotta take me to Fleetwood Mac tomorrow."

Geneva hung up the receiver. "Everyone said the same thing," she said without acknowledging Sylvie's arrival. "They got separated at Central Park and haven't seen him since. I'm calling Ilan."

The laces on Sylvie's chest tugged harder.

Her dad walked back to her mom. "Look, hun, we don't know all of his friends, and we don't know all of their numbers."

"But shouldn't one of these friends know the others? Maybe I could go over to the Firehouse." Already Sylvie's mom was dialing Ilan's number, which had been written out and stuck to the fridge weeks earlier. ILAN'S SUMMER HOME, Gary had written.

"He's got a lotta different groups he hangs out with," said Bernard. "He might have some college friends who don't know the GAA Firehouse friends, who don't know the high school friends, who don't know the neighborhood friends, who don't—"

"Dad. We got it." Sylvie peeled off her sneakers, dragged her duffel behind her to her room.

"Right. He's got a lot of friends," Bernard finished.

"Ilan? Hi, Ilan, it's Geneva—" Geneva seemed to only just realize her daughter was home and said, almost into the receiver, "Sylvie! Have you seen your brother?"

"I already asked her, dear," interrupted Bernard.

Ilan would have heard that, and Sylvie didn't want him thinking about her. No, that was bullshit. Of course she wanted him thinking about her. That was the *whole thing*. But he probably wasn't. She dragged her duffel a little faster, but she would hear most of this conversation even with her door shut.

After Gary's behavior two nights before, though, she *did* want to know where her brother was.

"I'm fine, yes—actually, I was wondering if Gary's there," Sylvie's mom continued. Her voice was cheery, but she was twisting the phone cord and frowning. "Uh-huh. And you haven't seen him today or yesterday?"

A pause.

Sylvie stepped into her room, trying not to be visible in the open doorway.

"Do you know anyone he might have spent time with?"

Geneva sighed. "Thank you, Ilan. Please keep an eye out for him."

"No sign?" asked Bernard.

"No. He gave me a couple names, but I've already tried them. Nelson wasn't home before, so I'll call again later, I suppose."

"You're sure Ilan's telling the truth? After Sunday night?" Her dad's voice had dropped, which meant Sylvie wasn't supposed to listen in. She gave them the security to speak more freely by closing her door a little and unzipping her bag. Then she promptly put her ear back to the door.

"If he's over there, at least he's safe," said her mom.

"Did he sound all right, Ilan? Sober?"

"He sounded the same as he ever does. But you don't know—we're the parents, Bernard. Kids know how to put on an act."

The same as he ever does? Then why hadn't he called?

Sylvie heard the floorboards creak as her dad walked away from the kitchen. "I really hope they're not getting into something."

"Makes me think you or I should go to that show with Sylvie tomorrow. Or maybe she could take one of her friends," said Geneva. She had followed her husband and gone into the living room.

Sylvie sighed and dug yesterday's clothes out of the duffel, dropping them in a hamper. They smelled like dance shoe leather and sweat. She walked back into the hallway and ambled toward the kitchen to get a glass of water.

"Marz's parents said Ilan was down here playing music last night, so *he's* not very worried," she said.

"Well, that's something, anyway," said her dad. "Why didn't you go see him?"

Sylvie shrugged. "Didn't know."

She could sense, in the pause before her parents spoke, that she had given a lot away. But she couldn't give away everything, or even the parts that mattered, so she braced herself for whatever they were going to say.

But they didn't say anything.

Gary hadn't shown back up by the time Sylvie had to go to dance, and she discovered that this meant having a chaperone all the way uptown and all the way back. It was hard to ignore how anxious she felt on the train, waiting for the first person to stare her down, not knowing how she would handle it in front of her dad.

Nothing happened on either trip.

Bernard let Sylvie separate from him at Prince Street, where Marz and Marybeth were smoking outside Fanelli's after Marz's band practice.

"Stay nearby, Sylvie. And you girls, don't smoke so much!" he said, and was gone.

They made their usual rounds of the street vendors, thumbing through paperbacks and art prints before hopping in and out of a few half-vintage boutiques (Sylvie used to like to see who had worn the old clothes, but today she kept her arms folded). After buying postcards at Untitled and a bag of potato chips at Zachary's, they began a loop down along Canal and back up again, saying hello to the people they knew and occasionally touching on Gary's disappearance after Sylvie explained it. Marz and Marybeth avoided the entire topic of Ilan, however, for which she was grateful.

Truthfully, with the sky growing dark, she was starting to freak out as badly as her parents were. So much of the last month was impossible to iron out. Jessie Baby's visceral reaction to Gary still hung in Sylvie's mind like a pendulum. Each time she wanted to blame drugs, the pendulum swung. Something was wrong with him, and now he was gone.

God, wouldn't it figure if the *son*, the *man*, was the kid who got hurt by some wandering killer? She knew there was more going on in the Village than a ghost dog on West Tenth Street—queer folks were picked off at the piers, and the papers didn't care half as much as they did about the co-eds in Queens—but she didn't ever imagine her brother getting mixed up in any of it. Maybe that was naive.

As they began walking east again so that Marz could head home for dinner, Gary reappeared.

"Wait—is that him?" Marybeth stopped and pointed ahead of them, where a figure with shaggy brown hair was crossing the next street. Whoever they were, they weren't walking like the condemned, which Gary certainly should be.

"It totally is," Sylvie said, the knot in her chest slowly loosening—but not untying. She hadn't expected the sight of him to make her nervous, but it did.

She hoped he wouldn't notice them, but as he looked for oncoming traffic to the west, he stopped. And he waved. They waved awkwardly back as he sauntered over. He was grinning. His hair needed brushing. His clothes looked slept in, all wrinkled and slightly stretched.

"Ahoy there, lassies," he said.

"Where've *you* been?" Sylvie asked. "Mom and Dad were calling around and no one's seen you."

"Oh, I met up with some people at the park and we took a tour of the nightlife," he said, easy and casual. Sylvie noticed the bruise on his wrist, smaller now than it was, less obvious.

"Seriously? You went clubbing all night? Where'd you go?" asked Marz.

He ran a hand through his hair, and it somehow settled where it should be. A piece of glitter winked in the sun. Sylvie didn't often think about how handsome her brother was or wasn't—except for when school friends might develop a crush and ask her about him— but she had to admit he looked pretty nice for someone who hadn't bathed in two days. He stood in a painfully careless contrapposto that Sylvie couldn't even make fun of without looking like a philistine. Compared to that, she was a dowdy old spinster on whom the sun didn't shine at all.

Yikes. The hell?

"Oh, shit, all over. I thought I'd get turned away from half of them, y'know?"

"I guess," said Marz, sounding skeptical that he would. Sylvie looked at her and found that both she and Marybeth were all but drinking him in.

This was freaky.

"None of this'll mean much to you three, but we started at Marie's Crisis, and later we hit Les Mouches, Crisco's, and some other places you've never heard of."

"Crisco's, like the grease?" asked Marybeth.

"The DJ booth is shaped like a can," he explained.

"Huh," all three of them said.

"Well, if you're not impressed by that, just know that I got into Studio *54*!"

"You did *not*," Sylvie scoffed. "*How?* Dressed like *that*?"

But why not? There was nothing wrong with denim and a tee. He made it look easy, the height of fashion.

"Did you see anybody famous?" asked Marybeth.

"Don't encourage his lies," said Sylvie.

"I wasn't paying all that much attention. I had to hook up with some new people because most of the group didn't get into Les Mouches. Actually, first I lost my wallet in a cab, but then some guy found it and that's how I ended up at Studio 54. And I got in for *free*."

"That's not possible," said Sylvie, who didn't know anything about how clubs like that one worked but *did* know that getting a wallet back wasn't that easy.

"Anything's possible, Cool Breeze."

"*How?*"

"I flashed my winning smile."

"I meant the wallet."

"Lucky night! Someone put extra green in it, too. Probably the person who jacked it. Joke's on them!"

"You're so full of it," said Sylvie.

"Of cash. Anyway, that's pretty much the last place I was at, I think."

"You think."

Gary shrugged, tossed his head a little to resettle his hair. "Busy night!"

"Did you see Ilan play last night?" she asked him, and she didn't sound jealous at all. She didn't even really feel jealous.

"I haven't seen him," he said, and his smile finally unhitched at one corner. But he quickly restored it.

"Well, good luck with Mom and Dad," said Sylvie. "They probably think you're in the river."

"I'd at least look a little sad when you walk in," suggested Marz.

"Or hungover," said Marybeth.

"And take a shower in Old Spice or something because you *reek*," added Sylvie. Then she ducked out of the way as he tried to ruffle her hair. Sylvie took the chance to grab his arm and turn it over.

"What'd you do to your arm?" she asked.

Up close, in the light, the wound was already green and scabbed—but the mottled edges looked just like a human bite mark should. It repulsed her. She was about to drop his arm, but he wrenched it away instead. She could see something pass across his vision, like he had stepped outside of himself for the briefest second, but then he was back to grinning and glowing in the golden hour and acting like Sylvie hadn't spoken.

"Well, I guess I'm off to the guillotine or whatever," he said. "Later days, chicas."

They watched him saunter off, turning the corner onto Greene Street for home. And all at once, Sylvie felt like she hadn't handled that well at all. It was a bit like a funhouse mirror had been between them and her brother, and now it was gone.

"I think you should wait until they're done with him," said Marz.

"Yeah," said Marybeth. "If you get sad being an only child, you can borrow one of my brothers."

"Did any of that seem funny to you?" Sylvie asked. "He's in way too good a mood."

"Funny-and-a-*half*," said Marz. "I'd just walk in and hand my parents the ax. Save them some yelling."

"Do you really think he got into Studio 54?" asked Marybeth.

"No way," said Sylvie. But lying about something that wouldn't really make Sylvie or her friends jealous was odd, too. Between Sylvie and Gary, he had always been the one eager for the club scene to open up in SoHo. Sylvie was content with the informal stuff and Marz preferred CBGB.

They followed slowly, letting him get a full block ahead, letting him go inside.

Arriving a few slow minutes later, Sylvie bid her friends farewell and they bid her good luck. Her nerves were spiking now. What if Gary started spilling more of her social life secrets? What if Jessie Baby was ripping his limbs off? Maybe she would just sit in the entryway for a while or take the stairs extremely slowly.

She tried both before giving in to impatience and easing her way inside.

She expected the powerful winds of her parents' shouting down at him, Gary trying to avoid telling them what he'd been doing, but all she heard was a canned laugh track off the boob tube. Jessie Baby came out of Sylvie's room, stopped in the doorway, and whined.

Whining was better than growling.

Her parents were on the sofa together, the distant rattle of pipes meaning Gary was probably in the bathroom.

"I'm back," she announced.

Her mom waved an arm in greeting. "Gary's home," she added.

"Safe and sound," said her dad. "How're the gals?"

"Fine." Sylvie just stood there, the door not even closed at her back.

"Did you kill him?" she ventured, because that would at least get a rise out of one of them.

"Of course not," said her mom.

"But he was gone for, like, two days."

"He's twenty, Sylvie," said her dad.

"Yeah, but—" *But this afternoon you were panic calling everyone he knew.*

"You hungry, kiddo?" said her mom. "Dad'll start dinner."

"Uh. Okay."

Slowly, confused, she shut the door. She kicked off her shoes. Jessie Baby whined again, and Sylvie walked over to her, began to pet her. From the end of the hall, she heard the shower turn off.

A fight would have been way better. A fight would have made more sense. Jessie Baby had brought her stuffed green (well, formerly green, now kind of gray) bear into Sylvie's room at some point, and as Sylvie shut her bedroom door, the dog lay down to chew it.

"What a total fry," Sylvie told her. "We're the only sane ones left."

CHAPTER TWENTY

June 29th

Sylvie half-expected Gary to tell her he no longer wanted to take her to Fleetwood Mac. She half-expected that he would tell her he had better, more exclusive places to be. When he went out late in the morning, she braced herself for his failure to return and the fact that she would be going with her dad or her mom. But then he showed up only a few hours later, dressed himself in his busiest, plungiest shirt and a pair of pressed Angels Flight bell-bottoms, and she relaxed—as relaxed as she could feel, anyway, which stretched the definition. He made her anxious, because Jessie Baby was still anxious, though she now consented to remain in the same room as him for a couple of seconds.

Gary never said where he went, and she didn't ask him. She wanted to enjoy the evening. She even tried blow-drying curls in the ends of her long, heavy hair, but they fell out by the time she was on the train. Oh well. She still had her second-favorite knock-off Gunne Sax peasant dress. Billowy sleeves, billowy hems, necklaces in her cleavage, just for Stevie Nicks. Maybe she should be done with boys altogether and find herself a nice, witchy girl with a shag cut.

"Call us before you head back, if you can get to a phone. And *stay together!*" was the last thing their mom said.

It turned out to be a great evening, to begin with. Her brother's mood was light and easy and when people watched them, they were *watching* him—but smiling, as though enthralled with his every movement. No train delays, no line to wait in—no line at all, because they were let right inside. The tickets were the cheapest they could get, but Gary led Sylvie in like they were VIP. Then someone offered them better seats because they were sadly going to have to leave before the show.

All good, all great, all amazing. Yeah, Stevie Nicks's voice was rough (they'd canceled Syracuse for vocal strain), but Sylvie didn't really mind. She just tried to soak in the fact that she was there, seeing her favorite band with her own naked (glasses-covered) eyes. And it was all good, all great, all amazing.

Until the middle of "Gold Dust Woman" (Stevie in a pointed witch hat), when Gary left his seat and didn't come back.

For three songs, Sylvie tried to brush it off. Maybe he ran into someone he knew and was talking. A lot. Maybe he got lost. Maybe he needed a smoke break.

She waited through the encore ("The Chain," "Second Hand News," "Songbird"), which she found hard to enjoy.

She waited until she had to go, to funnel out with the rest of the crowd. Gary wasn't waiting at the doors, wasn't in the lobby, wasn't even outside. It would be easy to miss him, though. He was another vaguely tall brunette white guy in a crowd full of them. Every mustache got a second glance, until Sylvie, panicking at first, then pissed off, waited for a pay phone to open up.

Her brother had ditched her.

"Concert over?" asked her dad when he answered.

"Yes, but I can't find Gary," she said.

"What?"

"He ditched me! He ditched me in the middle of the set! I can't find him *anywhere*!"

"Did he say where he was going?"

"No! I thought maybe the bathroom, but he didn't come back."

Sylvie plugged her free ear to hear above the chattering, hyped-up or high crowd. Her dad was talking to their mom; she could hear his muffled voice. Then he came back on the receiver.

"Are you still at the Garden?"

"Where else would I be?"

He ignored her backtalk. "Stay where you are. I'm coming in a cab to get you."

For twenty-five minutes, she waited out on the curb ignoring every person who attempted to talk to her. She even folded her arms so her boobs would disappear for a while—she didn't want the attention. Not here, not alone, not vulnerable. The thinner the crowd got, the more she hunched her shoulders. That .44 caliber killer only seemed to go for pairs, right? But a single, morose teen girl would be a lot easier to pick off. How could Gary leave her like this?

As soon as she saw her dad, she realized she was angry at him, too. "Why didn't you ground him when he disappeared? He probably thought he could get away with doing it again!"

The taxi cut through the thin traffic easily. Sylvie was slumped low in the seat, fingering the bangles on her wrist, twisting the rings.

"Because he's an adult, and it was a special occasion," said her dad, though he sounded less convinced.

"Yeah, what a real adult. Leaving his sister because he's embarrassed to be seen with her."

"Sylvie. I'm sure that's not it."

Sylvie didn't even understand what *it* could be.

It took her another couple of hours to wind down. She wanted to call Marz or Marybeth but couldn't do it this late. She shut herself up in her room and blasted a record through her headphones, wishing that she kept a diary so she could write BOYS ARE IDIOTS over and over.

When she finally did fall into bed, she was only asleep for an hour or two, because her parents' yelling woke her up. She felt around for her glasses to see it was after 3 AM.

At least he was catching hell this time. And half-asleep as she had just been, Sylvie found it remarkably easy to relight her anger.

Rolling out of bed, she stomped to her door and threw it open.

"You *scumbag*!" she yelled without even looking to see if her brother was actually home.

"Sylvie, don't even start," said her dad, but she ignored him and kept stomping until she was close enough to Gary to shove him. He looked at her as though he barely remembered he had a sister at all.

"Sylvie!" said her parents.

"What's the idea of ditching me? You want me to get kidnapped and assaulted, you giant ass!"

Their dad took Sylvie's shoulder and pulled her back, and their mom stepped in front of her.

"I don't know what's really going on with you," their dad said, "but you're getting a curfew until we feel like you've earned your freedom again. And that might not be until you go back to school."

Gary wasn't doing a lot of fighting back, which made Sylvie angrier. She leaned around her mom.

"Are you *that* embarrassed to hang with me? Did you turn Ilan against me, too?" she shouted at him.

"I haven't talked to Ilan!"

"Yeah, *right*. So he just suddenly stops calling and hanging out here for no reason, right?"

"It's not—it's not *no reason*!"

Sylvie felt a savage pressure in her chest. "So you *do* hang with him!"

"No—"

"It doesn't matter who you were with," said their mom, and she turned so she could gently push Sylvie away. "Sylvie, come on. Go back to your room."

"I'm—shocked isn't enough of a word, Gary, it really isn't," her dad was saying. "Your safety is one thing, and I think you need to take it more seriously, but your sister is only *seventeen*!"

Sylvie didn't want to go. Her nerves were on fire, her brain spinning. It was horrible, she realized, as her mom shut her door and left her alone again, to lose trust in her brother. He had always been so reliable and affable and *normal*, and she had needed those things when her view of the world got out of hand.

They kept talking outside for a while. Sylvie strained to listen, but it was just the usual parental disappointment and interrogation, and Gary wasn't giving anything up. His reasons for leaving didn't really make sense. He thought he saw someone he knew and then he lost track of time.

He didn't seem quite so insufferably jolly tonight, at least. She hoped he was wracked with guilt.

When everything quieted down, and Gary had gone to his room, Sylvie closed her eyes.

She woke up again after what felt like seconds. The lights were all still off, and she didn't hear the distant sound of trucks beginning their thunderous morning routines. Then she realized she was hearing something else—a soft, earthy whisper at the back of her mind. She'd heard that voice before, downstairs.

She sat up so fast that tiny dots flourished across her vision.

Outside her door, a floorboard creaked.

Sylvie's breath stopped. She stared at her door, at the knob, at the crack at the threshold that was only a strip of black.

Then she heard the creaking again, farther away this time.

Someone was walking around the loft. Maybe Gary had gone to the bathroom.

As her heartbeat eased, she heard the whispering again.

Another creak.

"Sylvie?"

Oh, lord, did it feel like her body and soul had been forcibly separated. Her vision flashed white, her muscles twitched. No part of her was prepared to hear her name at her door.

It was her brother's voice, whispering.

"Sylvie, you awake?"

Easing slowly off the bed, Sylvie considered ignoring him but didn't want him to keep saying her name.

"I am *now*. What is it?" she asked, the sound of her own voice setting goosebumps along her arms.

"I'm sorry, Sylvie. I really am." He sounded sorry, anyway. He sounded about as sorry as anyone could. "I don't know why I did it—I mean I do, but it wasn't . . . It wasn't on purpose. I thought . . ."

As he trailed off, Sylvie took a couple steps backward. "It's fine. Forget it." She wanted him to go away. She thought of the wound on his wrist. She thought of her dream. She thought of the voice in the dark of the studio. *Syyyyylvieee.*

"It's not fine, Sylvie. It's . . ."

"Just forget it and go to bed. We can talk tomorrow if you want."

"I didn't do it to hurt you. It's just the opposite. I don't want anything to happen to you, ever. Especially on account of me."

The conviction in his voice sounded like he was saying it as much to himself as to Sylvie, and that unsettled her. "Okay. I believe you. Just go to bed."

He didn't speak, but she could hear his weight on the floorboards. He didn't move away from her door for several more seconds. Then she heard the door to his room shut, saw the light flick on. He didn't turn it off again, and she didn't fall asleep.

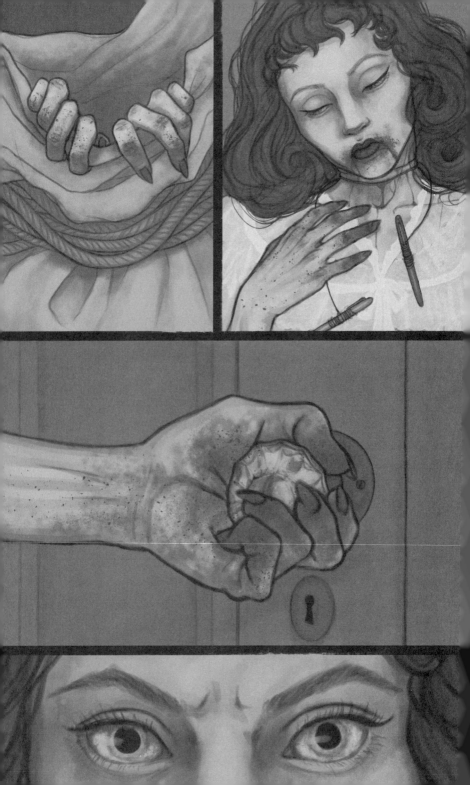

CHAPTER TWENTY-ONE

Sylvie only really went up on the roof in the summer, and not very often even then. It was soft and sloped and had patches of tar, not to mention it sweltered under direct sunlight. When she was younger and braver and dumber, she sometimes tried to dance up there, but her parents would hear it and tell her to knock it off, that she would kick the skylights or trip off the edge.

Sure, it was a decent view. The Twin Towers to the south and all the rest of the city to the north. And other rooftops on other buildings that often became makeshift stages or open-air studios.

Mostly, it was fun to watch the past up here. People seemed happy on the roof. They smoked and talked across generations. Sometimes they even stole naps or kisses or played a quick card game. The landscape of the roof barely changed. There weren't lines of laundry or children to watch—no families lived in the building before Sylvie's—but it was less harrowing than the machines and bustling people who filled the floors below. It was easier to pick out faces up here, too, and she knew almost all of them.

But she wasn't looking at any of it now, resting on an old beach towel in the shadow of the water tower, reading the June copy of *Teen Beat*. "Super Farrah Look-Alike Contest!" She made sure her legs and arms made no contact with the roof at all. But she thought about the people who had been up here before anyway. She wondered how many of them ever got to learn who Farrah Fawcett was. Surely one or two were still kicking.

She needed to be out of the loft. She needed to be alone.

Specifically, she wanted to be away from her brother.

Tonight was her last dance class before her first feis of the summer, and she had barely been thinking about it. There were so many other things getting in the way that she had sort of given in to inevitable failure. Feiseanna didn't really matter so much at Sylvie's level, but if Deirdre saw her flopping all over the place, she wouldn't let her anywhere near the oireachtas. And no oireachtas, no Worlds.

Besides, the older dancers had to help corral the young ones, so she would be there all day.

That was fine with her. She was up on the roof sunbathing because her brother was downstairs acting strange, and being out all day Saturday sounded good to her, too.

It was clear Gary hadn't slept. He skipped breakfast and sat in front of the TV set with the volume up just a little too high. He bounced his leg, seemed to forget how to blink. The wound on his arm was already gone, as far as Sylvie could see, which was as uncomfortable as it being there in the first place. Sylvie healed quicker than most people, but not *that* quick.

Their parents decided he was being penitent. He was home, after all, which was better than the last four days. But Sylvie was unsettled. Jessie Baby had stopped whining at him, but she still wouldn't come near enough to be petted. While their parents didn't seem to notice that, Gary seemed to have accepted it as part and parcel of his fate.

Eventually Sylvie would have to ask what was up, but she didn't want to do it right now. She had been free from strangers staring and everything else that came with it. Soon Deirdre would take her summer break, and Sylvie could forget Rynn altogether until August. And yeah, both solutions were temporary, but she was going to live in the moment.

She considered the whispers, then did not consider them again.

Music rose through the air, mismatching rhythms and instruments from different open windows. A couple of radios. Some kids shrieking in delight somewhere in the next street over. The traffic down on Broome Street and the unmistakable jolting rattle of empty trucks going down the cobblestones everywhere else. Honking on Houston or Broadway.

Sylvie took off her glasses and dropped the open magazine across her face. Lying flat on her back in jean shorts and a bikini top, she tried to imagine the life of a girl who would submit her photo to a contest or take notes on what Shaun Cassidy wanted in a girl. That seemed like a nice life. Well, actually it sounded boring, but she liked the sunny simplicity of it.

Hearing the door to the roof squeak on its hinges, Sylvie tipped up the magazine.

And there was Ilan.

Against the wild throb of her heart and stomach, Sylvie immediately sat up and put her glasses on. How should she even greet him? Big, open, and happy? Breathless and concerned? Pissed off? Or just sit there in stunned silence?

She settled on an awkward wave.

He didn't say anything, either, just sheepishly walked over to her with his hands in his jeans pockets. The closer he got, the more the sun glowed in his wavy blond hair. It was almost uncomfortably bright, but she couldn't look away. Her mind skipped all the noise and went right back to the moment on the windowsill.

He stopped a few feet away from her and slid his hands out of his pockets, still looking sheepish. She wondered why she wasn't talking to him, wasn't giving him his customary hug. What was she wary of, again? She was glad to see him. She was glad he was safe.

"Howdy," she said. "Long time no see."

"Your mom told me you were up here. I ran into her, outside," he said. His voice filled Sylvie in a way voices weren't supposed to. She could have hummed along to every word.

"Mind if I take some towel?" he asked, and Sylvie scooted over to give him more room.

He grinned at her, bright as the sun. The sheepishness was gone. "Thanks."

"How've you been?" she asked him, folding her legs up, turning a little toward him. "I was imagining a Collyer brothers situation."

"I don't have enough shit to be a hoarder. Nah, I wanted to say I'm sorry for the disappearing act. First, my schedule got busy out of nowhere."

"Marz's parents said you were playing a gig down here the other night," she said, and she didn't sound or even feel bitter.

"Yeah. That was wild-and-a-half. I was practicing at my place with the window open, and some guys shouted up at me and next thing I knew, I had to come play. I would've told you if I'd had the time. I guess I hoped your parents would be there, too."

"I was mostly out that day, anyway," she said, though she could barely remember the day. It was all fog.

"It made me think, y'know, about my future, and what I'm gonna do with it."

"Be a bigshot musician?" teased Sylvie. It was hard to be entirely sarcastic when looking at him. She just wanted to look at him, to watch how his lips moved and where his eyes focused.

"I've got some sessions lined up but honestly, it almost feels like—like why stay in school, y'know? Stanford's not really my scene, anyway."

"What'll your parents think if you drop out? Will you move back here?"

"Of course. And I guess they won't be shocked, since Tess dropped out, too. But at least I won't join a caravan of hippies, right?"

Sylvie smiled a half-smile. "I thought maybe you had."

"I really am sorry," he said, switching from laughs to a softer voice.

"Don't apologize," she said at once, desperate to make this point to him. All she could think of was the feel of his hand around hers, the way his eyes flickered to her mouth in his apartment, and down on that windowsill when they were so rudely interrupted—by what, she suddenly couldn't remember.

Her hair hung in two loose braids, and he gently tugged one, the way he liked to do. She could have fallen into his lap, and she would if he kept sitting there.

"Nah, I'm gonna apologize. Because I do care how you feel, y'know. I've cared for close to forever."

"I know. That's why I'm glad you're okay." Her mouth would speak before the thought had formed in her head. It was drawn out of her, untested and unthought, because she wasn't worried at all.

He was leaning closer. "I'm more okay now."

"We could improve on okay."

And closer. "I picked a shit time to leave last week."

"Yeah, you did."

"I won't do that again."

"No, you won't."

He was probably about to kiss her—he had leaned too close not to—but Sylvie grabbed his shirt and pulled him in just in case he wasn't. He made the tiniest noise in the back of his throat, but he didn't miss a beat. It was like they'd kissed a hundred times before. The only thought left in Sylvie's head was *finally*, and then that thought was gone with the rest.

It was like being filled and released all at the same time, and she didn't know what part of it was better. She wasn't even going to try to be a shrinking violet, pretending she hadn't hoped for this moment before now, hadn't imagined it in great, agonizing detail. No, this was the Summer of Ilan, starting now. The crush had bloomed wide open. She would remember it fondly, but she would remember this better.

Her glasses smudged, so she took them off. He barely gave her room, pulling her onto his lap. How had she liked *anything* before this?

His hands slid over her bare back, one continuing into her hair. The other hand went beneath the tie of her bikini top. He only pulled away to kiss down her neck, between her collarbones, leaning her back to find a spot on her chest, next to the fabric of her top, and he didn't let up until the skin was livid. He said things, sometimes, and she could barely take them in through the clouds in her brain.

Then he was back to kiss her properly again, and she felt her ties loosen, his hands move against her spine, and the door creak open as her mom said, "Sylvie—don't forget you've got dance!"

With a gasp, Sylvie sucked in the New York air once more and said, in a voice she thought sounded a little too throaty, "Yeah! I'll be down in a sec!"

Ilan hadn't even stopped—he was back on her neck, around which hung a very useless bikini top.

Her mind felt split. Her heart was racing at two different speeds. She heard the door shut, made sure her mom wasn't coming around the corner, and went back to kissing him.

No, Sylvie! Come on. She's going to come back up here! She might not even know Ilan is still over!

"Ilan. . . ." she trailed off, and he pulled away. His hair was messy, his lips bitten.

Oh, *cripes*, her mom was so gonna know they were up to something. She didn't want to parade it right in front of everybody.

She pulled herself back together half in a dream and half in a panic, but Ilan was completely unbothered.

"It'll be fine," he said, standing up and holding a hand out for her. "C'mon."

She stood up and he helped fix her top, taking his sweet time to brush aside her loose hair (she could have fallen to the ground—God, why was she so weak-kneed), then he grabbed the towel.

Now it was Sylvie's turn to look sheepish as she headed back into the apartment. Instead of vanishing, as he could have, Ilan followed her inside. She almost wanted to tell him to go, but one look at him and she changed her mind.

Gary was still in the sitting room, and at first he didn't react as Sylvie walked to her room to change. But then Geneva started talking to Ilan, asking him how he was, and as soon as Ilan said, "I'm all right," Gary bolted off the sofa and turned around.

"No," he said, so sharply that Sylvie came back out of her room.

"What the fuck are you doing?" he shouted. "Why the fuck are you here? You know you can't be here! No! Get the fuck out! Get out!"

As he shouted, he went to the door.

"Sylvie, come with me!"

"Huh? I have dance!"

"Good!"

Jessie Baby emerged from the back bedroom and let out an agonizing howl. Her hackles raised. She bared her teeth. Then she backed up, snarling. Sylvie ran over to her to corral her behind the door. Maybe she ought to have been more concerned, but her brain was fuzzy—with sun, with Ilan, with whatever Gary was doing now.

Ilan just stood there watching it all happen. Watching Gary shove on his sneakers, watching him retreat out the door, slamming it hard enough to rattle the chain locks.

His feet were heavy on the stairs.

No one knew what to say, except Geneva.

"What was that about?" she asked, gently.

Ilan shrugged. "I dunno. I haven't seen him much lately."

As though the entire episode hadn't happened, he and Sylvie's mom began an animated conversation about the news of his performance, and Sylvie pulled out her dance bag, her whole body still buzzing—in lust, sure, but increasingly in alarm.

Ilan left when she did. They got the train together, Sylvie not even thinking about how she tried to avoid them now. They kissed on the bench in the station, missing the first train, and Ilan almost missed his stop once they were on the second. She nearly followed him out. Gary didn't come back until after dinner.

CHAPTER TWENTY-TWO

Sylvie was surprised by her alarm just after dawn, as she'd forgotten there was a reason to set it. But her mom soon came in, chipped mug of coffee in hand, and said, "Good thing I noticed that. Up and at 'em. Take a shower, brush your teeth, do your hair. We're meeting everybody at seven."

Sylvie lay there for a half-second longer, yesterday's visit with Ilan already on repeat at the front of her brain. She had to compete today, and the only anxiety she felt was that she would be out all day and Ilan couldn't visit. Rolling out of bed, she went to work on cleaning up and gathering her good, unscuffed shoes and her old solo dress, then piled into a cab with her mom, where they took the train from Penn Station to Yonkers.

The feis was being held in an elementary school gymnasium, and the parking lot was overrun with kids and parents and teachers in various stages of sleep-dampened stress. After signing in and getting her schedule and number, Sylvie's mom went to find a seat with the other parents from Deirdre's school, and Sylvie met up with her friends.

"My heel broke," Nessa said instead of hello. "Can you believe it? The one time I told myself, oh, I don't need to bring my spares. It just snapped right off! *Look!*"

She held her hardshoes up.

"How does a heel even break like that?" asked Devon, already in his cream kilt, his burgundy suit coat draped over his arm.

"I don't know! But it *would* happen to me. I just got these two months ago!" With a groan, she shouldered her bag and went off to find her mom.

Though she wasn't scheduled to dance for two more hours, Sylvie changed in the gym locker rooms, checking that her hair was waved just right before pinning on her knit headband. Her mom helped secure a brooch to her shawl, to help keep it in place over her shoulder. It was second nature at this point in her life, though the dress changed from year to year. This was probably the last time she would wear this one.

The youngest kids were competing soon, and Caitlin was helping line them up and reminding them of the procedure. *Point your toe and off you go!*

"Remember when you were that age?" Sylvie's mom said to her, nudging her with her shoulder as Sylvie dropped into the chair beside her, careful not to crush her skirt.

Sylvie smiled. "Yeah. There's more kids every year."

"Maybe someday this won't be a secret little world anymore."

Sylvie could hear the accordion player warming up. "Doubtful."

For the next hour, Sylvie kept busy shuttling young beginners to their proper stages, and browsing the vendors set up along the back wall and out in the hall. She looked at some used costumes, wanting to trace her fingers over embroidery and lace but holding back. She waited for the butterflies in her stomach to emerge, for the brimming anxiety to spill over as the hours ticked by and her dances crested on the horizon. But she wasn't nervous at all. Where nerves might be, she dwelled on Ilan, replaying their time on the roof until her cheeks were flushed. It had been better than all the hundreds of scenarios she had played in her mind over the years, and they were only just getting started.

Not once did she think of how upset Gary had been. She had forgotten that part of the day completely.

The classroom across the hall from the vendors was a designated practice area, and behind the closed door you could hear teachers clapping the counts, lilting the steps. Feet thudded on the linoleum, heads bounced by the narrow window.

Deirdre had them in there fifteen minutes later, going over their softshoe dances until they were all just on the cusp of being sweaty and ruining their hair. Then she let them go back out to wait out the last twenty minutes.

They hung around in clumps near the stages until it was time to line up. Sylvie couldn't fathom how many times she had done this in her life as she shuffled near the middle of the line. In front of them, the adjudicator took note of the numbers, rang a desk clerk's bell, and the first two girls walked out. As the musician finished through the first eight bars of the slip jig, the girls started to dance. This was where Sylvie ought to feel even a pinch of nerves, but they were not coming. She'd dreamt Ilan was an adjudicator once, hadn't she? She pictured him out in the audience, watching her.

As the girls finished, two more replaced them. Then a third pair, leaving one pair before it was Sylvie and a girl from a school on Long Island. She was going over her steps and counting the music when she heard the rasp of a whisper. The hair stirred on her neck as a breeze circulated the room. She looked at the doors and Ilan was standing there—no, no, it was some other blonde guy.

And now it was her turn, and her heart was thudding as though she had already gone.

The last 8-bar of the slip jig was coming to its end. Sylvie stepped out of the line as she had stepped out a thousand times before.

Five-two-three-four-five, *six*-two-three-four-five, *seven*-two-three-four-five, and off you go—

Syyyylvieee

And she was stuck, high on her toes, calves sprung to launch herself forward. But she couldn't launch forward. She couldn't launch in any direction at all. She was suspended in the world, unmoving and unable to correct it. Even a marionette had more freedom.

Why do you shy from me?

Sylvie's eyes were wide and wild. She couldn't respond to the voice that rose in her head, rolling from one ear to the next, vibrating in her chest. All the sound in the room was gone.

You will have all that you dreamt of. You have nothing to fear.

The voice settled around her brain, soft, velvet, like a deep caress. There was nothing she could do to stop it, and then she didn't want to stop it. She smiled, and the room erupted back into order in the middle of her bow. She was breathing hard, her legs felt used, and the next dancers were already lined up to start. She'd done well at her slip jig, she thought, and when their group was done, her friends agreed.

"You looked a little dead behind the eyes, though," said Devon. "Deirdre's gonna call it out."

"*Nobody* smiles. I don't know why she cares so much," said Nessa, furiously working on breaking in her new hardshoes.

Sylvie had another forty-five minutes to wait until her next dance, so Deirdre ushered them all into the practice room again.

"You looked terrific, Sylvie," she said. "No notes on the steps but try not to look like an ax murderer. You lightened up during the last half of your second step, so keep that energy going."

When Deirdre turned away, Devon gave Sylvie a look. *See.*

Sylvie had placed first in the slip jig, and she took her small trophy to her mom for safe keeping.

For the next half hour, she watched the last age groups in her level compete, and changed into her hardshoes. And she thought back to her slip jig, trying to seek out memories of how it felt, but instead coming away with a slight sense of unease, as though she had forgotten something significant. She couldn't think what—she had won, after all, so nothing had gone wrong.

Then it was time for her to dance again. Sylvie lined up, closing and opening her hands by her sides, scanning the crowd, scanning the adjudicators, then retreating into her head to go over her steps.

You will win.

It wasn't her voice that said it, but the fear only held her for a brief second.

And she did win. And she won her final round, too, collecting three small trophies before she won the overall championship. Her mood was buoyed, her feet light, her thoughts untethered. She had expected to march into her first feis, in the midst of all this chaos in her life, and fall flat on her face. She had expected to disappoint herself, disappoint Deirdre. But instead Deirdre cheered and hugged her and said, "That's the girl I know!"

And Sylvie couldn't stop smiling.

✦

They arrived home late, having eaten dinner in Yonkers with most of her class. Gary's door was closed, and her dad was in front of the TV, whittling something onto a sheet of newspaper. She showed off her trophies and yawned through a recount of the day, then shuffled off to her room. Jessie Baby hovered in the hall, then retreated to the living room.

Sylvie held up the championship trophy. Her fingerprints had blighted the surface, but it still had that optimistic shine of a new win. She turned it over, glancing over the surface at the name of the feis and the placing (first). She remembered when she won her first trophy as a kid, how excited she was after acquiring dozens of tiny medals.

She looked at her reflection on the surface, at the stretched and distorted shape of her room and the chaos of posters and medal banners around her. She thought she could see a smile on her face, though she was pretty sure she wasn't smiling. A new solo costume on, with new embroidery and a new lace collar.

Impossible to see on the surface of a trophy, but it was clear as day in Sylvie's mind.

Shining hardshoes. Perfectly laced softshoes. The highest kicks, the strongest leaps, standing high on her toes in front of adjudicators so mesmerized that they forgot to give her a score.

A sash across her shoulder. A bigger trophy in her arms. A metal crown atop her head. A podium. A blonde adjudicator shaking her hand. She would change the face of Irish dance.

Now she did smile, a little, and as she set the trophy down, she noticed something just behind her. It rose up above her, a dark strip of something—a shadow too tall for the room. Gasping, she dropped the trophy and spun around, almost climbing onto her desk. But nothing was there.

She shoved the trophy away with her foot, not looking at it, and hurried out of her room to join her parents on the couch. Jessie Baby raised her head to watch her, thumped her tail once, but did not come any closer.

CHAPTER TWENTY-THREE

It was easy enough, with the distance of another day, to convince herself that she had just been seeing things in the trophy. Still, Sylvie left it on the floor, covered with a t-shirt.

It was less easy to convince herself that the events at the feis made any sense. Because they didn't. Most of it she no longer remembered at all. And as the morning turned to afternoon and Jessie Baby continued acting cautiously around her and her brother, jumping if either one of them made a sudden movement, Sylvie would watch Gary and a low panic, like a fever, began to take hold inside her.

But there was still a part of her that didn't really care. Obviously nothing had actually gone wrong or she wouldn't have won. It wasn't typical for her to sweep all of her dances, either, so maybe she had relaxed enough to shut off all her doubts, and she just wasn't used to that.

That's what she chose to believe as she went down into the studio to practice. She wanted to practice—she felt like she had to, that she would imprint upon herself some powerfully new level of skill if she ran through her steps *right now*.

As she unlocked the studio door, she heard footsteps on the stairs below. Fear came, but then it went, and then Ilan appeared.

She hadn't heard the buzzer, and his sudden appearance didn't startle her at all, which surprised her. Then she stopped thinking about it.

He kissed her a long hello.

"I was just gonna practice," she said by way of explanation and apology as she went into her dad's studio.

"I'll pretend to be a judge and look impressed," he said.

The needle on Sylvie's barometer twitched, briefly. She laughed. "Go ahead. But you're gonna be distracting."

The room was stiflingly hot, so she opened one of the windows. The back of the studio was cluttered with the usual melee of objects that might look terrifying from the corner of her vision, but she didn't think about it. Ilan was with her, and actually *with* her. They were crossing that bridge, and she was enjoying the journey.

Toeing off her sneakers, she rifled through her bag for her hardshoes and pulled them on.

"You've really killed the floor in here," Ilan observed as he crossed over it and sat back in the windowsill. The sight of it felt incredibly good. Calming.

"Yeah, it's pretty terrible, isn't it?" She went over to the stereo. "There's about to be a lot of accordion, just so you know."

As the first hornpipe began to thump its way from the speakers, Sylvie jumped around for a while, listening to the discordant notes of her shoes and trying to warm her body. She stretched the arches of her feet, flexed and pointed her toes, did some weak and ineffectual stretching of her hamstrings, then stood back along the wall.

As soon as she counted herself off, she jumped into motion, beating out her rhythms as though it was before everything. Before gunshots and screams and ghost dogs and all of that.

CRACK

A heel click without a hitch. Without a wince. She almost laughed, but there wasn't time. She had to dance. She frowned instead—no, Deirdre hated that—she relaxed, she relaxed right into her muscle memory, banging out the rhythms harder, wanting to leave gouges in the grain so deep that not even the best polish could seal it off. She would linger here long after her family was gone, and it wouldn't take someone with her useless hindsight to see it.

She could hear her steps echoing back around her, then cutting off as she stopped, breathing hard, a flash of sweat beginning to form at her temples and neck. The record moved to another track and as she went to stop it, the toe of her shoe snagged a sliver on the floor, scratching the leather.

That didn't matter. They'd get polished.

"That's pretty cool, actually," said Ilan. "It's like angry tap dancing."

Right. *Ilan!*

Sylvie snorted a laugh through her panting breaths. "Thanks. Hey, uh, Marz has a show tonight. You wanna come with me, or is your schedule all booked out?"

Ilan laughed. "Not tonight. I'm all yours."

Sylvie flushed, but as she was already flushed, his words only made her hide a wide, silly grin.

"And you're gonna see a lot of me, 'cause I told my parents I'm dropping out of Stanford," he said.

"No way! What'd they say?"

"They're a little pissed, but it's not like they can force me to go. Anyway, they'll save some money. That wasn't my scene. It'll be good."

And Sylvie believed that it would be. Believed that he knew what he was doing, because why wouldn't he? "Now you really gotta move out and come back to the neighborhood," she said.

He parted from the sill and came over to her and kissed her.

Good. She didn't need to practice, anyway.

It was so easy to kiss him and keep kissing him. It exceeded the drawn-out fantasy she had cultivated around getting to this part. He pushed her securely against the desk, his knee between her legs. One quick motion that didn't require stopping or starting. A dance in itself, the easiest choreography.

"Will they check on you?" he murmured, parting for air and for her neck.

"No."

The window was still open.

Good.

"Have you . . ." he whispered to her ear.

She didn't even hesitate. "Yeah."

"Come back to my place."

All she could do was nod.

He slid his hands up her shirt, around her back, to pull her away from the desk. She put her shoes back on in a daze and didn't even go upstairs to grab her purse.

They took a cab from Houston and parted for air only once or twice before stumbling back out on West Tenth. He had her hand in his at once and she started to cross the sidewalk to his apartment, but he pulled her the other way, back across the street. And at first, Sylvie just walked. She grabbed his waist and walked because she would have walked with him anywhere. But then he slowed down in front of the Mark Twain house. The House of Death. And that simmering note of panic began to steam.

"Hang on—where're you going?" she asked him, because she wasn't going to fuck anybody in a place like that, even Ilan. And Ilan had a bed (presumably, as she'd never seen it) just across the street. Not that a bed was important, but a place without mold and rats definitely was.

She had to pull her hand out of his. "Are you messing with me or what?"

Suddenly, so suddenly that Sylvie did jump this time, Ilan turned to look at her. She had never seen anyone look so afraid.

"Ilan?"

"No. No, no, no," he muttered to himself, turning around again, his hands threading through his hair in a gesture of pure panic. Only now did she see the raw, bruised mark on his arm—how had she not noticed it before?

She had been about to step closer to him, but he dodged her, walking toward the street, then looping back again, as though he was trying to outrun something.

Sylvie was aware that people were out there, coming toward them. "Ilan."

He looked at her again, but it seemed to hurt him to do it. He kept averting his gaze. His brow furrowed; his mouth quivered. "Oh, Jesus. Oh, Christ. What've I done." His voice wasn't quiet. He spoke as though he was alone.

"Can we please get the hell away from here?" She tried to grab for his arm, but he wrenched it away. Sylvie dropped her hands to her sides.

"I'm sorry. I'm sorry, Sylvie. It isn't—" He turned away from her, kept walking in circles. "We can't. I shouldn't have—I wanted to, but—it's not—"

"Spit it out!" she snapped at him, then she regretted snapping at him. He hadn't done anything wrong—*yes he had*. "Ilan—you gotta stop. Just stop! Let's just go to your place and calm down, okay?"

"No! No, Sylvie! You can't go to my place! You can't ever go to my place, no matter what I say!"

"What?" It caught her so off-guard that she thought she had misheard. Brain fog. Absolute brain fog. "But you just—Ilan, c'mon—"

"Sylvie. Please. I'm begging you. I'm *begging* you."

"You're not making any *sense!*"

"Gary's right. I shouldn't have gone to see you. That was stupid. Don't let me come near you again. Not until—this isn't safe." His eyes were bright, now, still terrified but threatening to spill tears. Sylvie couldn't even tell how she was feeling. Swells of anger, then deep confusion.

"What happened?"

This time, as he came near her, she grabbed hold of his arm, right below the wound.

"What *is* this? Tell me what happened!" She bent his arm as though he needed to see it to remember, and he pulled his arm back almost immediately.

"I'm sorry, Sylvie. I really am."

"What happened to you and Gary?"

"I wanted to—I've wanted to—I like you a lot. More than a lot. I love hanging out with you. I've always loved hanging out with you. But I—I fouled it up real, real bad."

"How? What did you guys *do*?"

He glanced at her, covered in so much shame she felt like pushing him into traffic.

"You owe me that much!" she said.

"This was a mistake. God, I probably—please don't come after me. Don't come near my place. Don't you dare come near my place."

"*I heard that already!*"

"Sylvie, listen to me," he snapped at her. Finally touched her—only to hold her arms in a firm grip. She clamped her mouth shut. "I love you, and I want you to live. Now get the fuck out of here."

He shoved her, slightly, as though she needed help to start her legs, and as he did it, a warm breeze kicked up the leaves in the trees around them, and something slithered around Sylvie's mind, bursting into her thoughts like radio static.

STAY WHERE YOU ARE.

Ilan almost dropped to the ground. Sylvie could see his legs weaken. He covered his ears. "GO, SYLVIE! RUN! GO *HOME*!"

All at once, like a cosmic drain being pulled, everything came rushing back down to her. Everyone on the block around them had stopped walking. And maybe it was Ilan's outburst that froze them, but Sylvie knew what was happening—knew and didn't know. The man walking his dog had dropped the leash, and the little white mutt was whining and barking at everything and nothing. In the distance, unseen, other dogs in other apartments began to howl.

Sylvie turned around and bolted down the street.

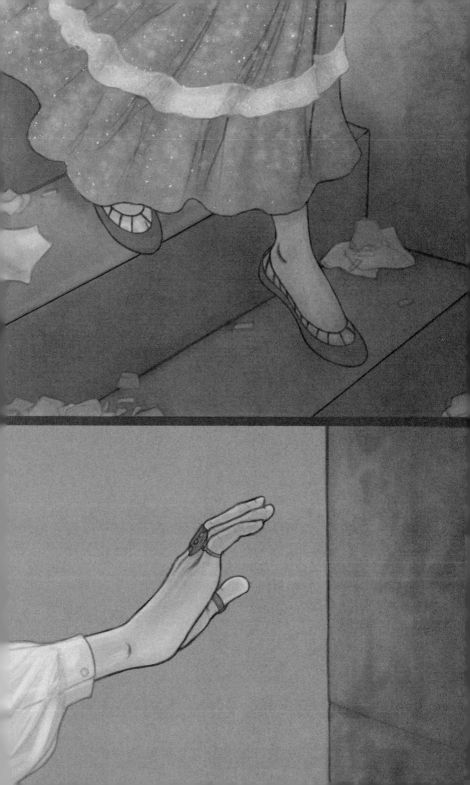

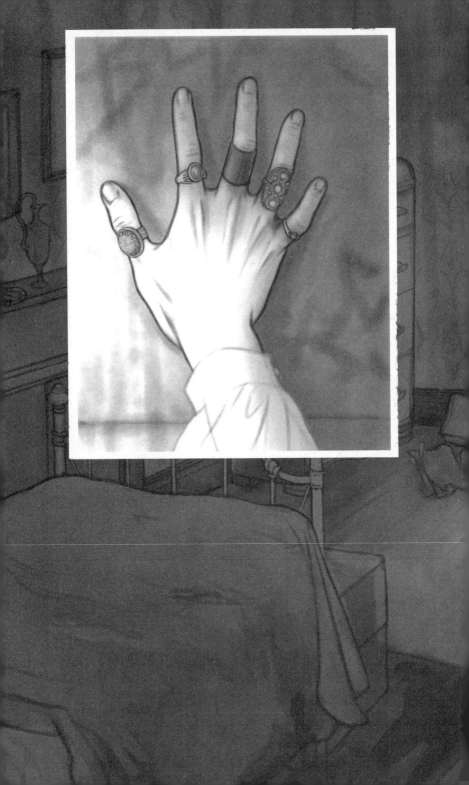

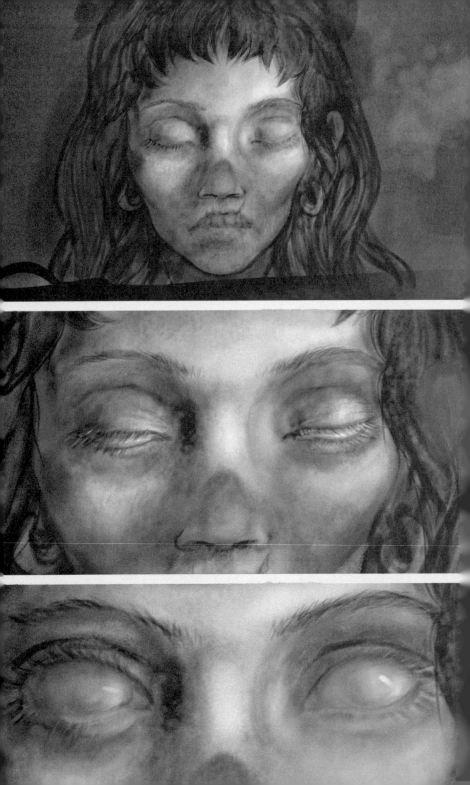

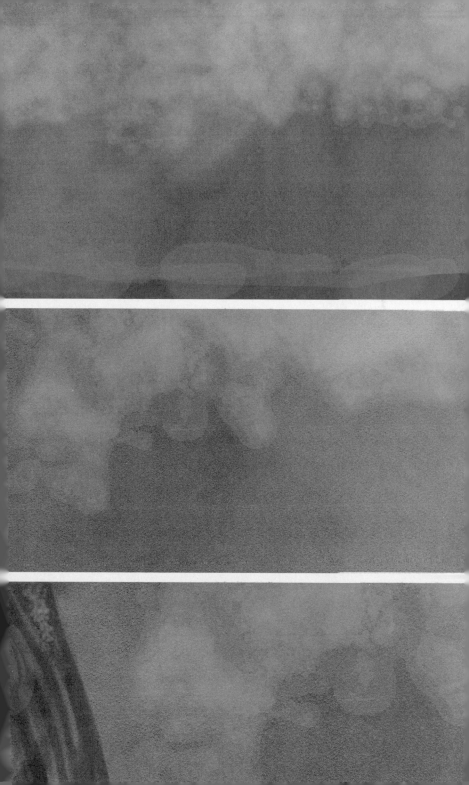

CHAPTER TWENTY-FOUR

People turned to her as she ran, so she ran in the street, dodging between cars that seemed almost to slow down for her. She didn't want to look back, but as she turned down Sixth Avenue, she couldn't stop herself. And there, sitting in the middle of the sidewalk several yards at her back, was the tall black dog.

Calling it black didn't even seem right. It was an absence of everything. Of light, of color. In the sun, its corrupted form was so much worse, and Sylvie marveled that they had been so calm the first time it appeared.

She wasn't calm now.

The air felt thick, though this had little to do with the sun. It also felt heavy, like her ears needed to pop. She ran for another block, dodging far more people—some of them stopping, most of them watching her with only a mild interest. A normal interest.

Waiting for the light, she looked back again and there it was— at the same distance, sitting in precisely the same way. It always sat, so that it looked like a long, thin column topped by sharp ears.

She ran into traffic, but it was harder to simply *run*. Everyone was out, going into and out of shops, looking for lunch, picking up laundry. Sweat trickled at Sylvie's temples. She looked back again and knew it would be there before she saw it. Sitting at the same distance. She didn't even notice how people gave it a wide berth, seeing it just as clearly as she did. To her, it had become her entire world.

Sylvie's run slowed to a fast walk. She sucked in shaky breaths of muggy summer air. As long as the dog wasn't getting closer, she didn't need to run. Running would get her home too quickly, anyway, and she couldn't go there if she was being followed by this thing.

Above her, she heard a funny rattling noise, then a much louder one. It carved through the air and landed with an ear-splitting collision of metal and rock right behind her. She felt the breeze as it stirred her hair. She heard several people shout in surprise. A fire escape ladder had come free.

Sylvie launched forward, but then there was another rattling sound and the next ladder fell. Then the next. She ran, one fell, she ran, one fell. The air was a cacophony of rattling metal and the screams of everyone around her.

She was going to die. This was how she was going to die. Crushed or impaled on a sidewalk outside a shoe repair shop.

Sylvie was gasping for air, now, and running without thinking. She kept to the far side of the sidewalk, jumping over the curb when she had to.

She didn't know where the hell to go or what to do, but her feet beat their customary path south, toward home. She kept her gaze up, the sound of the fire escapes still clamoring around her skull. She wanted to sit down and cry out for help, but she couldn't do that, either. Where was safe? Hide in a gallery? Hide in a store?

Behind her, she knew something was there, following at her heels. There was a presence in the air, a movement, a disturbance. The dog could probably nip her if it wanted to, if it could.

She shuddered and touched the wall of the nearest building as though the people there would save her. Like the memories stored here would form an army of the dead for her. The dog knew she was there, so what difference did it make if she used her powers now? She didn't even lift her hand away as she walked. She dragged it along one building, then the next, awkwardly climbing over stoops and loading docks to keep contact. Her eyes filled and she rubbed them. All around her, shadows of the past went about their lives unaffected and unafraid, consuming her in their midst, filling the air with obsolete street sounds and the familiar patter of conversation and confrontation.

She looked over her shoulder just once, and through the overlay of time she could make out the black hole shape of the dog sitting there, further back now than before, but the most visible thing in the world. Her heart raced, her skin felt cold. She pulled her hand back and returned to the outside edge of the sidewalk, knowing she looked no different to everyone out here, but feeling completely naked.

Turning down Greene Street was like pushing against the wind, and the sensation stunned her. She wanted to scratch at something that couldn't be scratched. She felt like people were watching her, murmuring to her, though there was no one even glancing in her direction. *Go up, Sylvie. Turn around. Check on Ilan.*

Afraid to go home, afraid she would bring something inside with her, she sat down on the marble stoop of the old, brick house she loved so well, and put her hands on the steps. The dog appeared across the street from her, then, in the middle of a blink. It came no closer.

And Sylvie sat there, buffering herself with visions she didn't need to pay attention to because she knew them better than a favorite film. If the dog came for her, if it sank spectral teeth into her leg and dragged her back to West Tenth, she would let it, she supposed. She didn't know what else to do.

She sat there as neighbors saw her and waved, saw the dog and avoided it. She sat there as tourists scouted for dinner and locals walked to the nearest gallery opening or a show down at Ali's Alley. She sat there until smoke from the long-ago fire in the floor above brought her back to herself.

Sylvie.

There was no sibilance in the word this time. It was harsh and cold like a crack in a frozen lake.

If you will not come to me, I will come to you.

She blinked. The dog was gone. She waited another minute before slowly rising back to her feet and running the rest of the way home. She didn't look behind her again. She knew nothing would be there now.

It was only when Sylvie arrived at her front door that she remembered she had left without keys and a dime to make a call. She leaned on the buzzer, backing up so she wasn't standing beneath the fire escape while she waited. She could still hear the phantom sounds of crashing metal.

When her mom let her up, Sylvie took the stairs two at a time. Her legs shook and her lungs squeezed and burned as she reached her floor and burst inside.

Her absence hadn't gone unnoticed. Nor did the fact that she had left her purse and her keys.

"You couldn't even leave us a *note?*" yelled her mom. "I go downstairs and not only is your bag there and the stereo on, the door is unlocked. And you're not there, you're not up here, you're not on the roof. I called Marybeth, I called Marz, I even called Ilan, though now I know why he didn't answer."

"I'm sorry!" Sylvie thought she would be gasping for air for the rest of her life.

"I don't understand it. What on earth were you thinking, just walking out the door without even change for the phone? I would've let you hang out with Ilan if you had just come up and told someone about it! For God's sake. You and Gary and these disappearing acts."

"I thought I was just gonna be right back, but things didn't work out like that," Sylvie said, knowing how ridiculously half-formed her defense was. She hadn't prepared one. She hadn't been in her right mind when she left, and now her mind was scrambled. She didn't care that her mom was angry. She didn't care if she punished or grounded her.

"And to go downstairs and see the mess you left—I can't believe it. I honestly can't believe it. First I thought some kind of lunatic had kidnapped you and left a calling card, but no!"

"Wait—what mess? I didn't leave a mess anywhere."

"Those handprints all over the studio!"

"I didn't leave any handprints anywhere!" Sylvie held up her hands to show they were clean. Sweaty and still trembling, but clean.

Geneva looked skeptical. "Well, somebody did, and you and Ilan were the only ones in there today!"

Sylvie frowned. "Ilan didn't do anything, either. Gary probably did it."

"I asked him." Geneva finally paused long enough to sigh and say. "I don't appreciate you kids messing with my work down there."

"We didn't! Mom, I swear. I don't know what you're talking about. Nothing was messy when I went down there to practice, okay?"

Her mom was already walking to the door. "Come downstairs with me."

Sylvie didn't want to. The first thought that sailed through her mind was that this wasn't her mother, but some elaborate doppelgänger trying to lure her into the jaws of a beast. It was only the fact that Jessie Baby was in the living room and not snarling from a corner that gave her the confidence to do what she was told. But when she saw what her mom had been trying to explain, she wished she had said no, anyway.

Large hands had impressed themselves in dense paths all over the floor of the loft, dodging the columns in a walking pattern. Not footprints—*hand*prints. Even Sylvie's bag had been touched, a fact that left her feeling like someone had walked over her grave.

"What the hell," she whispered. "Mom, this isn't normal."

"You're telling me! God, this is gonna take forever to clean up," said her mom, who was taking this in way more stride than Sylvie would—than Sylvie *was*.

"No, I mean—Mom, this is *crazy*. Those hands are *huge*. And there's no footprints! Is anything stolen?"

Geneva was walking through the room, her bare feet stirring up the dry clay impressions. Sylvie wished she wouldn't touch it. "Not that I can find. Stereo's there, and that's the most valuable thing."

"Are you sure?"

"I'll find out when we start cleaning up. But first I need you to go to the pet store. Which is what I wanted done earlier when you weren't here."

"Isn't Gary home?" Sylvie asked. She had already backed out of the room and was standing on the landing and deeply aware of the dark stairwell beside her.

"He already ran up to the Grand Union for me today. And you owe me, kid."

✦

She tried to make record time to and from Little Arf 'n Annie, which was only just down and around the block. With a bag of dry food in her arms on the way back, Sylvie's progress was slowed, and it made her feel like a sitting duck.

If that dog shows up, she thought, *I'll just throw this food at it. Maybe it'll eat it.*

The neighborhood was normal, but Sylvie didn't feel normal. The world felt far away, like the people who crossed her path weren't real, and the buildings were paper, and even the weight of the dog food bag was carried by someone else's arms.

Each step she took, she waited to feel something swipe at her ankles, grab at her knees. She waited for hot breath down her neck.

Check on Ilan.

Sylvie shook her head.

Check on Ilan. He might be hurt.

No.

CHECK ON ILAN. HE NEEDS YOUR HELP.

Sylvie threw herself inside and thundered up the stairs. The studio door was open, her mom mopping the floor with the radio blasting. She didn't notice Sylvie.

Bursting inside and dropping the dog food in the kitchen, she didn't know if her voice would even cooperate as she flung open Gary's bedroom door.

"Tell me what happened." It was a command, and she made it so, even through her gasps for air.

Gary almost backed off his bed, dropping the album he was looking at and pulling off his headphones before he could tangle himself in the cord.

"Jesus Christ," he muttered at her. He needed to shower. His hair was lank and heavy at the roots, his mustache untrimmed, days-old stubble coming in around his chin.

She flew at him, dropping onto his bed. "What happened to you and Ilan? Tell me right now."

Gary shook his head and got up, but Sylvie blocked him, shutting his door and standing in front of it.

"Tell me!"

"*No!*"

"Something's wrong and you owe me an explanation. *You owe me!*" She raised her voice as he kept shaking his head. "There's voices, Gary! There's voices and that—" she couldn't say it, "And all the damn fire escapes tried to fall down on my head!"

Gary stood there, looking thin and gray and exhausted. His eyes were red. "What?"

"Something's wrong with Ilan! And with you! That—that thing was following me around!"

"Down here?" Gary looked as though there was a window he could run to and shut, but his room was sealed off.

"No!" (Yes.) "Up in the Village!"

"You went up to the Village?"

"Ilan came by a few hours ago—"

Gary made a noise that could have been a groan or a choke.

"—and we went up to his place, and you know what he did, Gary? You know what Ilan did? He tried to take me into that fucking vacant house!"

"He what?" Her brother's voice was barely audible.

"Yeah! Yeah, that's right. He decided we'd go on a date to a rundown, boarded-up piece-of-shit house that's been tormenting him for weeks. That's what. And then he totally snapped and shouted at me to leave, so I did because I heard *whispering in my head*, Gary! Now tell me what you did!"

"Don't let him come down here again. If you see him, hide. Run. Call the police even! Just don't let him in here!"

"You have to tell me why or else I won't do it," she lied.

"Come on, Sylvie." The expression on his face, the fall of his voice, was like she had demanded he cut off an arm.

Sylvie knew she had caught him, and she kept going, "Come *on*? Something tried to *kill me* up there!"

Still, he didn't answer.

"Fine. I'll ask you questions, and you answer. You and Ilan had the same cut on your arm—what was it? How'd you get it?"

He shook his head, and Sylvie wanted to grab him and shake him harder. "That's not fair! You basically told Mom and Dad I'm a druggie burnout who should never be allowed out! Then you ditched me at the concert! So you *owe me*!"

She stayed in front of the door even as Gary turned away from her, raked a hand through his hair, sat down on his bed and stood up again.

"And you—earlier this week you strutted back home like a stupid peacock, sweating like you're strung-out! Gone all night, being a narc, *ditching me*—"

"Sylvie, seriously . . ." His voice was hoarse. "I don't want to tell you."

"Why *not*? I can try to help!"

There he was, shaking his head again, pacing back and forth between his bed and his dresser, unable to go anywhere else. He pulled at his mustache.

"Whatever you think you're protecting me from, it's already here! That—that dog followed me all the way home!"

Finally, Gary interrupted her, and his voice was clear and loud. "It's not the dog!"

Sylvie waited, and as she waited, she listened for her Mom's radio, wanting to make sure she stayed downstairs, at least for now.

Gary sighed and his voice lost its conviction, returned to gravel. "I mean, it is—but it isn't."

Sylvie kept waiting. Gary began pacing, knocked his fingers on his desk, walked back to her. Stopped. Waited. He didn't look at her.

"There's a woman." He said it so softly that Sylvie barely heard him.

"Huh?"

He closed his eyes, opened them again. They were redder now, and wet. He sniffed. He looked at the floor, at the walls, anywhere but at Sylvie, and kept opening his mouth to speak but saying nothing.

"Come on. Women aren't *that* terrifying," Sylvie joked, weakly.

"Sylvie, shut *up!*" he snapped at her. "Stop!"

Sylvie tensed her jaw.

He turned away from her again, carving almost a figure eight over his floor. It reminded Sylvie of the path the handprints made downstairs. "I thought I would forget about it or I'd wake up or something, but she's still in there. For a couple days—they were the *best* fucking couple days. But then she started talking again, and talking and *talking*. Go back up there, go back up there. And I can't understand the words, but I know what she's *saying*."

Sylvie opened her mouth to ask *who*, who was she? But she didn't need to.

"I went to check on Ilan because I was worried. Because I knew how much he was seeing that dog. Because he kept hearing whispers and wasn't sleeping. And he didn't want to tell you, and it's good that he didn't tell you. Because it's fucked, Sylvie. You don't even know how fucked it is."

"I think I have an idea," she murmured.

Gary didn't reply. Now that he was talking, he couldn't stop. "I don't like it up there anymore, y'know? I'd been trying to get him to rent a new place before he went AWOL. I think—"

He shook his head. The floorboards groaned beneath his bare feet. "Anyway, I went over there, and he let me up and he asked for my help. And I wish I had just said no. Because it didn't help either one of us. And it didn't help you. And it was supposed to."

Sylvie listened to the jingling of Jessie Baby's collar as she drank from her water bowl. As long as Jessie Baby was calm, she could be calm. Sort of. "What—what d'you mean?"

"It was awful, Sylvie."

CHAPTER TWENTY-FIVE
GREENWICH VILLAGE
June 26th

Gary hadn't seen or heard from Ilan all week. He had other shit to do than worry about his oldest friend, but Ilan never picked up the phone. That didn't sit right with Gary, but he had other shit to do. Tomorrow was the march. He had his ANITA BRYANT SUCKS ORANGES shirt washed and ready, and three of his friends at GAA had made a six-foot banner to match. His parents had taken out their WE LOVE OUR GAY SON shirts and were threatening to march with him instead of the growing contingency of proud parents, but Gary didn't mind so much. Each year it seemed less embarrassing and more of a blessing. Then on Wednesday was the Fleetwood Mac concert with Sylvie up at the Garden.

He wasn't in the right mood and didn't have the space in his brain to accommodate someone who was acting beyond wrecked *and* had the hots for his sister (which he'd suspected for years but never took seriously). It was all too weird.

One thing Ilan wasn't, was weird. He was cool—cool in attitude and presentation. Chill. Easygoing. Smart because he didn't rush anything. And California had given him a tan, which only increased his aesthetic value on top of everything going on inside. Gary'd never had a crush on him, but he understood the people who did, his sister included. Ilan had adapted easily to the difference in coastal cultures but growing up in the artsy muddle of SoHo had probably prepped him for it. Hell, his older sister had turned into a latent hippie. Plus, that's where his mom grew up, somewhere near Anaheim, way before Disneyland. It was in his genes to look like he should surf and act like he was judging the competition.

Not weird. Never weird. Not evasive. Never evasive.

There was always the possibility something else was going on in his life, Gary supposed. Maybe his parents' move was less about suburbia and more about divorce (which was probably also suburban). Maybe no longer being the smartest kid in his class by virtue of being the youngest had got to his ego, what ego he had.

Or maybe it was that house he lived across from now, that red brick thing that had been sealed up like a sarcophagus without a tomb. A dark stain Gary had never really noticed, but now it was all he could see.

The dog was one thing, and a god-awful thing. But it wasn't the worst thing. The worst thing was that the house had spoken—or something had spoken—that day on the sidewalk after the party. It spoke to him, and it spoke to Ilan, and without speaking to each other, they each decided to bury it.

He didn't know why he understood what it wanted or what it said. It could've been some sort of Enochian language, for all he knew. He didn't like to replay the sound of it, of the voice, dry like leaves, creaking like tree limbs. *Her.* That was what the house had commanded. *Her.*

A house shouldn't command anything.

They tried to play it cool afterward. Hanging out in the apartment, smoking whatever there was to smoke, windows open to let in the life that the Village was supposed to be full of. There was ivy on Ilan's building, and they listened to it rustle on breezy afternoons, but then the breezes blew in the voice. The leaves rustled louder.

I want her. Bring her to me.

The look on Ilan's face, the way the color had gone to gray beneath his tan, the way he had dropped his lit cigarette out the window, Gary knew he knew. Gary knew he heard. They closed the window, pulling it shut against decades of sticky paint, and shut the blinds.

But the voice didn't need the breeze to come in.

It dripped from the walls, came up through the floor, and down through the ceiling.

I will have her.

Gary decided not to come back.

They hung out anywhere else.

Sometimes he could still hear that voice, but it was faint. Chicken scratch on the surface of his mind.

Ilan, he knew, heard it all the time.

On the East Side, over late-night pierogi at Veselka, they talked about him finding a new sublet without touching on why. *Be closer to the old neighborhood, man.* Ilan would nod and agree and then pause and say, *It's only for the summer.* Like if he pretended the problem wasn't a problem, it would go away. The conversation went in circles. The spaces between sentences and topics were filled with someone else's demands, but Gary wasn't sure he was hearing them like Ilan was.

Come stay over with us more, Gary told him. Ilan would nod and then shake his head. *I can't.*

Secretly, Gary was relieved.

Neither of them thought to figure out what was going on because neither of them wanted to acknowledge anything was going on. Why would they? Who could help them? They'd be diagnosed with something and locked up.

What was this called? Abnormal psychology. Folie à deux. But which of them had started it?

Sylvie knew, though. At least, she knew about the dog. She'd seen it when they did. And Gary hated that most of all because it meant that *She* knew Sylvie, even if Sylvie didn't know. She might be starting to, though, and what would that mean? He didn't want to talk to her about it. He didn't want her involved. It didn't matter that she might get it.

Last Tuesday had been a whirlwind—he ran into Ilan on the way back from the supermarket. Surprised to see him leaving, he tried to ask what happened, but Ilan's face was blotchy, his eyes wide and afraid. Gary caught his arm and Ilan started to *cry*. Not, like, sobbing blubbering hysterics, but a glassiness over his eyes and a twitching mouth.

"Let me go, man," he said. "It's getting worse."

It's getting worse.

He hoped Ilan hadn't done anything permanent. He scanned the papers, pausing at the bodies found floating in the Hudson, off the docks. He never expected Ilan to be among them, but they could be other friends.

Ilan wasn't news, yet.

Gary had other things to do, but he couldn't live with himself if his friend got hurt when they should have been helping each other, formulating a plan. Not being so chickenshit. Sylvie depended on them maintaining a barrier, but they weren't doing that, either. Or maybe Ilan was now. And maybe Gary should leave him to it.

Gary would warn Sylvie off going up there again, but maybe he should tell her why.

No, she'd just end up going to see Ilan anyway.

After dinner, Gary hoofed it up to the Village, but he didn't take a direct line. He walked diagonally, skirting the periphery of NYU, going all the way to Broadway, weaving in and out of secondhand bookstores and record shops and only briefly scanning the titles. Maybe there was something about ghosts that would help them. Maybe he should keep going east and visit Marz, ask her.

No. This was for Ilan, and it was probably an emergency.

He decided to approach from above, turning at Fourteenth Street, walking down Fifth just long enough to stand at the church and murmur a clumsy prayer first, just in case. He thought it was probably way too late to get on any lists for help at such short notice, but better late than never. Then he looped back around the block to come in from the far side. Anything to avoid crossing in front of that house.

Maybe he went to his parents. Yes. Ilan went back home to his parents' place, and he's too ashamed to call. That's what Gary would have done—but he would have called, though. Maybe it was a hetero guy thing to avoid it.

He concentrated on all of the oblivious people walking along West Tenth. Happy people embracing the summer, many of them thinking of tomorrow, and the start of the march. People walking dogs, ordinary dogs who didn't seem bothered by anything and barely gave Gary the time of day.

Up to Ilan's door, Gary took a deep breath and buzzed. He held the damn thing down.

No one looked out the closed-up windows. No one came down the stairs.

Frowning, Gary stepped back down onto the sidewalk and looked up.

"Ilan!" he shouted. Some people gave him a look; most people just ignored it and moved on.

He heard no whispering, and it gave him courage, but he wasn't going to shout that he'd call the police for a welfare check. That would get him real attention.

"Fuck," he whispered, rubbing his mustache and scouring a hand through his sort-of-brushed hair. Now what?

I'm not calling the fucking pigs, Ilan. Show me proof of goddamn life.

He realized he didn't know Ilan's parents' new number, but maybe *his* parents did. And he'd have to be careful asking for it just in case Ilan wasn't actually up there. Or maybe that's exactly what he should be doing, getting the parents all panicked and forcing him out of his hole and out of the city—

"Gary?"

Gary hadn't noticed the window open, but there he was, less tan and more jaundiced.

"Ilan! Let me up! Where've you been?" Gary shouted at him.

Ilan just stared at him for a second before disappearing back inside. He left the window open. That was promising.

It felt like having daggers at his back, suddenly, to stand with the house behind him. It could see him, but he couldn't see it unless he concentrated on the reflection in the adjacent window, and like hell was he going to do that.

When Ilan came to the front door, it still managed to startle him.

Then Gary was just relieved. And relief is like a tidal wave that pushes every other thought out. "What it is, brother? Where've you been?"

Ilan looked way worse up close. He hadn't shaved and his fair stubble caught the fading sun. One eye was bloodshot, both were rimmed with red. He had tobacco stains on his fingers. His shirt was backward—somehow, that was the worst detail. The little tag flipped up below Ilan's neck.

Gary stared at him. "Your shirt's backward."

"Bad luck to fix it. I read that somewhere once," said Ilan, and his voice was rough. Rough like someone chain smoking and not sleeping. "Come up."

Gary didn't want to, but Ilan's voice and Ilan's gaze told two different stories. It was like he was trapped behind his own eyes, pleading, desperate, but someone else was speaking.

Exhaustion might do that.

Gary followed him up.

The apartment reeked of cigarettes, the air thick and gauzy. With the window still open, the smoke gently swirled through the hall as though a body had just passed through it.

"Ilan, this is messed up. If you won't stay with us, go to your parents," Gary said as soon as he shut the door.

Ilan turned around. If he had heard Gary, he ignored him.

"I need help," he said.

"I know. Get your stuff and come stay at our place. They won't ask—"

Ilan shook his head the entire time Gary spoke, then walked down the hall.

"Quit shaking your fucking head at me!" Gary followed him into the living room, through those clacking beads. Out the open window, he could see part of the row house, sitting there, windows dark, a struggling tree rustling green leaves in front of its face as though to block its vision.

"I've tried. I've really tried hard as I can," Ilan said, and it was difficult to listen to the sound of it. His voice was so dry it almost vibrated in his throat. "All night, every day. I used to go out, just walk around, but she follows me. She won't leave me alone."

"Who won't?" Gary stayed just inside the doorway, ready to bolt.

"I've tried so hard," Ilan started again. "I really have."

"I—I know you have, man." Was it smarter to cooperate or challenge him? Was it worse that Gary knew what he was talking about?

"It's gonna kill me. I know it's gonna kill me. All the talking, talking, *talking*." For a second, a spark, Ilan sounded angry. But it passed back into exhaustion. "Nothing I do changes anything. It's pointless. You have to help me."

Ilan had been speaking to the window (yes, to the *window*), but now he turned to face Gary. Gary tried to pretend that he hadn't been parting the beads behind his back, ready to bolt out of there.

"How? What?"

"I have to go in there."

"Go in—go in—" Gary almost pretended he didn't know what Ilan meant. "Go in that house? Are you fucking crazy?"

"I need to, Gary. I have to. It's the only way out of this." Ilan was begging. "I'm going in there no matter what but you're here and it's safer. I don't trust myself, but you've been safe."

"Barely. I see that fucking dog, and Sylvie—"

"*Don't!*"

Gary shut his mouth.

"Don't say her name."

Gary clenched his jaw.

"You gotta help me stop this. We gotta stop this."

"How, Ilan? How can we stop any of this? We don't know what *this* is!"

Ilan turned back to the window—not all the way, but enough to see out of it again. "The answer's in there. I'm gonna get it, and I'm gonna stop it. It's that place or it's me. Or it's her."

Finally, Gary broke away from the threshold and came over to him. "That's bullshit. You're totally fried, man. You're not thinking right. Come with me now, get far away from here, go to your parents' place. Dig?"

324

Ilan looked at him again and Gary froze. Ilan looked angry and it felt like a threat. "Have you heard it?"

Gary didn't answer.

"You've heard it."

"I don't know what I've heard."

Again, Ilan spoke as though Gary hadn't. "Say I leave the city—it won't matter. It's not really about me or you. We're just convenient. She's not gonna give up if we disappear on her. Maybe she'll use your parents or Sylvie's friends. Or maybe she'll use a stranger. And a stranger won't care so much about your sister, will they? They'll just go find her and snatch her off the street—"

"Jesus, stop! God! All right! Fucking Christ. I'll help you, okay? I'll help you. God. But can we not fucking wait in here until dark? Can we go somewhere else? Anywhere else? Can you do that for me?"

"Swear you'll help. I'll go with you if you swear it."

Ilan was serious, and sad, and tired.

"I swear! I swear I'll help you break into that place." What the fuck was he doing? He had shit to do this week! "But come on. Let's go to Sonny's or—"

Ilan shook his head. "No! Not to anyone we know. No. She'll follow. She follows me everywhere I go."

"Who is *she*?"

Ilan didn't answer.

✦

325

They found their way back at 2 AM.

Neither had spoken more about what they were going to do, but Gary called his parents from a pay phone to tell them he was staying with Ilan, that Ilan was a little stressed and needed company, and that he would be back home in the morning to grab his stuff for the march. Then he bought a flashlight at the first hardware store they passed. He didn't buy anything else that would help get them in there. He didn't want Ilan to feel encouraged or for anyone else to feel suspicious.

Gary wondered if they would be spending a night in jail instead, but as they stood at the curb, staring up at the four floors above ground and all its black windows, he couldn't help thinking that the police probably wouldn't care. It was odd no one had ever done anything about such an obvious fire hazard (and real estate get).

There were no lights on in either of the building's neighbors. He wondered what sort of things they experienced. What sort of things they heard through their shared walls. Were they bothered at all? Why was it Ilan who had the lure through his cheek and was trying a new method to wriggle himself free? Why would *Sylvie*, of all people, be the reason for this? Sure, sometimes Gary thought Sylvie had something else going on—she had panic attacks as a kid that gave *him* nightmares—but he was never comfortable enough to define what he thought that *something else* could be. Sometimes he actually believed her when she said she was psychic. Postcog.

He was definitely not comfortable now.

The front door and basement apartment windows were boarded up, but that was it. No warnings. No notices. There weren't even old, yellowing construction permits. It was as though someone, a long time ago (judging by how gray the plywood was), had closed it up and left, and in the meantime everyone had just forgotten there was a building here at all.

Even the graffiti across the plywood and red stone, thick though it was, was old. Weather-worn and chipped. The easiest to pick out had just never been tagged over, as though everyone had decided that was the final message they needed to share: SAVE BOSJWICK.

The happy plaque commemorating Mark Twain's stay here was so incongruous that Gary almost wanted to laugh at it.

He could hear the gentle rustling of leaves above them, but he couldn't feel a breeze. The Village wasn't dead at this hour, but it felt like they were standing under glass.

Ilan exhaled, sharp, and descended the steps to the place where the front door should be. It was dark down there, owing to the worn, metal awning that had long ago turned over a dark patina. The carriage lights were dead.

"Wait," Gary whispered, but wait for what? God, he didn't want to do this. He would sooner break into a bank. At least it wouldn't be so dark.

Ilan wasn't listening to him.

Reluctantly, a chill covering his exposed arms and neck, he followed. Above him, he noticed the underside of the awning was also riddled with tags. He half-expected to see bats hanging there, too.

They had brought no tools to do this, but it was obvious they wouldn't need any. Ilan gave the plywood one quick tug, and it broke loose where it had rotted around the nails. He gently dropped it as Gary stared at the maw that now faced them. The front door wasn't even closed all the way, and beyond it was darkness.

You didn't even need my help, he thought about saying, but he didn't want to abandon Ilan to this place. If there was nothing in there—and there wouldn't be—then maybe Ilan would finally calm down and listen to reason.

Again, he heard the trees rustling above, but this time he felt the breeze. Like the building had exhaled.

Ilan didn't even look back at him, didn't even appear to hesitate before pushing the door on its unused old hinges and disappearing inside.

"Ilan!" Gary whispered, desperately switching on the flashlight, casting one look across the street, and following him. "There could be rabid animals in there!"

The old tile entryway was covered in dust. Everything was covered in dust. On the wall to the left, three of the eight old mailboxes were open and empty, but for cobwebs. The stairwell was on the left side, with a door at the end of the hall, perhaps to the back garden, which had been crudely boarded up from inside. There was even a passenger elevator, the grille locked with a chain.

There was no sound in here but their soft footsteps on the neglected floor. Not even the skittering of tiny creatures into unseen corners. Water stains peppered the cracked ceiling.

It felt like they had stuck their heads in the jaws of a gator. Every time Gary moved his flashlight, he feared what it would fall on. He feared he wouldn't get out of here.

It's just a house. A house-turned-apartment hundreds of people had stayed in since it was built. If it was so terrible, so inherently evil, why had anyone lived in it at all?

He wanted desperately to come to terms with this place before he moved deeper into it, but Ilan gave him no choice. He was already on the stairs.

The stairs and Gary groaned as one. He looked back once, staring at the door with longing, then imagining it shutting and locking them in.

"I hate this," he whispered. Then he held his breath and began the ascent.

The building was suspended in time but there were few signs of its former inhabitants. Every floor was the same as the first. Each set of apartment doors was closed as though people were simply sleeping on the other side. Some of the numbers had fallen off. The windows were unblocked but the grime let in little light. The walls were papered, but the paper was peeling. Everything smelled of mildew. Gary fought back a sneeze, fought back a cough, as though the house might not know they were in here, somehow. As though it didn't feel them walking on its bones.

He didn't know what they were looking for, but he also understood why Ilan kept going, didn't stop to rattle the doorknobs or consult with him about what to do. There was an understanding planted in both of their minds, but the roots in Ilan were stronger.

The third floor smelled worse than the rest, and the top floor worst of all. If any animals had made this place a nursery or graveyard, they had done it up here, somewhere. Still, there were no signs of it. Gary covered his mouth and nose with his shirt and watched his steps, just the same.

There were two doors up here, like there were two doors on every floor. One to the west and one to the east. The landing space between them was narrow. The western door was closed like all the rest, but the other was cracked open, and the sight of it startled Gary so badly that he almost ran back down. His neck was damp with sweat, the hand clasping the flashlight white-knuckled and shaking.

Nothing was even there—just a strip of black abyss leading into the apartment—but he didn't like that it was open when nothing else was.

Worse still, in his opinion, was how there were boards stacked in front of it, loose nails piled next to them. Someone was planning to block the door but never got around to it.

The air was stifling and ripe with decay. The decay of the building and the decay of something else, something that must have once been alive. He prayed again, softly, that it was a raccoon or a den of rats.

Ilan didn't even pause before stepping over the two-by-fours and pushing the apartment door open. Gary expected the hinges to creak, but they didn't. He didn't want to shine the light in there. He didn't want to follow.

He couldn't leave Ilan.

Inside, the smell was so thick it might have been visible in better light. It would be yellow, it would be brown, it would pucker and curl. It had leached into the paper on the walls and slid between the dry floorboards. It had settled into the narrow runner carpet that extended down the hall and into the living room. It had sunk into the furniture there—a couch pushed against one wall and two stuffed chairs pushed against another, a table with a lamp, a fireplace. It looked habitable, once—he could see the goddamn Empire State Building through the square window—but now it was shrouded in dust.

There was a small kitchen across from the front door which had a narrow window covered by a rotting curtain. Gary had lost sight of Ilan, but his footsteps were easy to follow—he had turned left and gone down the long hall to the back, where the bedroom must have been, overlooking the garden. Must have been nice, once. Right now the way was blocked by a stack of dusty furniture—a dirty chaise, a curio cabinet with a mess of broken objets d'art behind foggy glass, a sideboard tipped up on its end, doors hanging open.

Gary stopped in the hall and watched as Ilan pulled everything away, gouging the floor where the carpet didn't protect it. He didn't ask for help, and Gary wouldn't have wanted to give him any. If a doorway was blocked by furniture, it ought to stay blocked.

"Be careful, man!" he said, but he discovered he didn't like speaking in here any better than out in the hall. He shone the flashlight into the kitchen and went in, pulling at the stiff drawers, hoping to find something to defend him—them—with. But the knife block was empty and only spoons were in the drawer. He didn't open the old fridge.

There was a soft thud out in the hall, then a larger one, followed by a grunt and a huge crack.

Gary ran out of the room, dusting off his hands on his jeans, prepared to find—he didn't know. He aimed the flashlight at the bedroom door. "Ilan!"

Ilan wasn't there anymore. The rotted door jamb was splintered at the lock.

Beyond this, Gary could see nothing.

"Ilan?"

Had he really expected him to speak? If he had, Gary would easily have pissed himself, anyway.

The hallway groaned under his feet.

Gary noticed the windows, first, when he shoved into the bedroom. Two square, paneled things that were too dirty to let in the world outside. Then he noticed Ilan, standing stock still and looking toward the eastern wall. His shirt glowed in the dusk.

Gary hated it. He prepared to shine his light over the rest of the room but stopped. He wondered why he cared to see. He wondered why he even wanted the light, really, and as he moved it to switch it off, the beam fell across a fireplace, and another person.

He should yell. He should run. He should maybe actually call the police. Or the feds. Anyone.

But he didn't. He stared at it. At *her*.

She had been—would always be, in a way—a young woman. Maybe a teenager, maybe a college kid. She had brown hair to her shoulders, but it was ratty and tangled. She had skin, but it was dry and tight and colorless, and stretched uncomfortably over her skull. There was no fat left in her, not anywhere. Her eyes, closed (thank God), were sunken and filled with shadow. Her dark lips had cracked and pulled from her dark gums, which had pulled from her blunt teeth.

Her clothes were rotting away, too, exposing a skeletal frame. She was wearing what looked like pajamas, an old-fashioned baby-doll nightie—frilly shorts, frilly dress, and a matching robe that had fallen from her wasted shoulders. All of it was blue. Her hands were in her lap, broken nails—painted pink, still—emerging from beds that had receded years ago. Some of her fingers were missing.

She sighed, and the dry skin across her bloodless chest stirred. It sounded like autumn leaves.

Her whole body was seconds from collapse, seconds from dust, and yet she sighed.

Then she opened her cloudy eyes.

How terrible, Gary thought. She needed help. He could help her. Ilan was right. Thank God they'd come. Thank God.

No—no—this wasn't right. This was a waking nightmare.

But she needs help.

When Ilan began to move again, Gary flinched. He couldn't find the words to tell him to stop, don't go near her, don't give her what she wants. The thoughts came to him and then slipped out of his mind, like so much sand.

He barely understood what he was seeing when Ilan offered his arm to the body and she bit into his wrist.

Gary could hear the skin split.

"Ilan—wait—Ilan, *no!*"

Ilan didn't react to him, and soon Gary didn't remember say-ing anything at all. He found himself next to Ilan, looking down at the wasted creature. Blood pooled over her thin lips. She did not speak but he could hear her talk. She was thanking him. She would show him how grateful she was. She would give him the world, if he wanted it.

He held out his arm, the flashlight limp in his grip. He knew enough to look away but the bite into his wrist hurt—it hurt so badly he dropped the flashlight onto her lap, and it broke her leg—tore her dry skin, cracked her hollow femur. The flashlight skidded across the floorboards. She didn't react.

Reality crashed right down on Gary's head with almost the same force. He backed away, colliding with Ilan, whose expression was suspended, thoughtful, calm, eyes brimming with tears.

"We need to go—we need to go right now, Ilan. *Right now.*" Gary pulled at him, ignoring how badly his wrist stung.

Ilan was rooted to the spot. He barely shifted on his feet. "It's good," he mumbled.

"What? No—come *on*, man. Come on. *Please.*" He would never see Ilan again if he left him here, Gary thought. It punctured his mind. "Don't do this. Come with me."

He begged. He begged and pushed and pulled and wiped angry tears, but Ilan would not come with him. And as Gary caught sight of the woman in the chair, he noticed she had lifted her head, had begun to sit straighter, like a person attempting to stand. He could not see her filmy eyes in so much darkness, but he knew she was staring at him. Ilan's blood, his blood, gently dripped from the corners of her mouth.

A dark shadow moved in front of her, a shadow so black that it absorbed even the flashlight's beam, where it lay in the dust on the floor. Human arms and human hands, padding noiselessly toward them.

Gary didn't need to see that dog to know what it was.

He left Ilan there, hating himself with each floor he descended, with each step he took. He pulled open the front door and burst out into the night, tripping up the stairs. He thought of running to a phone, calling for help. He even thought of going back in with a weapon this time.

And as he reached a phone booth, shoving a hand in his back pocket for his wallet and lifting the receiver, he suddenly stopped. He shivered. He looked at his wrist. Raw and bitten but no longer bleeding. In fact, it looked as though it was hours old rather than minutes.

A whisper at the back of his mind. Ice on a bruise.

Your fear is misplaced. The body is not mine. I will find a new one. I am grateful. I am so grateful. You will have your reward.

A tall shape unfolded behind the phone box, rose above it, darker than the night, so dark it seemed without dimension. Gary noticed it only obliquely.

No, Ilan would be all right. The thought was foremost in his mind, almost a shout.

He hung up the phone.

CHAPTER TWENTY-SIX

It was viscerally hot. Too hot to wear a pair of leather gloves, but Sylvie had to do it. She couldn't think anymore—her hindsight wasn't a gift anymore, and it wasn't even a curse; it was a lure. How else could she explain a dream that matched what Gary had just told her. How would she have known?

She had to shut off her brain just to get out of the house and over to Marz's place, but she couldn't shut off her brain. Her hands were coated in sweat inside the black gloves, her legs itching in her black dance tights, and all the discomfort did was remind her why she was hiding her skin at all.

Marz had a show, but Sylvie was having the longest day of her life and couldn't keep any part of it to herself.

While Marz lined her eyes in the oval mirror of her childhood vanity, Sylvie alternated between sitting on her bed and standing up. Marz's room was a host of contrasts, as it had never been made over since she was a kid. The paper was floral, the bed had a canopy, and the walls were covered in *Interview* magazine covers, and high contrast gig flyers for Pure Hell, the Velvet Underground, the New York Dolls, the Ramones, Suicide, Blondie, The Clash, The Stooges, Roxy Music, X-Ray Spex. . . .

Sylvie had always liked Marz's room, as it had a big, bay window and a real closet. Not to mention walls that fit and kept out the rest of the house. It had always been a bedroom, too, unlike Sylvie's square of drywall and brick, and Marz wasn't the only child to ever occupy it. (A very rich one grew up and climbed out the window to meet a man waiting beside a hansom cab, never to climb back in.) But every graphic shock of poster against pastel made her want to run back outside.

Marybeth and Marz noticed Sylvie's agitation right away, of course. She wasn't hiding it. She didn't want to. She waited a grand total of six minutes before telling them her brother's confession.

"Gary told me something super fucked up," was how she began, stopping on the well-trodden shag area rug. "Like, beyond fucked up."

Marybeth, leaning back on the bed and flipping through a copy of *CREEM*, sat up. Marz paused her eyeliner and looked at Sylvie in the mirror's reflection. "Spill."

"This is gonna sound really bizarre. And really unbelievable. More than anything else."

Her friends said nothing. Their belief was a given.

"Ilan and Gary broke into the Mark Twain house because—"

"Hold up, hold up, hold up. Say *what*?" Marz almost threw her eyeliner pencil across the room as she spun around in the chair. "They got caught?"

"No—just wait. Listen. They found a woman living in an apartment on the top floor. Gary says . . . well, Gary says she looks dead, but she isn't. And—" This part was going to be hard to repeat.

It sounded too extraordinary to be real. "She kind of hypnotized them or something and bit their arms."

"Like a *vampire*?"

"Yeah. I guess. And I gotta tell you, that day he came home and the next couple days he acted like a real piece of shit. You remember seeing him when he was missing all night?"

Marybeth frowned as though recalling something she didn't want to.

"And how he said he went to all those clubs that I *know* he wouldn't be able to on his own. Was that just luck? He says she promised him a reward. Plus, Jessie Baby was terrified of him. And then Ilan came by, and it felt the same way, and Jessie Baby was scared of him, too. He could've told me to jump off a cliff and I would've done it." The realization, as she spoke it, chilled her. Everything they'd done, she'd wanted at some point (still wanted now), but it had been directed by something outside of them both, hadn't it? And it hurt to know that the time they had finally kissed, which she hadn't yet told her friends, Ilan wasn't quite himself.

"And on top of that, he's out there getting gigs when he wasn't even trying to *be* a session musician. He said he was just playing music in his apartment, and someone heard him out on the street! Gary thinks Ilan keeps going back to that house. He won't go near him now."

Her friends said nothing. She could see them look at each other, then look inwardly, combing through their thoughts.

Marz spoke first. "So, you let this vampire chick bite you and it gives you, what? Luck? Confidence? Three wishes?"

Sylvie shrugged, helpless. "Not very good luck, because Gary's losing it. I guess that's why you'd go back. Once it stops working you have to. Or . . . I don't know. I don't know why she'd *care*. What does she get out of it?"

"That's some severe monkey's paw shit."

"Why did they want to break in in the first place?" asked Marybeth in a near whisper. "That place would be dangerous even without . . . any of that."

It took Sylvie a second to repeat her brother's fears. She didn't want to canonize them, to imprint them on the world. "He's— Gary's convinced, and Ilan is, too, that the woman in there wants me for some reason."

If you will not come to me, I will come to you.

"You? She wants *you*?" said Marz. "What for?"

"I don't know. To suck my powers out?" She shrugged again and dropped backward onto the bed, her legs dangling off the side. "She can have them."

"Sylvie." Marz got up and sat down beside her. Soon, both she and Marybeth were looking down at her. "No."

"I know. But—I just have this weird idea that the lady—that the lady is Rynn."

The pause after she spoke was brief.

"How would she suddenly be some kind of vampire, though? She was shot," said Marz. "And then kidnapped."

"She disappeared. They just assumed she was kidnapped," Sylvie reminded them. "Marilyn said she was starting to act weird. The papers said she was hanging out with a bad crowd."

"So she killed her family and fled to Manhattan?"

"Sure!"

"But why don't you see her at the house in the Village?" said Marybeth. "Wouldn't you see her there, too? You looked that one time."

"I don't know. Maybe I wasn't paying attention. I was looking for Mark Twain."

Marz snorted. "For real?"

"What if something happened to her when that guy shot his family? What if he, like, possessed her? Or if something had possessed him first and spread to her. And she's spreading it now, to Ilan and to Gary." God, what if Gary woke up tomorrow and stabbed them all in their beds? Is that what Rynn did? Is that what Gary feared Ilan would do?

I love you and I want you to live.

"We don't have any proof that Rynn is up there or that she's been turned into a vampire, or anything," reasoned Marybeth. "I think we should tell Ilan's parents he needs help and get him out of here. Then we just won't go over there anymore."

"Babe, we need a better plan than just not going into the Village ever again," said Marz.

"I *have* a plan," said Sylvie, staring up at the ceiling light. "I'm going to Brooklyn. I'm gonna look at that place, if the lot is still there. And I need to do it soon because Ilan is in deep shit."

"Are you serious?" Marz stood up and returned to the vanity as though this was all she had been waiting for and now she was content. "Okay. Let's do it."

"I don't think you should come," said Sylvie as she sat up.

"You shouldn't go out there by yourself," said Marybeth.

"If you think we're not going, you shouldn't have even told us," said Marz. "That proves you want us there."

"If something happens to either of you, I'll never be able to forgive myself."

Marz turned in her chair again and stared Sylvie down. There was no fear there, nothing but warmth and confidence. "Nothing's gonna happen. Nothing happened to Marilyn, right? Or her friends. If Rynn really went full Regan or something, then she and it are not there now. It's the perfect time to go."

"The other thing is—I'm gonna use my hindsight out there. I have to because I'm the only person who can see what happened. And I don't want to see it, I don't want to know it, but I have to. For Ilan's sake, and my brother's." She realized it as she said it, and it felt like a rock had dropped on her belly. *I'm the only person who can see what happened.*

"But I'm afraid. Every time I touch something, something weird happens." She wondered if she ought to tell them about the afternoon. About Ilan. About the fire escapes. Instead, she said, "Like, people stare. Or that dog shows up."

"Maybe being farther away from the Village will make it harder to detect you," said Marybeth, though she didn't look confident in it.

"You can't stop us," said Marz. "So what if people stare? They never do anything else. Yeah, it's creepy, but we can run. Besides, if we're all gone together, it'll be less suspicious."

"Or more suspicious," said Sylvie.

341

"No one knows what we're up to, right? So who'd ever guess we're in Brooklyn?"

"It's not really about getting in trouble for it—"

"I know. But let's pretend that's the biggest issue, because right now it is. Okay?"

Sylvie made sure her final sigh was as beleaguered as her lungs could make it.

Monday was the Fourth, so they agreed on Tuesday, when their parents were occupied by their work and their day jobs. They would meet up at Marz's and take the train from the East Side. It also gave Sylvie an extra day to prepare herself.

In the meantime, she kept indoors. And so did Gary. He left his bedroom door open and stood up every time he heard the front door or the elevator. He sat with Sylvie in the living room and constantly asked her where she was going, though she never went anywhere, even downstairs. And so it was inevitable that he would notice when she actually tried to leave the house on Tuesday, after lunch.

She had hoped he wouldn't. There were times he sat in his room listening to the Eagles and Led Zeppelin and Pink Floyd at a volume to make his ears buzz, but he wasn't doing it today. She felt like he knew she was up to something. But she acted casually as she grabbed her bag and unlocked the door.

"Where're you going?" he asked her. Though increasingly paranoid, he had, at least, trimmed his mustache and taken a shower.

"To see Marz and Marybeth," she said.

"Can't they come here?"

"No," she said, holding open the door, feeling the draft from the stairwell below. "We've got plans."

"Then I'm going with you."

"Gary!"

"I don't want you alone in case—I just don't want you alone."

"I'm not gonna be alone. I'm gonna be with my friends."

But he shook his head and was already heading for his sneakers. "No. Just pretend I'm not there."

"But—Gary, come on. We're gonna be fine!" Were they?

"I'll just feel better if I can keep an eye on you, okay? Can you humor me? Because aside from—there's a maniac with a gun out there and you'd be a prime target." He wasn't going to listen. She could run out the door, down the stairs—but that didn't feel fair or kind to him. And maybe it would be nice to have him with them. She already felt vulnerable and stupid for doing this at all.

She sighed. "Okay. Look." She sighed again. "We're going out to Bushwick."

He looked up at her, one shoe tied. "Why?"

"It's—it's complicated. I just—I want to figure something out. Something that could maybe help you and Ilan and . . . and everything else."

She expected him to argue with her, but all he did was keep asking questions. "What're you talking about?"

"Because—because I think there used to be a house out there maybe connected to the place on Tenth. And I need to figure something out." That was all she could say. He didn't know about Hell's

Kitchen, about the phantom of Rynn's death. That part of the story would make even less sense than a vampire.

She expected Gary to say no, don't you dare, but instead he said, "How's that possible?"

"I'll explain it later. I swear. But I need to go so we're back before dinner."

He shoved his foot in the second shoe. "Fine. But that's all the more reason I should come. I'm the only one of us who ever goes to Brooklyn."

CHAPTER TWENTY-SEVEN

July 5th

Sylvie hadn't gone to Brooklyn in months, and even then it was only to attend a fundraiser for another dance school in Brooklyn Heights. In summers, she went out to Coney Island once or twice, but usually they went to the Rockaways when they wanted to go to the beach. (And sometimes Gary went to Fire Island.) Her maternal grandparents had lived in Bay Ridge, where her mom was raised, but they moved to New Jersey when Sylvie was still a kid. Marz's parents had almost bought an old townhouse in Fort Greene instead of the East Village, but they hadn't wanted to do all the renovation (and her mom worried there was mold that would damage her lungs).

Bushwick was an easy journey over the river (*and through lost woods*). They hopped off the J and climbed down to Broadway below, bustling with activity even on a blisteringly hot afternoon. Remnants of firecrackers were impressed upon the sidewalks, and most of the businesses still had their patriotic bunting and Fourth of July scenes painted in the windows—fireworks and Statues of Liberty. A stuffed beaver in the taxidermy shop window wore an Uncle Sam costume.

From out of her shorts pocket, Sylvie pulled a scrap of paper with the address of the demolished Herkimer-Cropsey house, and a scratchy list of cross streets.

They walked under the shadow of the tracks, past family-owned storefronts. Carpets, laundromats, shoes, furniture, a bodega on each corner. In the afternoon sun, kids skateboarded in and out of the crowds and around the cars parked on the street. An ancient bike chained to a light pole had been carved down to the frame. Music blared from stores, from boomboxes, and from passing vehicles, competing sounds that became joyful noise. Elderly ladies with silk scarves over their heads chatted in doorways, fanning themselves. Bricks tagged, trash cans overturned into the street, newspapers swirling each time a train or a car blew by.

Most of the buildings were simple row houses covered in signage and aluminum siding, giving them that postwar, modern feeling. Lintels were chopped, stoops moved or removed, a sprinkling of windows broken and boarded up. People had lived here for generations, and Sylvie could feel it without touching anything. SoHo might feel like that, someday, she thought, but for now the only commonality was the trash and graffiti.

As they waited for traffic to ease or the light to change (which-ever came first), Sylvie noticed the shifting form of a brunette girl slipping through the dense clusters of people around her. And then—there, again, with her hair in a ponytail this time, just a flash as she walked over a newer portion of sidewalk and disappeared.

Rynn, as in life, not in the throes of what she probably thought was her death. Sylvie held her breath, unwilling even to blink, then wishing she could shut her eyes and walk without opening them again. It was inevitable that Rynn would run into her, and through her, though it shouldn't have been. She should have been contained in the brick and mortar of the places she knew, but instead she peppered the street: Rynn as a small girl, Rynn as a lanky pre-teen, Rynn as Sylvie knew her but wearing different clothes. The different clothes were more jarring than she expected. Rynn existed one way and one way only, with a single wardrobe like a cartoon character, and now she was coming back to life.

Except that she wasn't.

Marybeth and Marz could tell by Sylvie's face that something was going on. Gary stayed behind them, hands in his pockets, completely oblivious.

"What is it?" Marybeth whispered in Sylvie's ear.

"She's all over the place. Rynn is."

"For real?" Again, Marz looked around them as though she would see something, too.

The activity on Broadway helped mesh Rynn with her surroundings, making her less obvious sometimes, less surprising, but they weren't on Broadway for more than a couple blocks before they had to turn onto their first cross street.

It was a sunny, sweltering day, though, and everyone was out. A fire hydrant soaked the street, kids screaming and running through the spray in sagging clothes or swimsuits. Every stoop was occupied, every fence a leaning post as people stopped to chat.

Rynn was here, too, flickering in and out of existence, wearing all four seasons' worth of clothes, talking to an invisible friend or family member, needing her hand held to cross the street or running into it without looking. She went up one stoop—not her house, because this wasn't Bushwick Avenue where she lived. She was young and wore a little sweater, a frilly dress, and walked right through a man on a rocker. He didn't stir from his afternoon nap.

Sylvie was almost getting used to the sight of her—almost—after three long blocks.

"The corner, up there—that's where it used to be," said Marz, pointing up ahead of them.

Sylvie knew. Not because of some intuition, but because the buildings began to look shabbier and shabbier. Some lots were burnt out completely, others condemned for no visible reason. Most of the ones that ran up against where the demolished house should be were boarded up and left to rot. There were no people on the sidewalks except Rynn, and the only cars on the street sat on blocks and were coated in rust.

All they could see of the corner, as they got nearer, were overgrown grasses and weeds writhing in and around a sagging chain link fence.

"There's nobody out here," said Marybeth.

Except for Rynn—Rynn was everywhere. Turning the corner over and over and over again, mostly from the same direction they had come from.

Marybeth looked behind them. No one was looking their way. They might have walked behind a veil.

"This is pretty bleak shit," said Gary, his face tense, frowning.

Sylvie hoped, desperately, that the whole lot had been turned over and filled in, new houses built, new sidewalks laid, so that nothing Rynn touched was there any longer and she wouldn't have to witness the shooting from a whole new perspective. But as soon as the rest of the lot crept into view, as soon as they made the turn, Sylvie gasped. She couldn't help it. Rynn was *everywhere*. She moved over and through herself, crossing the street, back and forth and back and forth, retracing her steps on the sidewalk until Sylvie thought it was a wonder there was any sidewalk left.

But the empty lot was the worst of it, really, because her actions weren't so uniform. She started and stopped, short circuiting like a wire in a storm, appearing here, and there, clearly interacting with people and objects and rooms that no longer existed. Floors that no longer existed. The sight of her hovering, running, laughing, talking was disorienting. Her voice fluttered like an echo around them. Sylvie had never heard her speak before, but it was no different than standing in a crowd—every word blended together into noise.

Sylvie didn't even notice that the block was empty, because she couldn't. To her, it was teeming, overburdened with the brief life of one girl.

Sylvie forgot that her brother was there, that he didn't know.

"She's everywhere," she wailed. "My *God*."

"I wish I could see it," said Marz.

"No, you don't."

"What do you mean, she?" asked Gary. "Who do you see?" He looked pale, afraid, and grabbed Sylvie by the arm as though he was going to run off with her.

Sylvie then realized what he was probably thinking, at least a little, and she stammered out, "It's not—it's not what you saw."

Marz started walking toward the property first, and Marybeth gave Sylvie a meaningful look. "You still wanna do this?"

"No, but I have to."

The only consolation was how, from this distance, Sylvie couldn't really pick out one moment from another, and that Rynn's presence around the ghost of the house was fragmented, like the scene in Hell's Kitchen. She was always alone, even when it was clear she wasn't.

It felt awful, walking through the palimpsest of Rynn. Not that Sylvie could feel or touch anything, and not that her view of the past was as solid as watching a movie, either, but she kept flinching, anyway, and tried to concentrate, tried to do what she could to make it go, like she did with other buildings and their people. She even stopped and touched the sidewalk. Nothing happened.

"What do you *see*, Sylvie?" Gary asked, his voice tight, ready to crack.

"It's complicated!" she repeated.

"I told you about—you can tell me what's happening," he insisted.

"Just—just give me a minute, okay? I—" Could she do that? Could she tell him? "I'll explain it after we're done. But I promise it won't hurt you."

"Why won't you tell me?"

Sylvie moved away from him. "I *have* told you! I've told you and told you! All my *life* I've told you!"

350

The block had the usual turn-of-the-century row houses and a couple of two-floor standalones that must have gone up during or after the war. The sidewalks were covered in loose paper and trash that blew in from every place else. The only car on the street was parked in a short driveway overrun now with weeds. From the look of it, twenty years ago someone left it there and never came back.

These would have been prime canvases for skilled kids across the neighborhood and beyond, but there wasn't a mark on any surface.

Marilyn had been right to say it felt like this place didn't exist, that people didn't notice it, or didn't want to notice it, even if they couldn't avoid walking past. Whatever happened on this block, it was nobody's business but the Lord's, and the Lord had turned His back.

"It's so quiet," said Marybeth, and Sylvie wished she could hear that silence.

If she could, she would know it was not a peaceful, pastoral quiet. None of the city noise carried on the wind. No distant sound of the train along Broadway. No elderly Brooklynites sitting on their stoops or front porches. No kids making a playground out of the street. No stray cats. No barking dogs. No birds, not even a pigeon. No cars passing through or pausing with the windows down and music up. Latin and Funk had no place here. Nor any barbecues, nor laughter. It was like stepping into a vacuum.

The double lot that the old house once occupied still had more of the house than Sylvie was expecting. She had imagined a hole, or a pile of rubble, like so many empty lots in her city, but the remains of the fieldstone mansion looked down on her from a steep incline, and the demolition was crude. In fact, several walls around the first floor hadn't been completely razed, and they crumbled now due to the elements. The front steps still stood, leading down into a foundation filled with the detritus of the upper floors.

Slightly to the back of it was a giant, barren, old growth tree, which had a large gash across its bark, like the demolition was supposed to take that, too, and failed just as efficiently. The gash ran through a gaping hole big enough to swallow a person. It was a wonder no storm had ever felled it. It was as tall as a church spire and completely dead.

Marybeth and Sylvie, with Gary walking a funeral march right behind them, stopped alongside Marz at the fence.

Already, over Rynn's fluttering voice, Sylvie could hear the gunshots—three, this time. Rynn burst out of the house, right at the top of a porch or veranda that was no longer there—there was one hit, to the shoulder, just as Sylvie knew by heart.

Then that invisible hand pulled her backward. The vision fragmented, appearing elsewhere—what must have been interior walls, now outside, giving up their secrets. Two more shots unloaded into Rynn's chest, blowing it apart, and the memory abruptly stopped. Sylvie was so focused on it that she saw nothing else. How could that girl have survived such a thing?

Over the fence she went.

"Sylvie!" Gary called to her, but he didn't wait. He and the girls climbed over next, landing in overgrown, dry grass dotted with broken bits of the old mansion.

There were no memories of Rynn's body being dragged out, or left behind, or anything else after the last two shots. Not at this side of the house, anyway. Sylvie marched up the hill, steady, and walked up the badly damaged marble steps.

"Sylvie, be careful!" everyone called to her, but she didn't hear.

Through the gap where the doors used to be, she reached in, closed her eyes, and touched the broken interior wall. She concentrated on Rynn, peeling away the other layers of history for this one alone. Her heart beat so hard she could barely stand still.

She heard screaming, first. Not the one she knew by heart, but the screams of multiple people. A woman. A child. Then another. Then an older boy. They were cut off, one by one, until Sylvie heard Rynn and quickly opened her eyes as the first shot hit. It went right through Sylvie's chest and she gasped, though she felt nothing, and she stepped out of the way, as though it mattered.

A dark-haired man of medium height and thin build grabbed Rynn by the hair and began to drag her back. The size of him belied his apparent strength. He had been there all along, but Sylvie had never seen him before. Rynn hit at his wrist with her good arm, kicking and scrambling and sobbing—the scene in Hell's Kitchen had cut off by now—and as soon as he threw her back into what was once a foyer instead of a hole in the ground, he shot her four more times, blowing out her chest, exposing bone and tissue through her purple sweater. Sylvie couldn't help shutting her eyes in the middle of it, and when she opened them, when it was quiet again, Rynn's body was just lying there. Her eyes were open and unseeing—she *had* to be dead. The wounds gaped, ribs smiling like bared teeth, and blood pooled beneath her while the man stood above her, breathing hard, laughing or crying or maybe both.

Sylvie waited, her heart beating as hard as Rynn's wasn't—because it *wasn't*. Because Rynn was *dead*.

"There!" The sound of his voice startled Sylvie so badly she almost drew her hand back. He looked up and bellowed at nothing and no one in the now empty house. His voice echoed off walls that no longer stood. "Take your pick!"

As he walked away, he had to step over two other bodies, and as he did so he howled in rage or pain or something worse than both, and Sylvie immediately let the other memories of the house pour back in before he ended his life, too.

She took her hand away.

Stepping back, she realized she was shaking. She vaguely noticed her brother standing out in the weeds, watching as Marz and Marybeth investigated the injury to the tree. There were no shadow figures, no whispers carrying in on the breeze.

Through the other piles of rubble, Rynn carried on, laughing and talking with people Sylvie couldn't see. Sylvie cast one look back as she heard the shot, straight out of Hell's Kitchen, and noticed Rynn standing in the reconstructed hall—not staring, really, but looking at something. Then she appeared to open something, like a door—and it was difficult to see with so many other versions of Rynn tripping through her, so Sylvie touched her hand back to the wall and saw not just Rynn, but centuries of other people coming in and out of a jib door that Rynn now nudged open, too. Sylvie could watch her progress without touching anything, so she pulled her hand away.

She had to move, though, walking across a pile of boards and rubble to where Gary was standing at the dark maw of the old cellar, staring into it with a look of trepidation. His armpits and collar were damp with sweat.

She decided to walk around to him, because she didn't want him over there on his own. It gave her a closer view of what Rynn was up to, anyway, and she stood next to her brother and watched.

Rynn had descended a set of (invisible) steps and emerged into the cellar that had hooked Gary's attention. There wasn't much there now, only some old, rotting shelves and more rubble from other parts of the house. Whatever was down there back then, though, made Rynn gasp.

Sylvie had to let more history in to see what Rynn did, because there was nothing in the room with her.

The sight was confusing, then it was ugly. The room was a cellar, a larder, shrinking and expanding in size over the years and changes to the house. And there were women down there, dead and alive. Women with and without their heads. Men coming in—one in particular—to do the job. To bury their bodies in the soil—gone now, and history showed their bones uncovered and lifted away by different men in a different time.

But what had stolen Rynn's breath away was something even more disturbing—a tall, strange woman with long, brown hair that hung lank in her face and down her back. Her skin was mottled gray-green. Her wide-set, glassy eyes didn't seem fully human, nor did the shape of her face, which seemed like too many ideas for too many faces in one body. Nothing quite sat where you would expect

355

it to be. Sylvie was thankful for all the other activity that passed in front of her and across time, but the woman was more than a head taller than anyone who came down there and impossible to miss. She didn't seem to notice Rynn, but Rynn noticed her. Sylvie took her hand away and Rynn remained.

This was weird within weird.

Sylvie climbed into the cellar and touched one of the old shelves with one hand. She stuck her other hand into the over-turned dirt, until she felt some rotting boards—the woman was there, still unmoved by Rynn. And then a man entered the cellar through Gary, a man too far outside of Rynn's timeline to have overlapped. Too outside of any of the timelines this house suppos-edly saw. He wasn't the same man who slaughtered the women. He would not have ever met him. He reminded Sylvie of witch trials and Pilgrims, but he was dressed informally as he went down a dif-ferent set of stairs, no longer extant. There was no mansion back when this scene happened. There had been another house beneath it all, and this cellar was once a wooden lean-to with nothing in it but that woman.

The woman noticed the man at once and came forward, and he obediently held out his arm for her.

"Sssamuel," she said, in the voice that had been knocking around in Sylvie's head for weeks. Sylvie pulled her hands away, afraid the woman would notice her through time.

"Sylvie, what are you—" Gary was speaking, but Sylvie gulped the air and dug both her hands into the dirt. Something was hap-pening here that she needed to see.

Rynn had a close view of the man—Samuel—and the unnamed woman. Rynn shouldn't have a view of this at all, but she did, and as the woman leaned down, Rynn covered her mouth and fled. Sylvie covered her mouth for another reason.

Two, really, but one more than the other.

That woman had bitten the man's arm.

But *Rynn could see it.*

It was in the forgotten past and *Rynn could see it.*

Lost in what this might mean, frozen as her whole world suddenly shrank, Sylvie was there as Rynn returned—a different Rynn, a different day. Laughing, covering her mouth in a happier mood, she burst down the steps, and she wasn't alone. The father—the man who had ruthlessly taken a shotgun to his own family, had rendered Rynn's chest to pulp and exposed rib—was holding onto her waist, and once they reached the cellar floor, they began to kiss.

Sylvie pulled her hand away and averted her eyes to avoid seeing whatever they were going to do next. Then she backed up and returned to the grass, brushing the dirt from her skin, picking at it from beneath her nails. Gary had moved on, but he was looking at her with as much confusion as Sylvie must have had on her own face.

What the hell went on in this place? The papers said it was mass murder. Marilyn said it was ghosts. They didn't say anything about a woman feasting on blood. And then there was Rynn.

Sylvie's eyes followed Rynn everywhere else now. She had to know—she had to see if what she thought was true was *true.*

Everywhere Rynn paused, Sylvie attempted to see what she was looking at. And every reaction Rynn had, every way her head moved, matched the scene that Sylvie saw unfolding. A German-speaking man pointing at something in the paper, laughing and laughing until a woman came into the room and he showed her whatever it was. She started laughing, too. Rynn smiled at the scene. Sylvie was in shock.

Rynn could see everything Sylvie could. Rynn could see the past.

There was a Rynn at the back of the house who was very young indeed and appeared to be picking flowers and talking animatedly with someone Sylvie couldn't see. She was there several dozen times over, getting older, her hair getting darker. There were so many versions of her that Sylvie was sure they could all be her. And the flowers weren't just in the memory—there was a patch several yards from the tree even now. They didn't look healthy, were probably being pummeled by the heat. Were those the things Rynn had told Marilyn were good luck? They didn't look like much, but Rynn sure seemed to love them.

Sylvie thought of Marilyn, and she knew she could probably find her here, if she concentrated on it, but she couldn't bring herself to do it. It felt like a violation—and maybe everything Sylvie did was a violation, but she didn't know these people. She knew Marilyn.

Really, she just didn't want to stop following Rynn. She didn't need more proof, but she wanted it. She had entirely forgotten why she had come out to Bushwick at all.

There was Rynn out by the tree. Sylvie started to run over, but almost immediately came to a stop. A different girl had appeared—briefly—and there! Again! A golden blonde girl, sometimes wearing a cap or a hat, other times wearing a braid or a bun, centuries out of time. Sylvie had never seen her before, and she was spit from the memories of the dead tree, just like Rynn.

Rynn was watching the golden girl, too, with the same puzzled expression that Sylvie had when Rynn first showed up.

Sylvie wanted to see more of this new interloper, and she slipped through all the copies of Rynn and pushed her hand to the bark of the dead tree.

Instead of the golden blonde girl, a man came to the tree, frazzled, unshaven, unwashed. Samuel. He had the girl's same blonde hair, but it was lank. In his arms he carried bones and into the tree he tossed them. Then he dropped to his knees and prayed in a tongue even stranger than the whispers. He did this again and again, and Sylvie could mark the differences in days by the new strain on his face. He hacked at the knot, carving it wide open like a screaming jack o'lantern, spraying dirt and bark into his face. Sap oozed in thick rivulets. Sylvie winced at each blow. But at the same time, a stronger, healthier, cleaner version of Samuel dragged a bleeding head and dropped it near Sylvie's feet.

Between all these events, a figure climbed out of the tree's newly formed mouth.

The tall, brown-haired woman climbed out of the tree, looking like too many people and not like a person at all. Her too-long fingers of her too-large hands curled over the sap-covered, bleeding lips, and the rest of her unfolded from a diabolical, unseen womb. The entire trunk shivered, the bark creaked and split. The leaves began to blacken and fall. It was the woman from the cellar, the woman both she and Rynn had seen drinking from the man's arm. Sylvie was standing off to the side of the hole, and she knew this wasn't happening now, but it *had* happened, and it made her feel weak. She needed to look away, but she couldn't look away. She needed to scream but she was too shocked.

It's only a movie.

It's only a movie.

It's only a movie.

Then came worse things. Sylvie now realized the healthy version of Samuel had dropped the woman—the *creature's* head at her feet. Then he took the creature's headless body and shoved it back into the knot—in pieces. An arm. A thigh. Half of a torso. His body was saturated with blood and smelled even worse. Sylvie was grateful he had carved her up where she couldn't see it. Then, at the base of the tree, he began to dig. And he dug and he dug—and older versions of him prayed—and into the hole he put the head and covered it in dirt. Large, wide-set, glossy eyes stared up at him as he did this, but he didn't flinch. The lipless mouth was slightly open as though she had died mid-laugh, her pointed teeth stained pink.

When he was finished, he returned with a lamp and a guttering candle, but the flame failed in the rain. He wailed something in what sounded like old Dutch, raging at the sky, smashing his lamp against the trunk, trying to start a fire that wouldn't take.

In other moments, she saw the girl with the golden hair—fleetingly. She stood far from the tree, her foot touching a root without realizing it, impressing herself on the history of this place. She held white flowers. She stared at the tree in sadness. The creature came up behind her, towering over her, but did not touch her.

"Beautiful Metje, why do you shy from me?"

Desperate to push that woman away, Sylvie allowed in other layers of time. But few other people interacted with the tree, and it was easy to follow the moment of its desecration. She noticed one or two people attempt to climb it, or look into the terrible hole, but half of them left with anxious glances over their shoulders, or a hand clamped over their ears.

Sometimes she saw people simply standing in front of it. She saw a man do it, a man who first appeared in a brocade overcoat with powdered hair and was later reduced to a blood-spattered linen shirt and bare feet.

She saw Hessians in blue and white uniforms. She saw a young man come to the tree with a lady on his arm. He shoved her to the ground and wrung her neck. In the middle of this scene appeared a little boy who must have come from a century later, in his short pants and long curls. Sometimes he was there with his older sister, and she would hand him the white flowers and he would shake his head and run away.

After them, there were many other children, children from an increasingly dense and diverse neighborhood, who heard the stories of the skeletons and the ghosts and wanted to know. Teenagers laughing and drinking from one decade after another, before "teenager" was even coined, looking into the mouth of the tree for a scare and a laugh, then sometimes for a second glance.

Then came Rynn, and Rynn again, and then Rynn with a small, doe-eyed child in curls and a stiff, tartan dress. *Marilyn.* The little girl didn't like the tree, so they didn't linger, just looked for a moment before moving on to where the flowers grew.

"My mama said grandma made her pick 'em for protection. Mama always had a vase of 'em when I was little," Sylvie heard Rynn say. "Grandma said they're good luck flowers. When she picked them, she said they saved her."

"From what?"

"She just said that they make things quiet in your head."

Marilyn's tiny voice responded, but they were too far away, smothered beneath other sounds.

And then Sylvie saw Rynn's killer. She shouldn't have been surprised and yet she almost jerked away. He stared at the tree as often as Samuel had prayed, and sometimes he cried and begged it to give him peace, that he couldn't, *wouldn't.* He tried to swing an ax, but the head broke from the handle. Then sometimes he would smile or laugh or look at his hands as though they were filled with something beyond his comprehension, though nothing was there. Then the fear would return, and he would cover his ears.

Suddenly there were hands on Sylvie's arms, pulling her sideways. She snapped back to the present as though she hadn't been there in days. Or years. Or centuries. Seconds passed before she realized what was going on.

"We need to go." Marz.

"Your brother is cracking up." Marybeth.

Gary was in the patch of wildflowers, having walked a wild, restless path around the whole property to get there. On his knees, he was picking everything in sight, weeds and flowers alike.

Sylvie turned and carefully walked up beside him. She could hear him talking under his breath. "Gary? What're you doing?"

When he heard Sylvie, he jumped up and began shoving the flowers at her. "Take these," he demanded, almost throwing them at her and reaching down to grab more until she pulled on his arm.

"Gary, *stop!*"

He wheeled around and grabbed both of her arms and began pulling her away. His face was pale, his eyes were red. "Go. Sylvie. *Go.* We have to—you need to get away from here. She knows. She knows what—you have something she wants—she needs to get rid of it. The girl had it, and the last one had it, too. She needs to get rid of it and she needs a new body and it's going to be you because you'll heal once you're dead."

CHAPTER TWENTY-EIGHT

The girls couldn't get Gary to calm down, even as they peeled off the property like their feet were on fire. People stared at him, at them, as they sat on the train back to the city, and for once Sylvie understood why and wasn't afraid. Gary was quieter, but when he sat, he shook his leg, and he couldn't stop gasping for air and looking over his shoulders—as though someone would be outside the window, staring in at him, *Twilight Zone* style.

Nobody intervened, of course. It probably looked like he was having some kind of bad trip, which was what their parents thought when Gary kept raving long into the evening.

"You can't leave her alone!" he kept yelling at everyone. "She knows—she's known a long time and she's tried to use me—she's still using Ilan—she's not gonna stop!"

When Sylvie's parents asked her if she knew what was going on, Sylvie would only shrug. And it felt so unfair, but the truth wouldn't help. They'd only think both kids were losing it. And maybe Sylvie could take them up to the house on West Tenth, but that would risk her parents' safety, too.

Gary wouldn't eat. He paced in front of the living room windows. He turned the television set up so loud that Geneva immediately ran over to switch it off. Jessie Baby kept whining, kept retreating to their parents' room.

Eventually, they decided he needed medical attention.

Sylvie didn't know what to do then, either. Would he be safer in a hospital? They'd find nothing in his system and probably discharge him immediately, anyway. Maybe they'd put him in a psych ward. She felt burning guilt as their parents attempted to reason with him, and all she could do was let whatever was going to happen, happen.

"You can't leave her *alone!*" he kept yelling. He didn't seem to object to the hospital, only that Sylvie wasn't coming with them.

"I'll go," she tried to insist, but her parents looked at her and her dad said, with all the finality in the world, "No."

He called a cab company while their mom gently held Gary's arms and reminded him that Sylvie had been home alone countless times. That she wouldn't dare go out while they were gone, right? (Sylvie nodded.) That the doors would be locked, that Jessie Baby would be with her, that no one had ever broken into their building.

Gary would hear none of it, so in the end, Sylvie had to come, too.

She didn't mind. She didn't want to be alone, anyway. After their afternoon in Brooklyn, the world was suddenly very quiet without thousands of overlapping voices. She hadn't had any time to process a single second of it, but she could feel a tidal wave of thoughts trying to break through.

The hospital kept Gary overnight. They had to give him tranquilizers so he could sleep. He must have been grateful, at least, for that.

Sylvie's parents tried to tease more information out of her, but the only lie she could come up with was, "He and Ilan fell out, and I think it's really upsetting him."

"Why'd they fall out?"

Sylvie shrugged. "Ilan's been acting a little different, but I don't know what happened."

"Hasn't Ilan talked to you about it?" asked her mom.

"No. He's gotten really busy playing music and stuff, I think."

Gently. "And you haven't seen him lately?"

Sylvie shook her head.

Her parents gave each other looks only they could read before letting her go.

In her room, Sylvie flopped down on her bed. For a while, she let her brain turn to white noise. Then out of the static came her first coherent thought: *Rynn could read buildings, too.*

Was this an answer? Was this *the* answer? Was this why she could see Rynn and Rynn alone? It wasn't because her ability was broken; it was that it was on the same frequency as someone else. (Two someone else's, even, because there was that other girl there.) That was why she couldn't see the man pulling Rynn back inside. That was why she couldn't see Rynn after the attack unless she touched the surface that bore witness. Rynn had died after the third shot. The final two were to make sure of it.

But, wait—Rynn *hadn't* died, Sylvie kept having to remind herself. That was the whole thing! She hadn't died. She'd gone to a hospital and moved on with her life for another year. Or another twenty years, because she might be up there in that apartment, acting the part of a vampire. Just like that strange woman in the cellar.

Sylvie sat up.

Everything she had witnessed on that property was stirred up in her mind, but foremost of all was Marilyn's presence there. Sylvie couldn't stop thinking about the little girl in her tartan pinafore, hand in Rynn's, apparently wandering over to pick flowers at the back of the lot. She couldn't stop wondering how this ability was handed down and why it had to come to her. Because it truly felt like a trap now, more than anything else, and that burned her up. She had come to think of her powers as intrinsic as breathing, and now she felt like Marie Curie diving head-first into radiation.

She wanted to know more about what Marilyn did and saw on that property, but she didn't want to ask directly. Instead, she decided to phone Marilyn and ask about the archives, see if she had gone into them and learned anything new about Rynn's fate. But Marilyn didn't answer her phone.

It was a struggle to sleep. Sylvie kept dreaming of Rynn and Marilyn, hand in hand, both of them tiny little girls together, which was impossible. They skipped through a velvet garden of white flowers before stopping to pick some. The roots of the flowers were strong, and their small arms couldn't even snap the stems. They pulled and pulled, until a hand came through the dirt—five long-stemmed fingers ending in five bright, white flowers. Instead of screaming, the girls laughed hysterically. Then the shadow of the tree fell over the garden and the flowers withered up, and the hand receded into the ground, and the ground began to sink around them, and Ilan's body emerged from the dirt, bloodless and cold. Sylvie woke up so sharply that she slipped off her bed. She landed hard on her side, her hip bone digging into her arm beneath her.

She was too startled to feel the bruise until she officially woke up to the smell of her dad cooking bacon.

Gary wasn't coming home today, her parents later found out. His choice. They talked to him briefly before he asked to speak to Sylvie.

"Hey," she said.

"Hey, Silverado." A pause. "Sorry about, uh, me, I guess."

"How are you?"

"Strung out and loving it." And he did sound a little thick in the tongue. "Is everything okay over there? Has . . . anyone shown up?"

"Nope. Everything's okay here, except it's a hundred million billion degrees."

"That's an exaggeration!" called her dad.

"I'll probably go get an ice cream."

"Be careful, if you go. Take Marybeth or Jessie Baby. Actually, yeah, take Jessie Baby. She knows her shit." Gary's voice dropped to a near-whisper. "I need a couple days, I think. If it turns out to be a little too *One Flew Over the Cuckoo's Nest*, then I'll change my mind."

"I never saw that."

"Forget it. Just promise me you'll be careful. I know I sounded like an insane person but it's true. There's something about you that—anyway. Ilan knew it. He thought he was getting her off your trail, I guess. And I think I knew it, but I didn't want to admit it. I don't know how . . . I don't know how that thing found out about you—I don't even know what was up with you out there, either, by the way."

Sylvie eyed her dad, but he was looking at the TV.

"I told you," she said.

"Are you actually psychic?" He might have meant it as a joke, but he didn't laugh.

"Not in the way people think of."

"Can you see the future?"

"I don't even know what day it is tomorrow."

"Thursday. The past?"

"Postcog, all the way."

"You ever heard of James Randi's prize for genuine psychics? It's a few thousand bucks."

Sylvie snorted. "I know. He'd never believe me. No one ever believed me, except Marz and Marybeth."

A pause. "I always . . ." Another pause. "Explain later. Please. You were freaking me out."

"Sorry. But likewise."

"Sorry. Anyway, love you, Cool Breeze."

"Love you, too."

After lunch, Sylvie's parents dispersed into errands. Whether they had ever taken Gary's commands seriously or not, they weren't now. Her dad was off to buy sausage and cannoli on Bleecker, and her mom went to meet some people organizing the next artist talk. As soon as they left, as soon as the lock turned, Sylvie couldn't help feeling anxious. Part of her imagined that Ilan would step out of the elevator or climb in through the skylight. Maybe he had been lurking down below, in the studio, in the dark. It wasn't natural to be scared of him, and she knew that if she saw him, she would want to save him.

But Jessie Baby was in a very typical mood, drinking her water and going to her bed in the living room, where she curled up and promptly fell asleep. Above them, the ceiling fan whirred, gently playing with the sunlight that still streamed in even though the curtains were closed to keep it out. It was brutally hot.

Wally's. She was going to go to Wally's and get an egg cream or something. Something normal and something cold. Thinking back on what her brother suggested, she decided to wake Jessie Baby up and take her with.

Her leash hung with the coats by the door, and Sylvie half-heartedly peeled off her socks and shoved her feet into her sandals as she retrieved it. Turning around, though, Jessie Baby was already awake again, and standing up.

Sylvie whistled to her. "Wanna go for a walk, Jessie Baby? W-A-L-K?"

The whirring fan disguised the low growl, but it did not disguise the sharp barking. Jessie Baby's hackles were up, her ears down, her whole body rigid. Sylvie dropped the leash and almost tripped over her own feet trying to back away from nothing at all.

Jessie Baby's barking grew more aggressive, more frantic, as though she saw bears and wolves descending from all sides. She began to hurriedly back out of the living room, her entire body taut as a slingshot, her teeth bared. Could dogs go full *Exorcist*? Would a priest know how to handle that?

The living room curtains were gauzy and there was nothing out there that Sylvie could see except the shadow of the fire escape. But now she feared that Ilan was standing out there, and in that fear, she could almost see his shadow leaning down to peer inside.

It was her dog's unceasing barking that drove her to finally look outside, easing aside one curtain just enough to allow some of the street and the sidewalk on the opposite side to come into view. She was looking for Ilan, but she didn't find him. She didn't see the shadowy dog, either. But Jessie Baby was still growling, even as she retreated down the hall.

And that was when Sylvie noticed Marilyn. She stood stock still on the sidewalk, facing Sylvie's building, staring up at it, and Sylvie immediately stumbled away from the window.

"What the hell," she whispered. She didn't know what to do. She didn't really even know what she was seeing—already she thought she had dreamt the whole thing up, that it was just some other dyed blonde woman.

Then the buzzer rang, and Sylvie nearly shot straight to the ceiling.

Jessie Baby began barking all over again.

She just wouldn't answer—that's what she would do. But what if her parents came home? It was a split-second series of thoughts, because the buzzer still hadn't stopped. Someone was holding it down.

A minute passed. Sylvie held her hands over her ears, her mouth dry, her arms shaking. Jessie Baby alternated between howls and barks and even whimpers. She stood in the doorway of the master bedroom, unwilling to come out any farther.

It was mostly Jessie Baby's fear that made Sylvie open the door. She couldn't stand the idea of torturing her dog a minute longer.

She grabbed her bag, held her keys, and locked the apartment behind her—then wondered if that was a mistake. What if she needed to run inside quickly? But she wanted to keep people out. Maybe she should take the elevator, but she didn't want to get down to the front door that quickly—and it would open right there into the entryway, where Marilyn or whoever was at the door would see her immediately. If they didn't break the glass to get inside first.

What she really hoped was that Marilyn would go away before she got down there. She took her time, but taking her time freaked her out, too, because she had grown uneasy in the stairwell. She began to imagine someone behind her, slinking over the steps, ready to push her or grab her.

At the half-open door into the lobby, Sylvie—her heart loud in her ears—gently leaned out just enough to look through the windows in the doors. And there was Marilyn. And it was only half a comfort to her now.

Marilyn never came here unannounced, and it was the middle of a weekday.

Sylvie felt like she had run a marathon when she finally stopped hiding and opened the front door—immediately stepping outside to keep Marilyn from coming in.

Sylvie wanted to expect the usual smile and the cheerful, "Hey, Applesauce!" but wasn't surprised when instead Marilyn sort of grimaced. Her hair was frizzy, like she had styled it in the morning and forgotten it needed maintenance in the humidity.

"Hi, Sylvie."

When she didn't say or do anything else, just sort of blinked, and frowned, Sylvie began to feel weird. "What's up? Wanna go for an egg cream or something? That's where I was going." She gripped her purse strap. Tried to catch her breath.

"All right. That sounds nice!" For a second, Marilyn sounded okay, but as they walked, she drifted off again.

"I came to get you," she said, though it took her several seconds to finish the sentence.

"Came to get me?"

"Yes. I have—yes, let's keep walking." But as she said this, she stopped walking entirely. Sylvie turned to look at her. Marilyn beamed at her, touched her hair. "Oh, you're very pretty, Sylvie. Yes, you're a very pretty girl."

"Um. Thanks." Sylvie looked up and down the street, at the trucks stuck at angles in front of loading docks, and a man carrying an enormous canvas across the street. Life went on as usual.

Marilyn frowned again, her eyes became unfocused. She was the sort of person who would wear nice sunglasses no matter the weather, but today she wasn't. That little detail bothered Sylvie as much as the unkempt curls.

Sylvie glanced at Marilyn's arms, which were bare beneath a pussybow blouse suitable for work. Her skin was free of marks, free of bites. But her left hand was balled in a fist, and Sylvie realized she was clutching a few crushed white flowers in her hand. Her knuckles were white with the effort of holding them. Sylvie frowned.

Marilyn stumbled a little but caught her balance and kept talking. "We really shouldn't have gone out there. Oh, it was nice, the first time, when she was still around." She began to whisper. "But later it was strange."

What?

"You have to come with me, Sylvie," she said, stronger now, pulling on Sylvie's arm.

"Okay," Sylvie said.

"She told me to pick them for protection, but I think it all came to you!"

"What do you mean? The—the flowers? You've got them in your hand."

Marilyn ignored the question.

Each time they had to wait to cross the street, Marilyn would either turn to touch her hair and tell her she was pretty, or she would whisper about how she shouldn't have gone out there. She never explained where *there* was, though Sylvie had a good idea. She no longer needed an ice cream to feel a chill.

They were nearly to Wally's when Sylvie heard Marilyn say, "Yes, and Ilan thinks you're lovely, too."

Sylvie felt sick. Marilyn didn't know Ilan, had never met him. "What did you say?"

"The strangest thing happened to me today," Marilyn continued, frowning briefly.

"How do you know Ilan?"

"The strangest thing. A dog told me to come visit you!"

Sylvie stopped walking. "What?"

"Come with me, Sylvie," Marilyn said again, trying to get her to cross Prince Street. Sylvie had to pull her back to keep her from walking in front of a van.

She had no intention of following Marilyn. The day after Sylvie thought about her, called her, dreamed about her at the so-called Dutch house, she showed up at Sylvie's door acting like she was on quaaludes. Until now, until this moment, Sylvie hadn't considered that whatever was happening would step past Ilan and Gary and go after someone else in her life, unprompted. But the thing—whatever the thing was—knew Marilyn existed already, didn't it?

Sylvie went along with Marilyn's demands until they reached Houston Street. There, she pulled Marilyn near the curb and began to wave her arm, desperate. She didn't want to let Marilyn go, but she didn't know what else to do.

When a cab pulled over, Sylvie dragged her to the door and helped her get in the back. To Marilyn, she said, "This way will be faster." But Marilyn wasn't listening. Maybe it was muscle memory that encouraged her to get in. Sylvie assumed she took cabs everywhere. That seemed like a reporter thing to do.

Sylvie had to pass on directions and check that Marilyn had the bills to pay. The driver looked confused, more than a little annoyed, but the sight of the money changed his expression to resignation.

And maybe a glance at Marilyn, too. She did look put-together, but she was definitely out of it.

"She your sister?" he asked.

Sylvie sighed. "Yeah. Older sister. Bad trip or something." *Older brother. Bad trip or something.*

Sylvie handed back Marilyn's purse and shut the door. She noticed Marilyn suddenly wince and drop the flowers as though they had burned her. Then her head turned sharply in Sylvie's direction, giving her a hard stare before she lunged, slamming against the window just as the cab pulled away from the curb.

Though the taxi was gone, Sylvie still scrambled across the sidewalk and began to run.

Everyone she knew was in danger, but Marz and Marybeth seemed the most vulnerable of all now. They had been to the property, like Marilyn. They had seen the dog—and Marilyn had, too, all those years ago. But Marilyn had those flowers—a lot of good they had done her—and her friends had nothing at all.

But as Sylvie ran first for Marz's place, not wanting to be near her own house just yet, just in case her parents would come home, she decided she couldn't go into Marz's home, where her sisters were, and her parents. Something was flipping through Sylvie's brain like a Rolodex. She'd used her hindsight yesterday—that had been a mistake. The distance didn't matter. That *thing* would always know.

Bypassing Marz's house, Sylvie kept going east, into Tompkins Square Park. It had been a part of their ritual for years. They would visit Ray's Candy Store, buy some fries, and crash on a bench.

She couldn't fathom the thought of eating, but she crashed on a bench, anyway.

The most dominant sound was a Hare Krishna drum circle. On the next bench over, an elderly Ukrainian couple held an intense discussion over a paper bag of plums, while a girl walked by holding a slice of pizza between her teeth as she tried to re-tie the knit ribbon around her braid. Pepperoni dropped to the sidewalk, hitting her shoe. Walking past her was a young man trailing a thick smell of weed, his army uniform tattered at the elbows and knees.

Every boy with light, long hair snagged Sylvie's attention and almost sent her running. Every blonde woman with bouncing curls made her start. She hoped that Marilyn had gotten home. That the driver wasn't hurt—that *Marilyn* wasn't hurt. She wondered where Ilan was, what gigs he was playing, if he missed hanging out with her, with Gary, with everyone. She even considered going to a pay phone and calling his parents—but she didn't know their number.

"Sylvie."

Sylvie looked up, into the face of a dishwater blonde, white girl with long braids, walking a small dog. The dog had stopped to eat the pepperoni, but now it was staring up at its owner.

"Sylvie," the girl said again, and though her expression was empty, her voice was harsh. Her dog barked.

Sylvie jumped off the bench and ran out of the park.

She didn't really know what to do—go to that house on West Tenth, beg for whatever was in there to leave everyone alone?

Trade her life for theirs? She didn't understand what she was even up against.

If some blood-sucking corpse in an old house wanted her, was it noble or was it stupid to just give up and give in?

Stupid. It was stupid. She wasn't going to do that. Whatever was happening would just keep going, would just get worse. *Sylvie* was the one who could see it all, right? She was the *only* person who could find a way to cut it off at the roots. Or the head.

The head.

The woman (*women*) in the cellar. The figure in the tree.

The girl had it, and the last one had it, too. She needs to get rid of it and she needs a new body and it's going to be you because you'll heal once you're dead.

Rynn wasn't Rynn anymore. Sylvie knew this as certain as she knew the color of her sandals (white). Rynn had died during the shooting and something had slithered inside of her and turned her into a marionette. But she had been neglected all these years, and human bodies will do what human bodies will do—rot. So now that something needed someone new.

Why Sylvie's hindsight mattered, she didn't get it. When Rynn died, so had her powers. As soon as the last shot stopped her heart, Rynn no longer appeared without Sylvie's searching touch. The ghost, the voice, the creature—seemed to have gained nothing from it. So, then, why Sylvie? There were so many other bodies in the city.

. . . you'll heal once you're dead.

Rynn was dead, but her wounds had healed. The papers said so. It was a miracle.

Sylvie had no scars. Not even the smallpox vaccine left its tell-tale mark on her arm. Every injury healed completely, some- times as quickly as a day or two, if it was small enough. Her broken ankle took two weeks. But she'd never had surgery, or even had her wisdom teeth removed, so she had nothing major to use for scale. And she wasn't about to test the limits now. Rynn had died a gruesome death, one that was now destined for Sylvie if she didn't keep walking.

I'm not goddamn Wolverine.

She would rather deal with a vampire. A real vampire, whatever those were. Stake through the heart. Easy. Maybe in the time she hadn't seen Ilan, he had learned to be a Van Helsing. He was smart and capable and intuited things about the situation that no one else had, right? Sylvie stopped in front of Grace Church and thought of him and hoped it was true. But stopping and hoping weren't good enough. She wanted to talk to someone, even though she knew no one could help her.

Sylvie didn't know how on earth she was going to find one alleged psychic in a city lousy with them. Delilah Marie, that was what Marilyn called her. If Sylvie couldn't get her number out of the yellow pages or find it stuck to a random post some- where, she wouldn't go. Not just because it would take ages to find her, but because she didn't want to bother Marilyn about it, or about anything.

Sylvie hunted for the nearest pay phone that still had a weather-beaten directory shoved beside it. Three minutes later, she was almost relieved when she found the ad in the yellow pages:

DELILAH MARIE

READINGS AND CONSULTATIONS
DIAL _____
_____ 42nd Street

Sylvie picked up the receiver and opened her change purse. She definitely wouldn't have enough money to pay whatever this woman would probably want, but she plugged in her dime and dialed, anyway.

The phone rang and rang and rang and no one picked up, leaving Sylvie no other option but to head up to Forty-Second Street and meet Delilah Marie face-to-face. If she was even there. Sylvie quickly looked at the directory's date to make sure it was current.

The so-called psychic's building was off Eighth Avenue, a place her parents wanted her to venture even less than Times Square. It was a small, brick apartment with four floors. Delilah Marie's sign was in the window of a first-floor corner unit. Undoubtedly, the history here was rich and probably sordid, but all Sylvie did was ring the buzzer.

She hoped and didn't hope that no one would answer, and she didn't practice what to say. But a woman came to the door in a one of those kimono-style robes that were all the rage fifty years earlier, though it was probably younger than its wearer by a couple of decades or more.

"Yes?" the woman had a smoke-and-whisky voice. Her hair was brushed and rolled into a perfectly grandmotherish updo still stuck in the Sixties. Her face was fully made up, which probably looked better in dimmer light. She still had handsome cheekbones, prominent under her thinning skin.

Sylvie had no idea what to say to her. "Are you Delilah Marie?"

"Mmhm," she said. "Are you eighteen?"

The question, especially put forth in this neighborhood, almost made Sylvie balk.

"Sure," she lied.

"You're not. It's twenty bucks for a half hour."

What a damn racket. And an easy guess.

"I have eight. Can we do ten minutes?"

Delilah Marie looked her up and down behind a pair of fashionable glasses. Pearlescent plastic. Tinted lenses. "Come in, then."

Sylvie followed her into a small, square apartment that was dark and shuttered and filled with fans to keep the heat more bearable. It didn't look anything like all the obnoxious faux Eastern style rooms that Sylvie imagined. No tassels. Minimal red. No shaded lamps. Just a small wooden table and two wooden chairs by the closed window. The rest of the room was a living area with all the usual trappings: sofa, coffee table, side table, bookcase, carpet, radio (which Delilah Marie switched off as she walked by). The papered walls were covered in signed headshots like the ones in Sardi's restaurant. From a quick glance, Sylvie was fairly sure only her grandparents would recognize most of the faces. A cigarette smoldered in a brass ashtray.

"Did you tell all those people's fortunes?" Sylvie didn't know why she asked. She didn't really have anything to lose. She didn't know this woman and would never tell her who she was, lest this visit get back to Marilyn.

"Ten minutes goes by quick, sweetie," said Delilah Marie. "So, is it boys or school?"

"Do you—do you know anything about that Bushwick Murder House?"

Delilah Marie raised her pencil brows. "I'm sorry?"

Right. That name was probably made up by one person. "Cropsey is in the name. The name of the house. They demolished it."

"The Herkimer-Cropsey place."

Sylvie nodded. "Yeah, that one."

"What interests you about it?"

"The history of it. Everything."

"And what makes you think I know anything?" Delilah Marie tapped the ash off her cigarette.

"You know the name. Anyway, ten minutes go by quick."

Delilah Marie chuckled. "Touché." But, perhaps just to spite Sylvie, she paused to take a couple drags off her cigarette before continuing. "Well, it's where the legend comes from, you know. It's where they borrowed the name. Isaac Cropsey killed his wives in that house. He ran a cult that sacrificed them for wealth and success. Why does it matter to you?"

"I think—I think I'm being haunted. There's a black dog . . ."

Delilah Marie pressed her lips together, smearing her lipstick to redistribute the color. "Y'know, I used to be a hat check girl back in the '20s, when I was trying to join a chorus line. And I moonlighted with Miss Polly Adler—you're too young to know of her. Anyhow, when you're in those positions, you pick up a lot of information people won't tell nobody else. *Rich* people won't tell nobody else. And boy, some rich people in this city sure have some baggage."

"Black dog-shaped baggage?"

The so-called psychic cracked a thin-lipped smile. "And a headless woman."

Sylvie's heart felt like it stopped. She saw the head at the foot of the tree, glassy eyes staring up at her.

"And I started putting it all together, see. So, when I quit agenting—I was a talent agent after I finished my dancing and whoring days—and I set myself up here to help people, I knew I'd hear more stories. And once in a while, someone will come in here and confess that their grandfather talked about it. Or their mother got institutionalized for talking *to* it. Or their great-grandfather shot black dogs on sight. And there's some family tree that's got two generations crossed out in their Bible because they don't want anyone to know who they were."

"Really?"

"I know it's the same thing because most of them call that dog Samuel."

"*Samuel?*" Surely that man hadn't become the specter of a *dog*.

Delilah Marie didn't hear Sylvie, or didn't care enough to respond. "And these people were governors, mayors, businessmen, landowners. They've got their names on streets and towns and even goddamn Rikers Island."

"I don't understand. Why do they see the dog?"

"Black dogs are a bad omen, and it means they had family who did some bad things a long time ago. But it got them what they wanted, didn't it? Except for the inconvenience of the occasional reminder to say thank you. Because that mansion out there is cursed. And the land is cursed beneath it. Somebody did something they shouldn't have, and they seeded something in there that makes people turn wicked in the pursuit of their dreams. And the city was right to try and tear it down, but they couldn't just bulldoze that tree the way they did the house."

Sylvie thought back to the enormous gash in the side of the trunk, right across the scream of a hole. "I'm sorry?"

"You might be too young to remember, but back in '65 there was a pretty big blackout. They blamed some setting failure, but that wasn't it. Well, maybe that happened because of what *really* happened. I didn't know it at the time, of course. Not until there was a little article about it in the papers. They started demolishing that old house, and they didn't finish. Well, I could have told them they wouldn't be able to finish. After everything I've heard? They shoulda just burned it to the ground. Fire's a natural cleanser."

1965 was the year Sylvie gained her 20/20 vision. Her hindsight. Her powers. She remembered that blackout in vivid, horrifying detail.

"You're saying that whatever is out there was pissed off that they tried to destroy it."

"I sure am."

"And it did something to stop the demolition." Was that *really* how she got her powers? Wouldn't millions of other people have them, too? Like her brother, or parents, her friends? They had all been in the city when it happened.

"The men packed up and never went back. Nobody ever went back, except for foolhardy kids, I'm sure. There's always foolhardy kids." Delilah Marie blew out a cloud of smoke as though to make her point clearer.

"You don't think—you don't think you can get cursed just by going there, do you? Because I know a couple of people who went out there a lot when they were young." Not that Sylvie would say who they were.

"Not right away. You gotta take some action to make it stick."

"But who put the curse there?" Sylvie knew—Samuel, the man. She could still hear his strange praying and his anguished cries. His attempts to set fire to the tree. The woman feeding on his wrist.

"There's an old story that says some Dutch settlers made themselves a little enclave out there, when there were woods and all. Before Brooklyn was Brooklyn. They conjured up something evil to make themselves rich, and then they went into New Amsterdam and became pillars of the community. And their ancestors are still here, and none of them killed that thing. Some of them tried. It's still there, waiting. Of course, there's never been no evidence Dutch folks were there in that spot so early, but some people's family Bibles say otherwise. And anyway, no one ever dug the grounds up to check."

"I've been there."

"Well, you shouldn't go back. People die on that property. One family after another. They flee for the hills, or they stay and worship and kill each other and everyone who gets in their way. They do what that dog says." Delilah Marie held up a knotted finger wearing a giant paste jewel ring and began counting off.

"First on record, that Herkimer. He fled with his family. Never farmed a thing. Then that Cropsey family turns that Herkimer cottage into a mansion. They live there a long time, I guess, but in the end, they were destroyed. Battle of Brooklyn was right at their doorstep. They're Loyalists. Lost all the money and everyone in the family, except one son. Next, Hessians take over the place, but they attack each other and run off claiming they're seeing ghosts. And then the Cropsey son comes back, buys the house, gets rich as Croesus, forms that cult he called a fraternal order, and it turns out he's been murdering every woman he brings into his house. And then the fraternal order turns on each other.

"Then it starts over again. People try to live in it, can't bear it. People get hurt, hurt each other, hurt themselves. The Penzig brewing family buys it once it's fixed up, but nobody told them about the murders and the bodies. Their little boy jumps off a balcony, and even though he lives, he can't ever walk again. His sister is the one who buys the place back, to keep people from living in it. Of course, it don't matter. Nobody lives in it until that Italian family. The dad killed them all a year after moving in. He was a weak one. Then the girl who survived it starts worshipping that curse and her whole family gets murdered. The papers don't know the truth, but I can guess it. I've got clients who knew that girl and wouldn't trust her as far as you could throw her. She's probably in the East River now. But that evil is still spreading, and people are getting shot and others are getting carved up and dumped in the Hudson. And you know what? It's because there's always been a damn cult worshipping that curse out there. That's what."

The more Delilah Marie spoke, the more Sylvie realized that all the stories she'd heard from friends and acquaintances were really the same one. The same place. The same creature wanting a body, over and over and over again. The Hessians, the bodies in the ground, the Penzigs, the Brooklyn Murder Mansion.

"How do you get rid of it?"

"What did you do to see the dog?"

"Nothing! And none of my friends did anything, either. But it won't leave us alone. Ilan—he's my friend. He's getting gigs out of nowhere. He's a musician. And my brother—he went to all these clubs it's hard to get into. And I—it helped me win. It *made* me win." She would toss those trophies in a dumpster. They didn't mean anything.

"This happened after you went out there?"

Sylvie shook her head.

"This curse is all over the city now. It's in the roots. I suppose it's not surprising there's collateral damage."

"But how do I get rid of—"

"Burn that tree. Scrub that land clean. Though I'm not suggesting that *you* do it, and if you do, don't mention me." She glanced at her slim wristwatch. "It's been twenty minutes."

"I know—I'm—I just have one other question. Has anyone mentioned things other than a black dog and a headless woman? Like, has anyone mentioned having . . . weird powers or—like, maybe visions of past events?"

Delilah Marie raised her eyebrow but shook her head. "Only thing is someone once told me there's some flowers on that land that are supposed to offer protection. I've got a client with a daughter who picked them as a kid. Now she's a full-grown woman and the blossoms haven't died."

Sylvie resisted the urge to tell her she knew who that was. Resisted the urge to say the curse found a way in, anyway. But Marilyn had said something interesting in the midst of the spell, and Sylvie needed to know. "Do you think that protection can be passed on like that curse?"

"Why not? If the conditions are right, anyway."

"Say, like, if someone picked them or whatever while they were pregnant?"

"Seems like the best and easiest method." Delilah Marie narrowed her false lashes. "You're not pregnant."

Sylvie quickly shook her head. She realized she was clenching her fists and quickly rubbed her sweating palms on her thighs. "No ma'am. I'm on the rag."

"Someone you know?"

Sylvie shrugged and nodded at once. "She's not—she already had the kid."

"Well, go find that kid and talk to them. Because you're out of time with me."

"Um. I still only have eight dollars."

"You know my address. Mail me the other twelve when you get home. And don't have me opening the papers tomorrow to see arson fire at that mansion."

CHAPTER TWENTY-NINE

CHELSEA

July 13th

For a week, Sylvie walked a lot.

She called Marz and Marybeth once each, and talked just long enough to tell them that she couldn't be around them until she figured something out. It meant having to miss one of Marz's shows, but she walked by, across the street, and tried to listen to the sounds that carried out whenever someone opened the doors.

She called Marilyn once, too, but hung up when she answered. She just wanted to hear her voice for a second. Make sure she was okay.

She wore gloves. Her hands were constantly soaked in sweat as the temperatures climbed. She had strange dreams almost every night, of headless women and dark forests, of Ilan walking down an empty road paved in blood.

What consumed her now was keeping her parents out of it, oblivious and unaffected, and that was why she walked so much, trying to stay out of the loft, trying to seem too busy to talk. As soon as they asked the wrong question or Sylvie gave the wrong answer, she knew the claws would snatch them up. That one day she would come home and her dad would say, *There was a black dog running around the place. Don't know how it got in.*

And maybe it was just wishful thinking. The dog had already been there. It had left its mark all over the studio.

Without regular dance classes, Sylvie wouldn't have to see Rynn much until August. It was no longer the vision that bothered her as much as it was the ornament that carried her in it. Whatever it was, whatever it looked like, it had been attached to a place that felt like a violation. Like it knew Sylvie was there and used Rynn as bait to get her to do exactly what she did—find one house, then the other, and wake everything back up.

Sylvie's next feis was a week away, and she had a new dress to get fitted. It was a strange prospect, like that part of her life belonged now to someone else.

Monday blazed like all the rest. Though the sky was mostly cloudy, the clouds were clammy hands cupped around the city. Everything was too hot. Every surface seemed to have a fine layer of moisture that just stayed there, heavy.

It was exactly the worst kind of day to go get a wool dress fitted. Even after dinner, the air sat stagnant. Off on the horizon, you might guess it was raining, but it wouldn't rain here.

Sylvie's parents took a cab to Chelsea, where the seamstress lived in a first-floor apartment. They were going to visit Gary, too, so they dropped her off at the stoop of a brick townhouse and said they would be back to pick her up in an hour.

Sylvie had gone to this seamstress for every dress she'd ever danced in. Mrs. Haley's specialty was the Irish dancing costume.

Lace collars and embroidered knotwork were her forte. They took months to come together, but in the end it was living art. She liked to spend the fittings talking about her youth, how she had danced through her Catholic church, for a while, before losing interest. It didn't matter that Sylvie had heard the story since she was a kid.

"Just standing there with our arms locked straight for an hour or two after school on Thursdays. Never was so bored. Of course, it wasn't as flashy back then as it is now. Seems to me it gets more inventive every year. Oh, I do wish I'd stuck with it. Well, at least my children liked it better than I did." Her granddaughter Caitlin was in Sylvie's class.

Sylvie enjoyed her company. She had squashy furniture and an avocado green rug and had recently put wood paneling on the walls of her sewing room. She also kept a small, black-and-white television on a metal stand, and ran whatever was in syndication if she couldn't bear to listen to the news.

"It's all shootings and arsonry."

Sylvie's new dress was black wool with a goldenrod cape and two ubiquitous but eye-catching knotwork dragons on the skirt. She had chosen an assortment of colors for the embroidery, but the dragons themselves were a fiery red. Underneath she wore a white cotton shirt with a lace collar and wide knotwork cuffs and would have a matching lace headband.

"You grow about five inches each time I see you. Legs like a colt's."

Mrs. Haley also kept a tin of butter cookies, which she gave out freely once all the clothes were put away again.

Sylvie stood in the workroom with her arms out and her legs bare as Mrs. Haley pinned the lining in place. Occasionally she had to turn, but most of the time was spent standing quite still.

The shades were drawn to keep out the day. An old oscillating fan blew somewhere behind them, pointed away from the fabric and therefore not doing much good. The television was switched to CBS and a rerun of *Good Times*. Sylvie watched it without really thinking about it, then looked down at her dress again.

The skirt was lined with red satin that sat cool against Sylvie's skin. She wanted to spin in it or spread it out to see the dragons in full, but Mrs. Haley was behind her, pins in her mouth, carefully notching little chalk marks and folding up the fabric.

Then the buzzer sounded. Mrs. Haley paused and slowly stood up, her knees creaking.

"Probably your parents," she said.

And it was, but they weren't there to get her.

After a few words out in the vestibule, Sylvie's mom came down the hall and into the workroom. "Gary's gone."

"Gone? What do you mean, gone?"

"He's not there. His clothes are gone, he didn't check out— he left!"

"But—what do we do?"

"Dad's going home to see if he's there. I'm going back to the hospital. But I'll be back at 8:30, no matter what." And as she said this, she put a hand on Sylvie's shoulder and looked her in the eyes. "You hear me? Don't leave. Don't try to look for him. I'll be back in a half hour."

Sylvie nodded. Her mom left.

What fucking good was a new dance dress now? When Mrs. Haley knelt back on her little pillow to resume pinning, Sylvie wanted to jump away and tell her to stop. Gary might be on his way to disappear just like Ilan. What if he had given in and gone back to the House of Death? No one would know to look for him there.

She wanted to fix this. She needed to solve this. There was an answer out there, a switch someone should be able to flip to reset everything back to how it used to be.

It's all shootings and arsonry.

Sylvie wished she could set fire to the stupid house on Tenth, to the rest of the Bushwick house. Let them burn away to nothing and take all their history with them. Everywhere else was burned down, why not the two worst places of them all? Delilah Marie had practically told her to do it.

The set began to flicker, the picture cutting in and out as the tracking went. Frowning at it, Sylvie felt a sharp pain in one leg, then the other. She flinched and jerked away, two pins stuck just above the backs of her knees and Mrs. Haley grabbing another out of the collection in her mouth. She had a faraway look about her. Sylvie panicked. Her body went cold. She tugged her skirt out of Mrs. Haley's hand and stumbled away. Next she pulled the pins out, not looking as she did. Two small beads of blood welled up in their place as she ran to get her shoes—there was no time to change. She left her street clothes behind. She wanted her parents to know to look for her, really look for her, that something was very wrong.

Outside and still barefoot, she sat down on the stoop to shove her sneakers on. She could still feel the bite of the pins, and she remembered the dozen or so carefully tucked into the lining of her skirt. With shaking fingers, she extracted each one and dropped them into the garden. Then she looked back at the door of the building, certain she would see Mrs. Haley brandishing a knife like a horror movie villain, but of course no one was there. Maybe she should go back in—maybe the spell would already be broken. She licked her fingers and scrubbed away the blood, already coagulating in fine points.

Hell no. She was not going back in there. Her brother needed her. Ilan needed her. She wasn't going to sit idle now that she knew what to do.

Sylvie's fear began to crystallize into anger, and she jumped to her feet and started to walk.

She crossed Sixth Avenue and turned south. Everyone around her was getting hurt more than she was, and she knew it was deliberate. Each new incident was another needle in her skin, and she would pull them all out.

A corpse shouldn't have any power, and she would take that power away if it did. She would reduce it to ash and scrub the memory of Rynn—whatever Rynn had become—from the earth, if that was what it took. Rynn's body deserved to be free.

The House of Death had not been boarded up again. The rotten plywood sat discarded in the entryway. Sylvie barely noticed it, and no one noticed her as she shoved through the open door and stormed inside.

Up creaking stairs. The smell of mildew tugged at her, tried to get her to turn around, think about what she was doing, but she didn't stop. The smell worsened, but she didn't stop. She didn't stop until she was on the top floor, so filled with visions of chopping off a corpse's head that she almost flew into the only open apartment.

Then everything was truly dark, and in that darkness came the doubts. What if Sylvie was wrong? What if Rynn wasn't here, wasn't alive, had been a victim of a kidnapping that ended somewhere else? What if the thing she was going to walk in on, the thing she had imagined immolating, was—what?

Long, thin fingers sliding out of a tree.

She would go for that head no matter what. But she had nothing in her hands to accomplish it.

Sylvie looked back at the open door, heart hammering but now in fear. Sweat dripped into her eyes and she rubbed them, smudging her glasses as she did.

For a second, she reached out to touch the wall, to see what it would tell her, but she stopped. Doing that on the outside of the building had been a grave enough mistake. She wouldn't make it worse.

She went in deeper, into the living room, looking for something she could use to defend herself. A lamp, maybe, and she grabbed one off a dusty old side table, coughing when she stirred up air that had not been active in decades. Her bare hands felt vulnerable on the brass, but nothing happened. She could still control what she saw.

The place smelled awful. It was so old and so decayed that it was a wonder there weren't holes in the floor and ceiling. There were footprints, however, in the dust. Not even footprints, really, but a fresh path someone was taking—around the corner from the door and down the hall.

Sylvie gripped the lamp and followed.

The apartment was silent. It was like she had left the city, or even the planet. As she approached the door at the end of the hall, the musty, decayed smell began to take on a coppery tinge. Toppled furniture lay tipped against the walls and floor. She paused only once, to peer into the kitchen, hoping for a better weapon, but the open utensil drawer held only spoons.

She gripped the lamp tightly. She was too afraid to even take a deep breath. As she wove through the furniture blockade, trying not to touch anything, she thought she saw a flash of white reflected in a set of cabinet doors, but spinning around showed her no one was there.

Get this over with. Get it over with now.

Sylvie closed the gap and slipped into the open door, expecting to be jumped.

The room was empty. The windows glowed with the overcast sunset sky, but not brightly enough to hit the darkest corners of the room.

She frowned. There was a fireplace, a chair, a bed—a body.

Sylvie reeled back, dropping the lamp and breaking the old bulb. She looked away and felt her whole body seize up in shock. All the imagined scenarios of a flying rage, of beating bones to nothing, left her.

That body was dead. That body was beyond anyone's help or retribution. It lay on the floor, dried out in a tangle of fabric and hair, filmy eyes wide open but catching no light.

It didn't move, though Sylvie waited for it to do something. She didn't feel compelled to go to it beyond a savage curiosity that replaced the initial disgust.

Her heart felt heavy, though, because the longer she looked at the desiccated form of what had once been a teenage girl, the more she knew she had been right. This was Rynn. *Was.*

She didn't look older. She didn't look like she had been allowed to reach adulthood. But for how wasted she was, she looked like she had been frozen just as Sylvie last saw her.

The only thing—the only thing that was wrong, really wrong, was that blood had pooled beneath her body. Half-dried blood that still permeated the muggy air with an unmistakable tang. She could see it had dripped out of her mouth and nose, and where her left leg had been broken through the femur.

A body as decayed as hers should have had nothing left in it.

And that wasn't the only blood here—a pool of it sat mere feet away, almost in Sylvie's path. The air was so humid that the middle of the stain glistened, and someone had smeared it across the floor in a crude trail. Worse, in that trail of blood was a long fragment of bone from Rynn's missing leg, crudely broken to a bloody point at one end. The sight of the bone, more than the blood, made Sylvie's temples throb.

She had expected to find Gary here, but he wasn't, and she didn't feel relieved. That blood came from *someone*—it couldn't have all been Rynn's. There was a flashlight on the ground, too, and she wanted to grab it but instead heard a creaking somewhere in the apartment. Just one quick groan of the walls or the floors. Sylvie paused, heart hammering. What would she do if someone walked in on her? After a minute of silence, Sylvie decided the house had settled, unused to so much activity after years of no activity at all.

She could touch the wall. The place was empty, and she could reveal the secret that brought Rynn here. She felt she had to do it. That Rynn's abridged story deserved that much. If there was anything left in this building that could hurt her, Sylvie suspected it would already know she was here.

She turned to the wall behind her, looking at the dirty, buckling paper for a moment before recklessly pressing her hand to its surface.

She prepared for the chaos. For the decades to pass through and over each other, in front of her and around her and through her. But there weren't as many people as she expected. It was almost easy to pick through the generations.

And it was very easy to find Rynn.

Three men entered the room carrying a heavy canvas sack. They dropped the sack on the floor with a sickening thud, and immediately ran out again. One of the men couldn't stop screaming, *SHUT HER UP!*

But no one else was speaking.

They slammed the bedroom door behind them. Sylvie could hear banging and fumbling on the other side. And the sack moved, and arms emerged from the opening, followed by a familiar head and face. But her neck was bleeding—something was tied around it. She wore frilly, frosty blue pajamas that seemed absurd given the situation.

Sylvie let in other things. Over the top of Rynn flooded the previous generations, oblivious to what would happen here, oblivious even to the way the building was shaped into apartments—people walked through walls that hadn't existed a hundred years ago. This had been a servants' quarters once; it was clear from the uniforms the women put on and took off.

The Rynn of twenty years ago touched the wound and got to her feet. She tried the door and it wouldn't budge. She went to the windows. Sylvie watched multitudes of her pace, multitudes of her stand at the phantom of the closed door, then multitudes of her composure slipping. She howled into the empty room, clawed and scratched at the door and the walls, beating apart a dead girl's hands.

The sight of it almost made Sylvie stop looking, until she saw another familiar face.

There was Ilan coming into the room with the tides of history. But that wasn't possible. Not enough time had passed.

She pulled her hand away from the wall and he didn't go with it. He was really there, in the doorway, staring at her. And she hadn't seen him in so long that she actually smiled. A deep, rolling swell of relief washed over her, relief that he was still alive, relief that she wasn't the only living person in the building. She wanted to run right for him, grab him and take him away. *You did it! You destroyed her!*

And she almost did. She took two quick steps forward, but then she saw the blood covering his shirt.

CHAPTER THIRTY

Unease spread through her, quickly boiling into panic. Maybe it wasn't his blood. (It could be Rynn's.) Maybe it wasn't even blood at all. (She could barely breathe through the thick stench of copper.) Maybe it was superficial, and he had been trapped here for days. (Why hadn't he just walked out the open front door?)

Sylvie backed up until she touched the wall again, and she felt guilty for it.

"Ilan." Her voice struggled out of her. "Ilan, what happened to you?"

He turned his head slightly, as though to hear her better.

"You're hurt," she whispered. She cleared her throat. "You need to get help."

The stain on his chest didn't catch the light like the stain on the ground, which made it impossible to see where the wound was, what the wound was, only that the blood had so thoroughly robbed the shirt of its original color that from this angle it looked like only the sleeves were untouched.

"Sylvie," he finally said. The voice that came out of him might have sounded like Ilan at the edges, in the echo, but mostly it sounded like the scratching of stone, or the stirring of leaves. There was no human on earth who should make a sound like that. "I didn't think you would ever come. What a waste."

The strength left Sylvie's body, and she nearly sank down the wall, right to the floor. She shook her head, her throat tight, a hand squeezing the air from her chest. Panicked tears followed.

"No," she said, shaking her head. "No, no, no, no . . ." She couldn't stop saying it, like it would make a difference. Like it would either snap him back together or drive the pain out of her. She didn't even feel afraid. Fear was such a small thing compared to loss already in motion. Already complete.

"Come on, Ilan," she said, like it was some big joke. Like he would realize the prank had gone too far but she hadn't fallen for all of it. She didn't wipe her tears. "Don't do this."

Ilan finally moved again, stepping into the room with a soft look of concern. His movement was different, his stride a different rhythm than she remembered, than she knew. Sylvie flinched, knowing she had nowhere to go that wasn't through the door behind him—or through one of the dirty windows and straight down five floors to the garden below.

He spoke again but she couldn't understand the language, and she covered her ears to stop the sound of it getting in. The voice was every haunted corner of the earth, every stretch of desolate land. It was old and forgotten. Sylvie choked, sniffed, shut her eyes. *This couldn't be happening. It wasn't possible.*

She didn't want to speak anymore—for some reason, the idea of opening her mouth felt like a vulnerability, like he would shed his skin and crawl inside of her. Was that how it happened to him? Was there anything left of him in that body—or had he spilled out with the blood from that wound to his chest?

The expression on Ilan's face didn't change, and that impassivity made him even worse to look at. Everything about him was the same but not the same. His body was not doing what it should be. Visions of the last time she'd seen him erupted in her mind, as though forcibly drawn to the surface. Except he took her to his place, the way he should have, and—

"Don't." She had to choke it out. "Don't you dare."

Ilan spoke again, but this time it wasn't aloud, and though she couldn't understand the language, she knew what he was saying.

"Don't fight me, girl. I can find your brother. *He* will find your brother and then your brother will find *you*." There was none of Ilan's voice when he—when that *creature* spoke this way. It licked like a flame, sounding like a dozen different voices at once.

Sylvie continued to slide along the walls, trying to get in a better position to run. She had to find Gary—or find someone who could find Gary and protect him.

"Don't talk about my brother."

"Then what of your friends? I know them. I know their hopes and their dreams better than they do."

"No!"

"We don't have to hurt anyone, Sylvie. Make it easy for all of us. Stay here with us. Tend to us. Embrace us as a friend, and nothing more will happen. You're all we need."

Ilan stepped forward again and Sylvie frantically pulled a framed picture off the wall and lobbed it at him. She threw it too wide, and it hit the wall behind him, glass shattering in the door-frame and skidding across the floor. He didn't even look at it.

He spoke aloud once more, in that thin flicker of Ilan's voice. "Sylvie, this boy wanted you very much. If you had come but only a little sooner, none of this would have happened. Don't let his death be in vain."

She knew he was gone—but she wasn't ready to hear that he was dead. He could have been chopped into fifths, and she would have thought she could save him.

The room wasn't big enough to avoid this creature forever, and as Ilan's body came closer and closer, Sylvie's panic returned, but so did that burning anger. Her vision flashed white hot fear at the edges, a vise clamped down on her head.

Instinctively, she touched the wall at her back and the room returned to its past lives.

Ilan stopped, but he didn't retreat. People walked through him, around him, but he didn't notice, or he didn't care. He stared back at Sylvie and, though his empty expression didn't change, laughed at her. A chuckle. Like an amused parent. He wasn't going anywhere. She thought maybe it had been a shield that day, when the ladders fell like guillotines, but she was wrong.

"That failed to save sweet Metje. What good will it do you?"

Metje?

Sylvie jerked her hand away so she could see and hear clearly again. Tears fell but she didn't attend to them, didn't think about them, and blinked the last ones away before grabbing hold of a small end table and shoving it over, then throwing it at Ilan. Her aim was better because the object was wider, and it hit his legs.

The creature wasn't steady on Ilan's feet, not yet, and he stumbled to the side. Finally, the expression changed. Finally, the impassive stare became angry. Especially when Sylvie scrambled past him. She knew she had just run through the stain on the floor. She knew the stain on the floor had come from Ilan. He had tried to crawl away but his body failed. He had lain there for minutes or hours before he could stand up again (*oh, Ilan*). But it did not seem that he could run. He was not an infant, though, and he would learn quickly.

Out of the apartment, over the landing, down the stairs, now Sylvie was saturated with fear. A breeze cut across her, blew up the dust from the dark corners, sounding like a roar, like a freight train or a tornado.

On the next landing was the black dog, waiting at the foot of the stairs. She would have to run through it, jump over it—it would not stop her. She closed her eyes and felt the shock of frigid air burn the bare skin of her legs. It felt like raking nails trying to dig into her muscle, into her bone, and the two pinpricks on her thighs throbbed and began to bleed again.

Sylvie.

The voice crackled like a badly tuned radio station.

SYLVIE.

The dog appeared at the bottom of each flight, and each time she collided with it, her body felt worse. It was like someone had taken a baseball bat to her hips, to her knees. She knew she was slowing down, but above her she heard the floor creaking as something with actual weight began to give chase.

The dog followed at her heels, biting bruises into her legs with spectral teeth, grabbing at her with its human hands. Sylvie almost fell to her knees from the pain. Her nerves were on fire all the way to the top of her head. She grabbed at the wall, at the grille of the elevator, at the doorknobs of the other apartments, clawing her way to the open front door.

The dog couldn't hold her. The dog wasn't substantial enough.

THAT MAGIC WON'T KEEP YOU FROM ME.

In the doorway, now, the headless figure appeared. It swallowed the entire threshold, but Sylvie pushed through it. Her ears popped. Her eyes watered. Each tooth in her jaw felt attached to live wires. She almost doubled over, almost sat right down on the ground and closed her eyes. She could hear the building creaking, louder than ever.

I WILL HAVE YOU.

She limped quickly up the entry stairs and onto the sidewalk. The sweltering air was like static, like striking a match would blow everything up.

She began to run. At first, it was slow; each step like jumping from a great height. The normal impact of her feet to the ground rattled every part of her, jolted her head on her neck. It was a sensation like feverish body aches. She could feel her nose running, and when she rubbed it, the back of her hand was covered in blood.

Stopping wasn't possible, and Sylvie didn't look back because it would do her no good to know how close Ilan was. Eventually, the pain began to subside, or she got used to it, and she put real distance between herself and West Tenth Street.

Where could she go now? Where could she go that the creature inside Ilan wouldn't find her, and hurt her, and hurt anyone she was with? She had to find Gary, had to warn him (if it wasn't too late). Had to warn her parents, too. *Stay away from Ilan.* Over and over she thought it as she beat hell across the city. *Stay away from Ilan. He isn't himself.*

She—the creature—needed a body and she took his. She'd given up waiting for someone else to bring Sylvie to her. Whatever happened to Rynn that day she was shot, she had lived out her slow death in that apartment, driving the tenants mad, starving into powerlessness when no one came back to feed her. A human vessel lost, and no one there to give her a new one. Until Sylvie touched the building—she must have felt it. She must have been so overjoyed, if joy was a thing that creature could feel.

Sylvie headed east because she couldn't go home. Crossing Broadway, sweat coating her body beneath her wool dress, she finally looked back. Ilan wasn't there, of course—the night was too peaceful. But now that she'd lost him (in so many ways), she felt worse anxiety than before. She didn't know what he was capable of—what *the creature* was capable of. Every time she turned her head, she imagined he would pop up in front of her, sink his teeth into her neck.

She didn't understand why this hadn't already happened. Why something powerful enough to understand her dreams and desires and even who was most important to her, couldn't just hypnotize

WELCOME TO FEAR CITY

her the way it did Ilan and Gary and sort-of Marilyn. Hypnotize her and kill her and take her like she'd taken Rynn.

Sylvie was practically in the East Village now and despite her misgivings about seeing anyone, she needed to warn Marz. She had no change to make a call, so she kept running.

She didn't exactly stand out in an area known for standing out, but a few people wearing varying degrees of torn fishnet and thick eyeliner nodded at her dress. "Rough night?"

"The worst," she said.

She must have looked a fucking mess. She sniffed again, tasting blood, and licked the back of her hand to rub at her nose and lip. She couldn't walk into Marz's house like this—her parents would flip and call Sylvie's, and she could not risk that.

Marz's bedroom windows were open, thank fucking God. It would be a gamble as to whether or not one of her sisters was in there. Hell, it would be a gamble that Marz's parents didn't hear her as she called up, "Marz!"

She thought of dodging behind a bush or a tree. "Come on. Come *on*."

"Sylvie!" Marz called down. Marybeth's head poked out behind her. "Come up!"

Sylvie shook her head. "I can't. Come down for a sec. Please—hurry!"

The girls glanced at each other before disappearing and reappearing on the stoop. Sylvie waited at the curb, moving away to the front of the neighboring house so Marz's parents wouldn't have a total front row seat.

"What are you *wearing*?" Marz asked her.

Marybeth was looking at her face, though, and she said, "What happened? Is everything okay?"

"No. Rynn's dead—I mean, she's really dead—"

"Wait, what?" said Marz.

Marybeth gasped. "Sylvie, your legs!"

Sylvie looked down to find large, livid bruises across her knees, shins, thighs—everywhere.

Her friends made her turn around. "You're bleeding!" said Marz, immediately spitting on her hand and trying to rub the dried up streaks off the backs of her legs.

"Oh, my God, are those *bite marks*?" said Marybeth. "They're all over her legs. *Look* at that!"

"No—that one's a *handprint*. What in the hell?" said Marz.

Sylvie lifted one leg and almost immediately wished she hadn't. The skin wasn't broken, but deep, red teeth patterns, like those of a large dog's, mottled her skin like rotting flesh. And at her ankles and knees were the deep impressions of a grown man's fingers.

"Does it hurt?" asked Marz.

She put her foot back down. "A little—it hurt worse before."

"Where were you?" asked Marz.

"Just listen, please. Something was keeping Rynn alive in there but it's in Ilan now. If you see Ilan, stay away from him. Run. Just run. Don't let him come near you. It's not him anymore. It's something else."

Don't think about it. Don't think about Ilan. Don't cry about Ilan.

"How do you know? Did he—where're your parents? Did you *run* here?" asked Marz.

"I was at a dress fitting. My parents went to see Gary—I don't know how much time I have, so please just let me talk. Gary left the hospital without checking out. I don't know where he could be, but if Ilan goes to my place, they're screwed. So I have to stop it. I think it came from that tree, so I'm burning it down. I'm gonna burn it down. I saw a man do it, but he failed and I'm not gonna fail." As though this was a perfectly normal way to finish a conversation, she began to walk away. She had to find the nearest station to get herself back to Bushwick.

Marz grabbed her arm. "Hold the fuck up, girl. Do you even have pockets in that? Do you have tokens? Matches? You need help. I'm coming."

"No!"

"Girl, don't argue with me. Marybeth, stay with her and keep her here. I'm getting my bag."

"Grab mine, too!" Marybeth called after her.

"No!"

Marybeth softened her voice and said, "Hey. You can't just go alone. It'll be dark soon."

Sylvie shook her head. "I don't care. I'm out of time."

"Sylvie—"

"Ilan's dead. Ilan's really, really dead," she whispered. She almost wanted to say it until it meant nothing to her, but instead she felt something crack back open.

Marybeth wrapped her arms around Sylvie, but she couldn't bring herself to start crying again.

"If I don't end this, it's dominos. It's Gary, it's my parents—it'll be you, it'll be—she knows about you! She threatened me!"

"That's why we're coming. We'll help you. Look, ever since we went out there, I have these crazy dreams like I'm the youngest principal at NYCB or something. Balanchine's new muse. And I wake up and want to go to your place. Every time. And Marz told me she's dreamt of performing at CBGB and woken up at her front door with a set list in her hand. We didn't want to worry you, so we didn't tell you. But we're already in it. And it's not your fault we're in it. But we are."

Sylvie gripped her hand. "But it *is* my fault. If you guys get hurt, I don't care what happens to me."

"We won't get hurt."

"You can't know that. Ilan didn't do this to hurt himself and look what happened." *Don't talk about Ilan anymore.*

"If what you said—if Ilan is . . . then it's like you said. We can't just ignore it, can we? And frankly, I'd rather keep moving than stay here like a sitting duck."

Marz jumped down the stoop, skipping half the steps in her favorite old pair of winklepickers. She handed Marybeth her bag and hooked her arm into Sylvie's. "Marybeth's got her knitting needles in there. Those are good weapons. Now let's hoof it. I told Dad we're going to your place. It's not a good plan, but we're not gonna be in the city much longer, anyway. I'll deal with getting my ass beat later."

With Marz and Marybeth, Sylvie didn't have to think much about where they were going. They needed the J and, not wanting to transfer, Marz led them down to Delancey Street. They were all three covered in a sheen of sweat and the sun was sinking with them as they disappeared below ground. To Sylvie, it still felt like there should be a thunderstorm in the low hanging clouds, but nothing seemed to want to happen. She would have welcomed the rain. It might have felt nice on her legs.

Hopping on the next train, Sylvie stared out the window over the city lights as Williamsburg Bridge rose beneath them and carried them across the water. There was no moon. Their car wasn't overly crowded, and they were able to sit, which Marz encouraged because Sylvie's legs were a bit of a nasty spectacle. Because of the heat, most of the windows were open. One person held a boombox and nodded along to the beat, a towel around his neck.

Part of Sylvie wished she wasn't here, going away from her family, her home, and everyone she knew. She couldn't warn them now or throw herself in front of the danger. She wondered if her parents had found Gary, and what state the seamstress was in when her mom showed back up.

Another part of her wished the train would go a lot faster.

None of them wore a watch, so all Sylvie could do was stare out at the heavy horizon.

Then the lights went out, and the train abruptly screeched to a halt.

CHAPTER THIRTY-ONE

"The hell?"

"Look at *that*."

Manhattan was dark. Brooklyn was dark. Every skyscraper, every pier, every housing block reduced at once to silhouettes against the velvet sky. Headlights were the exception, and they cut through the dark as traffic sped along the FDR and all the side streets and bridges around them.

Everybody stood up, looking at each other, looking outside. Only an event bigger than themselves could bring the subway riders together like this. The only sound now, apart from the car traffic that continued across the bridge, was the boombox.

"Power's out everywhere!"

"Nothing works in this city anymore."

"It's the heat," said a woman. "I knew it. Been sayin' it all month. I said, something's gonna catch fire in all this heat. Now you see! You see!"

"Don't see much."

"Least we ain't in a tunnel, right?"

A couple people laughed.

With no ambient light from a moon, from a city, or from the train itself, they might as well have been in a tunnel.

"I can't just wait in here," Sylvie whispered.

Another minute or two passed, maybe, when the chatter began to slowly die away. The breeze coming in through the open window, off the water far below, was warm as breath.

There was a loud *thunk*. The boombox had fallen to the floor, but its owner didn't move to retrieve it. He didn't seem to notice it had happened at all.

The whitest faces were the easiest to see turning in her direction, but they weren't the only ones. Four faces, maybe five, maybe six. More at once than ever before.

"Syyyyylvieeee." Marz's lips were almost against her right ear.

"Stay where you are." Marybeth, on her left.

Then a white hot, searing pain in her left thigh rendered all of Sylvie's thoughts to nothing. She may have screamed—and so might some of the passengers, the ones who still had their own minds.

Marybeth's knitting needle was deep in Sylvie's thigh, blood already running over her skin and down her leg. Sylvie was sweating anew, blinking tears out of her eyes, as she stumbled out of the seat and limped away.

A soft, sibilant sigh stirred Sylvie's hair.

Sylvie. You can't outrun me.

Every step was fresh misery. She bit down on her fist and

grabbed the needle, pulling it out with a yell and throwing it—she didn't know where it landed. She could hear nothing but buzzing in her ears. Blood immediately gushed from the hole, and she struggled to cover it with one hand as she dragged herself toward the doors between the cars.

She couldn't tell the difference between genuine whispers and preternatural horrors. Sobs of shock escaped her closed-up throat.

They had been near the middle of the train, and as she moved unsteadily from car to car, she slowly picked up speed, ignoring how far she was above the water, ignoring how even the regular traffic had slowly snared to a crawl, frantic honking indicating all the signal lights were out. She couldn't think of anything beyond the searing pain in her leg and the warm blood that soaked into her shoe, leaving prints down every aisle, making some passengers gasp and back away—but some passengers were hooked, like Sylvie was the only bright object in a vast ocean of darkness. Those people rose in their seats and followed, leaving friends and partners behind to bewildered comment.

Eventually, Sylvie reached the front car. Instead of going inside it, she climbed down from the coupling and onto the side of the track. Every shift of her thigh muscle made her gasp and choke and pushed more blood out of the hole in her leg.

Car traffic stacked up on her right, giving her no escape on the road. She was dimly aware that people were shouting at her from both sides as she pulled away from the stalled train, hugging the narrow path between the rusting barricade that separated the road and the rail. The bridge's pedestrian path was high above her, but up ahead was a darkened switch with a medal ladder, and up that ladder she went. Her hands and foot were slick with blood and twice she nearly lost her grip. But physical pain was a lot easier to manage than whatever madness she had left behind on the train.

Sylvie couldn't see anyone else up here, but it was so dark it was difficult to truly tell. The walk to Bushwick would be lengthy but uncomplicated. She just had to stay on Broadway.

She ran at a staggered pace until the train tracks rose up and the traffic fell away. She ran until the pedestrian pathway peeled back and began to descend. Below her, as she approached the street, the honking was worse than ever.

A police officer was attempting to redirect traffic, acting now as a human stop light. Putting her head down, trying to cover her injury—a useless endeavor given the rivers of blood, fresh and drying, on her leg—Sylvie limped past him and kept going. She was thankful for the dark.

There were more people out now, mostly adults, mostly bearded fathers meeting at street corners, chatting to each other and pointing out toward the water. In any language it was obvious what they were talking about—*Do you see the city? It's not just us!*

Sylvie felt uneasy down here and wished she wasn't alone, wished she hadn't thrown away the knitting needle. In the moments when she felt almost numb to the pain, used to the exertion, she worried about Marz and Marybeth and hoped they had come to and escaped.

For several minutes, as she neared the Marcy Avenue subway station, people ignored Sylvie in favor of the excitement of the evening. But at the sound of a fender-bender, she chanced a look back and saw there were several people walking just behind her. It was too dark to see where they were looking, but Sylvie could take no chances. She looked up at the tracks shadowing the street and decided on a new course.

At the station, she hurried up the stairs, over the turnstile, and down the platform until she reached the end of it and delicately climbed down along the edge of the track. It was too dark to see where the next stalled train would be. A new rivulet of blood slipped down her knee.

This is insane.

Sylvie's thoughts were tied in knots, and she tried to walk without thinking about what she left behind and what she was going to. Below her, the worst of the traffic had long died away and was replaced by the occasional loud radio blasting dance music. Groups of people laughed and talked. Once in a while there was even a grill, as though this was a midday barbecue. A few windows had candlelight glowing on their sills. People stood on the roofs like they were going to watch fireworks. Some had binoculars, others had cameras. The city had never looked like this before and no one wanted to miss it.

Whenever she came upon a stalled train, she crouched down along the side and her punctured thigh burned with the effort. Many of the cars seemed empty, the doors standing open. Either people had jumped out or been evacuated. It had been so long without lights now that a sudden revival of the power grid seemed less and less likely.

The barbecues and party atmosphere in the streets below slowly began to change, with the first few ambulance or fire sirens launched in the distance—but that wasn't much different than an ordinary day. She could still smell smoke, but it was no longer rich and flavorful. In the quiet moments, distant building alarms sounded. Dogs barked.

She could hear more and more people below her. Shouting and talking. The occasional crash of something—maybe a trash can. A sharp laugh or two, followed by a yell. Then a louder alarm, throbbing out of a business somewhere. People hung out their windows, shouting down at the street.

Sylvie didn't look at anyone. She kept her head down. Hoped there wasn't enough light to see her by if you weren't looking.

Glass began to break. A window, maybe (probably). Triumphant yells.

What's happening down there?

An hour had passed, or maybe more, since she escaped the train. Sylvie's legs were sore in new ways now, and while the bleeding had stopped, the wound was still wet and angry. She was exhausted by the heat.

Every block was more intense than the one before it. There was more smoke, more shouting, more breaking glass. Curving along a bend in the track, avoiding another stalled train, she saw the first licks of flame through the grating beneath her feet. Something was on fire down there. Sylvie started to run again.

She saw more flames, higher flames, thicker smoke, the closer she got to the station—her stop. There was still occasional music, still occasional laughter, but mostly there was running. She wasn't even alone on the tracks sometimes, and no one gave her a second glance. Some of the people carried bags of groceries, others some electronics still in their boxes.

Fire alarms were constant.

With difficulty, her hands crusted with blood, she climbed back up onto the platform and hobbled down the stairs, through the station's open emergency doors and down to the street below.

There were hundreds of people around her now. Some climbed through the broken window of a corner shop, while others looked for another window to smash. The sound of it swelled up around her, pulling her in by its own gravity. On the corner, a trash can burned. A teenage boy kicked it over and ran off again, spilling burning debris into the street. Several others stamped it out.

Sylvie took a deep breath and marched resolutely through the building human storm. No one paid her attention—their focus, their ire, their adrenaline was on the buildings, the city, the very beast that had chewed them up and forgotten to spit.

The only thing that relaxed Sylvie was the lack of police.

She knew she was going to see Rynn soon, and she hoped the activity and the general darkness would prevent her from noticing, for now.

Clothing shops had been gutted; the denuded mannequins lying in the street looked like corpses bleached by the sun. Limbs here, a head there, chipped paint smiling vacuously up at the world. Glass eyes from the taxidermy shop spilled across the sidewalk and street. People crushed them or slipped on them or pocketed them with a laugh.

Sylvie had been trying not to think about the fire she was going to set, but she had to think of it now. The ones that kept popping up around her, naked flame and heat beckoning her, were reminders, and comforts. It meant hers wouldn't be noticed until it was too late to do anything. It was just an old, dead tree.

But she had nothing to start it with.

The first bodega had already been stripped almost to its rivets. The second one she found was little better. It seemed to be mostly food that had been taken, so she climbed inside, a couple of people reaching to help her, not quite seeing the state of her hands in the dim light.

She walked through the aisles. No beer or wine left. So much for that. Then she went to the counter and noticed nail polish remover and rubbing alcohol still sitting next to packages of condoms and boxes of Bic lighters. With no one there to stop her, she went around the counter and grabbed one bottle of rubbing alcohol, opening it up on her leg without thinking, sucking her teeth at the searing pain. Then she grabbed a second bottle and was about to reach for a lighter when someone seized her from behind.

Surprised, she dropped the bottle. It hit the linoleum and skidded off behind the glassy-eyed man who had hold of her arm. She twisted around until she could yank her arm back, then retrieved the fallen bottle and ran for it.

She was almost at the window when another person caught her, and she wheeled around. This man's grip was firmer.

"Get *off* me!" she shouted, knowing it would do no good at all. The man was beyond reasoning.

But not everyone was. A young man coming through the window noticed the scuffle and immediately grabbed the man's arm and pushed him. With his hold on Sylvie broken, the man seemed disoriented and almost fell backward onto the window frame, a piece of glass slicing deep into his arm.

"He do that to you?" the kid asked her, and Sylvie momentarily forgot her injury because she couldn't stop staring at the man.

"Oh, no. No. Thanks. I'm good. Thank you." But the kid was already gone to the back of the shop.

"Sylvie."

The man had spoken. Had ripped his arm free from the glass, dripping large coins of blood over the floor.

She bolted out of the shop.

The street was all obstacles. She jumped over empty boxes, broken merchandise, even an old couch someone had dropped on the curb. She held the bottle of rubbing alcohol like a football and cut onto a side street, out of the protection of the tracks, and out of the crowd.

Bushwick Avenue also swelled with people, but there were only homes and a church on this stretch, and the people who stepped outside were doing so to see what was happening everywhere else. Someone had taken out a hose and was spraying water on their house.

She cut across the carless street and into the residential blocks, where people stayed inside, candles lit in their windows but fiercely monitored as more plumes of smoke rose on the horizon.

Rynn was with her, in Sylvie's current and against her tide. Innocently moving through her life. The darkness made her harder to see, but Sylvie could hear her.

And as soon as she turned onto the empty street of the old mansion, Rynn's voice swelled all at once. She'd done a lot more talking here.

But Rynn—her story was over. Sylvie had to forget her now.

She climbed over the sagging fence and bolted into the dry, weedy grass. She focused in on the tree. She stared into the black maw that was its eye and its mouth all at once. Did it understand what it had unleashed? Did it understand what it had leached into the city its roots knew so intimately? She was so close now that she could begin to see its full silhouette—but there was something new, something brighter than the bark. The handle of an ax, an ax now buried in the lip of the knot.

Distracted by it, Sylvie's foot hit something solid, and she flew into the air, coming down hard on her side, only feet from the roots of the tree. Her glasses dug into her face, and she felt her new blouse rip at the sleeve. The breath went from her lungs, and she lay there, blood trickling down her nose, listening to the chattering of Rynn above and around her.

Dazed, Sylvie sat up and turned to see what she had tripped on, and there was Gary's body lying in the weeds behind her.

CHAPTER THIRTY-TWO

The wind went out of Sylvie's lungs all over again. She had barely recovered enough from the fall to use her voice, but that didn't stop her.

"No, no, no." Quiet, at first, as she crawled back over to him, then louder and louder until she was nearly screaming. Everything she wanted to do when she realized Ilan was dead, she began to do now. *"Gary!"*

She was afraid to touch him, afraid to know, but she couldn't just leave him there, and she couldn't pretend this wasn't happening. She grabbed his arm and it was warm, but the night was warm, and he might not have been here all that long. She rubbed her running, bleeding nose on the back of her hand and leaned over him, pressing her ear to his chest, trying not to make a sound so she could hear—his heartbeat.

She started to sob all over again. "Gary! Wake *up!*"

She touched his face, gently smacking his cheek, then shaking his shoulders. "Gary. Come *on!*"

No matter how she tried, Gary didn't stir. His breathing was shallow but steady and unlabored, and though he was unconscious she could feel his heart racing like he was awake, or dreaming.

Sylvie let out a groan of wild frustration. Gary had come out here, gotten an ax from somewhere, and tried to take down the tree. He figured it out just like she did, but he hadn't known all of it. He hadn't known enough.

She didn't have time to let her blood run cold. She had to do this, really do this. No backing out, no freaking out. She jumped up, wrenched the ax out of the bark and, for a moment, thought of doing the job that way—but it hadn't worked for her brother, just like it hadn't worked for any of the others who tried this method in the past. Hell, not even a bulldozer could settle it.

Sylvie stared up at the thick expanse of dark trunk, at the bare limbs and leafless branches. She was reminded of the husk of Rynn. Rynn, who kept touching the tree and crying out in fright as Sylvie stood there with the ax in her hands. Rynn, and the other girl, the blonde one, the wisp of a memory.

Now Rynn's body was finished and Ilan's had taken its place.

She knew things the others hadn't. She knew there was a head. She would dig it up and drop it in the maw with the rest of what she hoped were only bones now. Then she would do what the first man failed to do: burn the tree from its inside out, let the fever finally claim it, let it finally embrace the death it had been denied since the day the woman crawled out.

But that meant getting *Her* out of Ilan.

She didn't want to fucking cut off Ilan's head.

Sylvie touched that thought and moved on at once. First, she pulled Gary's limp body away from the tree. He still wore a hospital bracelet. Next, she dug through his pockets, hoping for a match or a lighter—they were empty. Even his wallet was gone. Maybe it had fallen out, but it was too dark to see.

With Gary closer to the fence now, Sylvie ran back for the ax. Then she began to dig with it. The head was there, not far below her. That was the easy part, and that's how she would begin.

It was harder than she expected. The roots hadn't weakened in three hundred years and there was a lot of packed earth. But she was desperate, and her bleeding leg nagged at her. She scraped at the dirt with the blade and her bare fingers, nicking the dry roots but unable to part them. Sweat dripping into her eyes with the effort, she managed to gouge enough of a hole to feel something strange—hair. She was feeling hair. She couldn't see it in the darkness, but it was there. The feel of it made her shudder and recoil.

Sylvie.

A breeze—a rustle through her mind.

Syyylvieeee . . .

Panicking, Sylvie turned to find Ilan's body standing in the weeds by the fence.

It was such a strange thing not to feel immediate revulsion or fear. Or maybe it wasn't, because Ilan had been in Sylvie's life since forever—she couldn't remember it without him around—and why should half an evening change that? That was his body, after all. No one else in the world looked like him.

That was his body, and it was unimaginably cruel to see what had been done to it. But he was only yards from her brother, and it was Gary she turned her thoughts to as she jumped up and, with a scream from deep in the well of her lungs, ran down the incline and straight into Ilan, pushing him into the chain link fence. His skin was slick with sweat—no, not sweat. Sylvie's palms and white blouse were smeared with something much darker than that. Blood.

"Don't touch him." Sylvie's voice snarled at the back of her throat.

Ilan's reflexes were not quick, but he was much stronger than Sylvie expected. His body grabbed Sylvie's arms, pushing her back, back toward the house, toward the tree.

"Sylvie. I'm not here for *him*." He pressed a hand to her face, smearing that fine sheen of blood over her cheek. It seemed to seep out of his pores, from his hairline, even collecting in his eyes. If he blinked, his tears would run red.

"Sylvie. Beautiful Sylvie, why do you shy from me?"

Sylvie shook her head, tried to look anywhere else, tried to pull out of his grip, but he was taller and broader, even now, even on strings, and he was *Ilan*.

No, he isn't.

"Don't," she choked, her nose bleeding, her eyes watering, her throat thick. "Please don't."

The hands that were once Ilan's and still bore the weight of him touched her neck, reached into her hair, bending her head back, making her look up at him as he continued to walk them backward.

Rynn slipped through him, then, a little girl with two plaits and patched coveralls.

Help me, Sylvie wanted to say to that little girl. But there was nothing Rynn could do anymore. She had done her duty more than she knew. She had kept that creature away, starved her into hibernation until Sylvie came along.

The creature inside of Ilan must have noticed Sylvie's attention was stolen for that brief second, because he tightened his grip.

"His mind was full of you," said the haggard voice that warbled in and out of Ilan's tenor.

"I don't want to know," Sylvie begged, twisting her body.

"Of course you want to know," Ilan whispered in that voice that contained a hundred voices. "You've always wanted to know. Your mind is full of him, even now."

Keeping a grip on her arm, bending it against her back, he leaned down to her neck and she felt dry teeth skim her pulse. She twisted harder, twisted until her shoulder hurt, visions of him biting down into her throat blooming before her eyes. She blinked tears through the streak of his bloody thumbprints on her cheeks.

"Stop," she whispered. "Please stop."

This close to him, she could smell the wound on his chest. It festered like death because it was death. Decomposition beginning at the hole through his heart. Rynn's fatal wounds had healed, but not his.

"If you let me in, it will be quick and it may be painless. I'm sure it was for him. I didn't even have to aid him. He knew what he had to do, and he did it."

"What do you want? What *are* you?"

Rynn, flittering across the yard, slipping through the pair of them like a ghost. Sylvie couldn't feel her, could only see her, but Ilan noticed whenever her attention was drawn away.

"Whatever you see won't help you now, you idiot girl. It didn't help Metje, and it didn't help *Rynn*. And the ones between them were weak. They ran, but I'm still here, and I will always be here."

"*What?*"

There was nothing Sylvie could do. There was no one to help her.

"Metje's mother meant to protect her, but instead she bore me a gift." Ilan held her face again. "Your incorrupt body."

He didn't even have to push her—she moved on her own, swallowed up by how much she didn't want these memories of Ilan's bloodless, bloody face, rotting shirt and oozing wound. Hands on her skin, soft as though it was really him.

She shut her eyes. "Please bring him back."

"Oh, Sylvie," sighed the creature. She felt Ilan's hand gently slip her tangled hair behind her ear, and she let out one quick sob. "Let's stop the pain."

She shook her head, then she felt Ilan's hands jerk away from her. He made a heavy, startled noise and she opened her eyes, terrified that he was going to—what? Unhinge his jaw and swallow her hole? But instead he had stumbled backward and there was Gary, holding the ax with the blunt side up. A hot wind blew up from nowhere. The dead tree groaned.

"Ilan! What the *fuck* are you doing to her?" His voice was rough as though he'd been sleeping for years.

Sylvie went to him, pulled on his arm. "Gary, no—"

"I told you to stay the fuck away—"

Sylvie pulled and pulled and pulled, Gary barely paying her attention until she had to scream, "That's not Ilan anymore! She has him, Gary! That's *Her*!"

The sight of Ilan, when Gary finally took it in, made it easy to believe Sylvie was right. She saw how his shoulders suddenly sagged.

Ilan smiled. It wasn't much of one, but it was cruel and joyful all the same, and quickly Gary recoiled, stumbling back, the ax falling from his grip as he covered his ears. As though that would help.

Gary's voice cracked. "Fuck you, you fucking moron! This was your grand fucking plan? This was how you were gonna protect Sylvie, you fucking piece of fucking shit? You shoulda just fucking *moved*! What was a dried-out old corpse gonna fucking do? Huh? Look what you fucking did to yourself! *Fuck you!*"

He reached back to take Sylvie's hand and pull her away. She stumbled over the rubble as the wind picked up, whipping around them, a harsh susurrus in their heads.

It's pointless.

It's pointless.

It's pointless.

Gary dragged Sylvie around the side of the house and into the wildflowers. They bent but did not break. The whispering stopped.

"Don't move from here."

"Are you nuts? I have to destroy the tree!"

"I already fucking tried it," said Gary.

"Yeah, but you don't know what I know!"

"What do you know, Sylvie? What could you possibly know?"

Ilan climbed over the hill of rubble to stare down at them. He wasn't steady, but he was strong. The dog appeared beside him, and behind him rose the imposing headless figure, a shadow darker than the night, even this night.

"There's a skull buried at the base of the tree, and it needs to be destroyed. I'm gonna burn it. I'm throwing a match in there, and I'm burning it down."

"How do you know any of that?"

"Because I told you! I can see the fucking past! And She—that thing knows it!" Sylvie left the flowers as she spoke, side-stepping

Gary and bolting for the fallen bottle of rubbing alcohol, light enough to stand out in the grass.

She had it in her hands, untwisted the cap just as she felt the biting pain in her legs, and she stumbled and fell. The bottle rolled back into the weeds, spilling out.

"Sylvie!" She heard Gary shout.

"Find the skull! Keep digging!" she gasped, not knowing if he heard her.

The dog kept biting at Sylvie, gripping at her legs with its long fingers, standing through her and around her with cold, burning—not skin, not fur, not anything.

You and Metje, scared little fools, the pair of you. The other girl knew better. She let me in without a fight.

A human hand on her leg now, dragging her back into the grass. She grabbed at exposed roots, at the dirt, at the weeds, kicking out until the phantom grip dislodged. As she scrambled onto all fours, the hand came down in her hair and pulled her back again. She gasped as she forced to stand up and turn around to face—Gary. It was Gary. He let go of her hair and immediately latched onto her neck with both hands. He didn't blink. He didn't make an expression at all.

"No—Gary—Gary, no!" Sylvie gasped, clawing at his fingers.

Behind him, Ilan came back down the rubble again. He didn't have to lift his feet anymore—the toes dragged along the ground.

This could have been finished by now, Sylvie. Your pain, the last thing you see, the final memory you will take with you—none of this had to pass. You could have come to me when I first called you. You could have listened.

Your brother will remember this when you cannot. It will haunt him in his dreams. It will destroy him. But, oh, have care that I will forgive him. I will help him. I will provide a way out of his misery when he comes to me. And he will come to me. And no one will know that he killed his sister. And when he thinks of you, it will be me.

Sylvie's eyes were wide. They stung with tears and the need to blink that wouldn't come. She could hear her pulse and the voice in her head and nothing else. Even Rynn receded from her consciousness. The corners of her vision began to crease. She tried to speak but could not do it. She gasped at nothing. She twisted and clawed until it was too hard to do either. Gary did not see her.

This couldn't be it. She wouldn't let it happen this way. Instead of clawing at his hands, she summoned up what remained of her strength and punched him hard in the face, colliding with his eye and nose, which began to bleed almost at once. She hit him again. He weakened. He blinked. Sylvie fell to the ground with a cry that couldn't be heard.

Sylvie felt like rags were stuffed inside her ears. She saw Gary stumble to his knees and reach for her—not a menacing reach, this time, but a desperate one. She saw Ilan standing over him, saw something bright in his hand—a long fragment of bone, already stained with old blood.

Sylvie came back to herself at once. Her throat burned, her lungs burned, her arms and legs felt cold and hot and her eyes watered, but she reached for the ax.

Once she had it, she was on her feet and screaming a hoarse scream that came up from the depths of her. She swung the ax wildly down and into Ilan's shoulder, right above the weeping wound. It sank into bone and Ilan dropped, landing on his knees. Blood didn't spray—there was no beating heart to pump it—but it oozed around the blade.

Sylvie wrenched the ax free, clavicle snapping, raking through rotting skin, and raised it again.

This body means nothing to me.

When Ilan looked up at her, Sylvie hesitated.

But it means everything to you.

The creature saw it. She saw the flicker in her eyes, the shift to thinking of him, wanting him back, not wanting to hurt the body she had grown up knowing but never knowing as well as she had hoped. Hoping now that there was still a chance—still a chance he could be restored.

He rose up again, and Sylvie did nothing to stop him. His joints creaked like the tree but his movement was fluid.

"But you, Sylvie—you are the one I desire above all," he said, and speaking it out loud meant that Ilan's voice was there to help carry the words. "He came to me to help you. To *save* you. And he saved me. Oh, I haven't forgotten. I will honor his memory. I will honor his memory by slipping inside of you."

He leaned down close to her. He had no breath, no warmth, but still her grip slackened on the ax, and it fell to the ground with a dull thud she didn't notice.

His mouth was at her ear, his hand gently lacing through her tangled hair. She could not smell the way he rotted. She could not see the blood creasing his skin. She could only see Ilan, golden in the sunlight of memory.

She didn't notice, either, how he held the fragment of bone, until he pressed it to her chest and the cotton of her blouse. Pressed harder, so that it pierced fabric and skin at once. And then he dragged it down, down her breast bone, slicing through both cotton and skin, leaving droplets of blood soaking into her shirt. And it hurt, but she was underwater in her mind.

"Do you think these are the first young men who have succored me? Do you think I am nothing and no one? I am in the very men who built this city."

"I'VE GOT IT! SYLV—" A sharp cry cut Gary off.

Ilan's hand froze. He straightened up. Then something came crashing down between them, slicing into forearms, breaking the bones, oozing blood and causing him to trip. And then there was Marybeth, jamming her knitting needle into his back as Marz held up the ax, ready to swing again. Sylvie surfaced back to reality and kicked Ilan's body hard in the stomach.

He dropped, a host weaker than the parasite within. In her head, through Ilan's open mouth, the scratching voice bellowed and screamed and even laughed—cackled, like brushfire. Cackled, like lightning striking the earth.

Marybeth began to pile broken fieldstone atop his stomach and Sylvie shook her head. "Help Gary! Go! Burn the tree—get the skull into the tree and burn it! Hurry!"

Marz and Marybeth both began to speak but Sylvie shook her head and bellowed, "GO! Please!"

Marz handed her the ax with a stare that Sylvie couldn't meet. Beneath her, Ilan's body laughed. It laughed and it laughed—*She* laughed. Blood dripped from his lips, coated his teeth. Beneath his elbows, his arms hung at odd angles, exposed bone and flesh glistening in the emerging starlight, and Sylvie wished it was a darker night—*somehow*, despite the blackout, it needed to be a darker night. She didn't want to see anything anymore. She couldn't do this. But she had to do this. There was a continuous scream in her head.

"I'm sorry," she said, blinking back tears. "I love you, too." Then she put her foot down on what was left of Ilan's chest and let out a wild yell, bringing the ax down on his neck. She closed her eyes before the impact—she couldn't help it. The blade hit bone and the feel of it traveled up her arms. She struggled to raise them, struggled to dislodge the ax. She wanted to throw up.

She sucked in a breath. She screamed it out. And she kept screaming. Kept raising the ax. Kept swinging it down. The creature's laughter died in Ilan's throat. Blood sprayed not from his neck, but from the blade as it swung. Sylvie could feel it hitting her face.

Finally, the ax gouged the earth with a hollow thunk.

She tossed it from her like a live snake and stumbled away.

The whispering didn't stop. It rattled with the wind. It tried to slip through the cracks in her mind and pull her back. But it wasn't strong enough anymore.

Sylvie opened her eyes and saw three pinpricks of light as Marz, Marybeth, and Gary dropped matches into the knot of the tree.

There was an explosion of embers, the sound of thunder from deep inside the earth. It cracked the trunk of the tree and rumbled out beneath them, shaking the ground with a primordial force. All four of them were blown off their feet and into the weeds and rubble.

Sylvie scrambled away as the fire burned blue for several seconds, licking the air. In those several seconds, the flames were the only sound—apart from the distant howl of dogs.

She lay on her back, staring up at the sky, Rynn stepping over and through her. It was as though the rug had been pulled out from under her, or taken out and beaten.

Gary let out a sharp shout and Sylvie was pulled back to the present. She jumped up and ran for him, Marz and Marybeth behind her.

Gary's mouth was set. His eyes were red, tear tracks through the dirt and blood on his face.

"Where is—"

He caught Sylvie with his free arm. "Don't go over there."

"Oh, Jesus Christ. Oh, my *God*." Marz. Sylvie instinctively flinched, and Gary had neither the strength nor, perhaps, the wherewithal left to grab her. He walked away, dragging the ax toward the tree.

Sylvie ran to Marz but before she made it another ten feet, she was hit by a foul, cloying stench that made her gag. Marz had already hurried off, hugging her stomach.

Looking down, Sylvie let out a strangled noise of surprise, then a louder scream, her hands flying to the top of her head, grabbing her hair.

Ilan was rotting.

Or had been rotting in a heatwave for what looked like weeks. Flies had already abandoned him, and now ants covered his empty eye sockets. His blonde hair was the only recognizable thing left of him, the only humanity apart from the bones that showed through peeling, sun-bleached skin. It wasn't even possible to see what had been done to him. Where the neck had been cleaved in two.

Sylvie turned away from the sight, pacing the property in broken circles until she simply dropped to the ground and heaved out racking, painful sobs.

She had hoped.

She had known better, but she had hoped.

Gary tossed the ax into the fire and stood there watching the flames blaze out of the hole like the mouth of an oven. The bark glowed as embers and small flames shot from cracks and knots. Soon the roots began to smolder, smoke rising from the ground. A branch collapsed with a loud crack as Gary walked away.

As the fire raged to an inferno, no one noticed how the wildflowers turned their faces to it, like the sun.

CHAPTER THIRTY-THREE

Sylvie's leg healed before the week was out, but she kept the bandages on and pretended it hadn't. She missed her next two feise-anna, which was something of a relief. And she didn't even feel bad about that relief, because getting on with things as usual didn't feel right.

The scar took a long time to fade, though, and it ached if she thought about it, which she often did. Occasionally, she glanced at it as she sat on the wooden sculpture in the NYU park, kicking out her leg just to test her muscle, to almost hope for a twinge so she could skip another competition and keep life from knitting itself back together, too.

The oppressive heat brought all the kids out to play in the jerry-rigged sprinkler, but Sylvie mostly ignored them. She kept her hands to the sculpture and cycled through memory after memory. Eight-year-old Ilan playing freeze tag with her and Gary. Ilan giving her piggy-back rides. Ilan and Gary graciously holding the rope so she and Marz and Marybeth could jump for a while. Ilan telling Sylvie he liked the mittens she was wearing that day, then bringing a pair of his own so she wouldn't feel self-conscious.

Sylvie knew she shouldn't look, but she couldn't stop herself. She hunted for him everywhere, longing to speak to him—and she often did, though he couldn't hear her. His eye line never quite met hers, either, no matter how she positioned herself. He was just a little kid. A happy kid who loved music and his friends. A hundred murmured apologies and never enough to assuage the guilt she felt. That she had killed him. That everything he went through was entirely her fault.

Every week, almost every night, she dreamt of him. When she woke, she often forgot the details. Maybe that was her punishment—to never remember those fantasies. Or maybe her brain was taking some pity on her. Dreaming of Ilan was never wholly pleasant, that much she knew. It made her think of the other dreams, the dreams with the woman. The dreams of him walking the bloody road. The day she dreamt of his bloodless body rising from the dirt.

Sometimes Sylvie walked up to West Tenth and stood in front of the Mark Twain house—the House of Death. She didn't know what she expected the first time she did it. That it would suddenly be fixed up, maybe. That people would suddenly move back in. She leaned against the tree, and every breeze caused her to strain, listening for something that didn't come. No one had fixed the plywood yet. No one had cleaned off the graffiti. The building stood frozen in time, but she suspected that stray animals might find a home there now. They would find Rynn's body. Ilan's blood. Rynn deserved to be buried, and Sylvie had a half-finished letter to Marilyn that would tip her off.

Every time she visited the Mark Twain house, her thoughts slipped to the night of the party. The embarrassment that had prompted her to make such a grave mistake. She should have known, but how could she? She'd looked at thousands of buildings and thousands of objects, but nothing had ever looked back at her. Even now, when she gazed down the block, she hoped to see him, sun illuminating his blond waves, a grin visible yards away. When she looked up at the windows, she wished for his ghost—but, oh, how awful to spend eternity in that place.

Then, inevitably, the guilt thickened in her chest until she couldn't stand still anymore, had to walk or risk coming undone. What if a part of him was still there, curled up in a brain that was obstructed by a monster, screaming and desperate to be heard? Sylvie's own powers had maybe primed her to accept a chthonic parasite, but it was still so difficult to believe that Ilan would die that way.

She tried to think of Rynn, how there was no way she had survived her injuries, that the last twenty years of her life weren't actually hers—that Ilan had been just as lost. But it didn't make Sylvie feel better. There was no expert to consult, not even Delilah Marie. No one but her friends to promise her that Ilan wasn't there anymore when the ax fell. But what did they know? What did *any* of them know?

She never looked at his apartment window. His parents had come and taken his things away before the funeral.

Explaining the trip to Brooklyn was simple. Sylvie had gone to find Gary, of course. And that was only half a lie. She had gone to find Gary when the power started flickering and it freaked her out.

Mrs. Haley had no memory of what had happened, to her or to Sylvie, and ended up calling for an ambulance because she thought she
was having a stroke or a heart attack. On top of that, Sylvie's mom
had shown up later than she meant to. No one was in the house, so
she went around to the neighbors. But then came the blackout.

As for Gary—Gary had heard rumors that Ilan had accidentally pissed off some shady people, he said. And when Ilan disappeared, those rumors started to get more pointed. Gary couldn't
point any fingers back, though; he didn't know who those people
were. No one Ilan had briefly played with understood the disappearance, either.

When Gary went to find Ilan, and Sylvie went to find Gary,
they'd been swept up in the chaos of the blackout until someone had
recognized Gary, knew he was a friend of Ilan's, and roughed him
up to stop him from asking questions.

Ilan's body was found before they could report it. The fire
in the tree—and maybe a deep understanding that the block had
changed—attracted the attention of the neighbors. He had been
dead, the coroner's report said, for almost two weeks.

Ilan's homicide was blamed on the drug scene. The police
liked it because it gave them a reason not to do anything. He wasn't
the only mutilated corpse on the docket, and as long as he didn't
have a .44 caliber bullet in his brain, they had other things to do.

Every day, Sylvie wanted to tell them the truth. Ilan had been
trying to help her, but he was out of his depth. She even wrote
everything down. Folded it up. Put it in her desk drawer. To his
parents, she insisted the police couldn't be right. Maybe he'd been

kidnapped. Maybe it was a case of mistaken identity. That's what the city had come to, right? Unchecked violence against the young.

Marilyn heard all the gruesome details at work.

Like Mrs. Haley, she was all right, too, after finding herself standing outside her apartment building, a headache gripping her neck and spine. She went to a clinic, but they couldn't find anything wrong. The only thing bothering her was that those white flowers she kept in her living room had disappeared. She'd picked them as a girl, she said, with Rynn. They'd gone to that old Bushwick mansion and Rynn called them good luck flowers—said her mother called them that, and so had her grandmother.

"Oh, but, speaking of Rynn's grandma, I finally got some time to go into the archives."

"Find anything interesting?"

"A couple little tidbits. First, they never found her, as far as I can tell. Never found who killed her family, either. And I guess there was an accident at the mansion back in the 1890s. A little boy fell off a balcony or something. He had a sister, and that sister was Rynn's grandmother. Well, step-grandmother. Her grandfather's second wife. Rynn always called her grandma. Anyway, step-grandmother bought the Herkimer-Cropsey mansion in the '30s and kept it vacant, as I guess you would. When she died the city took control of it."

Sylvie knew half of it, and the other half wasn't surprising at all.

"I also found interviews with some of Rynn's friends and neighbors after she was brought back home. All of her friends said they didn't associate with her anymore. She tended to, and I quote, 'hold court' with a lot of men, who used to visit her house at all hours. Her family refused to comment. Some of these men would later wind up shot and dumped in the river, by the way. One of them lost his mind, ran up Fifth Avenue tearing off his clothes and got hit by a car. That was around the time Rynn disappeared. I guess they were into gambling and other fun things like that. They were questioned about Rynn but released."

"Sounds like she made herself a little cult," said Sylvie, thinking of the men she had seen in the memories of West Tenth, how they had stacked furniture in front of the door to keep Rynn inside. Tried to strangle her but she wasn't alive enough to kill.

"Doesn't it? How funny. She was always a little fast, as my perpetually hypocritical mother would say, but a gambling ring is pretty out there." Marilyn sighed. "Well, they say trauma can change a person, and what's more traumatic than what she went through? Poor kid."

✦

In August, it was back to dance class, where Rynn was waiting for Sylvie as though nothing had changed. And she couldn't stand it. Oh, she pitied the girl, but it was easier when she was a contextless crime. Easier when Sylvie thought the crime had happened there, across the street. The idea of that mansion being anywhere near her, even in fragments, was unsettling. And maybe Sylvie deserved to remember it, maybe she should let it follow her, but after two classes, she couldn't do it. As much as she wanted life to be suspended, for the world to go on as though Ilan was still in it, Sylvie knew it would either be Rynn or her dancing, and she still wanted to dance. It felt different to her, but she had told Ilan the truth; it was what she was good at. It was there when nothing else made sense.

She thought of what Marz had said once—throw the ornament in the river. Get rid of it. And the idea wouldn't get out of Sylvie's mind. After all she had seen, all she had done, she didn't think twice about it.

She told her brother. She told her brother everything about Rynn, and Rynn's body, and the vision of her. She told him everything she knew of herself, and he believed her because he probably always had.

They snuck out of the loft after midnight and headed uptown, and together they hauled off a pair of stone reliefs that were still stacked outside the near-finished café. They were beautiful, carved with a series of flowers, and Rynn kept jumping out of them, screaming into the night.

They fell into the river with two hard splashes.

Gary dropped his arm across Sylvie's shoulders. "How's it feel?"

"Do you really have to go back to school?"

He didn't respond at first. She'd taken him by surprise. "Soon as I'm gone, you'll change your mind."

"I won't."

Gary didn't say anything. He hugged her tighter.

"Maybe I'll come with you," she said.

"After I hauled this a mile so you could dance in peace?"

"It wasn't *a mile*."

A pause. "You'll be okay, Silverado. If you stayed sane after seeing strangers getting their fingers and hair ripped off every time you touched things at home, you'll stay sane through this."

"This is different. I knew him."

"I'm not saying the situation isn't fucked. It's fucked. He thought he was doing the right thing. You didn't know. He didn't really know. I should've stopped him, frog-marched him to our place or something. Locked him up. Called his parents. But it's not useful to think like that. At the end of the day, something dangerous is gone. It can't hurt anybody else. So. Well. I guess there's that." He sighed.

Sylvie watched the lights of New Jersey across the river and leaned her head against her brother's shoulder. The breeze off the water was cool and quiet and gently stirred her hair. "I know. But I miss him."

"I know. I miss him, too."

The next day, the .44 caliber killer was caught.

EPILOGUE

BUSHWICK

1978

It took thirteen years, but the foundation was finally disappearing.

Or it was going to, shortly—there was a big pile of dirt just waiting for the shovels, and bulldozers waiting to break down the remaining walls—but archaeologists were allowed to look first. After all, the previous demolition had uncovered an even older part of the house, probably built by the Dutch, even though there was no record of a settlement out here. No one was sorry to see it go, but if the place really predated the charter, it would have been a real historical blunder for the city to fuck that one up, too.

The only original part of the actual Dutch house that remained was a deep corner of the cellar—a larder, probably. It was cool and dark even now, even today, but its yield was pretty unremarkable. The cellar had already been informally excavated, after all, when those Cropsey murder victims were found a hundred years earlier. Most of what was left—broken dishes, pieces of furniture and wall coverings, a second staircase into the remains of the mansion— were too late to have come from the Dutch at all.

The old elm was ash and charcoal limbs that stuck up at wild angles. No one knew if it was a victim of the blackout, or if lightning had finally hit its target after all these centuries. It was a shame to lose such an old tree, but it had been dead longer than it had ever been alive. It was a miracle a strong wind hadn't blown it down years ago. No one in the neighborhood shed a tear when they came out into the smoky dawn and saw it wasn't there anymore—except those who wept with joy.

The team dug up the garden near the cellar, and that, it turned out, was where all the treasures were.

Bodies. Two of them, in total. The clothes they wore gave them away—these were some of the unknown settlers. These were the people whose names were lost because they were never properly inscribed anywhere.

One of the bodies, a woman who must have been the mother, was bones and clothing and hair.

The other body looked as though it had only been there since the winter. She was mummified in such a way that every pore, every winkle, every motion her face once made was preserved for all to see now. She was a teenage girl with golden hair still in a long braid and, when they eventually looked beneath her long lashes, gray eyes. She wore a stained night shift like she had gone to sleep and not woken up.

That she was preserved this way wasn't even the most remarkable thing about her. No, what was remarkable was that out of her skin had erupted the stalks and stems of an unknown flower. Some of the crushed petals appeared to have maybe once been white, but they were brown now. No one could remember ever seeing such a thing before.

The age of the bodies would have been enough to study them.

The girl would have been enough.

But what was even stranger was that both bodies had been decapitated after death, the heads placed between their feet.

No one could remember ever seeing anything like that, either, but it reminded a few people of early superstitions. Ways of preventing the dead from rising again. They assumed that the rest of the family—there had to be someone who buried them—had left. Probably an illness or a string of bad luck drove them back home or into the city. It was obvious, now, why history had skipped over them. They had failed to thrive.

The researchers collected the bodies, and the next day, the bulldozer and steam shovel finished leveling the lot.

While dust clouds roiled in the still air, birds landed on the fence to watch, silent.

Acknowledgments

This novel took its final form with the help of many people (and no human sacrifice). Michael Lauritano, my partner in crime (writing and illustrating) and life. Sunny Lee, for reading and giving feedback on whatever I send her. The SVA Illustration as Visual Essay crew remains strong. And also tired.

My mom, Nancy, who loves a scary book or movie. My dad, Gary, who did not. They let me go to art school twice.

My agent, Linda Camacho, who gently poked me about finishing this project for years.

And to my team at Union Square Kids, who had to figure out how to make this weird hybrid novel work: Suzy Capozzi, Ardyce Alspach, Marcie Lawrence, Stefanic Chin, Grace House, Amelia Mack, Tracey Keevan, Renee Yewdaev, and Sandy Noman.

Eternal thanks to Yukie Ohta and the SoHo Memory Project, one of the greatest archives of New York City history.

For teaching me about the House of Death, I credit Jan Bryant Bartell, author of *Spindrift: Spray from a Psychic Sea*, and New York City's Boroughs of the Dead.

For answers to the mysteries of Irish dancing (including pronunciation guides), visit my website all about it: irish-feet.com.

(If you're in driving distance of Portland, Maine, come join the Stillson School of Irish Dance.)

For all things Sylvie's world (and beyond), visit dvojack.com/welcome-to-fear-city.

About the Author

Sarah Dvojack was born and raised in Washington state, where she was brought up on her parents' music and developed a passion for all things weird, historical, and Irish dance. She graduated from Seattle's Cornish College of the Arts with a degree in graphic design and went on to study in the School of Visual Arts' MFA Illustration as Visual Essay program. After a decade in New York City, she now lives with her partner and cats in that bastion of American horror and children's books, Maine, and works as a book designer. You can visit Sarah online at dvojack.com.